HAVE YOU HEARD THE ONE ABOUT...

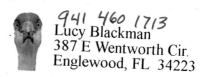
941 460 1713
Lucy Blackman
387 E Wentworth Cir.
Englewood, FL 34223

HAVE YOU HEARD THE ONE ABOUT...

Aging

By Lucy Blackman

iUniverse, Inc.
New York Lincoln Shanghai

Have You Heard The One About…
Aging

iUniverse books may be ordered through booksellers or by contacting:

iUniverse
2021 Pine Lake Road, Suite 100
Lincoln, NE 68512
www.iuniverse.com
1-800-Authors (1-800-288-4677)

ISBN-13: 978-0-595-37072-6 (pbk)
ISBN-13: 978-0-595-81472-5 (ebk)
ISBN-10: 0-595-37072-1 (pbk)
ISBN-10: 0-595-81472-7 (ebk)

Printed in the United States of America

GETTING OLD AT WORK

What happens when people of different occupations get old?

Old accountants never die, they just lose their balance.

Old actors never die, they just drop apart.

Old archers never die, they just bow and quiver.

Old architects never die, they just lose their structures.

Old bankers never die, they just lose interest.

Old basketball players never die, they just go on dribbling.

Old beekeepers never die, they just buzz off.

Old bookkeepers never die, they just lose their figures.

Old bosses never die, much as you want them to.

Old cashiers never die, they just check out.

Old chauffeurs never die, they just lose their drive.

Old chemists never die, they just fail to react.

Old cleaning people never die, they just kick the bucket.

Old cooks never die, they just get deranged.

Old daredevils never die, they just get discouraged.

Old deans never die, they just lose their faculties.

Old doctors never die, they just lose their patience.

Old electricians never die, they just lose contact.

Old farmers never die, they just go to seed.

Old garagemen never die, they just retire.
Old hackers never die, they just go to bits.
Old hardware engineers never die, they just cache their chips.
Old hippies never die, they just smell that way.
Old horticulturists never die, they just go to pot.
Old hypochondriacs never die, they just lose their grippe.
Old investors never die, they just roll over.
Old journalists never die, they just get depressed.
Old knights in chain mail never die, they just shuffle coils.
Old laser physicists never die, they just become incoherent.
Old lawyers never die, they just lose their appeal.
Old limbo dancers never die, they just go under.
Old mathematicians never die, they just disintegrate.
Old milkmaids never die, they just lose their whey.
Old ministers never die, they just get put out to pastor…
Old musicians never die, they just get played out.
Old number theorists never die, they just get past their prime.
Old numerical analysts never die, they just get disarrayed.
Old owls never die, they just don't give a hoot.
Old pacifists never die, they just go to peaces.
Old professors never die, they just lose their class.
Old photographers never die, they just stop developing.
Old pilots never die, they just go to a higher plane.
Old policemen never die, they just cop out.
Old preachers never die, they just ramble on, and on, and on, and on….
Old printers never die, they're just not the type.
Old programmers never die, they just branch to a new address.

*   *   *   *

HOW TO KNOW THAT YOU ARE GROWING OLDER

Everything hurts and what doesn't hurt, doesn't work.

The gleam in your eyes is from the sun hitting your bifocals.

My little black book contains only names ending with M.D.

I get winded playing chess.

Your children begin to look middle aged.

You finally reach the top of the ladder, and you find it is leaning against the wrong wall.

You join the health club and don't go.

You begin to outlive your enthusiasm.

You decide to procrastinate but never get around to it.

Your mind makes contracts your body can't meet.

A dripping faucet causes an uncontrollable bladder urge.

You know all the answers, about nobody knows the question.

You look forward to a dull evening.

You walk with your head held high trying to get used to your bifocals.

You turn out the light for economic rather than romantic reasons.

You sit in a rocking chair and can't get it going.

Your knees buckle and your belt won't.

You regret all those mistakes resisting temptation.

You're 17 around the neck, 42 around the waist, and 96 around the golf course.

You stop looking forward to your next birthday.

After painting the town red, you have to take a long rest before applying a second coat.

Dialing long distance wears you out.

You're startled the first time you are addressed as an old timer.

You remember today that yesterday was your wedding anniversary.

You just can't stand people that are intolerant.

The best part of your day is over when your alarm clock goes off.

You burn the midnight oil at 9 pm.

Your back goes out more than you do.

A fortune teller offers to read your face.

Your pacemaker makes the garage door go up when you watch a pretty girl go by.

The little gray haired lady you helped across the street is your wife.

You sink your teeth into a steak and they stay there.

$$*\qquad*\qquad*\qquad*$$

GOOD MORNING

My face in the mirror
Isn't wrinkled or drawn.
My house isn't dirty.
The cobwebs are gone.
My garden looks lovely
And so does my lawn.
I think I might never
Put my glasses back on.

*   *   *   *

An old man walked into a crowded doctor's office. As he approached the desk, the receptionist asked, "Yes sir, may we help you?"
"There's something wrong with my penis," he replied.
Flustered, the receptionist said, "You shouldn't come into a crowded office and say things like that."
"Why not? You asked me what was wrong and I told you." He said.
"Because" replies the receptionist. "You've obviously caused some embarrassment in this room full of strangers. You should have said there is something wrong with your ear or something and discussed the problem further with the doctor in private."
The man walked out, waited several minutes and re-entered. The receptionist smiled smugly and asked, "Yes?"
"There's something wrong with my ear," he stated.
The receptionist nodded approvingly. "And what is wrong with your ear, sir?"
"I can't piss out of it!" the man replied.

*   *   *   *

Everyone has a photographic memory. Some, like me, just don't have any film.

*   *   *   *

Never be too open-minded, your brains could fall out.

*   *   *   *

If you look like your passport picture, you probably need the trip.

*   *   *   *

By the time you can make ends meet, they move the ends.

*   *   *   *

Three old ladies are walking down the street. I think their names were Kathy, Judy and Mary Lou...anyhow, they are all hard of hearing.
One: "whew, it's windy today!"
Two: "No. Today's Thursday!"
Three: "So am I! Let's go to a bar!"

*   *   *   *

GAMES FOR WHEN WE ARE OLDER
1. Sag, you're it.
2. 20 questions shouted into your good ear.
3. Kick the bucket.
4. Red rover, red rover, the nurse says bend over.
5. Doc doc goose.
6. Simon says something incoherent.
7. Hide and go pee.
8. Spin the bottle of Mylanta.
9. Musical recliners.

*   *   *   *

An elderly couple had been dating for some time and decided it was finally time to marry...

Before the wedding they embarked on a long conversation regarding how their marriage might work...

They discussed finances, living arrangements and so on...

Finally, the old man decided it was time to broach the subject of their sexual relationship.

"How do you feel about sex?" he asked, rather hopefully.

"Oh, I like to have it infrequently," she responded.

The old guy thought for a moment, then asked, "was that one word or two?"

*   *   *   *

SIGNS OF MENOPAUSE

1. You sell your home heating system at a yard sale.

2. Your husband jokes that instead of buying a wood stove, he is using you to heat the family room this winter. Rather than just saying you are not amused, you shoot him.

3. You have to write post-it notes with your kids' names on them.

4. Your husband chirps, "Hi Honey, I'm home." And your reply, "Well, if it isn't Ozzie Nelson."

5. The Phenobarbital dose that wiped out the Heaven's Gate Cult gives you four hours of decent rest.

6. You change your underwear after every sneeze.

7. You're on so much estrogen that you take your Brownie troop on a field trip to Chippendales.

*   *   *   *

"OLD" IS WHEN....
Your sweetie says, "Let's go upstairs and make love," and you answer, "Pick one, I can't do both!"

"OLD" IS WHEN....
Your friends compliment you on your new alligator shoes and you're barefoot.

"OLD" IS WHEN....
A sexy babe catches your fancy and your pacemaker opens the garage door.

"OLD" IS WHEN....
Going bra-less pulls all the wrinkles out of your face.

"OLD" IS WHEN....
You don't care where your spouse goes, just as long as you don't have to go along.

"OLD" IS WHEN....
When you are cautioned to slow down by the doctor instead of by the police.

"OLD" IS WHEN....
"getting a little action" means I don't need to take any fiber today.

"OLD" IS WHEN....
"Getting lucky" means you find your car in the parking lot.

"OLD" IS WHEN....
An "all-nighter" means not getting up to pee.

*   *   *   *

The older you get, the tougher it is to lose weight, because by then your body and your fat are really good friends.

*   *   *   *

I intend to live forever—so far, so good.

*   *   *   *

They were celebrating their sixtieth anniversary. The couple had married as childhood sweethearts and had moved back to their old neighborhood after they retired. Holding hands they walked back to their old school. It was not locked, so they entered, and found the old desk they'd shared, where Andy had carved "I love you, Sally."
On their way back home, a bag of money fell out of an armored car, practically landing at their feet. Sally quickly picked it up,

but not sure what to do with it, they took it home. There, she counted the money and it's fifty-thousand dollars.

Andy said, "We've got to give it back."

Sally said, "Finders keepers." She put the money back in the bag and hit it in their attic. The next day, two FBI men were canvassing the neighborhood looking for the money, and knock on the door. "Pardon me, but did either of you find a bag that fell out of an armored car yesterday?"

Sally said, "No."

Andy said, "She's lying. She hid it up in the attic."

Sally said, "Don't believe him, he's getting senile."

The agents turn to Andy and began to question him.

One says: "Tell the story from the beginning."

Andy said, "Well, when Sally and I were walking home from school yesterday…"

The first FBI guy turns to his partner and says, "we're outta here."

$*$ $*$ $*$ $*$

I used to have Saturday Night Fever…now I just have Saturday Night hot flashes.

$*$ $*$ $*$ $*$

Any woman can have the body of a 21-year-old…as long as she buys him a few drinks!

*   *   *   *

My memory's not as sharp as it used to be. Also, my memory's not as sharp as it used to be.

*   *   *   *

Know how to prevent sagging? Just eat till the wrinkles fill out.

*   *   *   *

I've still got it, but nobody wants to see it.

*   *   *   *

I'm getting into swing dancing. Although not on purpose. Some parts of my body are just swinging.

*   *   *   *

It's scary when you start making the same noises as your coffeemaker.

*   *   *   *

I think I've reached my sexpiration date.

*   *   *   *

People our age can still enjoy an active, passionate sex life! Provided we get cable.

*   *   *   *

These days about half the stuff in my shopping cart says, "For fast relief."

*   *   *   *

I've tried to find a suitable exercise video for women my age. But they haven't made one out of putty.

*   *   *   *

Don't think of it as getting hot flashes. Think of it as your inner child playing with matches.

*   *   *   *

Don't let aging get you down…it's too hard to get back up.

*   *   *   *

Remember: You don't stop laughing because you grow old. You grow old because you stop laughing.

*   *   *   *

Jacob age 85, and Rebecca age 79 are all excited about their decision to get married. They go for a stroll to discuss the wedding and on the way go past a drugstore. Jacob suggests that they go in. He addresses the man behind the counter:

"Are you the owner?"
The pharmacist answers, "Yes."
Jacob: "Do you sell heart medication?"
Pharmacist: "Of course we do."
Jacob: "How about medicine for circulation?"
Pharmacist: "All kinds."
Jacob: "Medicine for rheumatism?"
Pharmacist: "Definitely"
Jacob: "How about Viagra?"
Pharmacist: "Of course."
Jacob: "Medicine for memory?"
Pharmacist: "Yes, a large variety."
Jacob: "Perfect! We'd like to register here for our wedding gifts."

*   *   *   *

The Perks of Being Over 50…
1. Your supply of brain cells is finally down to manageable size.
2. Your secrets are safe with your friends because they can't remember them either.
3. Your joints are more accurate meteorologists than the national weather service.
4. People call at 9PM and ask, "Did I wake you?"
5. People no longer view you as a hypochondriac.

6. There is nothing left to learn the hard way.

7. Things you buy now won't wear out.

8. You can eat dinner at 4. P.M.

9. You can live without sex but not without glasses.

10. You enjoy hearing about other peoples operations.

11. You get into heated arguments about pension plans.

12. You have a party and the neighbors don't even realize it.

13. You no longer think of speed limits as a challenge.

14. You quit trying to hold your stomach in, no matter who walks into the room.

15. You sing along with elevator music.

16. Your eyes won't get much worse.

17. Your investment in health insurance is finally beginning to pay off.

18. You can't remember who sent you this list.

*   *   *   *

If you are feeling a little older and missing those great old tunes of your younger days, there is good news. Some of your old favorite tunes have been re-released with new lyrics to accommodate aging audiences. Some examples:

Carly Simon—"You're So Varicose Vein"

The Bee Gees—"How Can You Mend a Broken Hip"

Roberta Flack—"The First Time Ever I Forgot Your Face"

Johnny Nash—"I Can't See Clearly Now"

The Temptations—"Papa Got a Kidney Stone"

Nancy Sinatra—"These Boots Give Me Arthritis"

ABBA—"Denture Queen"

Leo Sayer—"You Make Me Feel Like Napping"

Commodores—"Once, Twice, Three trips to the Bathroom"

The Beatles—"I Get By with a Little Help From Depends"

Steely Dan—"Rikki, Don't Lose Your Car Keys"

Herman's Hermits—"Mrs. Brown You've Got a Lovely Walker"

The Rolling Stones—"You Can't Always Pee When You Want"

Credence Clearwater Revival—"Bad Prune Rising"

Procol Harum—"Whiter Shade of Hair"

Marvin Gaye—"I Heard It Through the Grape Nuts"

Paul Simon—"Fifty Ways to Lose Your Liver"

The Who—"Talkin' 'Bout My Medication"

The Troggs—"Bald Thing"

*   *   *   *

A man was out walking one day and went by a retirement home. As he passed the front lawn, he saw 9 old ladies basking in the sun in lounge chairs. When he looked closer he realized that they were all stark naked. He went to the door and rang the bell. When the director answered the door, the man asked if he realized there were 9 naked ladies lying in the sun on the front lawn. The director said, "Yes" and went on to explain that the old ladies were all retired prostitutes living at the retirement home, and they were having a yard sale.

*   *   *   *

The Cat In The Hat On Aging

I cannot see
I cannot pee
I cannot chew
I cannot screw
Oh, my God, what can I do?
My memory shrinks
My hearing stinks
No sense of smell
I look like hell

My mood is bad, can you tell?
My body's drooping
Have trouble pooping
The Golden Years have come at last
The Golden years can kiss my ass

          *   *   *   *

An elderly Floridian called 911 on her cell phone to report that her car had been broken into. She is hysterical as she explains her situation to the dispatcher: "They've stolen the stereo, the steering wheel, the brake pedal and even the accelerator!" she cried. The dispatcher said, "Stay calm. An officer is on the way." A few minutes later, the officer radios in. "Disregard." He says. "She got in the back-seat by mistake."

          *   *   *   *

A little old lady was running up and down the halls in a nursing home. As she walked, she would flip up the hem of her night-gown and say, "Supersex." She walked up to an elderly man in wheelchair. Flipping her gown at him, she said, "Supersex." He sat silently for a moment or two and finally answered, "I'll take the soup."

          *   *   *   *

80-year old Bessie bursts into the rec room at the retirement home. She holds her clenched fist in the air and announced

"Anyone who can guess what's in my hand can have sex with me tonight!!" An elderly gentleman in the rear shouts out, "An elephant?" Bessie thinks a minute and says, "Close enough."

*   *   *   *

Two elderly ladies had been friends for many decades. Over the years, they had shared all kinds of activities and adventures. Lately, their activities had been limited to meeting a few times a week to play cards. One day, they were playing cards when one looked at the other and said, "Now don't get mad at me…I know we've been friends for a long time…but I just can't think of your name! I've thought and thought, but I can't remember it. Please tell me what your name is. Her friend glared at her. For at least three minutes she just started and glared at her. Finally she said, "How soon do you need to know?"

*   *   *   *

As a senior citizen was driving down the freeway, his car phone rang. Answering, he heard his wife's voice urgently warning him, "Herman, I just heard on the news that there's a car going the wrong way on Interstate 77. Please be careful!" "Heck," said Herman, "It's not just one car. It's hundreds of them!"

*   *   *   *

Two elderly women were out driving in a large car-both could barely see over the dashboard. As they were cruising along, they came to an intersection. The stoplight was red, but they just went through. The woman in the passenger seat thought to herself "I must be losing it. I could have sworn we just went through a red light." After a few more minutes, they came to another intersection and the light was red again. Again, they went right through. The woman in the passenger seat was almost sure that the light had been red but was really concerned that she was losing it. She was getting nervous. At the next intersection, sure enough, the light was red and they went on through. So, she turned to the other woman and said, "Mildred, did you know that we just ran through three red lights in a row? You could have killed us both!" Mildred turned to her and said, "Oh, crap, am I driving?"

*   *   *   *

With age come skills. It's called multitasking. I can laugh, cough, sneeze, and pee all at the same time.

*   *   *   *

We went to breakfast at a restaurant where the "seniors' special" was two eggs, bacon, hash browns and toast for $1.99.
"Sounds good," my wife said. "But I don't want the eggs."
"Then I'll have to charge you two dollars and forty-nine cents because you're ordering a la crate," the waitress warned her.
"You mean I'd have to pay for not taking the eggs?" my wife asked incredulously. "I'll take the special."
"How do you want your eggs?"

"Raw and in the shell," my wife replied. She took the two eggs home.

*   *   *   *

GOOD SHORT TEST
Take your time and see if you can read each line aloud without mistake. The average person can't.

This is this cat
This is is cat
This is how cat
This is to cat
This is keep cat
This is an cat
This is old cat
This is person cat
This is busy cat
This is for cat
This is forty cat
This is seconds cat.

Now go back and read the THIRD word in each line from top down and I bet'cha you can't resist passing it on.

*   *   *   *

Thought I'd let you know that I am now in the Snapdragon part of my life…

Part of me has lost its snap, and the other part is draggin!!!!!

*   *   *   *

California vintners in the Napa Valley area that primarily produces Pinot Blanc and Pino Grigio have developed a new
hybrid grape that acts as an antidiuretic and will reduce the
number of trips an older person has to make to the bathroom
during the night.
They will be marketing the new wine as Pinot More.

*   *   *   *

An old women and her daughter were sitting on a park bench
outside the local town hall where a flower show was in progress.
The old woman leaned over to her daughter and said, "Phooey,
life is so boring, we never have any fun these days. For $5.00, I'd
take my clothes off and streak through the flower show!"
"You're on!", said her unbelieving daughter, digging in her purse
and holding up $5.00.
As fast as she could, the old woman fumbled her way out of her
clothes and, completely naked, streaked through the front door
of the town hall. Waiting outside, her daughter heard a large
commotion inside the hall, followed by loud applause. The
naked old woman burst out through the door surrounded by a
cheering crowd.
"How'd it go?" asked her daughter.
"Great!", she said, "I won first prize as best dried arrangement.

*   *   *   *

A man was telling his neighbor, "I just bought a new hearing aid. It cost me four thousand dollars, but it's state of the art. "Really," answered the neighbor. "What kind is it?" "Twelve-thirty."

*   *   *   *

Conspiracy, We Must Stop This

Have you ever noticed that when you're of a certain age, everything seems up hill from where you are? Stairs are steeper. Groceries are heavier. And, everything is farther away. Yesterday I walked to the corner and I was dumbfounded to discover how long our street has become!

And, you know, people are less considerate now, especially the young ones. They speak in whispers all the time! If you ask them to speak up they just keep repeating themselves, endlessly mouthing the same silent message until they're red in the face! What do they think I am, a lip reader?

I also think they are much younger than I was at the same age. On the other hand, people my own age are so much older than I am. I ran into an old friend the other day and she has aged so much that she didn't even recognize me.

I got to thinking about the poor dear while I was combing my hair this morning, and in doing so, I glanced at my own reflection…Well, REALLY NOW…even mirrors are not made the way they used to be!

Another thing, everyone drives so fast today! You're risking life and limb if you just happen to pull onto the freeway in front of them. All I can say is, their brakes must wear out awfully fast, the way I see them screech and swerve in my rear view mirror.

Clothing manufacturers are less civilized these days. Why else would they suddenly start labeling a size 10 or 12 dress as 18 or 20? Do they think no one notices that these things no longer fit around the waist, hips, thighs, and bosom?

The people who make bathroom scales are pulling the same prank, but in reverse. Do they think I actually "believe" the number I see on that dial? HA! I would never let myself weigh that much! Just whom do these people think they're fooling?

I'd like to call up someone in authority to report what's going on—but the telephone company is in on the conspiracy too: they've printed the phone books in such small type that no one could ever find a number in here!

All I can do is pass along this warning: Maturity is under attack!

$$*\qquad*\qquad*\qquad*$$

WHAT IS A GRANDPARENT? (Taken from papers written by a class of 8-year-olds)

Grandparents are a lady and a man who have no little children of her own. They like other people's.

A grandfather is a man grandmother.

Grandparents don't have to do anything except be there when we come to see them. They are so old they shouldn't play hard or run. It is good if they drive us to the store and have lots of quarters for us.

When they take us for walks, they slow down past things like pretty leaves and caterpillars.

They show us and talk to us about the color of the flowers and also why we shouldn't step on "cracks."

They don't say, "Hurry up."

Usually grandmothers are fat, but not too fat to tie your shoes.

They wear glasses and funny underwear.

They can take their teeth and gums out.

Grandparents have to be smart.

They have to answer questions like "why isn't God married?" and "How come dogs chase cats?"

When they read to us, they don't skip. They don't mind if we ask for the same story over again.

Everybody should try and have a grandmother, especially if you don't have television, because they are the only grown ups who like to spend time with us.

They know we should have snack-time before bedtime and they say prayers with us every time, and kiss us even when we've acted badly.

"She lives at the airport, and when we are done having her visit, we take her back to the airport."

*   *   *   *

I have been guilty of looking at others my own age and thinking…surely I cannot look that old…I'm sure you've done the same…You may enjoy this story…

While waiting for my first appointment in the reception room of my new dentist, I noticed his certificate, which bore his full name. Suddenly, I remembered that a tall, handsome boy with the same name had been in my high school class some 40 years ago. Upon seeing him, however, I quickly discarded any such thought. This balding, gray-haired man with the deeply lined face was too old to have been my classmate.

After he had examined my teeth, I asked him if he had attended the local high school.

"Yes," he replied.

"When did you graduate?" I asked.

He answered, "in 1957."

"Why, you were in my class!" I exclaimed.

He looked at me closely and then asked, "What did you teach?"

* * * *

In a Thurmont, Maryland, cemetery:
Here lies an Atheist
All dressed up
And no place to go.

* * * *

John is 73 years old and loves to fish. He was sitting in his boat the other day when he heard a voice say, "Pick me up." He looked around and could not see any one. He thought he was dreaming when he heard the voice again, "Pick me up."

He looked in the water and there floating on the top was a frog. He said, "Are you talking to me?" The frog said, "Yes, I'm talking to you. Pick me up and kiss me and I'll turn into the most beautiful woman you have ever seen and will give you the most wonderful sexual pleasures that you have ever dreamed of." John looked at the frog for a short time and then reached over and picked it up carefully, placing it in his front breast pocket. Then the frog said, "What are you nuts, didn't you hear what I said? I said kiss me and I will give you sexual pleasures like you have never had."

He opened his pocket, looked at the frog and said, "At my age I'd rather have a talking frog."

*   *   *   *

Back in the old days, when Great Grandpa put horseradish on his head, what was he trying to do?
George Gobel: Get it in his mouth.

*   *   *   *

When I'm an old lady, I'll live with my kids,
And make them so happy, just as they did.
I want to pay back all the joy they've provided,
returning each deed. Oh, they'll be so excited.
When I'm an old lady and live with my kids.

I'll write on the wall with reds, whites and blues,
and bounce on the furniture wearing my shoes.

I'll drink from the carton and then leave it out.
I'll stuff all the toilets, and oh, how they'll shout.
When I'm an old lady and live with my kids.

When they're on the phone and just out of reach,
I'll get into things like sugar and bleach.
Oh, they'll snap their fingers and then shake their head,
And when that is done I'll hide under the bed.
When I'm an old lady and live with my kids.

When they cook dinner and call me to meals.
I'll not eat my green beans or salads congealed.
I'll gag on my okra, spill milk on the table
And when they get angry, run fast as I'm able.
When I'm an old lady and live with my kids

I'll sit close to the TV, thru the channels I'll click,
I'll cross both my eyes to see if they stick.
I'll take off my socks and throw one away,
and play in the mud until the end of the day.
When I'm an old Lady and live with my kids

And later in bed, I'll lay back and sigh,
And thank God in prayer and then close my eyes
And my kids will look down with a smile slowly creeping,
Say with a groan. "She's so sweet when she's sleeping."
When I'm an old lady and live with my kids.

*   *   *   *

I've sure gotten old. I've had 2 by-pass surgeries. a hip replacement and new knees. Fought prostate cancer, and diabetes.
I'm half blind, can't hear anything quieter than a jet engine, take 40 different medications that make me dizzy, winded and subject to blackouts.
Have bouts with dementia. Have poor circulation, hardly feel my hands and feet anymore. Can't remember if I'm 85 or 92. Have lost all my friends.
But…Thank God, I still have my Florida driver's license!

*   *   *   *

Reporters interviewing a 104 year-old woman:
"And what do you think is the best thing about being 104?" the reporter asked.
She simply replied, "No peer pressure."

*   *   *   *

God, Grant me the senility
To forget the people
I never liked anyway,
The good fortune
To run into the ones I do,
And the eyesight to tell the difference.

*   *   *   *

An elderly woman from Brooklyn decided to prepare her will and make her final requests. She told her rabbi she had two final requests.

First, she wanted to be cremated, and second, she wanted her ashes scattered over Bloomingdale's.

"Bloomingdale's!" the rabbi exclaimed. "Why Bloomingdale's?"

"Then I'll be sure my daughters visit me twice a week."

*   *   *   *

There are recent rumors that Julie Andrews did a concert for AARP. Ms. Andrews sang a favorite from the Sound of Music, Favorite Things. There were a few changes to the words, to fit in with the AARP theme.

Here are the new words to this tune:

Maalox and rose drops and needles for knitting,
Walkers and handrails and new dental fittings,
Bundles of magazines tied up in string,
Hot tea and crumpets, and corn plaster for bunions,
No spicy hot food or food cooked with onions,
Bathrobes and heat pads and hot meals they bring,
These are a few of my favorite things.
Back pains, confused brains, and no fear sinning,
Thin bones, and fractures and hair that is thinning,
And we won't mention our short shrunken frames,
When we remember our favorite things.
When the joints ache, when the hips break,
When the eyes grow dim,
Then I remember the great life I've had,

And then I don't feel so bad.

*   *   *   *

One night, an 87-year-old woman came home from Bingo to find her husband in bed with another woman. Angry, she became violent and ended up pushing him off the balcony of their 2nd floor apartment, killing him instantly.
When brought before the court on charges of murder, she was asked if she had anything to say in her defense.
Well, Your Honor, she began coolly. I figured that at 92, if he could have sex, he could fly!!!

*   *   *   *

I'm not aging; I'm ripening to perfection.

*   *   *   *

Top 25 Signs that you've already grown up.

1. Your potted plants stay alive.
2. Fooling around in a twin-sized bed is absurd.
3. You keep more food than beer in the fridge.
4. 6:00 AM is when you get up, not when you go to sleep.
5. You hear your favorite song on an elevator.
6. You carry an umbrella. You watch the Weather Channel.
7. Your friends marry and divorce instead of hookup and breakup.

8. You go from 130 days of vacation time to 7.

9. Jeans and a sweater no longer qualify as 'dressed up'

10. You're the one calling the police because those darn kids next door don't know how to turn down the stereo.

11. Older relatives feel comfortable telling sex jokes around you.

12. You don't know what time Taco Bell closes anymore.

13. Your car insurance goes down and your car payments go up.

14. You feed your dog science diet instead of McDonald's.

15. Sleeping on the couch makes your back hurt.

16. You no longer take naps from noon to 6pm

17. Dinner and a movie = The whole date instead of beginning of one

18. MTV News is no longer your primary source for information

19. You go to the drug store for Ibuprofen and antacids, no condoms and pregnancy tests

20. A $4.00 bottle of wine is no longer 'pretty good stuff'

21. You actually eat breakfast foods at breakfast time.

22. Grocery lists are longer than macaroni & cheese, diet Pepsi & Ho-Ho's.

23. "I just can't drink the way I used to" replaces "I'm never going to drink that much again"

24. Over 90% of the time you spend in front of a computer is for real work

25. You don't drink at home to save money before going to the bar.

*   *   *   *

How To Tell You're Over the Hill

You no longer laugh at Preparation H commercials
Your arms are almost too short to read the newspaper
You buy shoes with crepe rubber soles
The only reason you're still awake at 2a.m. is indigestion
People ask you what color your hair used to be
You enjoy watching the news
Your car must have four doors
You no longer think of speed limits as a challenge
You have a dream about prunes
You browse the bran cereal section in the grocery store
You start worrying when your supply of Ben Gay is low.
You think a C.D. is a certificate of deposit
You have more than 2 pairs of glasses
You read the obituaries daily
Your biggest concern when dancing is falling
You enjoy hearing about other peoples operations
You wear black socks with sandals
You know all the warning signs of a heart attack

*   *   *   *

Just before the funeral services, the undertaker came up to the
very elderly widow and asked, "How old was your husband?"
"98," she replied. "Two years older than me."
"So you're 96," the undertaker commented.

She responded, "Hardly worth going home is it?"

*   *   *   *

A 97-year-old man goes into his doctor's office and says, "Doc, I want my sex drive lowered."

"Sir," replied the doctor, "You're 97. Don't you think your sex drive is all in your head?"

"You're right it is!" replied the old man. "That's why I want it lowered!"

*   *   *   *

MIDLIFE

Midlife is when the growth of the hair on our legs slows down. This gives us plenty of time to care for our newly acquired mustache.

Midlife women no longer have upper arms, we have wingspans, we are no longer women in sleeveless shirts, we are flying squirrels in drag.

Midlife has hit when you stand naked in front of the mirror and can see your rear end without turning around.

Midlife is when you bounce (a lot) but you don't bounce back. It's more like splat!

Midlife is when you want to grab every firm young lovely in a tube top and scream, "Listen, honey, even the Roman Empire fell, and those things will too!"

Midlife is when you realize that if you were a dog, you would need a control top flea collar.

Midlife is when you go to the doctor and you realize you are now so old, you have to pay someone to look at you naked.

You know you are getting old when you go for a mammogram and you realize it is the only time someone will ask you to appear topless in a film.

Midlife brings the wisdom that life throws you curves and that you're now sitting on your biggest ones.

Midlife can bring out your angry, bitter side. You look at your latte-swilling, beeper-wearing know-it-all teenager and think, "For this I have stretch marks?"

Midlife is when your memory really starts to go: the only thing you retain is water.

The good news about midlife is that the glass is still half-full. Of course, the bad news is that it won't be long before your teeth are floating in it.

You know you've crossed the midlife threshold when you're in the grocery store and you hear a Muzak version of "stairway to Heaven in the produce department. It's very hard to "get jiggy with it" in midlife. Jiggly, yes; jiggy, no.

Midlife is when your 1970's Body-by-Jake now includes Legs-by Rand McNally.

Midlife is when you start to repeat yourself and your chins follow suit.

You become more reflective in midlife. You start pondering the "big" questions: what is life, why am I here and how much

Healthy Choice ice cream can I eat before it's no longer a health issue?

*   *   *   *

Dear Son,
I have become a little older since I saw you last, and a few changes have come into my life since then.
Frankly, I have become a frivolous old gal. I am seeing five-gentleman everyday. As soon as I wake up, Will Power helps me get out of bed. Then I go to see John. Then Charlie Horse comes along, and when he is here he takes a lot of my time and attention.
When he leaves, Arthur Ritis shows up and stays the rest of the day. He doesn't like to stay in one place very long, so he takes me from joint to joint. After such a busy day, I'm really tired and glad to go to bed with Ben Gay. What a life. Oh yes, I'm also flirting with Al Zymer.

Love, Grandma
P.S. The preacher came to call the other day. He said at my age I should be thinking of the hereafter. I told him, "Oh I do it all the time. No matter where I am, in the parlor, upstairs, in the kitchen, or down in the basement." I ask myself, "Now, what am I here after?"

*   *   *   *

I am hereby officially tendering my resignation as an adult. I have decided I would like to accept the responsibilities of an 8 year-old again. I want to go to McDonald's and think that it's a four star restaurant…I want to sail sticks across a fresh mud puddle and make a sidewalk with rocks. I want to think M&Ms are better than money because you can eat them.

I want to lie under a big oak tree and run a lemonade stand with my friends on a hot summer's day.

I want to return to a time when life was simple; When all you knew were colors, multiplication tables, and nursery rhymes, but that didn't bother you, because you didn't know what you didn't know and you didn't care.

All you knew was to be happy because you were blissfully unaware of all the things that should make you worried or upset.

I want to think the world is fair.

That everyone is honest and good.

I want to believe that anything is possible. I want to be oblivious to the complexities of life and be overly excited by the little things again.

I want to live simple again. I don't want my day to consist of computer crashes, mountains of paperwork, depressing news, how to survive more days in the month than there is money in the bank, doctor bills, gossip, illness, and loss of loved ones.

I want to believe in the power of smiles, hugs, a kind word, truth, justice, peace, dreams, the imagination, mankind and making angels in the snow.

So…here's my checkbook and my car-keys, my credit card bills. I am officially resigning from adulthood. And if you want to discuss this further, you'll have to catch me first.

*   *   *   *

A 60-year-old man went to the doctor for a checkup. The doctor told him, "You're in terrific shape. There's nothing wrong with you. Why, you might live forever. You have the body of a 35 year old. By the way, how old was your father when he died?"

The 60 year old responded, "Did I say he was dead?"

The doctor was surprised and asked, "How old is he and is he very active?"

The 60 year old responded, "Well, he is 82 years old and he still goes skiing three times a season and surfing three times a week during the summer."

The doctor couldn't believe it. "Well, how old was your grandfather when he died?"

The 60 year old responded again, "Did I say he was dead?"

The doctor was astonished. He said, "You mean to tell me you are 60 years old and both your father and your grandfather are alive? Is your grandfather very active?"

The 60 year old said, "He goes skiing at least once a season and surfing once a week during the summer. Not only that," said the patient, "my grandfather is 106 years old, and next week he is getting married again."

The doctor said, "At 106 years, why on earth would your grandfather want to get married?"
His patient looked up at the doctor and said, "Did I say he
wanted to?"

*   *   *   *

Just a line to say I'm living
That I'm not among the dead,
Though I'm getting more forgetful
And more mixed up in my head.
I don't know, when I stand
At the foot of the stair,
If I must go up for something
Or just came down from there.
I stand before the fridge so often,
My mind just filled with doubt:
Have I just put food away
Or should I get it out?
And there's times when it's dark out,
With my nightcap on my head
I don't know if I'm retiring
Or just getting out of bed.
So if it's my turn to write you
There's no need of getting sore;
I may think I have written,
And don't want to be a bore.
So remember I do love you
And I wish that you were here.

But now it's nearly mail time
So I must say goodbye, dear.
There I stand beside the mailbox
With a face so very red
Instead of mailing you my letter
I had opened it instead

        *   *   *   *

It's hard to be nostalgic when you can't remember anything.

        *   *   *   *

Self Improvement Workshops
Overcoming Peace of Mind
Creative Suffering
You and Your Birthmark
Guilt Without Sex
The Primal Shrug
Ego Gratification Through Violence
Holding Your Child's Attention Through Guilt and Fear
Dealing with Post Self Realization Depression
How to Overcome Self Doubt Through Pretense and
Ostentation

Business/Career Workshops
Money Can Make You Rich
Talking Good: How You Can Improve Speech and Get A Better
Job

I Made $100 In Real Estate

Packaging and Selling Your Child: A Parent's Guide to the Porno Market

Career Opportunities in Iran

How to Profit From Your Own Body

Under-Achievers Guide to Very Small Business Opportunities

Filler Phrases for Thesis Writers

Tax Shelters for the Indigent

Looters Guide to American Cities

Health and Fitness Workshops

Creative Tooth Decay

Exorcism and Acne

The Joys of Hypochondria

High Fiber Sex

Suicide and Your Health

Bio-Feedback and how to Stop It

Understanding Nudity

Tap Dance Your Way to Social Ridicule

Home Economics Workshops

How to Convert Your Family Room Into A Garage

How to Cultivate Viruses In Your Refrigerator

Burglar Proof Your Home With Concrete

Basic Kitchen Taxidermy

Sinus Drainage At Home

101 Other Uses For Your Vacuum Cleaner

The Repair and Maintenance of Your Virginity

How To Convert A Wheelchair Into a Dune Buggy
What To Do With Your Conversational Wit
Christianity And the Art of RV Repair

Craft Workshops
How to Draw Dirty Pictures
Needlecraft for Junkies
Gifts For the Senile
Bonsai Your Pet
Mobiles and Collages with Felt
Cuticle Crafts
How to Use Plaster To Improve Your Attitude
Self-Actualization and Your Genes

*   *   *   *

Older Dilemma
A. I was thinking about how a status symbol of today is phones that everyone has clipped on. I can't afford one so I am wearing a garage door opener.

B. You know, I spent a fortune on deodorant before I realized people didn't like me anyway.

C. I was thinking that women should put pictures of missing husbands on beer cans!

D. I was thinking about old age and decided that it is when you have something on the ball but you are just too tired to bounce it.

E. I thought about making a movie for folks my age called "Pumping Rust."

F. I have gotten that dreaded furniture disease…that's when your chest is falling into your drawers!

G. You know when people see a cat's litter box, they always say, "Oh, have you got a cat?" Just once I wanted to say, "No, it's for company.

H. Employment application blanks always ask who is to be contacted in case of an emergency. I think you should write…A Good Doctor!

I. Why do they put pictures of criminals up in the Post Office? What are we supposed to do…write to these men? Why don't they just put their pictures on the postage stamps so the mailmen could look for them while they deliver the mail?

J. I was thinking about how people seem to read the Bible a lot more as they get older then it dawned on me…they were cramming for FINALS.

*   *   *   *

If you lived as a child of the 40's, 50's, & 60's, congratulations on being a survivor of the times…Looking back it's hard to believe that we have lived as long as we have.

We licked the beaters and didn't have anyone telling us we were going to become deathly ill from eating batter with raw eggs in it!

At Easter time, we had our dyed Easter eggs in a nest on the counter and they sat out at room temperature for the week after Easter. We would peel one whenever we felt like it. I can't believe we made it!

As children, we would ride in cars with no seat belts. Riding in the back of a pickup truck on a warm day was a special treat.

Our baby cribs were covered with bright colored lead paint.

We had no childproof lids on medicine bottles or doors, but we got our butts spanked if we opened them, and no one called Child Protective Services.

When we rode our bikes, we had no helmets. Not to mention hitchhiking to town as a young kid!

We drank water from the garden hose.

We would spend hours building our go-carts out of scrap and rode down the hill, only to find out we forgot the brakes. After running into the bushes a few times we learned to solve the problem.

We would leave home in the morning and play all day, as long as we were back when the streetlights came on. No one was able to contact us all day. No cell phones. Unthinkable.

We got cut, broke bones and broke teeth, and there were no lawsuits. They were accidents. No one was to blame, but us. Remember accidents?

We had fights and punched each other and got black and blue and learned to get over it.

We ate cupcakes, bread and butter, and drank sugar soda but we were never overweight...we were always outside playing games. We did not have Play stations, Nintendo 64, X-Boxes, 99 channels on cable, video tape movies, surround sound, personal cell phones, Personal Computers, Internet Chat rooms...we had friends. We went outside and found them.

We rode bikes or walked to a friend's home and knocked on the door or rang the bell and just walked in and talked to them. Imagine that. Without asking a parent. By our-selves!

Little League had tryouts and not everyone made the team. Those who didn't, have to learn to deal with disappointment.

Some students weren't as smart as others so they failed and were held back to repeat the same grade. Tests were not adjusted for any reason. Our actions were our own. Consequences were expected.

The idea of a parent bailing us out if we broke a law was unheard of. They actually sided with the law. Imagine that!

The past 50 years has been an explosion of innovation of new ideas. We had freedom, failure, success and responsibility, and we learned how to deal with it all.

* * * *

Two elderly ladies are sitting on the front porch doing nothing.
One lady turns and asks, "Do you still get horny?"
The other replies, "Oh sure I do."
The first old lady asks, "What do you do about it?"
The second old lady replies, "I suck a lifesaver."
After a few moments, the first old lady asks, "Who drives you to the beach?"

* * * *

The old lady was standing at the railing of the cruise ship holding her hat on tight so that it would not blow off in the wind. A gentleman approached her and said: "Pardon me, madam. I do not intend to be forward, but did you know that your dress is blowing up in this high wind?"

"Yes, I know," said the lady, "I need both hands to hold onto this hat."

"But, madam, you must know that your privates are exposed!" said the gentleman in earnest.

The woman looked down, then back up at the man and replied, "Sir, anything you see down there is 85 years old. I just bought this hat yesterday!"

*   *   *   *

Ethel and Mabel, two elderly widows, were watching the folks go by from their park bench. Ethel said, "You know, Mabel, I've been reading this 'Sex and Marriage' book and all they talk about is 'mutual orgasm.' 'Mutual orgasm' here and mutual orgasm there—that's all they talk about. Tell me, Mabel, when your husband was alive, did you two ever have mutual orgasm?" Mabel thought for a long while. Finally, she shook her head and said, "No, I think we had State Farm."

*   *   *   *

Now that I'm "older" (but still refuse to grow up), here's what I've discovered"

1. I started out with nothing, and I still have most of it.
2. My wild oats have turned into prunes and All Bran.
3. I finally got my head together: now my body is falling apart.
4. Funny, I don't remember being absent minded….
5. All reports are in: life is now officially unfair.

6. If all is not lost, where is it?

7. It is easier to get older than it is to get wiser.

8. Some days you're the dog: some days you're the hydrant.

9. I wish the buck stopped here: I sure could use a few.

10. Kids in the back seat cause accidents.

11. Accidents in the back seat cause kids.

12. It's hard to make a comeback when you haven't been any-where.

13. The only time the world beats a path to your door is when you're in the bathroom.

14. If God wanted me to touch my toes, he would have put them on my knees.

15. When I'm finally holding all the cards, why does everyone decide to play chess?

16. It's not hard to meet expenses…they're everywhere.

17. The only difference between a rut and a grave is the depth.

18. These days, I spend a lot of time thinking about the here-after. I go somewhere to get something and then wonder what I'm here after.

*   *   *   *

A forty-ish woman was at home happily jumping on her bed and squealing with delight. Her husband watches her for a while and asks "Do you have any idea how ridiculous you look? What's the matter with you?

The woman continues to bounce on the bed and says, "I don't care. I just came from the doctor and he says I have the breasts of an 18-year-old. The husband said, "What did he say about your 41-year-old-ass?"

"Your name never came up," she replied.

*   *   *   *

One evening the old farmer decided to go down to the pond, as he hadn't been there for a while, and look it over. He grabbed a five-gallon bucket to bring back some fruit. As he neared the pond, he heard voices shouting and laughing with glee.

As he came closer he saw it was a bunch of young women skinny-dipping in his pond. He made the women aware of his presence and they all went to the deep end of the pond. One of the women shouted to him, "We're not coming out until you leave." The old man frowned, "I didn't come down here to watch you ladies swim naked or make you get out of the pond naked." Holding the bucket up he said, "I'm here to feed the alligator."

Moral: Old age and cunning will triumph over youth and enthusiasm every time.

*   *   *   *

There will be no nursing home in my future...When I get old and feeble, I am going to get on a Princess Cruise. The average cost for a nursing home is $200 per day. I have checked on reservations at Princess and I can get a long-term discount and senior discount price of $135 per day. That leaves $65 a day for:
1. Gratuities, which will only be $10 per day.

2. I will have as many as 10 meals a day if I can waddle to the restaurant, or I can have room service (which means I can have breakfast in bed every day of the week).

3. Princess has as many as three swimming pools, a workout room, free washers and dryers, and shoes every night.

4. They have free toothpaste and razors, and free soap and shampoo.

5. They will even treat you like a customer, not a patient. An extra $5 worth of tips will have the entire staff scrambling to help you.

6. I will get to meet new peoples every 7 or 14 days.

7. T.V. broken? Light bulb needs changing? Need to have the mattress replaced? No Problem! They will fix everything and apologize for your inconvenience.

8. Clean sheets and towels every day, and you don't even have to ask for them.

9. If you fall in the nursing home and break a hip you are on Medicare. If you fall and break a hip on a Princess Ship they will upgrade you to a suite for the rest of your life. Now hold on for the best. Do you want to see South America, the Panama Canal, Tahiti, Australia, New Zealand, Asia, or name where you want to go? Princess will have a ship ready to go. So don't look for me in a nursing home, just call shore to ship.

P.S. If you die they just dump you over the side, at no charge.

I'm facing it with a grin. I'll just check into the Holiday Inn.

*   *   *   *

A teenage granddaughter comes downstairs for her date with this see-through blouse on and no bra. Her grandmother pitched a fit, telling her not to dare go out like that! The teenager tells her "Loosen up Grams, these are modern times. You got to let your rosebuds show!" and out she goes. The next day when the teenager comes downstairs, the grandmother is sitting there with no top on. The teenager wants to die. She explains to her grandmother that she has friends coming over soon and that having no top on is not appropriate….

The grandmother says, "Loosen up, Sweetie. If you can show off your rosebuds, then I can display my hanging baskets."

*   *   *   *

Just got this from a reliable source. It seems that there is a virus out there called the C-Nile Virus that even the most advanced anti Virus programs cannot take care of, so be warned. It appears to affect those of us who were born before 1958!

Symptoms of C-Nile Virus:
1. Causes you to send same email twice.
2. Causes you to send blank email.
3. Causes you to send to wrong person.
4. Causes you to send back to person who sent it to you.
5. Causes you to forget to attach the attachment.
6. Causes you to wonder who all the people in your address book are.

7. Causes you to hit "SEND" before you've finished the letter.

*   *   *   *

YES, I'M A SENIOR CITIZEN!
I'm the life of the party…. even if it lasts until 8pm.
I'm very good at opening childproof caps…with a hammer.
I'm usually interested in going home before I get to where I am going.
I'm awake many hours before my body allows me to get up.
I'm smiling all the time because I can't hear a thing you're saying.
I'm very good at telling stories; over and over and over and over…
I'm aware that people's grandchildren are not nearly as cute as mine.
I'm so cared for long term care, eye care, private care, and dental care.
I'm not really grouchy,
I just don't like traffic, waiting, crowds, lawyers, loud music, unruly kids, Toyota commercials, Tom Brokaw, Dan Rather, barking dogs, politicians, and a few other things I can't seem to remember right now.
I'm sure everything I can't find is in a safe, secure place somewhere.
I'm wrinkled, saggy, lumpy, and that's just my left leg.
I'm having trouble remembering simple words like…
I'm beginning to realize that aging is not for wimps.
I'm sure they are making adults much younger these days, and when did they let kids become policemen?

I'm wondering, if you're only as old as you feel, how could I be alive at 150?

And, how can my kids be older than I feel sometimes?

I'm a walking storeroom of facts...I've just lost the key to the storeroom door.

*   *   *   *

The preacher, in his Sunday sermon, used "Forgive Your Enemies" as his subject. After a long sermon, he asked how many were willing to forgive their enemies.

About half held up their hands. Not satisfied he harangued for another twenty minutes and repeated his question. This time he received a response of about 80 percent.

Still unsatisfied, he lectured for another 15 minutes and repeated his question. With all thoughts now on Sunday dinner, all responded except one elderly lady in the rear. "Mrs. Jones, are you not willing to forgive your enemies?" I don't have any."

"Mrs. Jones, that is very unusual. How old are you?"

"Ninety-three."

"Mrs. Jones, please come down in front and tell the congregation how a person can live to be ninety-three, and not have an enemy in the world."

The little sweetheart of a lady tottered down the aisle, very slowly turned around and said:

"It's easy, I just outlived the sons of bitches."

*   *   *   *

This is an actual job application that a 75-year-old senior citizen submitted to Wal-Mart in Arkansas. They hired him too because he was so honest and funny.

NAME: George martin

SEX: Not lately, but I am looking for the right woman (or at least one who'll cooperate).

DESIRED POSITION: Company's President or Vice President. But seriously, whatever's available. If I were in a position to be picky, I wouldn't be applying here in the first place.

DESIRED SALARY: $185,000 a year plus stock options and a Michael Ovitz style severance package. If that's not possible, make an offer and we can haggle.

EDUCATION: Yes.

LAST POSITION HELD: Target for middle-management hostility.

PREVIOUS SALARY: A lot less than I'm worth.

MOST NOTABLE ACHIEVEMENT: My incredible collection of stolen pens and post-it notes.

REASON FOR LEAVING: It sucked.

HOURS AVAILABLE TO WORK: Any.

PREFERRED HOURS: 1:30-3:30 pm. Monday, Tuesday and Thursday.

DO YOU HAVE ANY SPECIAL SKILLS?: Yes, but they're better suited to a more intimate environment.

MAY WE CONTACT YOUR CURRENT EMPLOYER: If I had one, would I be here?

DO YOU HAVE ANY PHYSICAL CONDITIONS THAT WOULD PROHIBIT YOU FROM LIFTING 50 POUNDS? Of what?

DO YOU HAVE A CAR? I think the more appropriate question here would be "Do you have a car that runs?"

HAVE YOU RECEIVED ANY SPECIAL AWARDS OR RECOGNITION? I may already be a winner of the Publishers Clearing House Sweepstakes, so they tell me.

DO YOU SMOKE? On the job-no, on my breaks-no.

WHAT WOULD YOU LIKE TO BE DOING IN FIVE YEARS? Living in the Bahamas with a fabulously wealthy dumb sexy blonde supermodel who thinks I'm the greatest thing since sliced bread. Actually, I'd like to be doing that now.

DO YOU CERTIFY THAT THE ABOVE IS TRUE AND COMPLETE TO THE BEST OF YOUR KNOWLEDGE? Oh yes, absolutely.

SIGN HERE: Sagittarius.

*   *   *   *

Senior citizen to his eighty-year old buddy,
"So I hear you are getting married?"
"Yep!"
"This woman, is she good looking?"
"Not really."
"Is she a good cook?"
"Naw, she can't cook too well."
"Does she have lots of money?"
"No, poor as a church mouse."

"Well then, is she good in bed?"
"I don't know."
"Why in the world do you want to marry her then?"
"She can still drive."

*   *   *   *

Now that food has replaced sex in my life, I can't even get into my OWN pants.

*   *   *   *

Someone who teaches at a Middle School in Safe Harbor, Florida forwarded the following letter. The letter was sent to the principal's office after the school had sponsored a luncheon for the elderly. An old lady received a new radio at the lunch as a door price and was writing to say thank you. This story is a credit to all human kind.

Dear Safety Harbor Middle School;

God bless you for the beautiful radio I won at your recent senior citizens luncheon. I am 84 years old and live at the Safety harbor Assisted Home for the Aged. All of my family has passed away. I am alone now and it's nice to know that someone is thinking about me. God bless you for your kindness to an old forgotten lady. My roommate is 95 and always had her own radio but before I received one, she would never let me listen to hers, even when she was napping. The other day her radio fell off the nightstand and broke into a lot of pieces. It was awful

and she was in tears. She asked if she could listen to mine, and I said, "kiss my ass." Thank you for that opportunity.
Sincerely,
Edna Walters

*   *   *   *

A passer-by noticed an old lady sitting on her front step: "I couldn't help noticing how happy you look! What is your secret for such a long, happy life?"
"I smoke 4 packs of cigarettes a day," she said. "Before I go to bed, I smoke a nice big joint. Apart from that, I drink a whole bottle of Jack Daniels every week, and eat only junk food. On weekends I pop a huge number of pills and do not exercise at all."
"This is absolutely amazing at your age!!!!", says the passer-by. "How old are you?"
"Twenty-four."

*   *   *   *

I don't do drugs anymore…I get the same effect just standing up fast.

*   *   *   *

After a spring break, a teacher asked her young pupils how they spent the holidays. One child wrote the following:

"We always used to spend the holidays with Grandma and Grandpa. They used to live here in a big brick house, but Grandpa got retarded and they moved to Arizona.

Now they live in a place with a lot of other retarded people. They live in a tin box and have rocks painted green to look like grass. They ride around on big tricycles and wear nametags because they don't know who they are anymore.

They go to a building called a wrecked center, but they must have got it fixed, because it is all right now. They play games and do exercises there, but they don't do them very well. There is a swimming pool too, but they all jump up and down in it with their hats on. I guess they don't know how to swim.

At their gate, there is a dollhouse with a little old man sitting in it. He watches all day so nobody can escape. Sometimes they sneak out. Then they go cruising in their golf carts. My Grandma used to bake cookies and stuff, but I guess she forgot how. Nobody there cooks, they just eat out. And they eat the same things every night. "Early Birds." Some of the people can't get past the man in the dollhouse to go out. So the ones who do get out bring food back to the wrecked house and call it potluck. My grandma says Grandpa's worked all his life to earn his retardment and says I should work hard so I can be retarded someday too.

When I earn my retardment I want to be the man in the dollhouse. Then I will let people out so they can visit their grandchildren.

978-0-595-37072-6
0-595-37072-1

Printed in the United States
52980LVS00006B/397-498

Principles of Real Estate Management

Thirteenth Edition

JAMES C. DOWNS, JR., CPM®

(1905–1981)

Principles of Real Estate Management

Thirteenth Edition

Introduction by
Anthony Downs

IREM **Institute of Real Estate Management**
of the **NATIONAL ASSOCIATION OF REALTORS**®
430 NORTH MICHIGAN AVENUE · CHICAGO, ILLINOIS 60611

Library of Congress Cataloging-in-Publication Data

Principles of real estate management. -- 13th ed.
    p. cm.
  Rev. ed. of: Principles of real estate management / James C.
Downs, Jr. 12th ed. c1980.
  Includes index.
  ISBN 0-944298-59-1 :
   1. Real estate management.   I. Downs, James Chesterfield, 1905–1981
Principles of real estate management.   II. Institute of Real Estate
Management.
HD1394.P74   1991
333.33'068--dc20   91–2127
                                                  CIP

Printed in the United States of America

2 3 4 5 6 7 8 9 10 Printing / Year 00 99 98 97 96 95 94

Publisher's Preface

Principles of Real Estate Management, Thirteenth Edition, has been completely revised and updated to provide an academic foundation for property managers of the 1990s. It reflects the professional experience and expertise of numerous CPM® members of the Institute of Real Estate Management (IREM).

The text begins by providing a historical background on the profession of property management. Subsequent chapters cover principles of economics as they relate to real estate management, the objectives of property owners, and reasons for investment in real property. There are separate chapters on the most important facets of property management—financial issues, accounting, and record keeping; the importance of management planning and the management agreement; fundamentals of marketing and leasing rental space; the role of the property manager as an employer; and the importance of maintenance to the condition and the value of real property.

Management of residential property is highlighted by discussion of rental apartments and condominium ownership, as well as coverage of other types of residential properties. Unique aspects of maintenance and insurance coverage in residential management are also outlined. The dominant types of leased commercial properties—offices and retail space—are described in detail, with special emphasis on the differences in rental rates and lease terms in commercial leasing. The final chapter covers essentials of the business of real estate management.

ACKNOWLEDGMENTS

The Institute has drawn upon the experience and expertise of its CPM® membership at large in compiling the new edition of *Principles of Real Estate Management.* The book manuscript has been scrutinized by members who not only manage real estate on a daily basis but also teach others the skills of property management—both in courses organized and offered by the Institute of Real Estate Management and as instructors in colleges nationwide.

Special thanks and acknowledgment are due the following individuals who served as **Editorial Consultants** throughout this project. All are members of the Institute's faculty and participate in its educational programs in addition to actively managing large portfolios of diverse income-producing properties. Their contribution includes a peer-review assessment of the entire manuscript for both accuracy of content and ease of reading and teachability. This assures not only a good reference for the real estate professional—one that reflects current accepted property management practices nationwide—but also a well-formulated college-level textbook for training newcomers to the profession.

Julia A. Banks, CPM®, of Banks and Company in Denver, Colorado, has been a professional property manager for more than 20 years. Her experience includes management of the entire spectrum of residential and commercial properties. Ms. Banks has been active in the Institute of Real Estate Management, both locally and at the national level, since she achieved the CPM designation in 1978. In 1988, she was named Property Manager of the Year by the Northern Colorado Chapter of IREM. She has been a Regional Vice President, served on and chaired the Publishing Committee, served as Director for the Course 201 faculty, and is a member of the IREM National Faculty. For the last ten years, she has regularly taught chapter-sponsored offerings of Introduction to Real Estate Management which uses *Principles of Real Estate Management* as a textbook. Ms. Banks is an Adjunct Professor at the University of Denver, and she teaches property management in the Continuing Education Department at the University of Colorado.

Edward J. Childers, Jr., CPM®, of Centennial, Inc., in Nashville, Tennessee, has been a real estate professional for more than two decades. Since achieving the CPM designation in 1971, he has been active with the Institute of Real Estate Management, including service as a Regional Vice President, Senior Vice President of the Communications Division, Director and Vice Director for the Course 201 faculty, member of various national committees in the Education Division, and an elected Governing

Councillor. In addition, Mr. Childers has frequently taught Introduction to Real Estate Management which uses *Principles of Real Estate Management* as a textbook.

Richard F. Muhlebach, CPM®, President and CEO of TRF Management Corporation in Bellevue, Washington, has more than 20 years experience in managing, leasing, and developing commercial and residential properties. Since achieving the CPM designation in 1975, Mr. Muhlebach has been active in the Institute of Real Estate Management both locally and at the national level. In particular, he has served as Vice Division Director for the Education Division and chaired committees in both the Education and Communications Divisions. He is a Senior Instructor on the IREM National Faculty and has taught Introduction to Real Estate Management which uses *Principles of Real Estate Management* as a textbook. In addition to the CPM designation, Mr. Muhlebach has been awarded the designations of Certified Shopping Center Manager (CSM), Counselor of Real Estate (CRE), and Real Property Administrator (RPA) by other professional associations. He is also an instructor for the International Council of Shopping Centers and frequently teaches throughout the United States. Mr. Muhlebach is co-author of *Managing and Leasing Commercial Properties,* published by John Wiley and Sons, and author of more than 30 articles on real estate topics.

Lyn Weiland, CPM®, of St. Augustine, Florida, has been active in property management since 1976. After achieving the CPM designation in 1981, she served on a number of national committees of the Institute of Real Estate Management, including chairmanship of the Publishing Committee. In the IREM Education Division, she was appointed to the Course Content Board which determines the substance of IREM qualification courses as well as its educational courses and seminars. Ms. Weiland is a member of the IREM National Faculty and has served as a Course Board Director (Course 400). An active educator, Ms. Weiland has taught college-level courses at universities and for IREM across the nation. She has also been awarded the Certified Commercial-Investment Member (CCIM) designation and is a co-author of the IREM book, *The Successful On-Site Manager.*

Other Acknowledgments

A number of CPM members of the Institute regularly teach IREM Course 201, Introduction to Real Estate Management, which uses *Principles of Real Estate Management* as a textbook. The following faculty members provided additional guidance for the development of the Thirteenth Edition of *Principles of Real Estate Management*: Georgia B. Ascher, CPM®; Bodie J. Beard, CPM®; Robert E. Eaton, CPM®; Owen M. Ellis, CPM®; Paul A. Fessler, CPM®; Jules Galanter, CPM®; Joseph J. Glennon, CPM®; James A. Krizman,

CPM®; Robert M. Lattimore, CPM® Emeritus; Charles S. Lowen, CPM®; Kathleen M. McKenna-Harmon, CPM®; Charles R. Nicholson, CPM®; David C. Nilges, CPM®; and Richard J. Stampahar, CPM®.

In addition, thanks are due Lawrence M. Mages, of Bell, Boyd, and Lloyd in Chicago, Illinois, who provided legal review of information in the text, especially the discussion of eviction procedures; and Russell Schneck of Russell Schneck Design in Chicago, Illinois, who provided dustjacket art, cover design, and specifications for the interior of the book. The photo on the dustjacket is from T. Dietrich/H. Armstrong Roberts. The frontispiece is a portrait of James C. Downs, Jr., painted by Rick Farrell.

The Building Owners and Managers Association—BOMA International—is the acknowledged source for precise instructions for measuring office space for leasing. The instructions reproduced in exhibits 10.1 and 10.2 are necessarily incomplete, and the exhibit captions identify the publication which contains the complete measurement specifications and explanation.

The Institute also thanks Anthony Downs, Senior Fellow at The Brookings Institution, for writing the Introduction to the Thirteenth Edition. In it, he establishes the crucial importance of property managers and the services they provide to real estate investors and owners in the 1990s—a decade in which institutional ownership and global investment are expected to increase markedly, and changes in the U.S. population (proportionately larger numbers of senior citizens and growing cultural diversity in the work force) will have profound effects on the way the professional manages real property. He also shares with the reader the importance of professional real estate management to his father, James C. Downs, Jr.

AN APPRECIATION

James C. Downs, Jr. (1905–1981), was one of the founders of the Institute of Real Estate Management in 1933 and holder of CPM® key number 1— the first property manager to receive the CPM® designation. As a practicing real estate manager, James Downs was among the first to realize that the best means of developing qualified property managers for the future is to teach them specific skills. To this end, he wrote *Principles of Real Estate Management*. The first edition of his book was published by the Institute in 1947, and he revised the work repeatedly—through the twelfth edition published in 1980. The measure of his success is the more than 9,000 CPM® members of the Institute of Real Estate Management in 1990 and the thousands of others who were introduced to their careers in property management through college courses that relied on *Principles of Real Estate Management* through twelve editions as their textbook.

Always Mr. Downs sought to state the basic principles of property management and to set them in a context of contemporary examples. The editorial consultants and IREM staff have striven to perpetuate James Downs' principles and purpose throughout this new Thirteenth Edition. In appreciation for all that he contributed to the Institute of Real Estate Management—including the first twelve editions of *Principles of Real Estate Management*—this all new Thirteenth Edition is dedicated to James C. Downs, Jr., CPM®, in memoriam.

Contents

Introduction

SOCIETAL AND FISCAL INFLUENCES ON PROPERTY MANAGEMENT

It was 1980 when the twelfth and last previous edition of my father's book, *Principles of Real Estate Management,* was published—one year before he died. Since then, revolutionary developments have occurred in the world of real estate. Those developments have greatly affected both the environment in which the profession of property management is practiced and the proper way to practice it. Nearly all these revolutionary changes have served to increase the relative importance of property management compared to all the other major functions in real estate (development, design, finance, construction, leasing, and sales). This introduction seeks to explain why this is so and just what implications it has for property management as a profession.

Recent General Trends Affecting Real Estate

As my father said in his last Preface, "Real property . . . reflects the society it houses . . . by accommodating contemporary lifestyles and standards . . . [and adjusting] to the nation's social, financial, economic, and political condition." Hence understanding property management's current situation requires examining how it has been affected by certain general trends in American society before looking at real estate trends in particular.

Population Trends.   During the 1980s, the population of the United States rose by 23 million persons—about the same absolute increase as in each of the two preceding decades. But the trend toward smaller average household size continued, with a growing percentage of all households consisting of single persons living alone. At the same time, the annual rate of new household formation slowed to 1.3 million in the late 1980s compared to 1.7 million in the 1970s. It will be about 1.1 million in the 1990s, when total population will grow much less than in the three preceding decades. These changes will reduce the rate at which the overall demand for housing increases in the future.

The aging of the huge "baby boom" generation, born between 1950 and 1965, has caused each age group below 35 to experience a rapid acceleration in members for a while followed by a rapid decline. During the 1970s, this process oriented American culture more toward youth than ever before. In the 1980s, the "baby boomers" passed through young adulthood. During the 1990s, they will be advancing further into maturity. As a result, the number of young households with heads under age 35 will decrease by 4.2 million, but the number with heads aged 35–54 will increase by 12.6 million. So the cultural orientation of American society will shift more toward mature adulthood. In addition, the demand for rental apartments will grow much more slowly than in the preceding two decades because of reduced formation of young households. That will intensify competition among apartment properties, increasing the importance of managing them well. Moreover, the dearth of young people entering the work force will produce a worsening labor shortage during the 1990s.

At the same time, massive immigration from abroad is intensifying the diversity of ethnic groups in America. Between 7 and 9 million immigrants entered the United States in the 1980s, both legally and illegally. Most were from Latin America and Asia rather than from Europe as in the past. In the future, more than half the nation's population growth will come from immigration instead of natural increase. The resulting diversity poses new challenges to property managers concerning both their tenants and their work force. For example, children attending the Los Angeles public schools come from homes speaking 110 different native languages! Between 1986 and the year 2000, 28 percent of all net additions to the work force will be Hispanic, 17 percent will be black, and 11 percent will be Asian; so at least 56 percent will be members of ethnic minorities. Property managers must cope with workers from a greater variety of backgrounds than ever before.

Unfortunately, the nation's educational system has been doing a poor job of training American children to master the skills necessary for performing well in a high-technology society. As a result, levels of competence among a sizable number of American young people are below those necessary for many property management roles. This will place a new demand upon quality property managers—providing on-the-job training that overcomes the deficiencies that the educational system has left in many potential workers.

A final population trend consists of two continued migrations. One is out of central cities into suburbs—which now contain 45 percent of the nation's population. The second is a further flow of migrants from the Northeast and Midwest to the South and West. For the past two decades, more than half the nation's population growth has occurred in just three states—California, Florida, and Texas. That will remain true in the 1990s.

Economic Trends.   Since 1945, productivity has risen steadily in agriculture and considerably in manufacturing. As a result, employment has fallen sharply in farming and remained stable in manufacturing, despite huge increases in the output of both. So nearly all the growth of jobs in the U.S. economy has been in services, many of which are carried out in office buildings. That is a major reason for the explosive growth of office development during the 1980s. Management of office space is now a major real estate industry.

Concerning other types of property, the dominant trend has been toward ever-greater specialization. Hotel chains have developed several tiers of properties: budget motels, "standard" motels, business-class hotels, luxury hotels, suite hotels, residential hotels, resort hotels, and super resort hotels. Retail developers have created strip shopping centers, regional malls, discount outlets, community shopping centers, "power" centers, and manufacturers' outlet centers. Even industrial properties have been divided into warehouse space, research and development space, office and display space, light manufacturing space, and "flex" space that can assume different forms. Residential specialty properties include nursing homes, retirement colonies, downtown residences, and golf-course and resort condominiums, as well as plain apartments and townhouses. Each of these "narrow niches" provides new challenges to professional property managers. Furthermore, more projects are being developed with mixed uses that combine two or more of the specialized property types mentioned above. Managers of these big, complex mixed-use projects must be familiar with appropriate methods of handling several types of property, not just one.

Since 1973, average real wages—corrected for inflation—have risen little for the vast majority of American workers because of a drastic slowdown in overall productivity growth. American households have managed to keep their living standards from falling only by working longer hours, having more members—especially women—take jobs outside the home, and saving smaller fractions of their incomes. There has been some movement toward a shrinkage of middle-income groups and a greater division of the nation into low-income and high-income groups. This poses new challenges to property managers concerning both their tenants and their work force.

Another economic trend has been an enormous growth in the use of computers in almost all lines of business. Most management functions initially done by hand in pen and ink have become fully computerized. Sophisticated computer programs permit managers to obtain more information sooner and analyze it in more complex ways than ever before possible. This trend threatens to overwhelm managers with more detailed data than they can fruitfully absorb. Hence understanding how to use computers and their outputs effectively has become an essential part of property management.

Other General Trends.   Many U.S. communities have experienced rapid population or job growth and prolonged prosperity since 1982. Some of them have also been plagued by big increases in traffic congestion and infrastructure costs. As a result, their residents and governments have adopted strong antigrowth attitudes and often established policies designed to slow down new development.

This situation has changed the way developers must approach relations with the communities where they hope to create new projects. Merely because a developer owns a specific site no longer means he or she has the right to decide how to develop it. Developers must now regard nearby residents as their partners in every project, right from the start. Hence, in designing and planning each new project, developers must consult with nearby residents and community organizations and take their views into account.

This new relationship has definite implications for property management. Because developers must be more sensitive to the impacts of each new project upon the local community, they should pay more attention to how the operations of a project will affect surrounding residents once it has been built. To do so, they should confer with experienced property managers from the earliest phases of every new project. Only in that way can they take ongoing operational factors fully into account. So property management professionals should participate in every phase of the creation of any new development project.

Another social trend relevant to property management is the increased value many Americans place on their time. The economy contains millions of relatively well-paid, two-worker households whose lives are packed with activities. This is also true of the executives running most business firms. Hence such people are willing to pay higher prices for services designed to minimize the time they must spend receiving them. This fact should influence the way property managers organize the services provided by such properties as hotels, restaurants, retail facilities, and even office buildings and apartments. For example, retail centers should permit shoppers to get in and out quickly, and office buildings may attract more tenants if they provide day-care facilities, exercise rooms, and other special services on site.

Major Developments in Real Estate Finance

Four fundamental changes in real estate finance—deregulation, institutionalization, globalization, and syndication—have had profound impacts on real estate management during the past decade. The first three will continue to influence it during the 1990s. These changes had four major consequences—a development boom, the resulting finance-driven over-building of most commercial space markets, a shift toward institutional ownership of major commercial properties, and the collapse of the thrift industry.

In the late 1970s and early 1980s, federal financial authorities and the U.S. Congress changed the rules under which the main institutions of real estate finance had functioned for 40 years. The authorities removed the legal ceilings on interest rates that banks and savings and loans could pay their depositors; they also removed many restraints on how those institutions could invest their funds. This *deregulation* ended the periodic "credit crunches" that had marked real estate development in the past. Formerly, when short-term interest rates rose above the legal ceilings on what banks and thrifts could pay, some of their depositors withdrew funds to seek higher rates elsewhere. That caused an acute absolute shortage of funds; so these institutions had to stop making real estate loans. Thus, most new development had to cease whenever short-term rates rose during business cycles.

After deregulation, however, these institutions could pay depositors enough to retain their savings even when short-term rates rose. So they kept on making real estate loans, though at higher rates. Moreover, operators of savings and loans could now invest directly in land and commercial real estate equities—and had strong incentives to do so. Thus, the periodic constraints on new development that "credit crunches" had caused was removed, and new development could proceed right through the business cycle, at least in theory.

At the same time, three new sources of funds appeared in the 1980s. One came from foreign investors able to shift funds to the United States because of the *globalization* of finance in general. World capital markets became linked electronically through telecommunications and computer networks, and money could be transferred almost anywhere instantaneously. Also, deregulation in many nations permitted more institutions to invest funds abroad. So foreign investors flocked to U.S. real estate markets.

The second relatively new source of real estate capital consisted of pension funds, whose total assets soared to above $2 trillion. Their managers were pressured by laws concerning fiduciary responsibility to diversify some of their funds into real estate equities. They usually did so through pooled funds operated by insurance companies and special investment firms. Thus, massive investment by pension funds, insurance companies, and other pooled investors constituted a new *institutionalization* of ownership.

A third source of capital was tax-benefit-driven *syndication* legalized by the Tax Act of 1981. Syndicators attracted capital from high-bracket earners seeking to shelter their income from taxes, without much regard to the real need for the property they were funding. Although this syndication source was ended by the Tax Reform Act of 1986, it helped generate an immense flood of capital into real estate during the 1980s.

The first major consequence of this flood of capital was a commercial property development super boom from 1978 through 1989. In 10 of these 12 years—all except 1982 and 1983—more than 900 million square feet of new industrial and commercial space were placed under construction contracts, whereas that had occurred in only one previous year since 1945. The universal availability of capital removed the traditional restraint on new development. Previously, most buildings had to be substantially preleased before construction could be financed. In the 1980s, institutions flush with funds bankrolled developers building structures purely on speculation. Developers created new projects, not because of any strong demand for space by tenants, but because they could "finance out" by raising more than 100 percent of their costs on a nonrecourse basis from capital suppliers. They were willing to build new space almost regardless of conditions in the space market, since they could earn big development fees and keep their organizations busy.

Unfortunately, this orgy of development had generated massive *overbuilding* of nearly all commercial space markets by about 1987. The office vacancy rate in more than thirty cities tracked by Coldwell Banker rose from less than 5 percent in 1981 to more than 20 percent in 1987, and stayed there through 1990. Competition for tenants among operators of brand new, half-empty buildings became so intense that deep rent concessions became the rule. Instead of rising around 5 percent per year, as almost all pro formas had projected, the actual level of effective rents began to *fall* after about 1984.

The third consequence of all these trends was the shift of ownership of major commercial properties from the developers who built them to the financial institutions which supplied the capital. This shift occurred in two stages. At first, many financial institutions seeking equity in office buildings, shopping centers, and other properties were content to become joint venture partners of the developers whose properties they financed. The developers still owned part of these properties and usually managed them. Later, however, these institutions wanted 100 percent ownership; and many developers got into financial trouble because of the difficulties generated by overbuilding, so they had to give up their equity positions. In addition, foreign investors and some pension funds wanted 100 percent ownership of the properties in which they invested right from the start. So gradually major institutions took over ownership of more and more of the nation's prime commercial properties.

The fourth impact of these forces—abetted by the collapse of oil prices in the mid-1980s, along with several other factors—was the destruction of much of the savings and loan industry in the late 1980s. Massive overbuilding of commercial properties and a severe local depression in oil-oriented metropolitan areas, coupled with other forces too complicated to discuss in detail here, caused thousands of these thrift institutions to go bankrupt in the last half of the 1980s. This removed what had been a major source of real estate capital up through the 1980s from effective operation in the 1990s. Although hundreds of solvent savings and loans remain in operation, the properties taken over by federal agencies from those that were bankrupt had to be disposed of on private markets. This posed yet another challenge for professional property managers who had to operate these properties, both when they were federally owned and after private investors had bought them.

These developments created triply powerful pressures increasing the relative importance of professional property management in real estate markets. In the first place, institutionalization meant that the owners of most big properties were no longer individuals who viewed those properties as their own personal wealth, to be cherished like family jewels. Rather, the owners were bureaucratic officials of large institutions who had no personal financial interest in any particular property. To manage that property, they needed someone who had the requisite professional skills. In addition, globalization meant that the institutions which owned many of these properties were in foreign countries. They were totally unfamiliar with the properties themselves, or their market areas, and too far removed to operate them on a day-to-day basis. Clearly they had to rely on local professional property managers.

Finally, overbuilding heightened the importance of management in achieving acceptable profitability from any property. When vacancy rates are low and rents are rising almost automatically because of general inflation, property management does not require consummate skill. However, 20 percent vacancy rates produce super-intense competition, widespread rent concessions, and bitter struggles over every potential tenant. Under such conditions, the skill and imagination of each property's manager make the critical difference between whether it will prosper or fail. Moreover, because tenants are in the driver's seat in overbuilt markets, they demand more intensive—and therefore more expensive—service from building managers in order just to remain where they are. That means average property management expenses will be higher in such markets than they have traditionally been in the past or are now in "tight" markets.

With rents flat or declining, and expenses still rising because of continuing general inflation, developers and all other property owners were increasingly squeezed. Big financial institutional owners had "deep pockets," but many developers were unable to maintain their debt payments. So they had to turn their properties back to the source of capital that had financed them. This process accelerated as we entered the 1990s. It further intensified institutional ownership of real estate and, therefore, the need for professional property management.

It is quite likely that the massive flows of capital into U.S. real estate from many sources during the 1980s will not be repeated on the same scale in the 1990s. Syndication has been largely negated by the Tax Reform Act of 1986. The unification of Western Europe and the shift of countries in Eastern Europe to market economies may absorb much European capital that formerly came into U.S. markets. Japanese capital will still come to the United States, but more of it than in the past may go into developing Asian nations. New federal regulations drafted after the collapse of the thrifts have largely nullified savings and loans as a source of capital for commercial properties, and federal regulators have put heavy pressure on banks to reduce their real estate lending.

If the flow of capital into real estate slows down, and the long economic prosperity of the 1980s continues with only minor interruptions, then the degree of overbuilding prevailing in most commercial property markets may gradually recede. That will again change the environment for property managers, perhaps easing some of the super-intense competition prevailing in the late 1980s. Even so, institutional ownership will become even greater and therefore the need for professional management's skills will not diminish.

Some Further Implications of Institutionalization and Globalization

Both institutionalization and globalization have increased the relative importance of professional property management for other reasons at a more profound level of reality. They have changed the very meaning of the term "ownership," which is a key part of the basic definition of property management. My father defined that function as "the administrative operation and maintenance of property according to the objectives of ownership." However, "ownership" of an office building in Minneapolis by a pension fund in New York City or by a bank in Tokyo is different in kind from ownership of the same property by a Minneapolis developer who designed and built it himself. In the early days of real estate property ownership, most owners lived in the same community as their properties, took a personal interest in managing them, and intended to hold them for long periods of time—perhaps until they died and passed them on to their heirs. They had what might be termed a "truly proprietary attitude" toward these properties. Each property was considered a cherished asset to be well-maintained over a long period of time. Its unique characteristics, imparted by the inherently unique nature of its location—since every location is unique—were recognized by its owners.

However, institutional owners—especially those located abroad—do not have the same view of real properties. The people who run those institutions regard each property as simply one unit in a certain class of assets that their institution owns. With rare exceptions, their attitude is entirely impersonal and abstract, not particularized to that property. They even view real estate assets as a class as just one of several classes, along with stocks, bonds, and cash. From their perspective, the reason for ownership of such assets is solely to produce financial returns for their institutions, not to provide property services to local users in the markets concerned. Of course, property owners have always been motivated by earning profits and capital gains, but they had traditionally also taken a personal interest in how well their properties served their patrons.

In contrast, institutional officials essentially view all these assets as *generalized commodities* rather than individual properties. Each asset is essentially interchangeable with every other in terms of the traits that matter to them—market value and yield. Moreover, these owners have no commitment to hold on to real properties—or any other assets—for any long period. They are perfectly willing to sell them at any time, even immediately after buying them, if it seems financially expedient to do so. To them, all assets are like chips in a poker game: They may be of different colors, but their significance to the players is entirely based on how much money they stand for, not any traits they may have in themselves.

This attitude is quite different from the attitude necessary to manage a specific real property effectively. Every real property is unique because it is located at one and only one place on the earth. Even two McDonald's hamburger outlets that are identical in design, size, layout, and food served are nevertheless different because they must be situated at different locations. The very nature of location includes uniqueness because of the structure of physical reality. The manager of every property must be fully aware of the unique qualities of its location and its surrounding markets in order to run it properly. That means property managers cannot in practice regard individual properties as abstract commodities. They must instead regard all real properties as particularized and unique items, even if the methods used to manage them are quite general and transferable.

Thus the shift of property ownership toward large institutions introduces a possible divergence of perspective between the officials who run those institutions and the persons who manage the properties on a day-to-day basis. True, both are interested in the financial returns that the properties produce. But the managers must have a much more particularized perspective than the owners. This difference in perspective poses a special challenge to property managers. They must convince the usually absentee owners to make sufficient investments in the maintenance, operation, repair, and promotion of their properties to maximize the properties' long-run profits and market values.

Another aspect of this same situation involves what I call the schizophrenic nature of modern property management. "Schizophrenia" is a mental illness in which a person has a split personality, with each part behaving as though it had traits different from the other. Today, there is a schizophrenic relationship between the *financing* of real property on the one hand and its *management* on the other.

Because of the globalization of finance, today any property—even your house—can be financed with funds that come from almost any part of the world. Moreover, the instruments used to finance properties have become extremely complex thanks to the influence of Wall Street investment bankers. They slice ownership interests into many specialized packages to fit highly particular investment requirements of special fund sources. These instruments essentially treat a property as an abstract asset, as discussed above. One of the goals of such securitization of real estate ownership is to create financial instruments that can be bought and sold by anyone like shares of stock or bonds. As a result, ownership is almost totally abstracted from the unique characteristics of the underlying properties. Thus the financing side of real estate ownership requires global knowledge of world financial markets plus detailed knowledge of complex financial instruments that can be used to divide ownership into different bundles of rights.

In contrast, the management of any real property requires highly localized knowledge of both the property itself and its immediate markets. They are usually mainly located right around its site. True, some real properties—such as resort hotels—serve national or even worldwide markets, but most properties other than hotels draw their main patronage from the metropolitan areas in which they are located. This is true of office buildings, retail outlets, apartments, theaters, restaurants, industrial properties, warehouses, and most of the more specialized types of properties. Therefore, skillful property managers must have detailed knowledge of their local markets and competitors and must treat both their properties and those markets as individualized, particular realities—not abstract commodities.

It is rare indeed—almost impossible—for any one person to have detailed knowledge of both global financial markets and complex financial instruments on the one hand, and the local markets for a specific property on the other. Therefore, professional property management firms which become involved with the financing aspects of the properties they manage have two options. One is to become large enough to have specialists with both types of knowledge on their staffs. The other is to enter into cooperative arrangements with other persons or firms that specialize in the business of global finance.

Property Managers Face Greater Challenges and Greater Opportunities

In spite of the immense changes in general and real estate conditions that have occurred in the past decade, and those that will occur in the future, the basic skills necessary for professional property management have not changed all that much. As my father said in the twelfth edition:

> "The principles of managing real estate have remained relatively constant. Marketing techniques, personnel management, management plans, tenant and public relations, the solicitation and treatment of clients—in fact, the entire professional bearing of the property manager and the skills that must be mastered—remain much the same."

However, I believe that both the range and complexity of the skills required have increased notably. Relations between managers and owners have been altered subtly by the fact that most owners today are large financial institutions located far from the properties they own. The globalization of finance means that property managers must interact with a whole new cadre of specialists in property finance. Those "wizards" have a completely different type of knowledge from that required for effective property management. The ubiquity of computers means managers must understand how to use them without being overwhelmed by meaningless data. The increased intensity of relationships between property developers, owners, and managers on the one hand, and local community residents and advocates on the other, requires even more sensitivity to local feelings and attitudes than ever before. A looming shortage of labor, plus the increased fraction of the work force that will consist of recent immigrants, means managers must know how to deal with more diverse cultural viewpoints than in the past.

All these intensified requirements demand more skill and training for today's professional managers. However, the same trends and conditions that have produced these greater demands have also immensely increased the relative importance of property management in the success of real estate as an investment, for reasons explained above. Therefore, the opportunities that property managers face today have grown even more than the difficulties of taking advantage of those opportunities. If the 1960s were the decade of suburban development, the 1970s were the decade of inflation of property values, and the 1980s were the decade of commercial development, then the 1990s will be the decade of property management. More than ever, those professional property managers who have a broad understanding of how their role fits into society and its larger trends will have a huge advantage in taking advantage of these opportunities. The remainder of this book aims at providing property managers with such a breadth of vision, as well as with the detailed "tools of the trade" necessary to make them true professionals.

Anthony Downs
Senior Fellow
The Brookings Institution

The views expressed in the Introduction are solely those of its author and not necessarily those of The Brookings Institution, its Trustees, or its other staff members.

Quotations are from *Principles of Real Estate Management*, Twelfth Edition, by James C. Downs Jr., CPM®, copyright © 1980 by the Institute of Real Estate Management.

An Overview of Real Estate Management

Professional real estate management is the administrative operation and maintenance of property according to the objectives of the owner. It also encompasses planning for the future of the property by proposing physical and fiscal programs that will enhance the value of the real estate. Real estate management as a profession is the result of three major occurrences: (1) development of a legal system that granted individuals the right to own real property, (2) increased complexity and size of buildings and their components, and (3) changing economic conditions that required professional administration and advice to achieve sound fiscal operation of income-producing property. The history of real estate management has direct bearing on the functions and skills of property managers today.

HISTORICAL PERSPECTIVE ON REAL PROPERTY

In the United States, individual ownership of real property is a right that is taken for granted in the twentieth century, but the concept of holding individual title to property is a radical departure from historical precedents. Private property rights were so important to the American colonists that many of the fundamental rights in the United States Constitution and the Bill of Rights pertain to property ownership.

The basis of American property law came to the United States with the founders of this country. European systems of government, most notably

1

the English, had a profound influence on individual ownership of real property. In the age of *feudalism*—a period lasting from the ninth century to the fifteenth century in Europe—the king was the principal landowner in any sovereign state. Land was the symbol of wealth in a society that initially did not have money as a medium of exchange. The land in the country was usually divided among the king's family, who were the barons and lords of the estates. (Through primogeniture, the estates could be passed to their descendants.) The barons subdivided and redistributed their land to vassals (tenants) in return for expected services. Usually the service was a military obligation, and often a share of the crops or livestock raised on the land was required as well. Land was held in fee, meaning that to use the land, an obligation was owed to the lord of the land. Just as the vassal was bound to the lord, the lord was bound to the next higher authority in the hierarchical chain, and that nobleman was bound to another higher authority, until ultimately everyone in the country—from peasants to dukes—gave their allegiance to the king. In this manner, the land was inseparable from the notion of government and sovereignty, and the right to use land carried an obligation to defend the sovereign. Even though inheritance among the lords was sometimes instituted, land was not owned. The king, as the embodiment of the government, was the one who would be regarded as the landowner in today's concept of holding property title.

Improvements in agricultural production and the advent of money as a medium of exchange lowered the demand for the vassals' labor and created the opportunity for them to buy back their military and service obligations from their lords. Eventually, agricultural surplus and manufacturing advances made feudalism impractical. Through centuries of political and economic change, the absolute power of the king gradually diminished. Money, not land, became the primary measure of wealth, and hundreds of years of change produced a powerful merchant class. The wealth of this class eventually surpassed the wealth of the barons. As a result, land became another commodity that could be bought, sold, or traded.

With the founding of colonies in the New World, the merchants, not the barons, were accorded land rights for the most part. The Revolutionary War broke the bonds between the British colonies and the crown and created the United States. However, many of the rights to land today are remnants from English common law as it was applied to and evolved in the colonies. A property tax, which was common in many societies, was a means by which states and communities could raise funds for common services. The government has retained the right of *eminent domain*, meaning the state can condemn private property, give fair compensation to the owner, and redevelop the property for public service—even if the property owner is unwilling to part with it. Restrictions on the use of land today for preservation of natural resources, for economic reasons, for protection of other property owners' rights, or for other specific reasons are another carryover.

Common Law and Property Ownership

For citizens of the United States, the notion of common law is difficult to understand. Americans are more familiar with statute law—written law that has been enacted by a governmental body. Common law comprises laws that are not specifically superseded by statute law. In other words, common law is court interpretation when no statute is in place. These interpretations are based on precedent—the inherent beliefs of the society and previous court decisions. In England, legal precedent reaches back at least to the reign of William the Conqueror (1066–1087 A.D.). Common law can be interpreted as the principles of a common people, as distinguished from rules (statutes). England, which has a constitutional government, has no written constitution. Its constitution is common law.

The common-law interpretation of property ownership contributed to the crumbling of feudalism and also changed as the feudal system disintegrated. Feudalism was replaced by the allodial system, under which an individual could hold property in fee simple (conditional) or fee simple absolute (unconditional) ownership. The word "fee" in its earliest forms meant livestock, cattle, property, or money. Later, under the feudal system in England, a fee was the real property accorded to someone in return for and on the condition of homage and service to a superior or lord. The fee was inheritable in England, but the sovereign still owned the land. The ability to purchase and sell land and to have absolute power over the land owned (as a sovereign would have) is allodialism. In some respects, the term "fee simple absolute" is misleading. The governmental powers of eminent domain and zoning are two obvious restrictions on absolute power over the use of one's land.

Although we live in an allodial system, elements of the feudal system still persist. In many downtown commercial areas, land is occasionally leased for long terms (e.g., 99 years). A developer who builds on leased land owns the improvement (the building) but not the land itself. The owner of the improvement has only a leasehold interest in the underlying land. This is similar to the feudal privilege to use land and will it to descendants even though the king was the absolute owner of the property.

In some states, real property can be sold on a fee simple basis or a leasehold interest basis. When a leasehold interest is purchased, the improvement (house or condominium) is all that is owned outright; the underlying land is leased from another owner. In fee simple ownership, both the underlying land and the improvement are purchased. Fee simple ownership is usually preferred by buyers. Assuming locations of equal appeal, fee simple properties are usually valued higher than properties built on leasehold interests. One state where this distinction is seen is Hawaii, where land ownership evolved from a monarchical system of government.

EVOLUTION OF PROPERTY MANAGEMENT

The growth of the property management profession coincides with the growth of cities and with market demand for space to rent. After the American Revolution, cities began to increase in size and number. The intensive use of land in cities created new investment opportunities. For wealthy capitalists, real estate was an alternative for investment of surplus funds. However, they were not always proficient (or successful) in managing real property because that was not their primary business; often they considered such management a burden. A few people did find property management a profitable opportunity in this early period, but real estate brokerage was still the more lucrative activity.

Cities continued to grow in response to the Industrial Revolution. Increased mechanization moved production of materials and goods out of the home and into factories. The development of railroads allowed large amounts of food and other consumables to be moved across the United States quickly. At the close of the American Civil War, the population of the United States again grew rapidly and urban construction increased. The population was no longer as dependent on agriculture as a way of life because better understanding of farming and better tools for planting and harvesting increased the number of people who could be fed from an acre of land and increased the number of acres that could be farmed by one person. Office buildings and large hotels became more prevalent, and these properties required specific management. At the same time, most multiple-unit residences were small and owner occupied and retailers commonly lived in apartments above their stores, so there was little demand for professional management of these property types during this period.

The growth of the cities during the nineteenth century created greater demand for residential and commercial space. Better engineering and construction techniques led to development of larger buildings to meet that demand. However, fewer individuals could afford to own a building by themselves because larger buildings cost more to build and maintain. Ownership by groups (pooled capital) and financing by outside sources became prevalent. Because such buildings were no longer one person's concern, management became very important. Large size meant these buildings were more valuable; they were more costly to replace than smaller buildings. They required full-time attention to maintain their value, and cash flow from the property was crucial to offset the financing. The complexity of the ownership arrangement created an administrative role for a property manager.

Beginning in the 1880s and 1890s and continuing throughout the twentieth century, several major trends have affected urban land use. Land prices in cities rose because of heightened demand for space. Among other things, this prompted the construction of larger multiple-unit residences, and over time, residential conditions and equipment were upgraded—central heating, air conditioning, additional bathrooms, and improved insulation became standard features in apartment buildings. Maintenance requirements increased with each additional feature, creating an increasing need for management of residential property.

Advances in structural engineering led to development of tall steel-frame buildings known as *skyscrapers*. The earliest of these were office buildings. With every floor that was added, the possible number of tenants increased, and reliance on a full-time staff to serve these tenants also increased.

Improvements in transportation and electrical networks made possible the development of suburban areas and ultimately changed the living patterns of Americans. Local stores in the suburbs carried limited stocks of merchandise, and downtown shopping districts were inconvenient for suburban residents. To meet the needs of these growing markets, shopping centers were developed. The evolution of these centers from strips of independent stores to large enclosed malls with unified themes led to a parallel need for management of these complex retail properties.

Over time, these trends in residential, office, and retail development sparked an increasing demand for property management and ultimately led to specialization by type of property. However, in the formative years of construction of large buildings, property management was not very complex, and owner-management was still the common practice. Most of the buildings constructed in the early years were sold to individuals who had retired from other lines of business. Such buildings were an attractive medium of investment at retirement, and property management was often considered a post-retirement occupation.

Expansion in the 1920s

Primarily because of rapid business expansion and a consequent demand for rental space, owner-management lost favor in the early 1920s. Those who had purchased property to assure themselves of a modest living after retirement were suddenly quite wealthy. Dreams had become realities, and many of these investors chose to travel for long periods or moved to warmer climates. The result was extended absences from their real estate investments.

Being far away from their properties prompted these absentee owners to ask real estate agents to collect rents, order fuel, pay the janitor and the utilities, and forward the net proceeds to them. An owner's specific authorization was usually necessary for any other expenditures, and the owner usually negotiated leases personally, so the extent of property management during the 1920s was still limited.

In most cases, real estate agents performed these duties for the absent owners as an accommodation to a potential sales customer. A clerk was assigned to collect the rents, and a bookkeeper sent the owner a simple statement of receipts and disbursements at the end of each month. However, in neighborhoods where rents were highest and multiple dwellings were most common, the volume of this business became significant and real estate management became a profitable activity by itself. Suddenly, there was a drive to capture more of this business by providing exceptional service for clients and their properties, and competition for property management business evolved.

Before 1929, most large buildings were owned by business mavericks who had made their money in specialized fields. These entrepreneurs often imposed the practices of their main line of business on their real estate holdings. Property managers were hired to collect the rent and carry out the owner's policies, not to counsel the owner on the best use of the property. The fledgling profession of property management suffered from inefficiency. The newly established management companies usually had as many different management policies as they had clients. They did not have sufficient freedom to try different methods of management because of the risk that the owners would terminate their agreements with the managers. It was virtually impossible to persuade a client to change his or her decision, even when an order was mistaken or unsatisfactory.

The availability of financing also had an effect on income-producing property and its management in the 1920s. One financing trend was the *split mortgage*—the division of a loan into small-denomination bonds for sale by investment bankers. Other financing arrangements also came into being. Limited knowledge of real estate investments and the competition for loans produced widespread overlending. Prior to the Great Depression, it was common practice to finance property with a "standing loan." This usually had a term of five years, and the entire principal was due at the end of the term. Normally these loans required payment of interest only, and they were expected to be renewed (rolled over) at the end of each five-year period. However, these became problematic during the Depression. When banks were unwilling or unable to renew these loans, borrowers had only one option. They defaulted on the loans and the banks foreclosed. In the reorganization following mass foreclosures, heavily mortgaged properties presented a significant opportunity for property managers.

Unparalleled urban prosperity characterized the 1920s. Building construction was at a high level of activity, financed primarily by private sources such as insurance companies and building and loan associations. Power machinery, improved mass-production techniques, standardized parts and processes, and electrification markedly increased industrial efficiency. The U.S. economy developed at an unprecedented rate. Corporate profits and personal income expanded with the improvements in production. The availability of credit and of consumer goods to purchase with it made installment purchases popular. Coast-to-coast networks of chain stores emerged, and this growth in retail business held great promise for property managers.

The Great Depression

The foundation of the expanding U.S. economy collapsed altogether in the stock market crash of 1929, although the market for income-producing real estate actually began declining a year earlier. Most of the country's income-producing real estate (especially multiple dwellings and commercial buildings built from 1920 to 1929) defaulted to the mortgage holders. This economic devastation was the true origin of modern property management; for the first time, a large volume of property was gathered under one ownership, one policy, and one common perspective.

Early in the Depression, the lenders-turned-owners studied the existing property management organizations and often concluded that their interests could be served best by creating their own management departments. Not being familiar with the complexities of building management, they believed that the operation of real estate was limited to collecting rents and maintaining the physical structures. The personnel of these new departments were usually builders, architects, and contractors whose work was supplemented by routine collectors and perhaps a law graduate. Analysis, merchandising, and real estate economics often were overlooked because they were unknown to most of these executives; they had not thought such disciplines important enough to demand training in them.

After the first years of the Depression—years of trial and error as experience in management broadened—other views came to be accepted by the executives responsible for the operation of lender-owned real estate. The need for adequate analysis, market research, and scientific administration was widely recognized, and many organizations began to fill this need.

Recovery and World War II

Property ownership, which had been concentrated among lenders because of mass foreclosures from 1928 to 1933, was redistributed during the recovery years. Real estate promised once again to be a profitable opportunity for investors. Individuals and partnerships (sometimes called syndicates) purchased property from the lenders that were reducing their real estate portfolios as they prepared to resume their pre-Depression activities. In many cases, property managers were retained by the new owners to ensure that the properties were put to their highest and best use.

The recovery period (1934–1939) was characterized by an upsurge in occupancy, rental rates, and property values. When the United States entered World War II in 1941, the demand for urban real estate was so high that the demand for professional property management diminished somewhat. From 1941 until 1957, there were more renters than places to rent. This factor combined with federal residential rent controls, which prohibited rent increases during the war and afterward, meant that residents were so happy to find space that landlords could reduce services, virtually neglect interior maintenance, ignore the merchandising process, and still maintain high occupancy.

Postwar Period through the 1980s

Phenomenal construction from 1946 until 1956 satisfied the postwar demand for property. At the end of this period, the number of residential units being built exceeded the demand for new space. Much of this construction occurred in newly developed suburbs, which had become more numerous as a consequence of increased automobile ownership. Vacancies appeared beginning in 1957, and by the end of 1963, local markets assumed more standard rates of growth. Rental rates stabilized and occupancy levels fell, and property owners once again sought professional management.

For many, the suburbs became the place of choice to live, but the cities grew as well. Mid- and high-rise apartment buildings became popular in metropolitan areas beginning in the late 1950s. A towering structure could house hundreds or thousands of residents in the area of a city block. Such a concentration of population intensified service requirements and consequently increased the demand for property management.

The advent of the condominium in the 1960s and 1970s offered property managers still more opportunities. Professional management was usually a necessity for large multiple-owner properties.

The postwar period was also characterized by an enormous demand for office space. Several factors accounted for this growth. A greater number of people were employed in government and service industries, so their work was based in office buildings. As businesses prospered, they outgrew their existing quarters. At the same time, the complexity of office operations increased, and businesses required more room for computers and other types of office equipment. The heightened demand for office accommodations dramatically increased the opportunities for professional management. Rental retail space was also being developed during this period, and there was a phenomenal growth in the number and size of shopping centers, especially in the suburbs.

A sharp increase in the supply of mortgage money during the 1960s and 1970s affected the property management industry because it permitted the development of numerous large income-producing properties. A significant mortgage money source was *real estate investment trusts (REITs)*. This form of investment permitted those with limited capital to participate in large real estate investments. However, many REITs became suspect in the mid-1970s because of imprudent loans to developers and builders. The troubles of the REITs proved to be a windfall for property managers, who were asked to sustain the properties financed by the failing trusts. The problems experienced by REITs were ironic because the real estate market was thriving in most areas of the United States at the time. In the 1980s, REITs rebounded, but they are always subject to fluctuations in the real estate market, the integrity of the administration of the trust, and changes in governmental policy.

Between 1980 and 1982, the United States suffered the worst recession since the Great Depression. During this period of rampant inflation, real estate was viewed as a way to preserve capital. The recession finally gave way to a period of prosperity that lasted the rest of the decade. Demand for real property sent the median cost of single-family homes above $100,000 in many markets, and construction was booming. Many cities in the United States experienced a record increase in new office space, most of which was readily absorbed early in the decade.

One reason for the nation's rebound from recession in 1983 was the availability of credit. This resulted from changes in federal regulations related to banks and savings and loan associations (S&Ls). The ceiling on the interest rate that could be paid on savings accounts was raised, and the maximum amount insured by the federal government was increased from $40,000 per account to $100,000 per account. Savings and loan associations (also called *thrifts*) previously had been prohibited from lending money for commercial real estate development and from investing in real estate directly, but those restrictions were removed in the early 1980s.

These changes, combined with the Tax Reform Act of 1980 which offered numerous incentives for real estate investment, fueled unprecedented development. Numerous syndicates and partnerships were organized to take advantage of credit and tax opportunities. Other institutional investors, namely pension funds and insurance companies, also began to take an active interest in real estate as a means to diversify their portfolios and to capitalize on the rapid appreciation of real property developments. The record growth eventually faltered because of two significant and almost concurrent events:

1. The development boom began to slow down in the mid-1980s. As a result of overbuilding, there was a glut of rentable space on the market. Many developers lost their properties because high vacancy rates reduced their cash flow and prevented them from making their loan payments. Massive foreclosures ensued.
2. The federal government enacted the *Tax Reform Act of 1986,* which repealed most of the real estate-related income tax incentives granted through the 1980 Act. In particular, rental income from real property was defined by the new law to be *passive activity income* when the investor does not materially participate in earning those funds. Similarly, losses from such passive activities, which had been deductible from *active income* (i.e., salary) under the 1980 Act, could no longer be deducted from active income under the 1986 Act. This affected syndicates and partnerships in particular, forcing many of them into dissolution or bankruptcy.

The oversupply of vacant property, coupled with hundreds of poorly conceived developments and numerous failing syndicates and partnerships, lowered the value of the seized property even more. As a result, many of the banks and thrifts holding the properties went bankrupt and were seized by federal regulators. By early 1989, it was clear that a significant portion of the savings and loan industry had collapsed. Thrift failures were so widespread that the Federal Savings and Loan Insurance Corporation (FSLIC), the agency of the U.S. government that insured deposits in federal savings and loan associations, was dissolved. What was needed was an organization to efficiently manage and dispose of the assets from the thrifts that had been placed in receivership. Several new governmental agencies were created, two of which are particularly important: the Office of Thrift Supervision (OTS) and the Resolution Trust Corporation (RTC). The OTS was created to manage surviving thrifts; the RTC was instituted to liquidate the assets of failed thrifts. While the U.S. Department of the Treasury governs the OTS, the RTC is managed by the Federal Deposit Insurance Corporation (FDIC), which retained its responsibility for insuring deposits in participating banks. When the RTC was created, it became the largest landowner in the United States. For the RTC to retain any value whatsoever in the property it held, it recognized from the outset that capable, professional property managers were essential to its efforts in resolving the savings and loan catastrophe.

PROPERTY MANAGEMENT AND PROFESSIONALISM

Compared to other professions, the role and responsibilities of property management developed rather suddenly. Unlike accounting, law, medicine, or other professions that had existed for many centuries, property management developed virtually overnight as a result of dire circumstances. Businesses that survived the stock market crash in 1929 were in a precarious position; they had already suffered substantial losses, and poor management of their real estate holdings would have perpetuated their losses. The need to establish standard practices of property management and a method to accredit property managers were recognized by pioneers in the profession.

Founding of the Institute of Real Estate Management

In 1933, fourteen property managers gathered to establish an association of responsible real estate managers. As a result of their efforts, 100 property management firms joined together to form the Institute of Real Estate Management (IREM), an affiliate of the National Association of Real Estate Boards (the NATIONAL ASSOCIATION OF REALTORS® today). Each firm was required to pledge itself to certain practices: (1) The firm would set up separate accounts for its funds and those of its clients; under no circumstances were the funds to be commingled. (2) The firm would carry a fidelity bond on all applicable employees. (3) The firm would in no way benefit financially from a client's funds without full disclosure to and permission from the property owner.

Although the initial reason for organizing the Institute of Real Estate Management was to adopt specific ethical standards of practice, the association and the scope of its standards continues to grow. In 1938, the founders of IREM agreed that accrediting individual property managers was more fundamental and beneficial than recognizing the integrity of management firms—which had been the practice until that point. The standards of a management firm can change with staff changes, the founders reasoned, but individuals' standards generally apply throughout their lives. Therefore, the Institute of Real Estate Management reorganized as an association of individuals and inaugurated the *CERTIFIED PROPERTY MANAGER® (CPM®)* designation to acknowledge individual professional achievement. A CERTIFIED PROPERTY MANAGER subscribes to a Code of Professional Ethics, has proven his or her ability by successfully completing a series of property management courses, and has worked a prescribed number of years in the profession with a required size portfolio. Other factors involving his or her professional experience are also considered.

More than 13,000 individuals have achieved the CPM designation from the Institute of Real Estate Management, and more than 9,000 CPM members of IREM are actively engaged in property and asset management. These professionals manage more than $1 trillion worth of real estate assets. Although the careers of many CPM members of IREM involve property management only, some members are also active in brokerage, syndication, consultation, development, and appraisal.

As the Institute has grown, it has also responded to and accommodated changes in the property management profession by developing two additional designations. The ACCREDITED MANAGEMENT ORGANIZATION® (AMO®) designation was created in 1945 and is related to the original Institute program—accrediting management firms. In addition to the original practices that were required for a firm's membership in IREM, the AMO designation stipulates that at least one executive of the firm must be a CPM member of IREM. This is in addition to strict insurance and financial requirements.

A major aspect of property management is site management of residential properties. To recognize this specialization, the Institute established the ACCREDITED RESIDENTIAL MANAGER (ARM®) service award in 1974. The prerequisites of successful coursework, professional experience, and agreement to uphold the ARM Code of Ethics are similar to the qualifying steps for the CPM designation, except that the focus of the ARM service award centers on residential property management and specific site-management responsibilities.

Property Management Skills

The property manager works closely with both tenants and property owners, and many skills are necessary to successfully serve these two groups. Diplomacy is essential to effectively negotiate delicate matters that may arise between the two parties. Knowledge of advertising and business promotion are valuable skills because the typical rental property is not large enough to warrant the services of an advertising agency. Familiarity with the market of the property being managed—and its competition—is critical for maximizing the financial return from as well as the occupancy of the property. Understanding of economics, accounting, statistics, and valuation calculations is essential to set realistic rents for the present and future and to ensure a healthy economic life for the property.

Property management education is a vital qualification for the professional manager. Every real property is unique, and economic, social, and political changes will affect each property differently. A property manager who is trained in these areas is generally able to isolate these different factors, determine how they affect the property, and create a program to respond to them appropriately. The foundation of this flexibility and foresight is education.

Even though the property management profession has grown exponentially since the early 1930s, it is still essentially a personal service profession. Because of the individual relationships property managers have with both building owners and tenants, conscientious managers are aware of the ongoing need for self-improvement and adherence to a strict code of ethics.

Primary Responsibilities of the Property Manager

By definition, *real estate* refers to land and any improvements on it. Farms, mines (both underground and at the surface level), golf courses, forests, and even deserts are real estate. However, the definition is often limited to nonagricultural property that houses individuals or families or accommodates commerce, industry, professions, or other activities. Any changes or new trends among these property users directly affect real estate and its management. As society expands and changes, property managers respond to a diversity of problems—either to capitalize on or to minimize the effects of changes on the real estate in their care (depending on the projected outcome).

Primary Property Management Responsibilities
* Maintain the property
* Respond to tenants' needs
* Collect rents
* Pay expenses
* Prepare budgets
* Develop marketing plans
* Negotiate leases
* Report to owners
* Hire and supervise personnel

Real estate management is growing steadily as a profession because of three significant trends. First, simultaneous growth of the population and its requirements for space has increased the total number of all types of buildings. Second, a larger percentage of real estate is considered investment property. Third, there is a wide acceptance of the fact that property management requires special training and education. The training, education, and duties of the property manager can be categorized under four different responsibilities: management of the physical site, management of on-site and off-site personnel, management of funds and accounts, and management of leasing activities and tenant services. These different types of responsibilities are all components of the manager's overall responsibility as the agent of the owner. An *agent* is a person who enters a legal and confidential arrangement with the owner and is authorized to act on behalf of the owner. In the role of agent, the manager is the owner's *fiduciary,* entrusted to act in the owner's best interests. Property management often involves fiduciary responsibility for millions of dollars in assets and cash flow. For this reason, property owners should choose property managers with strong ethical backgrounds to be their agents.

Site Management.   The title "property manager" encompasses a wide range of roles, depending on the amount of property that is overseen. The manager of a 100,000 square-foot office building is a property manager, but someone in this role may also be called a *site manager,* and he or she may report to an *executive property manager.* An executive property manager may have numerous site managers reporting to him or her, and he or she may report to a property manager at yet a higher level. Regardless of the level of responsibility or whether the manager is responsible for one site or many, management of any site hinges on the following fundamentals.

Property managers regularly inspect the sites they manage and use appropriate and accepted checklists for this inspection. Although maintenance staff members are usually assigned to regularly examine particular sections or components of the property, the manager should be available to consult with the staff and the owner on any problems that are noted. The manager is consequently the expert who identifies, analyzes, recommends, and implements any major maintenance or remodeling projects. Because the manager is ultimately responsible for such activity and is not necessarily an expert on every aspect that warrants attention, he or she should rely on the advice of knowledgeable staff or contractors.

Energy use and conservation are ongoing concerns of property managers. In the effort to reduce costs and conserve natural resources, property managers monitor the energy efficiency of properties in their care and investigate new equipment that shows promise of reducing or at least controlling energy consumption.

Many property managers today have become *asset managers,* a title that expands their responsibilities. An asset manager views a property from the perspective of its present and potential value to the owner. Even though the property may be considered solely from an investment standpoint, effective asset management requires the manager to be as familiar with, proficient in, and attuned to property inspection as a conventional property manager. A thorough inspection can lead an asset manager to identify and analyze alternate uses of a property. If an alternate use (e.g., conversion of an aging office building into residential units) seems feasible, the property manager or asset manager must be able to implement a plan to effectively change the property's use. Yet another aspect of asset management that pertains to physical structure is analysis of properties to identify and recommend to clients what should be bought or sold.

The term "site management" often implies maintaining the physical structure, but updating documents and records is also a principal aspect of this role. Aside from accounting records, there are numerous other forms and documents (insurance policies, tenant files, the management agreement, and other property-related documents and information) that must be maintained in a logical and chronological order. All insurance records should be placed where they can be referred to immediately when the need arises, and a manager should be able to quickly retrieve the files of tenants who enter the management office. In addition, a cross-referencing system is necessary so the manager can refer to specific time-sensitive documents well in advance of their expiration. Insurance policies are generally renewed annually and many residential leases also follow this pattern. The effort to keep records timely ensures continuity in the operation of a property and gives the manager more time to invest in other management responsibilities.

The owner should be primarily responsible for compliance with governmental regulations with respect to the property, but the property manager must be knowledgeable in this area in order to avert (or at least minimize) any liability for noncompliance and to advise the owner regarding applicable regulations. Changes in income tax laws, fair housing and other antidiscrimination laws, environmental regulations, zoning ordinances, or property taxation rules are just some of the ways in which government at all levels can affect the operation of income-producing property. It is also the property manager's role to advise the owner when to seek legal counsel. Such advice is based on the manager's knowledge of the legal and tax ramifications of certain actions.

Although the responsibilities of property management are broadly applicable, the skills required to carry out these responsibilities may be refined or tailored to a specific type of property. The duties and requisite skills for operating a skyscraper office building can differ substantially from the requisites for managing a twenty-unit multiple dwelling in the suburbs. Perhaps the most challenging type of property to manage is the mixed-use development where office, retail, and residential uses can be combined in a single property.

Personnel Management.   Many of the duties of a property manager are in fact performed by staff members. Unless a property manager's portfolio is small, it is difficult for one individual to perform all of the accounting, maintenance, leasing, and administrative functions that are required. A support staff is usually necessary to give clients effective service. Some staff may be assigned to a particular site; others may not work at a particular site, or their responsibilities may not require them to work on site. Contractors are often hired to perform specific functions that are not regularly encountered or otherwise do not warrant a staff assignment. Those who are contracted and those who are employed must be managed on an ongoing basis, and it must be ascertained that subordinates who have staff members reporting to them are also complying with management standards. The chain of command must be monitored to verify its efficiency and maintain its flexibility in order to effectively serve new needs as they arise. Clear communication is crucial to assessment of work performance and verification of adherence to specifications and safety regulations.

Staff members and contractors require operating policies and procedures to guide them in the performance of their jobs. Such policies and procedures should be neither so rigid that they stifle innovation nor so elastic that they provide no guidance at all. Operating policies and procedures must be established, monitored, and enforced for every operating department of a property and for each job title. These include working hours, training procedures, productivity expectations, and accountability for tools and equipment. Supervision of on-site and off-site personnel and development of policies and procedures are the responsibility of the property manager.

Financial Management.   Managed property is usually owned for the purpose of producing income, and a property manager is hired in large part to maximize that income. This mandates a property manager to be capable of administering property funds and accounts. The manager should have the authority to incur expenses, up to a prescribed dollar limit for any single expense. He or she should be permitted to decide which items or services to purchase, determine the quality and quantity of purchases, approve invoices, and negotiate or approve contracts for services.

All journal entries, records of accounts, bank deposits, progress reports on the collection of delinquent and slow-paying accounts, and filing of receipts should be reviewed by the manager to ensure consistency, accuracy, and honesty. Controls to safeguard receipts and disbursements should also be established through management information systems. The manager should prepare, review, or verify the monthly operating statement and submit it to the owner. He or she should meet with the owner to review financial requirements and, when appropriate, recommend sources of additional funds. The owner should be advised of estimates of the value of the property and the implications these estimates have in comparison to similar properties.

As part of the responsibility for funds and accounts, a property manager should determine the validity of the assessed valuation of the property, its insurable value, and its insurable risks. Based on his or her familiarity with customary coverage, the manager should recommend an appropriate insurance program to the property owner.

While daily and monthly maintenance of funds is a continual process, projection of future income and expenses is also a recurring responsibility. A property manager must be able to develop seasonal, annual, and long-range operating and capital expenditure budgets. Even though it is understood that a budget is merely an estimate, such estimates must be as accurate as possible to ensure fiscal strength and predictable cash flow. Variances will inevitably occur, however, and the property manager is responsible for controlling variances from the budget.

Leasing and Tenant Management.   Most work of a property manager is done with the property owner in mind, but managers must also provide their tenants with effective service. Property managers must be genuinely dedicated to responding to tenants' needs because the space they lease is the space in which they live, work, or exchange goods. Such direct attention to tenants is an indirect service to the property owner—good service fosters renewals and minimizes turnover. Foremost among the manager's responsibilities is supervision of renting and lease renewal. To maximize income from the property, the manager must determine the amount of rent to charge and authorize any deviations from it. If special improvements or additional tenant services are necessary, the manager should determine the appropriate amount of additional rent.

The property manager should meet routinely and personally with building occupants to discuss management matters. While this may be on an individual basis for items such as maintenance or lease renewals, the manager may also be required to meet with all occupants or tenants at once (for example, the homeowner members of a condominium association or the retailer members of a merchants' association in a shopping center). In the effort to lease available space, the property manager prepares marketing plans and selects the media, format, and volume of advertising to carry out those plans.

SUMMARY

The professional property manager's role is to oversee the operation and maintenance of real property according to the objectives of the property owner. Inherent in this definition is the concept of private property, without which individual ownership and use of real estate would not be possible.

The development of property management as a function within the real estate industry resulted from a number of factors. The major demand for management expertise arose in the 1930s after lenders foreclosed on thousands of mortgages and discovered that the management of these properties required specialized skills. Since that time, the need for professional property management has intensified because of absentee ownership of real estate, ownership of property by groups of investors through syndicates and partnerships, and increased urbanization, as well as recognition that professional management is often necessary to maximize income.

Recognizing the need to establish standards of professional property management, a group of property managers gathered during the Depression and founded the Institute of Real Estate Management. The Institute grants three awards: the CERTIFIED PROPERTY MANAGER® (CPM®) designation for individuals; the ACCREDITED MANAGEMENT ORGANIZATION® (AMO®) designation for management firms; and the ACCREDITED RESIDENTIAL MANAGER (ARM®) service award for apartment managers. Recipients must meet personal education and experience requirements, and all pledge to adhere to ethical business practices.

The primary functions of a property manager are management of the site, management of on-site and off-site personnel, management of funds and accounts, and management of leasing activities and tenant services. Through the educational programs offered by the Institute of Real Estate Management and from their professional experience, CPM members of

IREM seek to continually improve their abilities to expand and refine the services they offer to their clients.

Key Terms
ACCREDITED MANAGEMENT ORGANIZATION® (AMO®)
ACCREDITED RESIDENTIAL MANAGER (ARM®)
Agent
Asset manager
CERTIFIED PROPERTY MANAGER® (CPM®)
Ethics
Feudalism
Fiduciary
Institute of Real Estate Management
Passive activity income
Property management
Site manager
Thrift

Key Points
The evolution of American property ownership rights
The scope of property management from 1920 to 1929
The effects of the Great Depression on property management
The development of professionalism in property management
The importance of ethical standards
Primary property management skills and responsibilities

Real Estate and Economics

The goal of the manager of real property is to preserve and increase the value of the managed property. This is best accomplished when the property is put to its highest and best use. In economic terms, that is the use which produces the highest yield in terms of income or profits, or both. To determine the highest and best use for a particular property, the manager analyzes the range of possible alternative uses. This analysis includes a study of the impact of social, political, and economic trends on each proposed use over its economic or productive life. Economic trends, in particular, have a significant impact. In order to understand the impact of economic trends on real estate, one must first understand the fundamental principles of economics.

BASIC ECONOMICS

Economics is the study of the range of activities necessary for the satisfaction of human needs. These activities include the production, distribution, and consumption of manufactured goods and agricultural products as well as the various services provided to individuals and businesses. Fundamental to all of these actitivies is the use of land and the construction of buildings to house these activities—real estate is an important component of economics in general. In fact, ownership of land was once the principal measure of wealth.

Functions of Money
* Medium of exchange
* Standard of value
* Store of value

Today wealth is measured in terms of money. The material substance of wealth—an automobile, one's home, the furnishings in it; stocks, bonds, and other investments—is expressed as the money value of those items. If *money* is defined as the accepted medium of exchange within a community, the *value* of an item is its relative worth in terms of the amount of money that must be given in order to obtain the item. In the United States, the medium of exchange is the U.S. dollar.

The interrelationship between money and the goods and services that can be purchased with it goes beyond money's role as a *medium of exchange*. Money allows comparison and measurement of the values of goods and services that are otherwise not readily comparable or measurable; it serves as a *standard of value*. Money itself has value based on its purchasing power; it serves as a *store of value* during the time between specific transactions. The value of money fluctuates over time because of changing factors in the marketplace (e.g., interest rates, inflation, the money supply).

The Marketplace

In any study of economics, an important element is the *market*—the place in which the exchange of goods and services between willing sellers and buyers actually takes place. The town square "market," a retail store, and a real estate office are all markets. In these markets the purchases and sales take place between people who are face to face. In other markets—e.g., the New York Stock Exchange, Chicago commodity markets—the seller never sees the buyer. The marketplace has become complex and multi-faceted. Many different elements are part of or have an effect on the market for a particular item. Price, supply, and demand are important components of the market. In particular, they have a direct effect on rental space and employment levels. These phenomena are themselves affected by changes in technology and in the value of money. It is these particular elements of the market that are of interest to property managers.

Price.   The value of one product or service is based on the value of the other products or services that would be exchanged for the desired item. In a complex economy, money is the medium of exchange used to measure the value of goods and services. The *price* of an item is the amount of money required in exchange for a unit of it. Price is therefore a component of value.

Price is the value of an item at which exchange takes place; it must be acceptable to both the buyer and the seller. The price of any item is determined by market factors. If the price the seller wants is higher than the amount a buyer is willing to pay, no transaction will take place. In a barter economy, the exchange of one item for another item can be effected only when both parties to the transaction are in agreement. The trade itself may be negotiated in terms of greater or lesser amounts of the items being exchanged. When money is the medium of exchange, however, such negotiation usually takes place only in such major transactions as the purchase of an automobile, a house, or other real property, or the leasing of commercial space for long periods.

Supply and Demand. Prices vary in the marketplace. They are subject to the quantity of available goods and services and the relative value of money. When the amount of merchandise available for sale exceeds the amount that people are willing to buy, the excess volume reduces the value of the individual units and therefore lowers the price. This is most readily demonstrated with agricultural products. When there is a bumper crop of grain, the price of a bushel of grain will be relatively low. Crop failures generally cause higher prices. The availability of goods and services is called *supply*. Availability of goods and services for sale is related to price, and more goods or services will be offered as prices rise.

Price is not the only factor limiting supply, however. The supply of one item can be affected by the price of another related item—the supply of corn will drop if the price of soybeans rises because farmers will choose to grow the more profitable crop. Supply of a finished product depends on the price and availability of its components—the supply of cotton dresses is reduced when the price of cotton goes up. An increase in the number of sellers of a specific product will increase the supply of that product—reduction of import restrictions permits foreign-made goods to compete with comparable domestic products and increases the overall supply. Sellers' expectations are another consideration—for example, oil production may be temporarily reduced (i.e., delayed) if prices are expected to rise in the future.

Another market factor that affects price is *demand*—the amount of goods or services for which there are ready purchasers. Conversely, demand is affected by price. Generally the amount purchased will increase as prices drop. Demand is also affected by factors other than the price of an item. The price of related goods is one example—demand for tea increases when the price of its substitute, coffee, rises. On the other hand, demand for sugar, a complement to coffee, drops when coffee prices go up. Because the price of "coffee with sugar" rises as the price of coffee

---

**The Laws of Supply and Demand
Relative to Price**
• When demand exceeds supply, prices rise.
• If supply exceeds demand, prices drop.
• When supply equals demand, prices are stable.

---

rises, reduced coffee consumption will lower the demand for sugar. Another example is income—people spend more as their income rises, thus increasing demand. People's preferences are also a factor in demand, and preferences may be altered by advertising—high-fiber cereals owe their popularity to advertisement of their health benefits. (A high-fiber diet is claimed to reduce one's chances of developing cancer of the colon.) An increase in the number of buyers will increase demand for goods or services—the baby-boomer segment of the U.S. population continues to have high impact on different product markets as it ages. Buyers' expectations are also a consideration—people tend to stock up on consumable items such as coffee when prices are expected to rise; conversely, they will delay buying a car if automobile prices are expected to be lower in the future.

Over time, prices tend to be stable when supply meets or is equal to demand. When supply is less than demand, prices tend to rise; when supply exceeds demand, prices tend to fall. Taken together, these statements are considered the *laws of supply and demand*.

Rental Space.   These same phenomena occur in the real estate market. When demand for rental space is strong, rents go up. Growth in the number of new households being formed increases demand for apartments. A growing work force signals a need for more office space. Rising income encourages consumer spending, and this creates demand for retail businesses and store space. Rising rents stimulate investment in existing income-producing properties (apartments, office buildings, shopping centers) as well as construction of new ones. New development eventually increases the supply of apartments, offices, and store spaces beyond the demand for them, and rents stabilize or go down. The value of the real estate holding also decreases as its rental income is reduced.

Employment Levels.   The labor market, too, is subject to the laws of supply and demand. The work force consists of all those who are employed plus all those who are unemployed. Full employment is an ideal that cannot be fulfilled; new jobs are being created at the same time that other jobs are being removed from the market. So full employment in economic terms can only result when the ever-shifting labor market is in balance. Unemployment has many negative connotations, but there are

Employment, Unemployment, and Rent

During the 1930s—the period of the Great Depression—unemployment peaked at roughly 25 percent. It descended to around 15 percent before 1940 and then rose to nearly 20 percent during the Second World War. Prior to World War II, the unemployment rate was below 5 percent between 1905 and 1910 and again in 1920. It went above 10 percent and then dropped to around 2 percent before 1925 and remained below 5 percent till 1930 when it rose dramatically. After World War II, the rate fluctuated between 2 and 7 percent through about 1975, when it increased sharply.

The unemployment rate is the number of unemployed divided by the number in the labor force (the number of employed plus the number of unemployed). Employment is measured by the Bureau of the Census, which surveys 58,000 households every month to gather information on their labor-market activities during the preceding week. From these data, the Bureau of Labor Statistics estimates the number of employed and unemployed that month. It classifies everyone over age 16 as employed, unemployed or not in the labor force based on a specific definition of employment.

For property managers, levels of employment and unemployment, particularly as they change within a localized area, reflect people's—and businesses'—ability to pay rent. They also indicate whether the need for housing or commercial space will increase or decrease.

types of unemployment that are not negative. Voluntary changing of jobs is an active part of a dynamic economy. On the other hand, unemployment can result from long-term decline of a specific industry or from a general downturn of the economy.

Unemployment affects the real estate industry in several ways, most notably as a reduction of the income stream of a property. People who are not working do not have income from which to pay rent for housing. Rather than struggle to meet expenses on their own, renters may double up to share expenses, or young adults may return to their parents' home. Inability to pay rent may force residents to vacate apartments or be evicted from them.

Reduction of the work force means businesses have fewer employees. For most businesses, fewer employees mean reduced work space requirements. Unemployed people are generally not consumers, so retail businesses may have to cut back the amount of space used to display merchandise for sale, especially if they reduce their sales staff. They may opt to relocate to smaller store sites. In factories, the initial reaction may be reduction of the length or number of work shifts, but eventually they may eliminate redundant equipment and then seek smaller sites. As the slowdown of business reduces demand for space, it also reduces the demand for new construction; the market cannot absorb additional rental space, and the market for a type of space becomes overbuilt.

The office building market is particularly affected by changes in the level of employment. High employment means that companies need more space to house their operations and personnel. The market for office space is usually healthy. However, high unemployment means companies need less space; they will also be less inclined to move because of the expense involved. If they stay and renew a lease, they may seek to reduce the amount of space rented. If they do move, it will be because they have found a smaller space that meets their current needs. The ultimate effect of unemployment on office space is higher vacancy levels and slowing absorption of new space.

Technological Change.   One of the most far-reaching causes of change in the marketplace is new technology. The twentieth century has witnessed greater efficiency in production, improved modes of transportation, innovations in communication, and development of totally new products. New technology can affect production and distribution, supply and demand. The jobs created as a result of technological change have a direct impact on the labor market.

Technology also has an impact on rental space. For example, development and widespread use of computers contributed to a growing demand for *new* office buildings because retrofitting of older buildings for the high-tech equipment used in many businesses can be very costly. Computers also altered inventories. While increased supplies of crops and manufactured goods usually increase demand for warehouse space, the ability to maintain accurate counts of items in stock coupled with manufacturers' ability and willingness to ship small quantities on short notice have reduced the need for storage space among distributors and retailers. The direct effect of this phenomenon has been increased demand for *smaller* store spaces. By-products of technology provide other examples as well. Prior to the 1980s, there was no such thing as a video store. However, video rentals can be profitable in just about any size store, and these operations currently lease space in every type and size of shopping center and provide additional profits to supermarkets, drug stores, and other types of businesses.

Money.   The U.S. *money supply* comprises all of the printed currency and coinage in circulation outside of banks, plus those bank deposits that are immediately convertible to cash (i.e., savings and checking deposits owned by individuals but held in banks), plus other negotiable instruments such as travelers' checks, credit union share-draft balances, and negotiable order of withdrawal (NOW) accounts. This amount of money, referred to as *M1,* is the most frequently cited measure of the U.S. money supply. More broadly, the money supply includes less liquid funds such as money market mutual fund shares and small time deposits (e.g., certificates of deposit) on which penalties are imposed for withdrawal before a specified maturity date. (This is added to M1 and called *M2.*)

The laws of supply and demand at work in the marketplace also affect the value of money, which is a reflection of the general price level. Fluctuations in prices and in the value of money are related to the amount of currency available, the number of times money changes hands, and the amount of goods exchanged in sales and purchases. The amount of currency available includes both cash and demand deposits in banks (savings and checking accounts). The greater the volume of currency, the lower the value of the individual unit of currency—e.g., the U.S. dollar. Because money is not consumed in transactions, the value of a unit of money is further defined by the number of transactions or exchanges in which the individual unit is used. One dollar used ten times in a year has as much value in the marketplace as ten dollars exchanged only once. The need for currency is based on the amount of goods exchanged—the volume of trade. The greater the volume of trade, the greater the need for money and therefore the greater the value of a unit of money. A disproportionate increase in the amount of currency in relation to the volume of goods available for purchase is *inflation*; the value of the currency is reduced and prices rise. It takes more of the less-valuable money to make a specific purchase. On the other hand, a decrease in the amount of currency in relation to the volume of goods is *deflation*; the value of the currency increases and prices drop. Periods of inflation and deflation are results— historically, prices were as likely to fall as to rise. Since World War II, however, deflation has been significantly absent from the U.S. economic scene. Inflation (or deflation) is frequently triggered by specific changes in the money supply, and governments have a key role in managing the supply of money.

The Role of Government

There are numerous ways in which the U.S. government has an impact on the economy. Its impact is felt at many levels. Sometimes government competes directly with private businesses, as when the Tennessee Valley Authority became a local provider of electricity. Government is also a purchaser of goods and services from private industry, and that stimulates production and fosters competition.

On the other hand, specific legislation and regulatory programs add to consumer prices and skew the costs of doing business (e.g., requiring governmental agency approval of drugs, pesticides, and other products before marketing; setting minimum wage rates; taxing specific products— tobacco, alcoholic beverages, gasoline). Price controls (supported prices for agricultural products, ceilings on airfares) and regulation of competition in U.S. markets (limitations on imports; subsidies for domestic products) are other examples. In a *laissez-faire economy,* government regulations are minimal or nonexistent. Such an economy permits flexibility of

Gross National Product (GNP)

The most comprehensive measure of the total output of the U.S. economy is Gross National Product (GNP). It consists of the market value of all final goods (tangible objects such as canned food and automobiles) and services (intangible objects such as entertainment activities and transportation) produced by an economy in one year's time. The U.S. GNP is currently measured in billions of dollars, and the amount is calculated by adding together the value of personal consumer purchases (durable and nondurable goods and services) and government purchases of goods and services at the federal, state, and local level, plus the investment of private capital in new plants and equipment, commercial buildings and residential structures (fixed investment), and new stocks of business inventory. The investment amount is adjusted for depreciation (using up) of the existing capital stock during the process of production.

Because foreign trade provides some of the goods and services purchased by Americans, its effects are also included in the measurement of GNP. The volume of goods and services exported to other countries is added to GNP and the volume of goods and services imported must be subtracted. When imports exceed exports, the net value is negative (as it was during the late 1980s in particular).

A rapidly rising GNP may signal rising interest rates or the beginning of a period of increasing inflation. A declining GNP may forecast falling interest rates or impending recession. (Some economists consider two consecutive quarters of declining GNP as an indicator of recession.)

Real estate is a significant portion (greater than 15 percent) of GNP. It comprises construction, professional services, and real estate finance accounts for designing, building, brokering, financing, and managing real properties (residential, office, retail, industrial) that are built or traded for investment but excludes building materials and construction of public facilities. Its contribution to GNP exceeds those of both durable and nondurable goods manufacturing, both wholesale and retail trade, and the cost of government as individual sectors.

wages, prices, and interest rates in the marketplace. However, the Great Depression of the 1930s had such wide-reaching effects in terms of unemployment and low general productivity that the marketplace has been heavily regulated ever since.

In addition to its participation in the economy, the federal government also measures economic activity. It collects information on wholesale and consumer prices, interest rates, the money supply, levels of production and consumption of goods, construction starts and permits issued, sales of new and existing homes, etc. Trends and changes in these indicators are used to chart economic growth, inflation, and the place of the U.S. economy in the world at large. Changes in the levels of employment and unemployment, especially in those sectors represented among residential and commercial tenants in a particular locale, signal possible changes in ability to pay rent. Growth in nonagricultural employment relates to new jobs, new businesses, and increasing demand for rentable commercial (office, retail, industrial) space. Declining employment may be the harbinger of increasing numbers of late rent payments possibly leading to rental vacancies as tenants seek less-expensive (smaller, lower rent) space. It may also be a reason for tenants' unwillingness to accept rent increases at lease renewal. Fluctuations in interest rates are a measure of the availability of funds for borrowing—for investment, construction, and operating capital. The U.S. Federal Reserve System may lower the discount rate at which it lends money to its member banks as a way to stimulate economic growth. The Producer Price Index (PPI) and the Consumer Price Index (CPI) are measures of inflation at the wholesale and retail levels, respectively. The CPI is often used as the basis for rent increases. The number of building permits issued, the number and value of construction starts, and absorption rates for newly constructed space chart the health of the U.S. real estate market in particular. Real estate professionals in general and property managers in particular follow many of these economic indicators as a matter of course.

Of all the functions of government, however, taxation, regulation of banking, and control of interest rates are among those of greatest interest to the property manager. (The specific role of the various levels of government in the real estate market is discussed later in this chapter.)

Taxation. The various functions of government, including the services it provides, have inherent costs. In order to pay these costs, the government must have income. Government derives its income from various sources, the most significant of which is taxes. In the United States, the federal government taxes the income of individuals and businesses. State and local governments impose taxes primarily on property.

The federal income tax, as its name implies, is a tax on personal and business income. Changes in the law have from time to time specifically encouraged or discouraged investment in income-producing property. In the early 1980s, the law provided for higher tax rates on higher incomes, but it also created a variety of *tax shelters*. It was possible to invest in property that generated little or no income and still make a profit. The level of continuing inflation essentially guaranteed a selling price higher than the property's purchase price. In addition, *losses* from real estate investments could be used to offset income from wages and other sources. This reduced the property owner's taxable income and placed him or her in a lower tax bracket. However, the Tax Reform Act of 1986 changed all that. Investment in real estate became less profitable because the tax incentives were greatly reduced. Losses resulting from real estate operation could no longer be used to offset other income, thus "sheltering" that income from taxation was blocked. Owners who had previously bought property for "tax breaks" found themselves in the position of having to use income from other sources to support their real estate investments that were operating in the red. Those who did not have "deep pockets" had few options, and they elected sale, foreclosure (default), and sometimes bankruptcy. Inflation slowed and property values no longer appreciated quickly, especially in overbuilt markets. As a result, the number of distressed properties on the market increased.

Financial Regulation.   A significant role of government relates to money. Government establishes the form of money and fixes its value. It also produces the nation's money—it coins metallic money and prints paper money—and regulates the amount of it in circulation. When governments mint and print additional currency, they create inflation. When they reduce the amount of currency in circulation, they cause deflation. Printed money and coinage were traditionally backed by some convertible commodity, with each country fixing a value of the commodity for its particular currency so that international exchange could take place. Gold was an accepted standard for more than half a century. The currency was considered a receipt for gold that could be exchanged for an amount of the metal at any time.

After World War II, nations moved away from an international gold standard, and the present "standard" involves a mixture of floating and fixed exchange rates. Exchange-rate stabilization is coordinated by the major central banks. The value of the U.S. dollar "floats" with respect to all the major currencies of the world. The desirability of the dollar in world markets has fallen sharply because of a negative balance of trade; the United States imports more than it exports—primarily petroleum. The government consistently spends more money than it collects in taxes and other revenues, and the federal debt is enormous.

The U.S. government also regulates banking. Once banks provided a variety of unique services, including loans for investment, and they were the only institutions that offered checking (draft withdrawal) accounts. By definition, savings and loan associations or thrifts were limited to savings deposit accounts and loans primarily for homeownership. Deregulation of the thrifts in the 1980s gave rise to several phenomena. Branch banking (and branch S&Ls) became widespread, and S&Ls were allowed to offer "checking" accounts (negotiable order of withdrawal or NOW accounts) and to lend money for commercial investment. Many banks and S&Ls entered the real estate market directly, often lending money in a manner that allowed them to participate in the property ownership. Many of these institutions had no prior experience in real estate investment, and they frequently made loans for development of marginal properties. In addition, assets held in reserve to reimburse depositors were allowed to fall below required levels (sometimes as a result of real estate assets having lost value). When the borrowers defaulted on the loans, the financial institutions foreclosed on the properties. By the end of the 1980s, the market was glutted with troubled properties. Failures of S&Ls became widespread, and the Federal Savings and Loan Insurance Corporation (FSLIC), which guaranteed the deposits in the institutions, was required to pay back the insured deposits. The Financial Institutions Reform, Recovery, and Enforcement Act of 1989 (FIRREA) enacted by the U.S. Congress transferred the responsibilities of the FSLIC to the Federal Deposit Insurance Corporation (FDIC), which is the insuring body for deposits in banks. The new law required the FDIC to eliminate differences that existed in deposit insurance coverages at banks and S&Ls, and it now insures deposits at both types of institutions.

Interest Rates.   As part of its regulation of banking, the U.S. government controls money supply by adjusting interest rates, and this has widespread effects. When the Federal Reserve System lowers the discount rate charged to its member banks (to stimulate economic growth), they, in turn, may lower the commercial "prime" interest rate they charge their best customers for short-term loans. This can lead to reduction in the interest rate paid on deposits as well. Conversely, the Federal Reserve may raise the discount rate to reduce the money supply or in an effort to discourage banks from excessive leniency in their lending and investment policies.

Interest is a major inducement for people to save. When an individual's income exceeds the amount required to take care of basic needs, the surplus income can be spent immediately for personal enjoyment (to acquire possessions, for recreation, etc.) or set aside for future use. When interest rates are high, individuals are willing to save more.

Savings deposited in banks and related financial institutions do more than earn interest for the saver. That money is put to work to produce more money. Savings deposits are used by banks to finance various types of lending. Consumers borrow money to purchase homes, automobiles, major appliances, recreational equipment and vehicles, etc. Businesses borrow money for operating capital—to purchase raw materials for processing into finished products or to provide inventory of products for sale. Money thus borrowed is paid back to the lenders with added interest. In fact, the amount borrowed often depends on the rate of interest being charged. When money is plentiful, interest rates tend to be low, and banks readily lend money to willing borrowers. When money is tight, however, interest rates tend to rise, and individuals and businesses tend to borrow less. High interest rates encourage saving and discourage borrowing. Controlling interest rates is one way the government controls the amount of money available for borrowing. Changes in interest rates are among the factors that contribute to inflation and deflation, and periods of inflation

---

Economic Indicators

A number of economic factors measured by the U.S. government on a regular basis are known to move upward and downward in the same pattern as the business cycle. Some of these indicators lead the cycle, some run concurrent, and others follow it. Of particular interest are the indexes of business activity—building permits, total output, employment, business formation, and new orders. Sustained downturns in one or more of these indicators are often followed by a period of recession.

Indicators that relate directly to real estate include the total value of new construction put in place (all property types), nonresidential investment as a percentage of gross national product, total manufacturing and wholesale trade inventories, and retail sales. Other indicators of interest to real estate professionals reflect the general economy. These include consumer and producer prices, net exports, employment, and interest rates (especially the prime rate).

Indicators that tend to rise or fall in advance of a general rise or fall in business activity are called *leading indicators*. They are the most important because they give advance warning of future economic events. Normally they turn down before a recession and up before an expansion of the economy. The U.S. Department of Commerce publishes a composite *index of leading indicators* that is a weighted average of twelve of their leading indicators. Four components of this index are new building permits, net change in inventories, stock prices, and the money supply. The index of leading indicators is one of the most widely used indicators in the U.S. economy; however, its accuracy in forecasting recessions is not absolute because components of this composite index do not move together in exactly the same rhythm.

---

and deflation affect the sale and purchase of goods and services, usually in a cyclic manner.

The Business Cycle

Periods of economic expansion or contraction may be short-lived (a few months), or they may go on for many years. Sometimes one region of the United States or the world will be affected more than another. Occasionally a single industry or a single market will be the focus of economic change, but that is rare. Businesses and industries today are interrelated in such complex ways that whatever affects one significantly will eventually affect most if not all of them. Poor sales of consumer merchandise slow down a retailer's business, the retailer orders less from wholesalers and distributors, and they in turn take less of a manufacturer's production. A raw material shortage curtails a manufacturer's production, there is less merchandise for wholesalers and distributors to move to retailers, and consumers cannot purchase products they desire. Changes in technology, development of new materials, and discovery of new uses for existing materials are some factors that contribute to massive economic changes. They may make current materials and technologies obsolete, or they may create whole new industries. Development of railroads in the mid-nine-

E X H I B I T   2.1

The Business Cycle

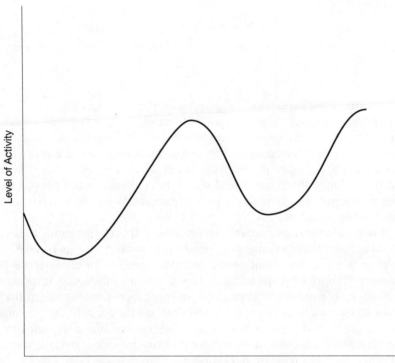

The business cycle is represented by a series of troughs and peaks over time. Slowing business activity shown as a downward slope is a period of *recession*; a deep trough indicates *depression*. Beginning growth or *recovery* (an upward slope) culminates in *prosperity* (the peak).

teenth century, mass production of automobiles in the early twentieth century, invention of plastics and downsizing of computers more recently are just a few examples.

When business is good, it is easy to sell goods or services. Demand exceeds supply, prices are high, and it is easy to make a profit. When business is poor, supply exceeds demand, prices are low, and profits are often replaced by losses. These various periods of inflation and deflation of an economy are known as the *business cycle*. There are generally four successive stages in the business cycle—recession, depression, recovery, and prosperity (exhibit 2.1). By convention, professional economists look at the downside first, perhaps because its causes and effects are more readily apparent.

The Business Cycle
* Recession
* Depression
* Recovery
* Prosperity

Recession.   During periods of prosperity, there is expansion of all sectors of the economy. The increased demand for goods tends to raise prices. Prosperity also results in higher wages. When personal income increases, there is a tendency to spend that income—buying a more luxurious car, paying more in rent for a larger apartment, etc.—but only up to a point. Once their needs and wants are satisfied, many people will store their surplus income in the form of savings. Money thus saved is not available for spending.

When individuals are actively saving money, there is generally a corresponding reduction in consumer spending. However, savings invested in banks or in stocks and bonds provide capital needed for commercial investment. Temporarily, spending by business firms offsets the absence of spending by consumers. The lessening of consumer spending affects businesses in two ways. Because merchants can no longer rely on the same level of sales, their income is reduced; they cannot afford to maintain a large inventory. Manufacturers still have to pay for raw materials, wages, and other costs of production. Competition increases as businesses try to maintain or increase their share of a dwindling consumer or industrial market. In order to maintain inventories and meet payroll expenses, businesses turn to bankers. Meanwhile, the bankers become cautious; their willingness to lend money to business for expansion may not extend to providing operating capital. The tightening credit also reduces the funds available for new construction. Prices cannot continue to rise in this environment. There are not enough buyers—demand has been reduced. This slowdown in business activity signals the beginning of a period of economic *recession.*

Soon manufacturing costs catch up with selling prices. Banks raise their interest rates and may even refuse to make loans; businesses cannot borrow additional capital. The inability to obtain funds from the bank leads to failure of some businesses, and this can have a domino effect. One business may be depending on payment from a second business in order to meet its obligations on a loan. When that payment is not forthcoming, the first business fails. Failures of businesses mean banks and S&Ls cannot collect their outstanding loans, and eventually the financial institutions themselves can fail.

Depression.   Ultimately there is widespread reduction in business activity. Employment is reduced, wages are lowered, and consumer demand declines. Surviving businesses try to sell all they can and buy as little as possible—in order to meet contractual obligations, pay their debts, and avoid failure. As demand continues to decline, so do prices. The most serious outcome of all of these negative factors is a period of *depression*. Stocks of goods diminish as inventory is sold and not replenished. The rate of production is slow and prices are low. Interest is down and so are wages. Unemployment is widespread. Depression eliminates the weakest businesses and banks—there is less competition in the marketplace.

Recovery.   During a depression, however, there is also a reduction in business costs because rents, wages, and prices for raw materials will have declined. Machinery and equipment that were not maintained or replaced during the depression will have to be replaced eventually. The need for new machinery creates a demand for capital equipment, and increased demand stimulates other businesses and leads to higher prices. These are early signs of *recovery*. Once recovery gets started, employment increases and more money is paid out in wages. Additional income increases demand for consumer goods and tends to raise prices. Production costs will not rise as quickly as prices because rents, interest rates, and wages—which react more slowly to change—will remain low for some time.

Prosperity.   When prices are rising faster than the costs of production, business income increases in the form of higher profits. The reviving economy is once again headed for *prosperity*. Prosperity is a period of good business. Businesses foresee opportunities for profits, so they borrow capital, increase their production, and try to enlarge their share of the market. Banks are willing to lend money for business expansion because such loans are easily repaid. Lending expands their business. The expansion of one business creates demand for the products of other businesses, and that tends to raise prices. High prices in the marketplace attract other businesses to it, resulting in competition.

Economic growth is also fueled by population growth. In particular, changes in the size of the population affect the size of the work force. A growing work force means larger numbers of consumers as well. The baby boom generation—people born between 1950 and 1965—increased the size of the work force dramatically beginning in the 1970s (exhibit 2.2). However, they have produced fewer offspring. As the baby-boomers pass into middle age in the 1990s, their children are entering the work force—but in much smaller numbers. This reduction in the labor pool will reduce overall demand for consumer goods; it also means that ultimately the large volume of new construction to meet the needs of the large numbers of baby-boomers will grind to a halt. Markets that cannot

EXHIBIT   2.2

Projected Population of the United States (percent)

Age Group(s)	1970	1980	1990	2000	2010
Total Population (thousands)	203,235	226,546	250,410	268,266	282,575
Percent Increase	—	11.5	10.5	7.1	5.3
Under 18 years	**34.3**	28.1	25.6	25.5	22.2
18–24 years	**11.7**	**13.3**	10.4	9.4	9.6
25–34 years	12.3	**16.4**	**17.5**	13.8	13.3
35–44 years	11.4	11.3	**15.1**	**16.4**	13.2
45–54 years	11.4	10.1	10.2	**13.9**	**15.3**
55–64 years	9.2	9.6	8.5	9.0	**12.5**
65 and older	9.8	11.3	12.6	13.0	13.9

Data compiled from *Statistical Abstract of the United States, 110th Edition, 1990.*

Aging of the baby-boom generation (those born between 1950 and 1965) is indicated in bold-face type.

absorb space rapidly will see increasing vacancies. By the end of the 1980s, some major markets were seeing office and commercial vacancies in excess of 20 percent. Until the late 1980s, many in the industry considered 5 percent the "natural" level of commercial vacancy.

Prosperity tends to feed on its own momentum. Employment levels rise as businesses expand. Business expansion leads to new construction of office, industrial, and retail properties. High wages permit workers to purchase luxury items and invest in homeownership. During these times, housing starts increase, especially single-family homes. Investment and savings are on the rise. Meanwhile, rents and interest rates begin to escalate as leases and contracts expire. The economy starts to slow down, checked by rising prices, wages, rents, and interest rates—all of which make money tighter—and the cycle repeats itself.

Throughout the business cycle, rents, interest, and wages do not change as quickly as other prices do. Rents and interest rates are usually fixed for a period of time; leases and other contracts run for months or years. Wages and salaries are also fixed for extended periods, sometimes by contract. As general prices are rising, rents, interest, and wages are slow to catch up. The disparity in these costs of production in relation to the prices commanded for goods is part of what fuels prosperity. Rents, interest, and wages eventually catch up with prices, however, and this has the effect of reducing profits and creating losses—ultimately fueling recession. The numbers of potential buyers will diminish, depressing real estate prices. Unavailability of capital precludes investment in improvements, and the real estate market will be glutted with distressed properties. In the long run, the credit crunch that results will promote recovery by limiting new building.

Recession is not always followed by a period of depression, and recovery is not always a separate stage in the business cycle. Sometimes periods of prosperity follow periods of mild recession; economic expansion and contraction are apparent but not pronounced. Often a scientific breakthrough or development of a promising new technology is a significant contributor to economic recovery. The real estate industry, while part of the general economy, reacts to the same economic pressures more slowly and more strongly. (The nature of the real estate cycle is discussed in a later section of this chapter.)

REAL ESTATE ECONOMICS

The amount of land available for use—the earth's surface—is strictly limited. Land cannot be produced. Nor can it be consumed or destroyed. The limited amount of land is what gives it value. Land also has unique characteristics based on its location and its inherent qualities, and these factors give value to land and affect its desirability. Ultimately, the use to which land is or can be put determines its market value. Fertile farmland that yields more grain per acre than another plot is more valuable than less productive acreage. However, neither will be as valuable if the grain cannot be transported to the marketplace. Location that includes ready access to transportation is a key factor in the value of farmland. Land in urban areas (city centers) is considered more valuable than suburban land because of the intense use to which it is put. Population density is very high for residential uses—a 100-unit apartment building may occupy the same amount of land as two or three single-family homes.

In urban areas, residents accept high rents as a tradeoff against long, expensive commutes to work. They expect that rent to be compensated by ready access to public transportation and the cultural and entertainment features of the city and by the amenities of the building where they live. Businesses willingly pay high rents for office space in urban areas because they have access to a large labor pool and to all the services available in a city. Often cities are also their major markets. Retailers will pay high rents to have store space in an area where wealthy people shop or to have access to very large numbers of potential customers. High rents mean higher property values because they return greater profits to investors in city land.

The Real Estate Market

Markets for specific products and services can be found wherever there are willing buyers and sellers of those products and services. The prod-

Consumer Price Index and Rent

The Consumer Price Index (CPI) is the most commonly used measure of inflation. The U.S. Department of Labor calculates the current year's cost of a particular array of goods and services consumed by a typical family and reports it as a percentage of the cost of that same array of goods and services in a base year (also set by the Department of Labor). Among the goods and services "consumed" are food and beverages, housing, apparel, transportation, medical care, and entertainment.

The CPI is computed and published monthly or bimonthly for most of the standard metropolitan statistical areas (SMSAs) in the United States. As a measure of inflation, the CPI is used as the basis for raising wages and for adjusting social security and pension benefits and income tax schedules. Property managers use it as a guideline for rental rate increases, especially for commercial properties.

Upward movement of the CPI favors the property manager whose leases include rent escalators based on it; the CPI provides a rationale (measure of inflation) and a rate (the percentage change) for the scheduled rent increases based on a reputable, nonbiased statistic provided by the government. Because the CPI measures inflation over time, annual rent increases based on the change in the CPI are usually realistic. However, downward movement of the CPI for any length of time can reduce or cancel the benefit expected. The CPI showed a price decrease in 1955; both before and since, it has always moved upward, most drastically between 1970 and 1980. Between 1982 and 1988 the rate of increase in the CPI slowed significantly, but it began to rise again as we entered the 1990s.

Annual Changes in the CPI Between 1980 and 1990*

Year	CPI	Amount of Increase	Percent Change
1980	256.2	—	—
1981	280.7	24.5	9.6
1982	293.6	12.9	4.6
1983	303.1	9.5	3.2
1984	315.3	12.2	4.0
1985	326.6	11.3	3.6
1986	330.8	4.2	1.3
1987	345.8	15.0	4.5
1988	360.5	14.7	4.3
1989	377.0	16.5	4.6
1990	400.7	23.7	6.3

Five-Year Changes in the CPI Between 1970 and 1990*

Year	CPI	Amount of Increase	Percent Change
1970	118.5	—	—
1975	165.6	47.1	39.7
1980	256.2	90.6	54.7
1985	326.6	70.4	27.5
1990	400.7	74.1	22.7

*Figures are for the month of November; comparison is to base year 1967 = 100. Note that the annual percentage increases in the CPI are very small over the decade of the 1980s, and this is reflected in the sharply reduced cumulative percentage increases for 1980–1985 and 1985–1990 compared to those for 1970–1975 and 1975–1980. The cumulative increase over the entire decade (1980–1990 = 56.4%) is less than half of the cumulative increase over the preceding decade (1970–1980 = 116.2%).

ucts themselves and the people who provide the services can be transported from one location to another. Land is fixed in location, however, so the market for land is usually local. Owners of real estate may not be local—large commercial properties, in particular, are traded at the national level and in international markets—but the ultimate users are locally based.

The value of land in the local market depends on its use and any improvements to it. Because buildings and other improvements to land have a long physical life, the commitment to a specific use is not readily subject to change. The general trend in real estate is *increasing* value. Land use is affected by many things, among them industry, population, and highways—and supply and demand.

Industry. Changes in industry and the economy also affect land value. Inflation, wide fluctuations in the availability and cost of mortgage money, and the cost and availability of foreign crude oil are factors that affect the real estate market at the regional, national, and international level. At the local level, empty factories on the edge of a city may no longer be useful as industrial property. Creative developers and architects can usually find a way to convert them to other uses. Vacant warehouses that could not be sold or were no longer usable for their original purpose have been renovated and converted to new housing. Factories, post offices, railroad stations, and historic buildings have been made over as shopping centers. Such changes, intended to increase the income from the property and therefore increase its value, also preserve landmarks and conserve raw materials.

Changes in a region will affect land use. Growth such as occurred in the so-called Sunbelt (the Southwest) in the 1980s had impact nationwide. Many industries relocated there from the northeastern United States. What they left behind became known as the Rust Belt. High-technology and petroleum were the booming Sunbelt businesses. They brought jobs that created demand for new office space. However, dependence on them to the exclusion of other types of industries eventually had severe effects locally. Increased importation of petroleum reduced domestic exploration and production. Higher prices for domestic oil increased production costs of products derived from it. When the oil and high-technology industries faltered, many cities—especially Dallas and Houston in Texas—suddenly had phenomenal amounts of vacant new office space and interrupted construction. Property values declined drastically.

Population. Changes in population size have a direct impact on land values. When the population in an area grows, land value increases. The increase in demand for the fixed amount of land leads to higher prices. Population growth is a direct result of formation of new industries that

provide jobs. New manufacturing industries also attract support businesses (suppliers of raw materials or parts and distributors of finished
goods), which also increase the number of available jobs. When the local
population declines in number—particularly if significant numbers of
people move away and others do not move in to replace them—demand
for land is reduced, land values decline, and prices are lower. Population
decline results when industries close down because they have become
obsolete or lost their share of the market. Those satellite businesses that
depended on the major industry may close down earlier because their
"supplies" are no longer needed or later because there are no products to
distribute. These shifts in industrial activity that affect population size also
affect the local economy by increasing and decreasing the amount of income available for discretionary spending.

Changes in the characteristics of a population can affect land use and
that has an impact on land value. As wages increase, individuals have more
discretionary income. Homeownership, once a dream, can now become
reality. The demand for housing soon becomes a demand for better
quality housing as renters opt to buy or choose to pay higher rent but only
in exchange for certain amenities. Shorter workweeks increase leisure
time and generate demand for recreational and entertainment facilities
(e.g., golf courses, sports arenas) where the disposable income can be
spent.

Ample discretionary income encourages shopping, and that creates
demand for shopping centers. In order to meet demand and create
unique shopping environments, major malls began to include "food
courts" where a variety of specialty fast foods (ethnic entrees, baked po-
tato meals, cookies, frozen yogurt) are purchased from self-service stalls
and eaten in an open area surrounded by the vendors. Many specialty
malls that cater primarily to tourists are dominated by food and food service businesses. Shopping has come to include eating as an adjunct activity. All of this is a reflection of changing American eating habits and follows a trend away from meals eaten at home.

The U.S. population is aging rapidly, and more people are living
longer than ever before. For many, careful retirement planning provides
high income after retirement, and an aging population increases demand
not only for retirement housing (which may be comparatively smaller and
is likely to be more expensive and to include recreational amenities), but
also for extended care facilities—nursing homes and health care.

Highways.   New highways provide access to distant land and open new
areas to development. Initial development may be only housing which
will draw residents away from urban areas because they can live in a less
congested environment while continuing to work and shop in the city.

Eventually there will be commercial development. Businesses will move offices and manufacturing from the city to the suburbs where there is less congestion and a developing pool of labor that may not demand the same wage scale as in the city. Computers and telecommunications have reduced the need to have all of a business's operations under one roof. It may be necessary to have a headquarters office in the central business district (CBD), but support functions (customer service, inventory controls, storage) can be located anywhere.

Enclosed shopping malls that offer a wide range of merchandise beyond clothing will not only meet the needs of suburban residents but also attract shoppers from nearby communities and cities. While highways provide access to cities by suburban residents, they also create reverse commutes. Some people who live in the city cannot find jobs there, and suburban commercial areas cannot always fill their labor needs from the nearby communities. So people may travel from the city to the suburbs to work—instead of the reverse.

Highways not only open land to development, they also lead to specific land uses. Travelers between cities create demand for roadside facilities, and there is a market for gasoline service stations, restaurants, and various qualities of temporary lodging (hotels, motels, etc.). Highway intersections that attract operators of roadside facilities eventually attract other businesses, and these businesses attract employees who become residents in the area. All of these factors that lead to land development also add to its value.

Supply and Demand.   In the real estate market, the laws of supply and demand are also at work. Generally the value of real estate in a given market is based on the present worth of projected future benefits to be derived from the investment. Stable values result when there is a balance between the supply of a given land use and the economic demand for that use. Supply is usually limited and is not quickly increased. Supply declines as a result of deterioration, demolition, and destruction by hazards (e.g., fire). Existing properties are part of the total supply even if they are not used. Demand changes, however, and there are many factors that influence it. Population, income, credit, personal tastes and preferences as well as governmental actions, taxes, and costs savings all have impact on demand. The imbalance between supply and demand means real estate investment can be more risky than other types of investments whose markets are more predictable.

When there is an oversupply of a use (e.g., office space, shopping centers, etc.), the value of that type of property declines. An overbuilt market is a renter's market. There is more space available than there are renters desiring such space, so prospective tenants can negotiate lower rents and other favorable terms—some or all of which can have negative long-term effects on the property value. An underbuilt market is more desirable to investors because it favors the property owner. When demand exceeds supply, the space that is available will command high rents because there is less competing space.

Government and Real Estate

Governments operating at all levels affect real estate transactions in numerous ways. Local governments tax real property based on its value—ad valorem taxes. The tax burden affects the value of a particular parcel of land and is therefore an important consideration in the investment in real estate. Local zoning ordinances impose limits on land uses, and compliance with them—or efforts to change zoning—can be costly. Appropriate zoning is particularly important in real estate development.

Federal regulations that affect financial transactions have an impact on the real estate market. Acceptable interest rates and availability of funds for mortgage loans determine how much can be borrowed. As has already been stated, high interest rates discourage borrowing. The amount of debt service (mortgage principal and interest payments) affects the return that can be derived from the purchase of a rental property. To meet debt service requirements, the property must produce more income generally. The amount of income needed to pay debt service reduces the amount the owner can keep.

Government ownership of land in national and state parks, highways and rights of way, public buildings, and military bases makes it a major participant in the real estate market. The presence of various government-owned properties can increase or decrease real estate values, depending on what they are and where they are located. A military base, for example, may be desirable because it brings jobs to an area. Conversely, if it attracts undesirable businesses to the area (e.g., bars or so-called adult entertainments), a military base will not enhance surrounding property values.

Numerous governmental subsidy programs have an influence on property values and real estate investment decisions. Some housing programs subsidize rents for lower income groups and may limit rental rates that can be charged for private properties participating in the program. Other programs encourage homeownership by offering more favorable terms for mortgage loans than are available in the private sector, in effect competing with it. (Government subsidized housing is discussed in more detail in chapter 9.)

Federal programs are often the key to land development or redevelopment. One such program is urban renewal, which opens land in cities to new uses. Urban renewal has both short-term and long-term effects. The short-term effects are often negative because urban renewal displaces the original users to land elsewhere and results in loss of property value in the sale. When urban renewal eliminates housing, the residents move elsewhere, often to the suburbs. It also encourages the movement of businesses and industries to the suburbs. The displaced owners may have to accept less than market value for their properties because that is all that is offered. (The sale price of a property may reflect low values of adjacent, blighted properties.) Long-term, however, urban renewal has many positive aspects, especially as it revitalizes the area. Development of a parcel of land for one use usually attracts development of adjacent land, often for a different use. Industrial development may attract research facilities and offices. Residential development tends to attract retailing and entertainment enterprises. Occasionally the reverse is true.

Rent controls are occasionally imposed by different levels of government, usually with the intent of setting upper limits on rental rates to maintain a pool of "affordable" housing. In general, rent controls interfere with the operation of the laws of supply and demand in the marketplace. In the absence of rent controls, more rents would tend toward the average rate rather than the extreme high (uncontrolled) and low (controlled) rates. Rent controls create an artificial lack of movement in rents at the lower end of the rate range. People tend not to vacate rent-controlled apartments. The stagnation at low and middle rental rates forces those who are moving to go to areas where rents are higher. When controlled rents are substantially lower than market rents, the demand for those units is often disproportionately high and demand for units at market rates is consequently low. The reduction in income that results when controls are in place means there is less money available for maintenance and repairs, so maintenance is deferred. The lesser income and the deferred maintenance both contribute to lowering of the property's value. In order to sell a property after rent controls have been in place, the owner may have to take a loss. A loss may result anyway through deterioration, which can remove the property from the overall supply and thus curtail rental income altogether.

Some regulations affect real estate both directly and indirectly. Laws enacted to protect the environment offer a useful example. Concerns about the presence of asbestos in buildings led to demands for containment or removal of the material from certain classes of existing buildings and use of other materials for fireproofing new buildings. The direct effect was tremendous costs to building owners for containment or removal of asbestos. There was also an effect on value because the presence of asbestos made a building less desirable to prospective buyers. The potential for long-term liability if asbestos were to be discovered after the sale of the building added to the problem. Although the demand for removal or containment of this potential hazard changed as more research was done, the effect on the real estate market did not go away. Environmental regulations can be enacted at all levels of government, and the most stringent requirements are the ones that apply in a given situation. Because of this, environmental aspects of a property will continue to be a major concern for property owners and managers as well as for potential investors.

One type of laws of particular interest to property managers are those laws regarding fair housing. Fair housing laws are promulgated by all levels of government, and they specifically regulate how houses are sold and apartments are rented. Practices that discriminate on the basis of race, color, sex, religion, or national origin have long been prohibited by federal law. The Fair Housing Amendments Act of 1988 expanded the bases of discrimination to include physical and mental handicaps and familial status (children).

Real Estate Cycles

Just as there is a cyclic nature to other businesses, there is also a cyclic nature to the real estate market. Statistics of real estate sales, new housing starts (single-family and multiple dwellings), mortgage lending, new construction, and absorption rates for rental space show periods of high and low levels of activity. The total of real estate transactions or sales recorded in real estate markets throughout the United States operates on a long cycle averaging more than 18 years. Some cycles have been longer while others have been shorter, the discrepancies in duration being related to important historical events (depressions, wars, major technological changes). There is also a short cycle lasting up to 5 years that is related to availability of mortgage funds, shifts in money markets, and governmental housing programs.

Like the business cycles discussed earlier, the real estate cycle has four components. They generally follow their business counterparts (exhibit 2.3, broken line). As a result of *overbuilding,* demand begins to decline, absorption slows, and rents weaken further just as building peaks. Overbuilding is a consequence of prosperity, which cannot last forever, and precedes and then coincides with recession. The real estate market then undergoes *adjustment*—demand continues to decline, occupancy diminishes further, and rent concessions become widespread. New building is decidedly slowed during periods of recession and depression. This is followed by *stabilization,* a period in which demand begins to increase despite declining construction starts, thus making inroads into the excess supply. This coincides with the depths of recession or depression and is the real estate equivalent of recovery. The last stage is *development.* As prosperity returns to the rest of the economy, occupancy is high, rents are rising, and absorption levels are high. Demand accelerates and new construction is needed to meet the increased demand.

E X H I B I T   2.3

The Business Cycle and the Real Estate Cycle

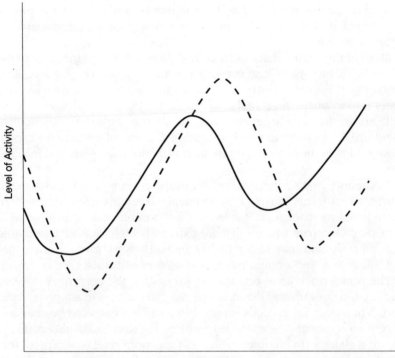

The solid line indicates the business cycle; the broken line shows the real estate cycle, which follows it. Slowing business activity (a downward slope) is characteristic of a period of recession. In the real estate cycle, new construction declines as a result of overbuilding (a peak) and leads to a period of adjustment during which occupancy declines and rent concessions are widespread. A deep trough indicates depression; occupancy and rents are reduced severely. An upward slope signals beginning growth or recovery. In the real estate cycle this reflects accelerated demand for rental space and increased new construction. The business cycle culminates in prosperity (the peak) which leads to new levels of overbuilding.

Real estate demand depends on activity in other sectors of the economy for its motivation. As a consequence, it tends to lag behind the upward movements in the general economy, but it also tends to exceed the heights of the peaks and depths of the troughs of the general economic cycle. Recovery and prosperity are reflected in high occupancy levels, high rental rates, strong real estate sales, large amounts of money available to lend at acceptable interest rates, and large volumes of new construction. Conversely, during periods of economic recession and depression, vacancies increase, delinquencies in mortgage and rent payments rise, and real estate sales decline both in numbers of sales and in prices. New construction slows and the numbers of mortgage loans and their dollar values decline.

Many of the factors that influence real estate cycles are inherent in the real estate market itself. Real estate is not always a mirror of the general economy. By its very nature it is local, and local situations will have greater impact on the local real estate market. However, real estate booms and busts are frequently generated by conditions outside the immediate market area. Globalization and institutionalization of investment capital had key roles in the U.S. real estate market in the late 1980s and into the 1990s.

Occupancy levels reflect the relationship between supply and demand at current rent levels. Changes in occupancy levels are of particular concern to property managers. However, it is the public that sets the tone of the market. Occupancy levels that are extremely high indicate a probable space shortage and may justify higher rents. High vacancy, on the other hand, suggests a weakening market, and renters will resist rent increases.

The rental price level reflects the strength of the current real estate situation. It moves up and down in response to changes in supply and demand. When demand exceeds supply, higher rental rates can be charged, and rent increases at renewal of leases or as automatic adjustments under escalation clauses (in commercial leases) are more readily accepted. It is critical for property managers to know the prevailing trends in rental rates in their area.

Mortgage lending reflects the lenders' confidence in the safety and desirability of real estate as an investment. Lenders must believe the property is sound, that it will retain its value or increase in value over time, and—most important from their perspective—that it will generate sufficient income to assure repayment of the loan. Property managers should keep abreast of current interest rates in their area because mortgage lending is affected adversely by rising interest rates.

Building activity is a measure of the economic potential of vacant land. Large-scale building increases the supply of a specific use and thus depresses the market for that space. When there is a surplus of space, construction is curtailed, and this has wide-reaching effects beyond the real estate market itself. Construction workers that are unemployed may not be able to pay rent. They certainly will not have income to spend for consumer goods generally, and that affects other segments of the economy.

Mortgage foreclosures reflect the inability of owners of real property to generate enough income from their properties to pay the debt on them. In general, foreclosures are an effect of economic recession or depres-

---

The Real Estate Cycle
* Overbuilding
* Adjustment
* Stabilization
* Development

---

sion. Real estate loses earning power as a result of reductions in occupancy levels and rental rates. However, the absence of foreclosures does not necessarily signify prosperity. It is important for property managers to understand the conditions that lead to foreclosures as well as be aware of foreclosure activity in the local market.

SUMMARY

The property manager's goal is to preserve and increase the value of a property through good management. This can best be done by trying to achieve the highest and best economic use for the property. An evaluation and understanding of economic trends is necessary to the accomplishment of this goal.

Economics covers the activities of production, distribution, and consumption of manufactured goods and agricultural products. Real estate is a part of the economic picture because land is fundamental to economic activity.

Value is attributed to the products of economic activity by agreement to exchange one kind of goods for another. The use of money facilitates exchange because it functions as a standard of value. It allows measurement and comparison of the value of goods and services that cannot otherwise be readily measured or compared. Money is also a store of value through its purchasing power.

The marketplace is subject to the laws of supply and demand. When supply is less than demand, prices tend to rise; when supply exceeds demand, prices decline. Changes in the supply of money in relation to the volume of goods available for purchase affect the economy overall. More money than goods signals inflation; the opposite signals deflation. Because government can control the supply of money, its actions can lead to inflation and deflation.

In general, business activity is cyclic in nature. Prosperity is a period of economic growth, but economic growth cannot continue forever. Workers having met their needs and wants tend to save their excess wages. When they are saving and not spending their income, banks and S&Ls have capital to lend to businesses for expansion. However, reduced consumer spending reduces business income, and financial institutions that lent freely for expansion become disinclined to lend money for operating capital. The economy slows down, and prosperity is followed by a period of recession. Supply exceeds demand, prices drop and production is reduced. Profits fall off and businesses have less income to pay for operating expenses. Wages are reduced, and unemployment increases. Borrowing is curtailed, and businesses fail. At its lowest point, the economy may enter a period of depression. Eventually, however, the surviving businesses take stock of their situations. Their inventories are reduced and they have to replace equipment. Orders for new merchandise and machinery create demand, which leads to increasing prices, and the economy begins to recover. Recovery soon becomes prosperity, which is a period of high demand in comparison to supply. This is reflected in high profits, high levels of borrowing, and increased production. There is little unemployment; wages are high, and prices for consumer products are high.

Real estate is part of the overall economic picture primarily because of the relation of land to economic activity. However, the real estate market is itself subject to the laws of supply and demand, and factors in the general economy of the nation and the world can have impact on it. The real estate market is also affected by governmental actions, both those related specifically to real estate and those that affect the economy at large. Real estate business is itself cyclic and follows a pattern similar to that of the business cycle except that changes in occupancy levels, rental rates, and mortgage financing are among the specific components of real estate cycles. Often the cycles of real estate are reflections of the state of the general economy, although they tend to follow other trends and to be more extreme.

Key Terms

Deflation	Prosperity
Depression	Recession
Economics	Recovery
Inflation	Value
Money	

Key Points

The laws of supply and demand in the marketplace
The cyclic nature of economic activity
The role of government in economic activity
The differences between the real estate market and the general economy
The role of government in real estate activity

3

Ownership Forms and Goals

The purpose of professional real estate management is to achieve the property owner's goals for the investment. A variety of reasons exist for investing in real estate, and the deed to a property can be held in one of numerous ways. The method of purchasing property, the reasons for ownership, and the form of property ownership itself, affect the management of a property. To achieve an owner's goals, a property manager first examines how and why a property is owned.

MEANS AND REASONS FOR REAL ESTATE INVESTMENT

Most Americans aspire to invest in real estate at some point in their lives. A principal dwelling is often the largest and most expensive item an average American purchases. Because people normally buy a home or condominium to live in, they may not consider the purchase of their principal dwelling primarily as an investment. A new homeowner usually says, "I bought a house," instead of, "I invested in real property."

Purchasing real property is always an investment, however, regardless of how the owner uses the property. The capital investment is generally preserved and can be recaptured by selling the property to someone else.

Liquid Assets
* Savings accounts
* Stocks
* Bonds
* Precious metals

Means of Investing

An investor or group of investors purchases a property through one of two means. Either it is bought outright as an all-cash purchase, or part of the purchase price is financed through a loan. Both types of purchases have specific advantages and disadvantages for the investor.

All-Cash Purchase.   An all-cash purchase will yield a greater return on a periodic basis than a financed purchase because payments for financing (debt service) do not consume a substantial portion of the income from a property. Even though an all-cash purchase promises a greater amount of income, this benefit is not without cost—because the purchase price of income-producing property is commonly quite high, an all-cash purchase may consume most of an investor's assets and limit his or her ability to diversify investments.

The ready availability of large amounts of cash depends on how it is held. Savings accounts, stocks, bonds, or precious metals are considered *liquid assets* because they can be converted into cash quickly and easily at or near their market value. Money can be withdrawn from a bank account for investment in stocks. The stocks can be converted back into cash and invested in platinum. The platinum can be sold to invest in bonds. The advantage of a liquid asset is the diversity it offers. The investor who owns $100,000 worth of platinum and decides to purchase $50,000 worth of stock can simply sell enough platinum to pay for the stock. On the other hand, real property is considered an illiquid asset. The only way to convert real estate into cash is to sell or refinance the property. Neither can be done very quickly and both require agreement on the property's value.

The "value" of an owner's investment in real estate is called *equity*. An all-cash purchase gives the owner 100-percent equity. If a purchase is financed, the investor's initial equity is the amount of the cash down payment. When a property is held over time, the owner's equity increases as the principal of the loan is paid down. If the property is then sold for more than the original purchase price, the increase in the market price is the result of *appreciation* in value, and the amount of appreciation becomes part of the owner's equity. For example, if an owner pays $10,000 down on a $100,000 real estate purchase and finances the remaining $90,000, the initial equity owned is $10,000. If the property sells for $120,000 five years later, the seller's equity at that time will be *at least* $30,000 ($10,000 initial equity plus $20,000 in appreciation *plus* whatever equity—if any—has accumulated through amortization).

Financing.   Borrowing funds to purchase an income-producing property is often necessary or desirable. For real property, an instrument called a *mortgage* is drafted when a loan is approved. Among other things, a mortgage promises the deed of the property to the lender if the borrower fails to repay the loan. (The property and its deed are held as *collateral* to secure the mortgage loan, and the lender is entitled to foreclose the mortgage, sell the property, and apply the proceeds to the outstanding debt in the event the borrower defaults on the loan.) In essence, the mortgage is the legally binding document that stipulates the conditions of the loan, but borrowers and lenders alike commonly use the words "mortgage" and "loan" interchangeably.

The mortgages for all real property loans contain three major conditions: (1) they require the principal (the amount borrowed) to be repaid, (2) they require interest to be paid on the principal, and (3) they require these payments to be made on a specific schedule. The process of repayment (debt service) is designed to address all three of these conditions. Debt service is usually paid monthly, and the amount of the payment depends on whether part of the payment is used to pay back principal, the interest rate for the loan, and the term (length) of the loan.

When the principal is paid in full, a loan is said to be fully *amortized*. This is often the result of gradual reduction of the principal as part of the debt service. In the early years of the loan term, most of the monthly debt service payment is allocated to interest, and only a small portion (as little as 5 percent initially) is applied to pay down the principal. However, if the payment amount is unchanged, the portion allocated to interest is gradually reduced as the principal is paid down over time, and the portion allocated to principal slowly increases. Whether and how much of the debt service payment is used to amortize the principal depends on the type of loan.

In a *fixed-rate mortgage,* the interest rate is constant over the term of the loan. This type of loan was once the industry standard. The individual monthly payments on a loan with a long amortization period (e.g., 30 years) are generally lower than those on a loan of the same type with a shorter amortization period (e.g., 15 years). Lower payments can be beneficial, especially when the income produced by a property is low. However, a longer amortization period usually has a much higher cumulative cost because the portion of the debt service payment applied to the principal is smaller, and more payments are made over time.

On the other hand, a *variable-rate mortgage* permits the lending institution to raise or lower the interest rate of the loan based on changes in a prescribed index such as the average treasury bill yield or the prime rate. Interest on most variable-rate mortgages is a few percentage points above the *prime rate,* which is the lowest interest rate available from banks for short-term loans to their best customers. An *adjustable-rate mortgage (ARM)* is a type of variable-rate mortgage in which the interest rate is adjusted at fixed intervals (e.g., semiannually or annually), based on changes in the appropriate index. Variable-rate mortgages often have an upper limit or "cap" on the amount of change allowed in a year and over the term of the loan.

Sometimes the debt service will require a fixed payment amount over the term of the loan with a very large *balloon payment* at the end. The monthly payments usually allocate only a small amount to the principal; the bulk of these payments is interest, and the balloon payment amortizes the remainder of the principal owed. The monthly payments are smaller than those for a fully amortized loan at the same interest rate. The difference is the maturity date. Thus a 15-year mortgage may be repaid in monthly installments comparable to those for a 25-year fixed-rate loan; the balloon payment is required for amortization because the shorter loan term precludes accumulation of the full amount of the principal from the smaller periodic payments. The requirement of a balloon payment compounds the risk inherent in borrowing. If funds are not available for the balloon payment, the borrower must refinance, and the interest rate and monthly payments for the refinancing may be higher. If unable to refinance, the borrower must sell the property to cover the debt or risk foreclosure.

In addition to monthly payments, most mortgages have start-up costs such as points and application fees. A *point* is one percent of the total loan amount. If two points are payable for a $100,000 loan at the closing of the purchase (beginning of the loan), the borrower will pay $2,000 to the lender to secure the loan. Because the purchase of real estate involves more than the selling price of the property, some owners consider these additional costs as part of their *investment base.* If additional funds must be invested in the newly purchased property in order to make it operational (i.e., rehabilitation) or to enhance its ability to generate income (i.e., installation of new appliances to upgrade apartments and achieve higher rental rates), many investors add the cost of these initial improvements into the investment base as well.

While there are many advantages to financing, the purchaser must understand that his or her equity in the property will be less than 100 percent until the principal of the mortgage is fully amortized.

**Financial Reasons to
Invest in Real Estate**
* Capital preservation
* Capital appreciation
* Periodic return
* Income tax advantage

Reasons for Investment

Even though real estate is an illiquid investment, the allure of owning property and the financial rewards of ownership make it one of the largest storehouses of wealth. The earnings of liquid investments usually derive from few sources. Growth in the value of precious metals is based on demand; metals are often bought to preserve capital. The value of stock can appreciate from both demand for the stock and increasing value (profitability) of the company. Stocks often pay a periodic dividend as well, while the only earnings from a savings account are periodic interest payments. Bonds purchased at less than face value have a fixed maturity date and accrue interest over the period they are held. While some bonds (e.g., municipal bonds) are tax-free, the income from others may be taxable only when the bond matures or is converted to cash. Real property, on the other hand, can provide all four of the following: capital preservation, capital appreciation, periodic return, and income tax advantage. While a major consideration in real estate investment is financial return, there are nonfinancial considerations as well.

Capital Preservation.   Investment in real property is considered a way to preserve capital. Property values tend to rise with the inflation rate if the property is in a good location and the economic environment of the area is healthy. Land and real property are similar to precious metals in having an *intrinsic value*. They are inherently useful. It is the intrinsic value of a property that should increase at least at the same rate as inflation. Investors interested primarily in the safety of their capital look for property with extremely low risk. Qualities that indicate low risk include the following:

* Prime location
* Durable construction
* An architectural style that will not become outdated
* Excellent potential to increase in value over time
* Established tenancy with leases that contain clauses allowing pass

through to the tenant of increases in certain operating expenses and rent escalations if the leases are long-term
- The ability of the property to produce sufficient income to pay expenses and debt service (if financing is elected or necessary)
- Intrinsic value of the property is nearly equal to its purchase price
- Absence of encumbrances (e.g., mechanics' liens or zoning restrictions)

Capital Appreciation.   Appreciation is the increase in the value of an asset over time. In real estate investment, capital appreciation is achieved when an owner sells a property for more than its original purchase price. Because it does not materialize until the property is sold, capital appreciation can be the ultimate goal of a long-term investment, although it is also possible for a short-term holding.

A property manager plays an important role in the capital appreciation of a real estate investment by positioning the property to meet its highest and best use, producing as much income as possible, controlling operating costs as much as possible, and maintaining, preserving, and improving the structure itself. Value can increase for several reasons. If income increases and exceeds any increase in expenses, the property will be more desirable and can sell for a higher price. An improvement in the economy of the area, greater demand for property in the area, rehabilitation of the property, or a change in its use can drive value up as well.

Periodic Return.   The relationship between purchase price and cash flow is a consideration for real estate investors who seek regular, periodic income from their property. In the same manner that a property manager can enhance capital appreciation of the property, he or she can influence periodic return. However, the amount of income that can be generated is subject to prevailing conditions in the market.

Income Tax Advantage.   Tax incentives for real estate investment are commonly granted by federal and state governments in the United States and elsewhere. Incentives for property ownership help to drive the U.S. economy. To increase the amount of housing stock available, federal and state governments allow income tax deductions for mortgage interest, operating expenses, and *depreciation* (loss of value) of income-producing residential property. The same kinds of deductions can be taken by owners of nonresidential income-producing properties. Deductibility of mortgage interest encourages borrowing, which keeps money in circulation. The demand for loans encourages lending institutions to seek savings and investment, which in turn generate additional tax dollars. Deductibility of operating expenses provides an incentive for the owner to reinvest in the property and keep it well-maintained.

Depreciation is particularly enticing because no money has to be spent in order to take the deduction. A building has a specific *useful life* in which it produces income. The government allows the owner to assume that the building will eventually fall into disrepair and ultimately have no value (depreciate). The depreciation period varies for different types of properties. In theory, if the depreciation period is 30 years, the property owner can deduct ⅟₃₀ of the purchase price of the property (excluding the land) each year for 30 years. Calculation of income tax deductions for depreciation is more complicated, however. The tax law sets the periods of useful life for various classes of property. For real estate investments, the depreciation period depends on the type of property (e.g., residential or commercial).

Depreciation also applies to *capital improvements*—investments in equipment or alterations that last for more than one year and increase the value and productivity of the property. The number of years allowed for depreciation of capital improvements varies. The Internal Revenue Service distinguishes between a capital improvement and a *repair,* which preserves the investment in a property but does not lengthen its useful life. As an example, adding new microwave ovens to existing apartments can be a capital improvement; fixing a hot water heater is a repair. The cost of a repair is tax deductible, but only for the year in which it was made.

Pride of Ownership. In addition to the financial reasons to own income-producing property, the property manager must understand that many investors own real property because of an inherent pride of possession. Real estate is in many ways more tangible than stock certificates or other assets. Property ownership can be a symbol of financial security, wealth, or power. A real property is in a specific location and serves a specific purpose; those aspects of the property make the owner a contributor to the community, and that alone can give an owner pleasure. In addition, the owner may live on the premises, have an office there, or possibly operate a retail business in the income-producing property he or she owns, so an owner's relationship to the property can have more dimensions to it than just derivation of income.

Even though pride of ownership cannot be measured in financial terms, those who truly care for their income-producing property usually profit financially from their personal interest in it. Property owners who take extraordinary pride in their holdings may not seek the highest financial return possible; often they prefer to reinvest a portion of the proceeds in repairs, maintenance, and improvements. They respect the need to set aside reserves for future maintenance. Even though such owners may not be seeking a maximum net income, their pride in the property is likely to increase net income anyway. Attention to maintenance and repairs has the potential to attract tenants; deductibility of maintenance and improvement

E X H I B I T   3.1

Characteristics of Ownership Forms

Ownership Form	Taxation Status	Investor Liability	Management
Sole Proprietor	Single	Unlimited	Personal
General Partnership	Single	Unlimited	All partners
Limited Partnership	Single	Limited	General partner(s)
C corporation	Double	Limited	No restrictions
S corporation	Single	Limited	No restrictions
REIT	Modified single*	Limited	Trustees

*Tax losses cannot exceed cash distributions.

costs offers tax incentives, and dedicated care makes capital preservation as well as capital appreciation a more likely outcome.

PRINCIPAL FORMS OF INCOME-PROPERTY OWNERSHIP

There are numerous ways for investors to own an interest in real property. Each of these different forms of ownership provides the investor with different capabilities and limitations in making a profit from the property (exhibit 3.1). No particular form is necessarily ideal; each has certain advantages and disadvantages. Depending on the property and the goals of the investors, one form can be more beneficial than others.

Sole Proprietorship

Sole proprietorship is a mainstay among ownership types. Most individual owners invest in small buildings—a second house to rent to others or a small storefront or apartment building. The sole proprietor does not often have real estate holdings worth millions or billions of dollars. The portfolios of those who have that much real estate are generally diversified through several forms of ownership.

Sole proprietors benefit directly from the profits produced by the property. They are also directly liable for any financial losses and may be able to take deductions for such losses on their personal income tax. However, deductibility rules vary. Because of this variability, both the owner and the manager should scrutinize tax provisions and seek the guidance of legal or tax advisors regarding the deductibility of losses.

A sole proprietor usually takes great pride in owning real estate and generally is more involved in management decisions than if the property is owned by more than one person. The involvement is understandable; such an investment is usually substantial for a single owner. Because the sole proprietor can take an exceptionally active interest in management, the demand on the manager's time may be disproportionately high. The owner may consider himself or herself the manager's only client. On the other hand, sole proprietors own many investment properties in the United States, and many of them direct the management of their property in a sophisticated manner. Every sole proprietor is different. By incorporating knowledge of the property and the owner's goals in a detailed management plan, the working relationship between a manager and a sole proprietor can be rewarding both financially and personally. (See chapter 5 for a detailed discussion of the management plan.)

Partnerships

The high cost of land and of the buildings on it makes group ownership a more realistic undertaking than individual ownership. A very common association of individual investors is a *partnership*. A partnership is an arrangement that allows each partner to participate in the profits and losses of their mutual investment. The partnership distributes all profits and losses to the partners based on the amount of their investment. The partnership itself pays no income tax; the income (or loss) of the partnership affects the tax reporting of the individual partners based on their share in the investment. A partnership takes one of two forms. It is either a general partnership or a limited partnership.

General Partnership. A general partnership involves two or more investors who agree to be associated for business purposes. Title to property is held in the name of the partnership. All partners share in the rights, duties, obligations, and financial rewards to the extent of their own participation or in accordance with the partnership agreement; however, the partners' personal liability for the debts of the partnership is unlimited. Any general partner can commit the other partners to a financial obligation without their consent or knowledge, provided the contract for the service or material is made on behalf of the partnership and not on behalf of the individual. A general partnership is usually entered into by a small number of investors who know each other well and are reasonably certain they can work together cooperatively.

Because general partners are personally and fully liable for the property, they can lose personal assets along with their investment in the partnership if the property faces bankruptcy or a lawsuit. Depending on state laws and the partnership agreement, a general partnership may have to be dissolved if one partner chooses to remove his or her interest. Even if dissolution is not mandatory, it may be unavoidable because it is difficult to sell a partial interest in an established partnership.

To manage a property for a general partnership successfully, it is best if all the partners are always in agreement—one dissenting general partner among five may have equal authority over the manager and the property, although the partners may agree that a vote must be taken on certain actions and that those who own the majority of the investment must be in agreement to enact a change. The manager is usually in the best position to reconcile any differing points of view, but this consumes time that could be spent more productively. If the manager reports to more than one person, multiple reports must be distributed, a process that uses even more time and resources. Even among the most cooperative partners, occasional differences of opinion are inevitable. To avoid financial harm to the property because of or during a dispute, the partners can name one of their number as a managing partner with whom the property manager will work exclusively. This maneuver centralizes the management control and places the obligation for settling differences where it belongs—among the partners.

Limited Partnership. A more popular form of partnership is the limited partnership. It consists of one or more general partners who supervise the investment, plus a number of limited partners who participate in the arrangement only to the extent of their financial investment. As in a general partnership, the liability of general partners is unlimited; the limited partners assume no liability beyond their capital investment. There are two forms of limited partnerships: *Private limited partnerships* have thirty-five or fewer investors and usually are not required to register with the Securities and Exchange Commission (SEC), although they may have to file a certificate with state authorities. *Public limited partnerships* have an unlimited number of participants and are required to register with the SEC when the number of partners and the value of their assets reach certain levels.

Individual investment in a limited partnership does not necessarily require a large amount of capital, so it is very attractive to an investor with limited resources who wants to participate in a large venture. As in a general partnership, the tax benefits and obligations pass through to the individual partners based on provisions in the partnership agreement.

Limited partners have no say in management policies, and they may consider this a disadvantage. The decisions made by the general partners in a limited partnership affect more than their personal investments; the potential exists to lose the investments of all the partners. If the property requires additional funds because of adverse economic conditions, the general partners are obligated to invest additional capital, but the limited partners are not. Limited partners may make additional contributions to protect their original investment, but they generally are not known to do so.

The challenges to management are about the same as in a general partnership. However, if some limited partners become frustrated with the general partners' decisions, they may try to appeal directly to the property manager. If a limited partner is permitted to have direct influence on the management of the property, the Internal Revenue Service can reclassify the partnership as an association that is taxable as a corporation, or the limited partner could be reclassified as a general partner and lose the liability protection extended to limited partners.

The manager may be obligated to report to *all* investors in a limited partnership, but such reporting is potentially expensive. The manager should seek to avert this reporting requirement and can do so by including in the management agreement a clause that clearly delineates the form and frequency of reports and to whom they are to be sent. To minimize or discourage conferences between the manager and anyone other than the general partners, the agreement should also state an hourly fee for discussion with limited partners, their attorneys, accountants, heirs, executors, or anyone else. In turn, the partnership agreement should provide for these special charges to be levied directly to the individual requiring the services. (See chapter 5 for the contents and purpose of the management agreement.)

Syndication. A real estate *syndicate* is a special type of partnership formed by any combination of owners who purchase the interest in a property together. The investor may be an individual, a general or limited partnership, a joint venture, an unincorporated association, a corporation, or a group of corporations. Syndication is a way to pool both capital and experience for a property's success. The advantage of syndication is that a formal agreement can be made between people of differing backgrounds to accomplish one specific goal. There is also flexibility of investment—a syndicate can be established to purchase a particular property, or it can be developed to rely on the experience of a *syndicator* to acquire property that appears promising. If more funds are necessary, additional partnerships can be sold.

Corporations

The difference between a corporation and any other association of investors in the United States is its recognition by federal and state governments. A corporation is chartered by a state and considered to have a legal life of its own; it is an independent legal entity. It can sue and be sued. If a corporation goes bankrupt or loses a lawsuit, the liability of the corporate owners (the stockholders) is limited to the amount of their investment. As an independent legal body, a corporation is obligated to pay local, state, and federal income taxes; it cannot transfer its tax deductions to its shareholders. Corporate profits therefore are subject to *double taxation*—at the corporate level and again at the individual shareholder level. In contrast, a partnership or other form of multiple ownership may be certified through its home state as a legitimate business entity and it has no independent legal authority; only the individual investor can be represented in court.

A corporation may own the building in which it conducts its business and derive additional income from the property by leasing any excess space. For example, a shopping mall may be owned entirely or in part by one of the major department stores that anchor it. A machining company may develop land around its factory into an industrial park. A bank, advertising firm, or other service company may build or purchase a premier office building for its business operations and rent out the space it does not use. Such rental income is generally secondary to the income generated by the main business operation of the corporation (e.g., retail sales, manufacturing).

Income tax law in the United States recognizes two types of corporations for tax purposes. Most corporations are legally defined as *C corporations*. These entities pay income tax and have no restrictions on the number of shareholders or the types of stock they issue. The obligation of a C corporation to pay income tax is the main limitation on its ownership of real estate as a primary business endeavor. Even so, the attraction of limited liability for all participants (directors as well as shareholders) is a positive feature for some real estate investors.

Unlike a C corporation, an *S corporation* combines the ownership features of a corporation with those of a partnership. It does not pay federal income tax, so there is no double taxation; profits (and losses) are passed directly to the shareholders. Because the investors are shareholders and not partners, their individual liability is limited to the value of the stock they own. Stock ownership inherently provides for the election of a board of directors, a factor that ensures centralized management. Also, ownership of the investment is more easily transferred through stock shares than it is in a limited or general partnership. To be eligible for classification as an S corporation, the corporation may have no more than 35 shareholders, and only one class of stock can be offered. All shareholders must be individuals or estates; other corporations or business ventures cannot hold stock in an S corporation. Classification as an S corporation is by choice; otherwise a corporation is classified as a C corporation. The eligibility requirements for classification as an S corporation are strict, and some states do not recognize S corporation status, so state corporate taxes may be imposed anyway.

Working as a property manager for a corporation may involve more administrative procedures because of corporate reporting to the government, its directors, and its shareholders. The board of directors may be the authority for management decisions, although the manager's contact may be someone other than a board member whose primary responsibility is unrelated to real estate. Formal documentation and board approval may be required for decisions involving the property. Budgets and financial statements for the property may have to conform to the accounting standards of the corporation, even though they may not be suited to real estate management. The corporation may also require one budget for the calendar year and another for the fiscal year if that is different. Annual audits and filings with the SEC may be added to the property manager's list of duties. Because working with a corporation can create the potential for uncomfortable compromises between confidentiality and mandatory public disclosure, all information must be maintained in strictest confidence by the manager and released only by the corporation.

Real Estate Investment Trusts (REITs)

The Real Estate Investment Trust (REIT, pronounced "reet") is another vehicle that permits small investors to engage in large real estate ventures. A REIT is a specialized trust fund that invests in real estate exclusively. It can take one of three paths for investment, either directly, through mortgage funds, or both. A REIT issues shares that can be publicly traded, and its passive losses cannot exceed cash distributions to the trust beneficiaries. For a REIT to avoid double taxation—if a REIT has any retained income, corporate taxation rules may apply—it must distribute at least 95 percent of its taxable income to the shareholders, and it must meet several requirements to assure that most of its income is derived from real estate. Investors in a REIT are liable only to the extent of their investment.

Because REITs operate through shares, they can offer greater security than limited partnerships by diversifying their assets among properties in several locations (provided the trust is astutely managed and the REIT is significantly large). If shares of the REIT are publicly traded, the beneficiaries have two distinct advantages—they profit from real estate investment and their funds remain liquid. However, REITs are obligated to distribute most of their earnings, and adequate reserves may not be available for capital improvements to or additional investments in a property owned by a REIT. Likewise, a REIT has few options for preserving its capital. If the real estate market becomes unfavorable, most owners of real property can liquidate their assets, possibly taking a one-time loss, and invest the remaining capital in something else. A REIT, by definition, must keep its money in real estate. Challenges of managing a property owned by a REIT are similar to those posed by corporate ownership.

Joint Venture

Any combination of ownership forms described previously can be used to establish a joint venture. The purpose is to jointly share the risks and the rewards by contributing the appropriate knowledge, skill, or asset that is necessary. The advantages, disadvantages, and tax obligations depend on the type of organization selected for the joint venture. Some of the most common joint venture relationships are between a developer and an institutional investor or lender undertaking a new project. The lender invests capital, land, or both, and the developer contributes knowledge to make the project succeed. Foreign capital is usually invested in real property in the United States via joint ventures. In this case, a domestic entity nurtures the development and the foreign investor provides the capital.

SUMMARY

A comparison of investment options reveals that real estate is a highly illiquid investment in comparison to stocks, bonds, and other investment vehicles that can be converted to cash with relative speed and ease. However, the various ways in which real estate can be owned and the many advantages of that ownership sustain its popularity as an investment.

The property owner can make the purchase using either all cash or a combination of cash and financing. Mortgage loans commonly have a fixed maturity and interest rate, but it is also possible to establish a mortgage with flexible terms to take advantage of market fluctuations. The terms of the loan can have a profound impact on the property's success based on changes in the property's income, the overall economy, and the owner's expectations from the investment.

The motives for owning real estate include capital preservation, capital appreciation, periodic return, income tax advantages, and pride of ownership. Any of these reasons alone may be sufficient for an investor to purchase a property. However, the investor usually examines the combination of these factors before making a purchase.

The principal forms of property ownership are generally sole proprietorship, partnerships, corporations, real estate investment trusts (REITs), and joint ventures. Each of these ownership types has advantages and disadvantages, and no single form is necessarily ideal. Each form has different effects on income from the property, payment to the investor, tax obligations, and the relationship between the manager and the owner. Understanding of the subtleties of how and why the property is owned is the basis for determining how it should be managed and how its productivity can be improved.

Key Terms

All-cash purchase
Collateral
Corporation
Equity
Financing
Investment base

Joint venture
Mortgage loan
Partnership
Real Estate Investment Trust
Sole proprietorship

Key Points

Real estate as an investment vehicle
Liquidity of assets and real estate equity
Differences among mortgage loans (terms and rates)
The financial reasons for real estate investment (capital preservation,
    capital appreciation, periodic return, income tax advantage)
Intrinsic value of real property
Distinctions among the types of ownership
Double taxation of corporate owners

Financial Management

Most income-producing properties have numerous sources of income and a multitude of expense items that must be received or paid in a timely manner. The nature of the income and expenses must also be recorded accurately to maximize income for the owner and avoid any financial penalties. For most rental properties, income and expenses are related to one of three categories—normal day-to-day operations, reserves, or security deposits. Funds received and paid out must be recorded in an accounting system which will be the basis for regular reports that are sent to the owner. Financial management goes beyond recording and reporting. It includes specific projections of income and expenses in the form of budgets.

Effective financial management of real estate is in some respects no more complicated than managing household finances. Over time, the level of income must be greater than the level of expense in order to achieve a positive balance of accounts. If spending exceeds income, it cannot do so for very long. The members of a household may keep thorough records of their income and expenses and conclude from those records that they should seek higher-paying jobs, secondary income, reductions in spending, or a combination of these alternatives if they wish to achieve greater financial security. The same objectives are inherent in financial management for real estate. Although comparing financial management of real property to household financial management is simplistic, the same fundamental processes are used for considering ways to achieve greater net income. The key to maximizing net income for an income-producing property is evaluation of the disposition of funds—both receipts and disbursements.

EVALUATION OF OPERATING FUNDS

For any income-producing investment, the measure of its profitability is the amount of income returned to the investor. For rental real estate, that measure is the cash flow that results from its efficient operation.

The Cash Flow Chart

The property management profession has adopted specific terms to identify the various types of income and expense related to cash flow as follows:

	Gross Possible Rental Income
minus	Vacancy and Collection Loss
plus	Miscellaneous Income
equals	Effective Gross Income
minus	Operating Expenses
equals	Net Operating Income (NOI)
minus	Debt Service (Interest and Principal)
equals	Pre-Tax Cash Flow
minus	Income Tax
equals	After-Tax Cash Flow

The property manager's involvement with financial management often ends with the production of net operating income. On the other hand, the owner's assessment of the property's value is usually based on pre-tax or after-tax cash flow. Although the property manager may have no control over these outcomes, he or she must be aware of how they are calculated and how they are evaluated by the owner. These terms are defined in detail in the following sections.

Gross Possible Rental Income.   The maximum amount of income the property can earn from rent is called *gross possible rental income.* It is a financial inventory of all the leasable space in a building at its maximum possible rental rate. Once established, this figure remains fairly constant in reporting from month to month. The only factors that can change gross possible rental income are changes in rental rates or a change in the amount of space that could be rented. Gross possible rental income does not indicate income actually received; it is a statement of the amount of income that would be received if the building were fully leased and all tenants paid their rents in full and on time.

Changes in rental rates occur most commonly when leases are renewed or when new tenants replace those that have moved out. Changes in the amount of leasable space are more complex. Older buildings may have areas that are used for storage or otherwise considered unrentable. Yet if these obsolete areas can be rehabilitated and leased, their estimated rent may be listed as gross possible rental income. In an older office building, for example, space in the basement that was originally rented as offices may only be used currently by the building maintenance department to store supplies and equipment. While the space may no longer be feasible for offices, it may be rentable to current tenants as space for storage of supplies and records. If the property manager decides to use the space in this way, the scheduled rental income for this space should be included in the gross possible rental income. On the other hand, conversion of a basement apartment into a laundry room makes it part of the common area and therefore unrentable. New developments commonly have model units and often these are regarded as unleasable. However, the models are usually in perfect condition and could command a higher rent than similar units to be leased. Setting a rent for the model unit and including it in the gross possible rental income category reminds the manager and owner that if the right prospect wanted to lease the model, it would be available for that purpose.

Vacancy and Collection Loss.   The actual rent received is rarely equal to the gross possible rental income. Vacant units produce no income, and rents not collected represent lost income. Both reduce the amount of rental income received. In the flow chart, the *vacancy and collection loss* amount is subtracted from gross possible rental income to indicate the actual amount of rental income for a given reporting period (usually a month). Delinquent rents and losses because of vacancies are usually listed separately. When finally paid, delinquent rent will be added to the income category, therefore nonpayment of rent is a true loss of income. On the other hand, vacancies simply reduce income; they do not represent a loss. The property manager has a duty to pursue collection of unpaid rent. If the nonpayment persists, however, the matter should be referred to a professional collection agency or an attorney for aggressive reinforcement of the obligation owed to the owner.

Miscellaneous Income.   Income derived from coin-operated laundry equipment, pay phones, vending machines, late fees, etc., is called *miscellaneous income* (or *unscheduled income*). Generally this is income from sources other than scheduled rent. Thus unscheduled income may also include previously unpaid rent that is recovered after a tenant no longer occupies the rental space, usually after the property manager has turned the matter over to a collection agency or an attorney.

Effective Gross Income. Subtracting the vacancy and collection loss amount from the gross possible rental income and then adding to it the miscellaneous income yields the *effective gross income* of the property. This figure should match the total amount collected (gross receipts) during the reporting period. In this respect, the effective gross income total can help to verify accounting for the rent and other receipts during the reporting period. Effective gross income, which can vary substantially from the gross possible rental income for the property, is the amount that is available to pay building expenses, debt service, and a return on the owner's investment.

Operating Expenses. The *operating expenses* of income-producing real estate include the costs of operating a business (payroll, office supplies) in addition to the costs of maintaining the condition of the property (maintenance, repairs, grounds keeping, etc.) and providing services to its occupants (utilities, decorating, security)—in other words, all the expenses of the property with the exception of debt service. Insurance, property taxes, and fees for legal and accounting services and management are also operating expenses. (Specific categories of expense are discussed in the accounting section later in this chapter.) One objective of tracking operating expenses is to calculate how much of the effective gross income remains after the bills have been paid. An even more important objective is to keep that remainder at a consistently high level.

Net Operating Income. What remains after operating expenses have been deducted from effective gross income is *net operating income (NOI)*. This amount is an impartial measure of the property manager's success. The property manager strives to attain the highest possible level of income with the least possible expense in order to maximize net operating income for the owner. Any variance in effective gross income, operating expenses, or both will cause net operating income to vary. Depending on the agreement between a property manager and owner, financial management of the operating funds may end with the manager's submission of the NOI to the owner, but other expenses are customarily paid from the NOI as well.

Debt Service. An owner's personal evaluation of a property will not stop at net operating income. The *debt service* obligation of a property—the amount required to repay the mortgage loan—is deducted from net operating income. Although this amount is a recurring expense, it is not

---

Managing Financially Distressed Property

Property that is in receivership (turned over to an impartial third party who controls and preserves the asset for the benefit of the parties affected) or foreclosure (repossessed by the lending institution to satisfy a loan that is in default)—or is bankrupt—has undergone a downturn in its financial management. When income falls short of meeting debt, the property manager or owner may reduce some services or offer less-expensive services instead. If tenants become dissatisfied, they move out, increasing the financial burden on the property. The loss of income forces the owner or manager to reduce services further, and more tenants may leave. Those who remain probably are in financial distress themselves and may not be paying rent regularly. At the point when a new property manager takes over, he or she may find the property to be entirely vacant and in need of repair.

In order to manage such property appropriately, the manager must know the owner's objectives and time frame. A lending institution may require only that status quo be maintained because it will try to sell the property quickly to avert additional losses. However, when the objective is to make the property profitable, the manager generally lists the conditions that require immediate attention and those that can be addressed in stages. The conditions may involve rehabilitative work, collections from tenants whose rent is past due, and evictions. These lists of items and their priority rankings can be the basis for a budget which indicates how much additional capital must be invested in the property to re-establish it in the marketplace.

---

an operating expense. An owner will want to know if a property will generate enough cash to service the debt and provide a satisfactory return on his or her investment. In some instances, the property manager is expected to handle the payment of debt service for the owner; other owners may prefer to make these payments themselves. Who will make the debt service payments is a subject for negotiation of the management agreement. (The management agreement is explained in chapter 5.)

Cash Flow.   The amount remaining after debt service has been subtracted from net operating income is the *cash flow*. It is the owner's pretax income or return on investment. (When the required debt service payment exceeds the amount of NOI, the cash flow is negative.)

Two important payments are made from the cash flow of the property. These are contributions to the reserve fund and personal income taxes. Although reserve funds come from the cash flow, the property manager usually deducts the reserve amount directly and maintains that fund. The owner generally calculates and pays his or her own income tax. Depending on the arrangement between the owner and the manager, the actual amount the owner receives in a check from the property manager—the *net proceeds*—can be the same amount as the cash flow. In fact, if there is no loan on the property or if the owner makes the mortgage loan payments and does not maintain a reserve fund, net proceeds can be equivalent to net operating income.

Other Considerations

The amount of the debt service payments depends on how much cash the owner used to purchase the property and the terms of the mortgage loan. The property manager may be called on to advise the owner on whether the owner or the property could benefit from refinancing the debt. *Refinancing* can provide extra cash by mortgaging the equity in the property. Depending on the current market, any existing loan can be refinanced for a longer term or for a larger or smaller principal amount. Sometimes refinancing is used to lower the amount of the periodic debt service payments.

The net operating income of a property will be the same regardless of whether the owner purchased the property with all cash or financed most of the purchase price. The constancy of the NOI of an income-producing property makes that sum a definitive measure of property value.

Property Valuation.   From the perspective of a property manager, the importance of maximizing net operating income is obvious: a manager who can produce enough NOI so the owner can pay debt service and receive a satisfactory return on his or her investment is more likely to have such an account renewed. However, the level of NOI represents more than the owner's month-to-month return on his or her investment; it also directly affects the *value* of the property. To calculate the estimated value (V) of income-producing real estate, the annual net operating income (I) is divided by the *capitalization rate* (R) as indicated in the following equation. (The capitalization rate or "cap" rate is a decimal constant.)

$$\frac{I}{R} = V, \text{ or } \frac{\text{Net Operating Income (NOI)}}{\text{Capitalization Rate}} = \text{Estimated Property Value}$$

Therefore, if the cap rate is 10 percent (.10 as a decimal) and the annual NOI of a property is $100,000, its estimated value is $1 million. The cap rate for a specific property depends on the property type, the cap rates on recent sales of comparable properties in the area, and market conditions, including interest rates. Variations in the cap rate have major effects on value—value declines as the cap rate rises. When the same cap rate is used in a comparison of similar properties in a market area, the property with the highest net operating income will have the highest estimated value. If the NOI of a property decreases and the cap rate does not change, the property value will be reduced. This is in addition to the reduction in periodic income resulting from the lower NOI. Thus any factor that helps to increase NOI also increases property value.

Income Tax.   A manager may have no involvement whatsoever in the tax paid on the income generated by the property he or she manages, but the growing complexity of income taxation and its effect on ownership increase the property manager's need to understand these taxes. Income taxes on profits from real property usually are levied against the individual investor's personal income. Stated very simply, if an owner makes $10,000 on a property and that amount is subject to tax at a 28-percent rate, the *after-tax cash flow* is $7,200 ($10,000 − $2,800 in tax). Because each individual's tax obligations are different, the property manager can only estimate *pre-tax cash flow* with any accuracy. Professional tax accountants and attorneys can best advise an owner regarding the taxes on investment income and the resulting after-tax cash flow.

Reserve and Security Deposit Funds.   The operating funds of a property are usually the most extensive and require the most attention, but reserves and security deposits also need continual monitoring to assure their preservation and growth. While operating funds are not necessarily held in an interest-bearing account, reserve and security deposit funds depend on regular earnings for part of their value.

Reserve fund.   A reserve fund is money regularly set aside to pay future expenses. If this money comes from the income of the property, it is deducted from cash flow. A reserve fund is commonly used to pay for capital expenditures (e.g., boiler or roof replacement); regular operating expenses are generally paid from monthly receipts.

The reserve fund is usually kept in an interest-bearing checking account. Because the reserve fund generally earns interest, some managers use it to accumulate funds for operating expenses that are not paid monthly. Property taxes and insurance premiums are often paid only once or twice a year; prorating the amounts and accumulating funds on a monthly basis means the money will be available when the payments are due, and cash flow will remain fairly constant from month to month. When the funds for these infrequently paid operating expenses are accumulated in the reserve account, it is important for the property manager to be sure the payments are properly recorded as operating expenses when they are paid.

Specific amounts deposited into the reserve fund for capital improvements can be a set percentage of effective gross income or net operating income. Because deposits to the reserve account are usually for a predetermined purpose (such as replacing carpeting in five years or re-modeling units according to an established schedule), the periodic payments into this account can be budgeted as a set amount.

Developing a reserve for capital expenditures usually requires accounting for the funds on a capital expenditure report and a ledger. The expenditure is paid as a check drawn on the reserve account. It is important to note that the accumulation of reserve funds reduces the amount of cash available to the owner from the income of the property. Because of this, an owner may be reluctant to allow the accrual of such funds. The owner and manager may also have different perspectives on the adequacy of reserve funds and their disposition. The availability of reserve funds is extremely important and is a subject for negotiation of the management agreement.

Security Deposits.   Tenants are usually required to pay a security deposit as a guarantee of their performance of the terms of the lease (payment of rent, preservation of the property, etc.). Many states regulate the way in which security deposits must be maintained. Some require lessors to hold the deposits in trust or in a separate bank account that is established and maintained exclusively for security deposits. Many states and municipalities require landlords to pay tenants interest on the amount held and may require that security deposit funds be held in an interest-bearing account. It is also common for these laws to stipulate the rate of interest to be paid to the tenants, but the rate is usually low enough so that earnings on the security deposit account may exceed what is owed to the tenants by a few percentage points, thus providing a small amount of additional income. However, the amount of this extra income probably will not pay for the process of accounting for security deposit interest and maintaining the account. The property manager must know and follow the applicable laws relating to security deposit collection and maintenance and any requirements regarding payment of interest.

For tax purposes, the interest earned by the account is reported as income to the owner if it is not distributed to the tenants. To reduce (or eliminate) the owner's tax obligation on the interest, it may be necessary to issue checks to the tenants annually and report this distribution to the Internal Revenue Service and to the tenants on the appropriate income tax forms. The property manager should be aware of the current tax laws and how they apply to such funds. Even if the amount of interest owed to each tenant is relatively small, the cumulative amount owed to all tenants could require the owner to pay much higher income taxes if the account is not properly maintained.

If the tenant has met all of the lease obligations, the security deposit is ultimately returned to the tenant. If not, part or all of a security deposit may be retained to pay for property damage (wear and tear above normal standards) or to compensate the owner for any debts owed by the tenant (such as late fees, past-due rent, etc.).

ACCOUNTING FOR INCOME AND EXPENSES

Rents and other regular income of the property (excluding security deposits and monies intended for reserves) are commonly deposited into a checking account to be used exclusively for the payment of expenses of operating the property. Records of income and expense must be accurate because these records are the bases for disbursing proceeds to the owners and filing income taxes. They must also be consistent so that duplications and omissions are avoided and budget projections can be verified. The best way to assure accuracy and consistency is to establish a *chart of accounts* (exhibit 4.1), usually with account numbers or codes for specific categories of income and expense.

No chart of accounts is necessarily definitive; most buildings have unique features that require separate categories, entries, or subentries. The type of property and its size will affect the scope of a chart of accounts. Depending on the level of detail desired, income and expense categories can be either subdivided further or grouped under more general headings. A detailed chart of accounts usually also provides account codes for security deposits and reserve funds, debt service payments, and income taxes as appropriate. Specific capital expenditures may also be assigned account codes. In this way, *all* income and expense items for a property can be identified, not only for purposes of accounting, but also for reporting to the owners and others and for preparing accurate budgets. The manager who is required to develop a chart of accounts for a new property or for new management of an existing property can seek advice from a professional accountant. In that way, he or she can be assured of identifying all of the separate accounts needed for a specific property.

Accounting records are commonly recorded in a *general ledger* showing both receipts and disbursements and the separate accounts to which the individual items relate. The owner and manager must agree on the method of accounting so that financial records and reports will be consistent, accurate, and easily understood. In *cash-basis accounting,* income is recorded when it is received and payments are recorded as they are made. *Accrual-basis accounting* records income when it is due and expenses when they are incurred, and the records may not reflect actual receipts and disbursements. The entire accounting and reporting system should conform to one of these two methods. However, a cash-accounting system

EXHIBIT   4.1

Common Categories for a Chart of Accounts

Operating Income
Rents
Miscellaneous Income

Operating Expenses
Management Fee and Administrative Costs
Personnel Expenses
Energy (Gas, Oil, Electricity)
Maintenance and Repairs
Supplies
Building Services
Security
Legal Expense
Grounds Keeping
Water and Sewer
Rubbish Removal
Interior Painting and Decorating
Recreational Amenities
Property Tax
Advertising and Promotion
Insurance

---

may utilize accrual accounting for expenses that are not due monthly (insurance, taxes). When such a "modified cash system" is used, records of net proceeds must be adjusted to reflect the partial accruals. All transactions, no matter how inconsequential, should be recorded on the day they are made, especially those involving petty cash. Use of a purchase order or other written record for every purchase over a set amount assures that the merchandise or service received is acceptable and matches what is ordered.

Specific Categories of Expense

Although amounts and types of expenses vary by property, there are some common expense categories recognized in the real estate management profession (see exhibit 4.1). Every property management company defines expenses in its own way, and some major categories may have to be subdivided to adequately account for the operating expenses of a specific property. In addition, property owners sometimes request unique expense categorization. The property manager must understand the management firm's categorization of expenses as well as the owner's and apply them consistently.

Management Fee and Administrative Costs. The compensation paid to the managing agent is generally a percentage of the effective gross income of the property. Usually there is a minimum payment if effective gross income is below expectations. Administrative costs is the heading under which one would list supplies, postage, and other common expenses associated with operating an on-site office if there is not a separate account for office expenses. At times, nonstandard charges such as fees for tax preparation may be listed as administrative costs.

Personnel Expense. The payroll and benefits category may be listed as a single item, but the various deductions and distributions usually require separate accounting for salaries, taxes, benefits, and the various employer contributions required by state and federal governments for social security and unemployment taxes, etc. Because of the complex accounting, the property manager may prefer to list each of these items as subaccounts under payroll. As an alternative to a distinct personnel category listed among the operating expenses, payroll may be recorded as a subaccount in the appropriate operating expense category on the basis of the employees' duties (administration, maintenance, grounds keeping, etc.). In such a case, subentries for salaries, benefits, and taxes would be listed under those subaccounts as well. How payroll is listed depends on the preference of the owner and the manager; the important point is to be consistent.

The payroll schedule can skew monthly reports and the monthly flow of cash through the accounts of the property. Rental income is generally received twelve times a year, on the first of every month; but a monthly payroll is rarely used, and a weekly payroll is impractical. Paying employees biweekly (twenty-six times a year) yields ten months with two pay periods and two with three pay periods. To avoid such variation, employees are commonly paid twice a month (usually on the fifteenth and the last day of the month), a system that balances payroll distribution against rental income. Because rent is usually collected on the first of the month, activities during the first week of the month usually center on processing incoming checks and issuing late notices for unpaid rents. The middle of the month is usually less active from an accounting standpoint, so a semimonthly payroll system can help to ensure steady bank balances, a monthly payment of proceeds to the owner that is fairly constant, and a manageable schedule of activities in the accounting department. A semimonthly payroll may require additional computations for employees paid by the hour because the number of workdays per pay period varies, but the savings that result from preparing payroll only twenty-four times a year instead of twenty-six may offset the additional work. No matter how payroll distribution is scheduled, additional accounting is required for hourly employees who receive overtime compensation.

Energy (Gas, Oil, Electricity).　This complex category of expense may require several subaccounts to provide accurate and appropriate records. Energy bills are usually issued and payable on a monthly basis, although the number of days in the billing period may vary without regard to the number of days in the month. The price of energy production and delivery also may increase or decrease monthly. These differences can cause variances in the monthly energy expense for a property even though consumption may remain fairly constant. Some utility companies, especially those whose rate structures vary based on the season of the year, offer programs to equalize bill payments. If utility costs are passed through to the tenants (as in commercial properties), additional accounting is required to prorate and collect the utility fees.

Maintenance and Repairs.　This category is used to account for all general maintenance and repairs, both interior and exterior. Expenses incurred for exterior painting and cleaning, elevator maintenance contracts, boiler inspection and repair contracts, air-conditioning service contracts, parts, small hand tools, and fire protection equipment are all commonly listed as maintenance and repairs. Other related expenses include plumbing, electrical, plastering, tuck-pointing, and carpentry services. If staff are employed to perform some or all of this work, their payroll expenses may be included in this category. Fees for maintenance contractors, however, should be a separate item in the maintenance category and not considered personnel expenses.

Because so many operating expenses may be regarded as related to maintenance or repairs, this category has the potential to become too broad in scope. To avert this, certain types of maintenance or repairs may be listed as separate subaccounts either because of their recurrent nature, the amount of expense they represent, or both. Grounds keeping expenses may be included in maintenance, although they are often substantial enough to merit their own category. Interior painting and decorating costs are almost always listed separately, in part because this work may be done for purposes of marketing and not just to maintain the leased units.

Supplies.　The supplies category accounts for items that are regularly replaced, although office supplies may be listed under administrative costs and cleaning materials may be included under maintenance and repairs. The property manager may use this category to record replaceable goods that are purchased in large quantities or those that are particularly expensive. Irregular purchases or materials that are replenished infrequently may also be accounted for in the supplies category. Except for specific recurring expenses, there may be little or no need for subaccounts under supplies.

Because price reductions are common for volume or bulk purchases, the property manager should consider the frequency of replacement and the cost of holding inventory compared to the discount being offered. A sale on light bulbs may offer a 10-percent discount on bulbs purchased in a lot of 100 or more. If that number of bulbs is replaced annually and the property has ample storage space, such a discount may be worthwhile. However, if only twenty bulbs are replaced annually, the initial investment and storage costs for the larger quantity may cancel the value of the discounted bulk purchase.

Building Services.   This category is used for expenses related to upkeep of the property that are infrequent or of too small a dollar value to be itemized into subaccounts. Striping the parking lot, having keys made, and repair or repainting of signs on the property are some likely expenses to be listed in this category. Seasonal and regional considerations may also apply. In the northern United States, pest control may be a building service; in the South, however, this expense is often a subaccount. Conversely, snow removal would be a subaccount in the North and a building service in extreme southern regions.

Security.   Because of the inherent liability risks, most properties that provide a security force contract with an agency for this service. Other security-related expenses are usually listed in the category that reflects their direct cost—e.g., night-time lighting of parking lots and common areas would be included in the electricity expense. Although the presence of a doorman or other attendant may deter criminal activity, the service provided by this staff member is usually regarded as a convenience to tenants and visitors rather than security as such, so the salary involved would be a personnel expense.

Legal Expense.   Charges frequently arising in this category include the costs of prosecuting unpaid rents and evictions, protesting property tax assessments, and periodically reviewing legal documents (leases, contracts). Depending on the size of the property and the frequency of legal consultation, a retainer may be a regular expense in this category.

Grounds Keeping.   The extent of this cost depends on the size of the area that must be maintained. Lawn mowing, picking up litter from the parking lot, fuel for power equipment, and similar recurring expenses can be listed in this category. Regular expenses, including landscaping, might be separate subaccounts. For a small property with a site manager who does grounds keeping as well as general maintenance, occasional costs of this type may be listed as building services if they are not considered maintenance.

Water and Sewer. This is an expense that fluctuates seasonally. Most communities bill water and sewer charges as one item, presuming that water intake at a property determines how much sewage it produces. Often this is a subaccount in a utilities category that includes energy expenses, telephone service, and garbage collection as well. As water tables are depleted and new, deeper wells must be tapped, water and sewer costs will increase. Conservation measures (watering grounds at night rather than in the heat of the day, replacing leaky faucets and pipes) will minimize this expense and preserve a valuable natural resource. Specific expenses (e.g., faucet and pipe replacement) would be categorized as maintenance or plumbing expenses.

Rubbish Removal. Large properties usually must contract with a private, licensed waste hauler to have trash removed from their sites. The charge is often based on the number of pickups at the site each month and the number of containers, although it may be based on the weight or volume (cubic yards) of material removed, or a combination of volume and number of pickups. As landfills near their maximum capacity, the cost of this service will most likely escalate. State and local legislators are enacting laws to require recycling of paper, glass, plastic, and metal items and to encourage composting of organic waste to reduce the volume disposed in landfills. Rubbish removal may be listed under utilities when a separate category is not required.

Interior Painting and Decorating. Painting and decorating of interior areas can be a large and frequently recurring expense, especially in residential properties, so it is often listed as a category separate from maintenance and repairs. In addition, the work may be performed solely to improve the appeal of the property, not strictly to maintain it. The interior painting and decorating category would also cover charges for such items as wallpaper, painting equipment, and contractors. If the property or management firm employs full-time decorators, their wages and benefits may be listed here or as a personnel expense.

Recreational Amenities. Recreational amenities were once limited to residential property, but many office buildings now offer such facilities for tenants' employees to use. The maintenance and servicing of exercise equipment, swimming pools, and other recreational facilities would be listed in this category, with subaccounts for each amenity as appropriate. If utilities for the amenities are metered separately, the charges may be listed here as well so the full cost of operating the recreational facilities can be seen at once. Otherwise, utility charges belong in the energy cost category. Salaries for lifeguards, exercise instructors, or other staff members dedicated solely to recreational services may be accounted here (for the same reason as utilities would be) or under personnel expenses.

Property Tax.   Many municipalities levy a tax on the assessed value of real property. The tax may be payable semiannually or annually; however, some property managers budget for this expense on a monthly basis to maintain a reserve for the tax when it becomes due. If the property is financed, the lending institution may require cumulative payment into an escrow account for the property tax. Under some types of commercial and retail leases, the property tax is passed through to the tenants on a prorated basis. The pass-throughs may be estimated and collected monthly, requiring the manager to maintain these funds in a reserve account until the tax is due.

Advertising and Promotion.   The frequency and amount of expenses incurred for advertising and promotion depend on the vacancy level, response to market demand, and the age of the building. New developments require more promotion than buildings that are established in the marketplace. For established properties, a twenty-word advertisement in the classified section of the newspaper may be sufficient. A new property may buy a half-page display advertisement in a local magazine for a year, or another type of major promotion may be desired. Because of this variance, the property manager and owner may decide to budget a fixed amount per reporting period and monitor these expenses separately.

Insurance.   Insurance premiums are paid on varying schedules, although semiannual and annual payments are most common. This category is usually limited to insurance on the property. Employee medical coverage and employment insurance taxes are accounted as personnel expenses. The types of insurance usually accounted for in this category are listed below.

- *Fire insurance* protects the policyholder against all direct loss or damage to the insured property by fire.
- *Extended coverage (EC),* usually purchased as an addition to fire insurance, covers loss from specific perils (windstorm, hail, explosion, civil commotion, aircraft, vehicles, smoke, and water damage from fire fighting).
- *All-risk insurance* covers any damage that is not specifically excluded from the policy; however, the exclusions can be quite extensive.
- *Boiler insurance* pays for any damage resulting from a boiler malfunction.

Reports to Owners
* Summary of Operations
* Rent Roll
* Vacancy Report
* Delinquency Report
* Explanation of Budget Variances

---

* *Property damage insurance* protects against liability for damage to property of others that occurs on the insured property.
* *Rent loss insurance* protects the owner from loss of income resulting from damage that makes all or part of the property unrentable.
* *Fidelity insurance* protects one individual against financial loss that might result from dishonest acts of another specific individual. This coverage is usually purchased by a management firm for its employees, meaning it would not be an operating expense for the property unless a policy were maintained for site employees who are employed by the property owner.
* *Owner, landlord, and tenant liability (OLT) insurance* covers claims against a property owner, a landlord, or a tenant arising out of injury to a person or persons on the property.
* *Umbrella liability insurance* provides additional liability coverage beyond the limits of the basic liability policy.
* *Automobile insurance* is purchased to protect employees who drive service vehicles owned by and operated for the property, and to protect the property owners from liability incurred as a result of operating these vehicles.

REPORTING ON INCOME AND EXPENSES

The documentation of all financial transactions pertaining to the property is an important aspect of the manager's responsibility. In addition to entering these transactions into a ledger or computer file when they occur, the manager is custodian of all receipts, bank statements and canceled checks, copies of purchase orders, and copies of receipts the manager issues for payments made to the property. Information from these records must be reported to the owner of the property on a regular schedule, usually once a month. In addition, there may be reports to tenants in the form of bills, receipts for payments, statements of interest earned on security deposits, damage assessments, and other financial transactions related to occupancy of leased space in the property. The property manager must maintain records and issue reports on the property as a whole and each unit in it. Clients who own several properties managed by the same firm may request comprehensive portfolio reports as well.

The principal record of income for a rental property is the *rent roll.* This is a record of the tenants, their unit or suite numbers, and their specific rental rates and lease terms, as well as whether rent has been paid or is past due. If certain operating expenses are prorated and passed through (as in commercial leases), the amounts due and paid are also recorded in the rent roll. If the rent roll information is computerized, it can be sorted based on different parameters, permitting convenient production of vacancy reports, delinquency reports, and reports on lease expiration, all of which are regularly sent to the owner. Year-to-date totals are particularly useful for monitoring delinquencies that exceed one month. The rent roll is usually compiled from the records maintained on individual tenants and is one of the reports regularly sent to the owner of the property.

The manager usually maintains a *rental ledger* for each rental unit. It lists the tenant's name, phone number, unit identification, rental rate, late charges, security deposit amount, move-in date, lease terms, recurring charges, pass-through charges, and other pertinent facts about the leasing arrangement. Various types of ledger forms are available commercially or a specific form can be designed for this use. Alternatively the ledger may be established as a computer file that is periodically updated and stored as print-out hard copies.

Commercial tenants may be sent a monthly rent bill (statement of rent due) because their leases usually include requirements to pay prorated pass-through charges (see chapter 10). When the rent is a flat rate (as in residential properties), a bill is rarely issued. It may also be necessary (or appropriate) to issue receipts, especially when a lease agreement is set up initially, if payment received is in cash, or when partial payment is accepted. Copies of dated rent bills marked "paid" are an effective verification of the monthly income records.

A *summary of operations* report is an at-a-glance view of the gross amounts of income and expenses of a property for the period. It emphasizes the *net proceeds* that are paid to the owner. For small enterprises, the summary of operations may be the only financial report. For large properties, this summary usually accompanies more detailed reports (rent roll, vacancy and delinquency reports, etc.).

A *narrative report of operations* should also be sent to the owner. This report is used to explain any differences or *variances* between the actual income and expenses and the amounts projected for them in the budget. If there is an extreme variance in either income or expenses, a personal meeting with the owner usually provides a better setting for such explanations. When the variations are minimal, a narrative report may not be required, but a personal note indicating that the property is functioning without incident is evidence of the manager's personal commitment to the property. This tangible offering of goodwill can also help the owner and manager work together more effectively when times are difficult.

Types of Budgets
* Operating (annual)
* Capital
* Long-range

Record keeping and reporting with respect to the individual tenant, the property as a whole, and the owner can be time-consuming and complicated. However, computerization permits the various calculations and data analyses to be performed easily, especially if a standard *spreadsheet* program is used. Tabulation of year-to-date (cumulative) results, comparison to the current-year budget, and comparison with performance from the preceding year are convenient functions of such programs.

BUDGETING

Budgeting is not an exact science. The actual income and expenses of a property will rarely (if ever) conform precisely to budget projections. A budget is a tool; the property manager uses it to establish the priority of spending based on the amount of income the property is producing and the expenses that are incurred. The budget helps the property manager in his or her effort to minimize variance of the property's net operating income and assess the cash position of the property at a given time. When an unexpected expense creates a cash shortage, the budget can guide evaluation of alternatives for meeting the expense.

There are several different types of budgets. Three that are commonly used in real estate management are operating, capital, and long-range budgets.

Operating Budget

The most commonly used budget is an *operating budget* that lists the principal (or regular) sources of income and expenses for the property. The amount listed as gross possible rental income in the income and expense reports for the property should be fairly constant from month to month. Every other item of income or expense for the property is added to or subtracted from the gross possible rental income to calculate net operating income. Any variance in individual entries is reflected in the net operating income. Therefore, even though gross possible rental income may be a fixed amount, the owner's income can vary substantially. A budget permits better projecting and monitoring of income and expenses.

Aside from indicating the sources of income and expenses for a property, a budget indicates *when the transactions are expected to occur.* Seasonal variations in energy consumption should be reflected in differing monthly amounts allocated for heat and air conditioning over the course of the year. Advertising expenses for an established apartment building may be minimal for most months, the greatest part of funds allocated for this expense being divided among the months of highest expected leasing activity. On the other hand, a new development or a property that is undergoing extensive rehabilitation may require a large advertising budget divided equally over the year to reflect the intensity of the leasing activity.

The budget is also the starting place to consider alternatives for paying unanticipated expenses. If winter weather is exceptionally cold and snowy, higher fuel consumption generally will increase the fuel expense for the property; greater demand for fuel usually leads to price increases, and that, coupled with increased consumption, can devastate a fuel budget. Other increases in season-related expenses, such as snow plowing, can have a significant effect on profits. When such extra expenses conflict with projections made in the budget, the property manager can review other projected expenses. If another budgeted expense can be put off temporarily (or omitted altogether for the year), that change may offer a way to offset part or all of the extra weather-related expenses. Otherwise reserve funds may have to be used. Regardless of the alternatives considered, the property manager should notify the owner of the action that is being taken.

The *annual budget* is the most common form of operating budget. To prepare such a budget, the property manager generally reviews income and expenses from previous years. If any departures from normal operations are anticipated for the upcoming year (e.g., temporarily high vacancies because of remodeling), the budget should account for these as well. The annual budget projects the whole year's income and expenses for each account (exhibit 4.2).

Possibly one of the most valuable aspects of this annual exercise is the presentation of the new budget to the owner. It offers a natural opportunity to discuss the past performance of the property and make adjustments to individual budget items as they preview the coming year. By reviewing each item in the budget, the manager can explain how anticipated income and expenses are expected to affect the property's performance. Planned increases in rents would be reflected in the gross possible rental income, vacancy and collection loss, and effective gross income categories. An increase in staff size or wage adjustments will affect personnel expenses. Each line item should be reviewed in detail because the owner and manager must agree on the budget before it is used.

Planning on a monthly basis is particularly useful when the manager reports to the owner on a monthly basis. Often an annual budget is developed in greater detail by allocating an amount for each line item on a month-by-month basis. Some items can be divided into twelve equal parts because they do not change from one month to another; others will vary

E X H I B I T   4.2

Items Common to an Annual Operating Budget

INCOME
Gross Potential Rental Income
Less: Vacancy and Collection Loss
Plus: Miscellaneous Income
Effective Gross Income

EXPENSES
Management Fee
Administrative Costs
Personnel
Electricity
Gas
Maintenance and Repair
Supplies
Building Services
Security
Legal Expense
Grounds Keeping
Water and Sewer
Rubbish Removal
Interior Painting
Interior Decorating
Recreational Amenities
Property Tax
Advertising and Promotion
Insurance
Other Expenses
Total Expenses

Net Operating Income
Less: Debt Service
Cash Flow

---

substantially from month to month based on seasonal and other factors. It is important to project income when it is expected to be received and expenses *when they are expected to be paid.* If an expense is normally incurred in March and paid in May, budgeting for that expense in March will result in variances for both months and the variances will require explanation.

The annual budget serves as a point of reference for the manager and the owner. However, actual income and expenses can differ significantly from such a budget as the year progresses. To compensate for such differences, property managers sometimes prepare quarterly budgets that reflect adjustments to the original projections made in the annual budget. These modified budgets can be more accurate than the annual budget because the projections are not made so far in advance. Also, quarterly budgets cover the approximate time of one season, so their projections of seasonally affected income and expenses can be more accurate. Occasionally new or adjusted monthly budgets may be necessary or appropriate for the same reasons.

Capital Budget

Because one purpose of a reserve fund is to accumulate capital for improvements, a *capital budget* is prepared showing how much to set aside in the reserve fund on a regular basis. In principle, the property manager can do this simply by calculating the cost of the improvement and dividing the total by the number of months before the change is to be implemented. However, if funds are to be accumulated over a period of years, inflation must also be considered. If the interest earned on the accumulating reserve is not substantially higher than the rate of inflation, the anticipated total accumulation will not meet the actual cost of the improvement. Furthermore, the cost of materials may rise faster than the inflation rate, so a larger monthly allocation will be necessary to assure a reasonable match between the amount of reserve funds and their anticipated use.

Long-Range Budget

Use of a capital budget often leads the property manager and owner to develop a *long-range budget* that illustrates the relationship between operating income and expenses over five or more years in the life of a property. The level of detail and precision is less in this type of budget than in an annual budget because projections cannot be as accurate for the longer time period involved.

A long-range budget can be used to show the owner what to expect over the period of time he or she holds the investment. It can illustrate the anticipated financial gain from a rehabilitation program, a new marketing campaign, or a change in market conditions. Long-range budgets illustrate expected income, expenses, and sources of funding. Long, major projects may require extraordinary cash contributions or financing arrangements by the owner in the early years of the holding period. Ideally, these extra contributions are paid back in the later years of the holding period, after the income from the property stabilizes at an amount greater than when the property was purchased or when the changes were implemented.

SUMMARY

The success of an income-producing property is measured by the amount of money it generates. *Gross possible rental income* is adjusted for *vacancy and collection losses* and for receipts of *other (miscellaneous or un-scheduled) income* to determine the *effective gross income* of the property. *Operating expenses* are deducted from that amount to find the *net operating income (NOI)* of the property. For some types of operations, NOI is the "bottom line." For most real estate investments, however, NOI is adjusted by deducting the expense of the mortgage loan (*debt service*) to yield *cash flow*. This amount is usually the *net proceeds* paid to the owner, who is then responsible for income taxes on it.

Financial management of a property involves establishing and maintaining thorough and accurate financial records for the property as a whole and for individual units or tenants. Every dollar of income or expense must be accounted for and categorized based on its source or destination as identified in a chart of accounts. The accounting records are the basis of the financial reports the manager sends to the owner each month. They are also used to develop budgets to project future income and expenses. The manager's objective is to maximize net operating income and minimize variances between actual and budgeted income and expenses.

Key Terms

Accrual-basis accounting	Net operating income
Capital budget	Operating budget
Capitalization rate	Operating expenses
Cash-basis accounting	Rental ledger
Cash flow	Rent roll
Chart of accounts	Summary of operations
Debt service	Valuation
Long-range budget	Variance

Key Points

Calculating cash flow
Net operating income in relation to property value
Cash versus accrual accounting
The purpose of categorizing income and expenses
The property manager's responsibility with regard to income and
    expenses
Importance of accuracy and consistency in accounting and reporting
Importance of budgeting and the different budget forms

5

Establishing Management Direction

A real estate investor usually has a specific purpose in mind for purchasing a property. The reasons to own income-producing property are often multifaceted and encompass more than production of a favorable financial return on the investment. When an owner contracts with a property manager, the goals he or she has for the property become the goals of the property manager. These goals and the methods for their achievement are stated in two types of documents—a management plan and a management agreement. A management plan is a logical, deductive, and intensive analysis of all factors related to a property, such as its location, physical condition, financial status, and future prospects. A management agreement is the formal contract that defines and explains the responsibilities of the owner and property manager and establishes their business relationship.

THE MANAGEMENT PLAN

An important element in the management of real property is a specific *management plan*—an analysis of the current physical, fiscal, and operational conditions of a property expressed in relation to the owner's goals. If these conditions are not suitable for attaining the owner's goals, the property manager commonly uses the management plan to recommend and support physical, financial, or operational changes. A management plan may also be developed to evaluate the feasibility or practicality of plans the owner has for the property.

Because of the unique aspects of each property, each property manager's management style, and each owner's expectations, there is no definitive form of management plan. For some properties, an operating budget and a list of the manager's observations may suffice. For others, a document that is hundreds of pages long may be necessary to give a complete perspective on the current conditions of the property and the programs required to make its operation effective. Regardless of the size or form of the plan, its appearance and presentation are always important. Logical assertions and conclusions, clear statements of the facts, and neatness of presentation exemplify the preparer's property management skills and his or her ability to communicate effectively.

The usual starting point for a management plan is a definition of the owner's goals for investment in the property. (Forms of ownership and types of goals are discussed in chapter 3.) The owner's goals narrow the scope of the manager's research and the recommendations made in the management plan. If the owner is seeking rapid capital appreciation from a property, the management plan may center on improvements that can be made in a short time. Ways to increase the rental income are another important inclusion because a higher yield from a property will increase its value. For owners who want consistent income from their investment, a property manager may create a schedule of gradual improvements that will maintain a high occupancy rate and create the potential for steadily increasing cash flow.

The goal of the manager, as exhibited throughout the management plan and the actual management of a property, should agree with and complement the goal of the owner. That goal is usually for the property to reach its *highest and best use*, meaning that it generates the highest net operating income possible and is being used in the best possible way based on its location, size, and design.

In developing a specific management plan, the property manager usually undertakes the following exercises in the sequence shown.

Regional analysis
Neighborhood analysis
Property analysis
Market analysis
Analysis of alternatives
   Operational changes
   Structural changes
   Changes in use
Cost-benefit analysis
Management plan conclusion

The most important aspect of a property's value is its location. To gain a clear understanding of the effects of supply and demand on a property because of its location, it is essential to define and thoroughly describe its surroundings. Two identical buildings, one located on Wall Street in Manhattan and the other in a small rural town, obviously will have different dollar values even though their designs and structures are the same. A building cannot be readily moved, nor can the inventory of space in it be easily changed. The value of any income-producing property is affected by the demand for space in it. The amount of income it can produce depends on the number and quality of all the units available locally and their proximity to the property being analyzed.

Regional Analysis

Because value is dependent on location, the property manager must understand the economic, governmental, and physical conditions that affect a property. After major national concerns have been outlined, the most logical place to begin the evaluation is with the region. General economic and demographic conditions, as well as geographic features of the area surrounding the property, are outlined in a *regional analysis*. These conditions affect tenancy and the demand for space in a particular property.

Demand is what ultimately gives value to real estate. People and their economic means create demand. To understand the level of demand for a property, the property manager investigates pertinent information about the general characteristics of the region. This is done by collecting historical data and growth projections for all facets of the region, including the people who live there (*demographic profile*), business and industry, tourism and recreation, public improvements and facilities, transportation and traffic conditions, the educational system, and the economy. The manager then evaluates these data, seeking trends that signal (1) future growth and opportunity, (2) little or no change from the current conditions, or (3) eventual decline. The government and social climate of a region also greatly affect the value of its real estate, so a manager must carefully analyze these regional components as well.

Most of the data for a regional analysis in the United States come from statistical compilations available from many sources, including the federal government (Department of Commerce, Bureau of the Census; Department of Labor, Bureau of Labor Statistics; and Department of Housing and Urban Development). Statistics compiled by the U.S. government may be localized by commercial firms. Professional associations (Institute of Real Estate Management, NATIONAL ASSOCIATION OF REALTORS®, Building Owners and Managers Association, International Council of Shopping Centers) publish reports for regional and national comparisons. However, the most valuable information is found within the region itself, through state and local governmental agencies, utilities, local industries, financial institutions, chambers of commerce, and local economic development agencies.

Sources for Demographic Information

The primary source for most demographic data about the United States is the census the federal government conducts every ten years in years ending in zero. The census data are sorted and tabulated in numerous ways to show specific relationships. Although the tabulations themselves are objective, extrapolation of trends from the statistics is somewhat subjective. By themselves, numbers will not indicate whether a development will attract enough tenants from a region or neighborhood to succeed. That must be projected from evaluation of the data.

The advent of the computer has reduced the time necessary to compile raw data into usable studies. There are numerous private companies that prepare and publish such computer analyses of data. Many of these firms are subsidiaries of companies that already maintain vast databases (e.g., insurance companies, savings associations, mailing houses, phone companies, etc.). They may combine their data with census results or just compare their results with correlative census figures to verify accuracy. These companies specialize in analyses of very small geographic areas. Data can be sorted on the basis of census tracts, city blocks, zip codes, area codes, phone prefixes, or any other specific boundaries identified by the customer. Such reports are fairly economical in consideration of the time necessary for compilation. A further convenience is that many research companies promise delivery of the reports within a few days' time.

In addition to publishing decennial results, the United States Department of Commerce, Bureau of the Census, produces many other statistical profiles on its own and in conjunction with federal departments and agencies. *The Census Catalog and Guide* lists the reports that are available and when they are published. A few publications that are especially valuable to property managers are the *American Housing Survey for the United States,* which is conducted every other year in odd-numbered years, and the *Census of Retail Trade,* which is conducted at five-year intervals in years ending in two and seven. The annual *Statistical Abstract of the United States* is a compilation of more recent information added to the census data. It is an easy-to-read, compact resource.

Demographic reports about specific regions and neighborhoods may be readily available through local civic groups, REALTOR® boards, and business councils. The chamber of commerce is often the best starting point for any demographic research. It may have specific data on hand or it may have information on where local data can be found.

For property management purposes, demographic data must be viewed in the context of local property values and rents. A source for this information is the annual income and expense analyses for specific property types (office buildings, shopping centers, federally assisted apartments, conventional apartments, and condominiums, co-ops, and PUDs) published by the Institute of Real Estate Management. These reports contain national summaries, metropolitan area reports, and regional compilations.

Neighborhood Analysis

The next step is an in-depth study of the immediate neighborhood. The *neighborhood analysis* is a detailed look at the population and real estate near the subject property. Similar to the regional study in content but more narrowly focused, the neighborhood analysis is an evaluation of data related to nearby sites and the competition. Because the neighborhood analysis centers on the immediate surroundings, this study may seem more important than the regional analysis; without a thorough regional analysis, however, the neighborhood analysis can be too optimistic or pessimistic. Just as a property is affected by changes in its neighborhood, the neighborhood is affected by changes in the region.

Analyzing a neighborhood requires first that its boundaries be defined. The neighborhood of a particular property may consist of a few buildings adjacent to it or comprise an area of many square blocks. Often the neighborhood boundaries are natural or constructed barriers (rivers, lakes, ravines, railroad tracks, parks, and streets) that separate discrete areas which have common characteristics in population or land use. Sometimes neighborhood boundaries are not visually discernible; the manager may have to compile information from such sources as the United States census, municipal and county governments, local government offices, local utility companies, newspaper reports, the local library, the school board, and welfare agencies in order to precisely map a neighborhood. The objective in analyzing the neighborhood is to characterize the population, economic elements, and property types that are dominant in it. Such things as ethnic groups, income levels, institutions (e.g., colleges, hospitals), etc., are part of what characterizes a neighborhood.

Once the boundaries of the neighborhood are defined, the property manager can evaluate the data that have been collected. A neighborhood is not a static environment; it changes continually and these changes affect the property. Therefore, the manager examines the changing neighborhood conditions and includes definitions of these trends in the neighborhood analysis, explaining why he or she thinks they are taking place. Population shifts are indicated by changing numbers of individuals in different age and income groups and changes in household sizes. Economic shifts are reflected in fluctuating real estate sales prices and rental rates. Differences in types of property development (new versus renovated), changes in land value and use, and vacancy rates are other indicators of specific trends.

A physical inspection of the neighborhood is also essential. The manager wants to know whether the neighborhood is well-maintained. General cleanliness and neatness, so-called *curb appeal,* is very important. In reporting the analysis, the property manager may single out particular features in the neighborhood that favor the subject property. For example, the manager may comment on the location and quality of schools, accessibility to stores, and the level of public transportation service in the neighborhood analysis for an apartment building. Transportation, restaurants, and types of business services would be important components of the neighborhood analysis for an office building.

If results of the neighborhood analysis seem incomplete or uncertain, the manager should investigate further. A complete and fair perspective is essential to an accurate market analysis later. For instance, population growth often indicates prosperity for a neighborhood; it can also signal the reverse. A population increase because some hotels in the neighborhood have become rooming houses usually indicates deterioration. A manager would be unwise to predict a change in land value from a single statistic. Evaluation of its cause in the context of other specific statistics is essential to understanding a particular trend and its impact.

The more a property manager knows about a neighborhood, the better. The best neighborhood study is one that is updated continually. The manager must monitor current trends to know whether conditions are improving, staying the same, or declining.

Property Analysis

The same analytical method is next applied to the property itself. A *property analysis* includes the results of a careful inspection of the building, along with a description of its rental space and common areas, its basic architectural design, its overall physical condition, and factors related to its recent operation. The following are some of the questions a property manager should be able to answer from a property analysis. The unique features of each property will suggest additional considerations.

- *Building size.* How many units or leasable square feet does the building contain? What are the sizes of the units? (For an apartment building, include the number of rooms per unit as well.)
- *Condition.* What is the physical condition of the building structurally and with regard to maintenance (roof, masonry, elevators, HVAC, other mechanical equipment, windows and trim, doors, other hardware)? Can obsolescence be corrected? How could functional inadequacies be corrected? Should a structural engineer or other professional be consulted about the condition of any elements of the building?
- *Common areas.* What is the condition of the heavily used elements (floors, floor coverings, lobbies, entrance halls, stairways, blinds, storage, laundry room)?
- *Tenants' individual spaces.* How attractive is the rentable space (layout, exposure, view, features)?
- *Occupancy.* What is the current occupancy level and what has it been historically? What is the composition (and character) of the tenancy (two adult roommates with no children in apartment 101; a law office with 100 employees in suite 1800; a convenience store in unit 3)?
- *Curb appeal.* How desirable is the property (visual impression, age, style, grounds, layout, approaches, public space)?
- *Building-to-land ratio.* What is the relationship between the build-

ing and the land on which it is located (parking, current zoning)? Can the building or the land be used more efficiently?

- *Compliance status.* Is there any evidence of violations of health, safety, or environmental standards?
- *Current management.* What are the current standards of building management? What policies and procedures are in effect for tenant selection, hiring and training of staff, maintenance, rent collection, purchasing control, and administration?
- *Staff.* How is the property currently staffed? What are staff attitudes, capabilities, training, and goals?
- *Financial integrity.* What is the status of the property with respect to net operating income? What is its level of debt? Are expenses high or low compared to competing properties?

In the examination of the property and analysis of the information obtained, the manager should keep in mind that the owner's ultimate goal is usually to achieve the greatest return on his or her investment by putting the property to its highest and best use. Thus far, only part of the picture has been revealed. The information gathered in the regional, neighborhood, and property analyses is used again in the market analysis.

Market Analysis

The term "real estate market" is interpreted differently in relation to such diverse aspects of real estate as mortgage loan interest rates, development, property cost, property value, and even rental rates. All of these except mortgage interest rates relate in some way to the level of competition and the demand for rental space in a particular property. The level of demand for rental space in a specific building is determined in comparison to the demand for space in competitive buildings by a process called *market analysis.*

Market analysis entails gathering information about specific comparable properties and comparing their features to those of the subject property. Once the property manager learns what the other buildings offer, he or she evaluates the advantages and disadvantages of the subject property accordingly. Most important, the market analysis must only account for competing buildings within the neighborhood and the region in which the neighborhood itself is located, based on the information derived from the regional, neighborhood, and property analyses. After comparing the property to its competitors, the manager analyzes regional and neighborhood factors that affect, or could affect, the performance of the subject property. The manager conducts this study based on the current condition of the property; it is premature at this point to speculate on how the property would fare in the market if it were remodeled or improved.

Examining the property in its current condition first establishes a point of reference to measure whether or how much difference a projected change can or will make. The principles of conducting the market analysis are essentially the same for all types of property; for consistency, the following explanation (examples and general discussion) relates most directly to residential property; important distinctions for commercial property in particular are noted as well.

The manager first singles out the buildings that are in competition with the subject property. To determine which buildings are legitimate competitors, the manager examines the subject property at the submarket level. A *submarket* is a segment of the overall market that is limited by a particular market influence. These individual markets include office markets, store markets, apartment markets, and single-family residence markets. This categorization reduces the numbers of potential tenants and potential competitors. Other factors narrow the field even further. Prospective tenants usually prefer one portion of the region in which to locate, so they will limit their search to the part of town they prefer. They also commonly search for a particular type of rental unit (i.e., households of two or more people do not look at studio apartments; convenience store owners do not seek supermarket-sized spaces, etc.). Because prospects narrow their focus in such a manner, the property manager should narrow the focus of the market analysis to determine the true competition. The subject property is compared to similar properties in the neighborhood or general vicinity, not to property that is across town or in another region (unless it is concluded that the "neighborhood" of the property includes these areas). However, even if property across town is not in direct competition with the subject property, its standing in the market will have an influence because it is a part of the market as a whole. This is accounted for in the narrative description of the market.

Facts learned in the regional and neighborhood analyses should indicate which buildings are in competition with the subject property. Generally they are of comparable size, with units of similar size at similar rental rates. Once these properties are identified, their features and amenities can be compared with those of the subject property and rated appropriately. Prospective tenants usually assign a dollar value to different amenities based on perceived benefit. For this reason, when comparing the subject property to the competition, a property manager should list those features and amenities that are expected to influence a prospective tenant to sign a lease. The following considerations pertain to most markets.

- The number and types of units (or space) available within the area
- The average age and character of the building in which they are located

EXHIBIT 5.1
Comparison Grid (Residential Property)

	Subject	Comparable Property #1		Comparable Property #2		Comparable Property #3	
Name/Address							
Type of unit							
Square feet in unit							
Rental Rate							
Rate/square foot							
Categories	**Description**	**Description**	**+ / − adj.**	**Description**	**+ / − adj.**	**Description**	**+ / − adj.**
Location							
Age							
BUILDING CONDITION							
Exterior							
Grounds							
Common Areas							
PARKING							
Condition							
Open/Covered/Garage							
Ratio							
Other							

E X H I B I T   5.1 (continued)

Comparison Grid (Residential Property)

Categories	Description	+/− adj.	Description	+/− adj.	Description	+/− adj.
APARTMENT INTERIOR						
Floor/Carpet						
Drapes/Blinds						
Stove/Refrigerator						
Dishwasher						
Washer/Dryer						
Closets/Storage						
Air conditioning						
Other						
AMENITIES						
Laundry room(s)						
Swimming pool(s)						
Other						
Total Rent Adjustments						
Adjusted Rent/Unit						
Adjusted Rent/Square Foot						

- Features that are similar in most units within the market—layout, equipment, size, amenities (what defines a typical unit)
- The current rent for an average unit on a monthly (and square-foot) basis
- The occupancy level of all units of a given type; the occupancy level of units of the type that are superior in the market, average in the market, and inferior in the market
- Rental rates and occupancy levels in recent years (the trend for each)

The manager should ask whether the rent and occupancy trends compare with real estate market trends in general; how vacant units in the area compare to those in the subject property with regard to size, age, condition, amenities, and rents; and, based on the results of the neighborhood analysis, whether there is an increase or decrease in the number of prospective tenants for the subject property.

Comparison Grid. To make an effective comparison, the property manager categorizes the features of the competitive properties with respect to the subject property using a *comparison grid* (exhibit 5.1). Specific features to be compared are listed at the left, and the comparable properties are indicated as column headings. Some categories are straightforward (age of the building, for example); others (location, condition, and appeal) are subject to interpretation. Still others may require additional explanation. A "pets allowed" category may be listed as a straight yes or no for most residential properties, but some apartments may have very specific provisions. (Dogs may not be allowed at all, while cats may be allowed if a higher security deposit is paid.) For commercial properties, rental rates would be subdivided to account for additions to base rent (e.g., pass-through expenses, percentage rents or "overages"), and a comparison of anchor and ancillary tenants would be included.

Consistency in rating or ranking is most important. In preparation of the comparison grid, the same rules of assessment for each category of analysis must be used for all properties. It is difficult to describe and rate location on the comparison grid, yet the location of a property within the neighborhood is its prime marketable feature. For instance, being a block from a supermarket or a mass transit stop would ordinarily be a promotable feature for a residential property; being next door to the bus depot or to the parking lot of the supermarket would not. On the other hand, being next door may be more attractive than being three blocks away from these same amenities. Because most factors involving location are relative and complex, a separate location analysis (exhibit 5.2) can help the property manager evaluate the property's location and discern more precisely how it affects demand.

EXHIBIT 5.2

Factors Influencing Location Quality

Access to Transportation
Proximity to major roads
Proximity to interstate highway(s)
Proximity of mass transit stops
Relative convenience of different modes of transportation

Convenience of Local Facilities
Central business district (CBD)
Convenience store or center
Neighborhood shopping center/supermarket
Regional mall or larger shopping center
Major employment locations (if different from CBD)
Schools and colleges
Parks, sports and fitness centers, and other recreational centers
Cultural/entertainment centers
Social services (government and human services centers)

Neighborhood and Surroundings
Reputation and acceptance level of the neighborhood
Conditions and reputations of areas traversed to reach local facilities

Personal and Property Safety
Crime against people
Crime against property
Access to police, fire, and emergency medical services

Comparison grid analysis allows the property manager to determine how the units in the subject property compare to similar units in the market on a feature-by-feature basis. The purpose of the exercise is to show whether a particular feature at a comparable property is better than or not as good as the same feature in the subject property and how the total of these features affects quoted rents. By attributing a dollar value to each feature, a market-level rent can be determined for the subject property based on the comparison. If the feature in the subject property is better than in a comparable property, the rent for the comparable is adjusted upward; if the feature in the subject property is not as good, the rent for the comparable is adjusted downward. The adjustment amount (negative or positive) is based on what the property manager estimates a tenant would pay for the feature or would not pay because of its absence. For each property, the adjustments are totaled and its rental rate is changed to reflect the net adjustments. Rents for the comparable properties are then analyzed to determine a market rent on either a per-unit or a per-square-foot basis. (Typically, a comparison grid analysis is done for each type of unit.)

Setting Rents. Quoted rents and occupancy levels of the competing rental units are evaluated to determine the rent that can be charged for the subject property based on quality, amenities, and other attractions (e.g., a view). The comparison grid indicates whether rents for the units in the subject property are below, at, or above market rates. Based on this information, the manager can evaluate the current *rental schedule* of the subject property and compare it to the rental schedules of other properties on the comparison grid. Any of several methods may be used for this comparison. One relatively accurate method is the *base-unit-rate approach,* in which the typical unit within a specific submarket (either an actual unit or a perceived ideal) is used as a standard against which all similar units are measured. To determine whether the current rental schedule of the subject property should be adjusted, the property manager searches for an optimum balance between vacancy and maximum income. While the ideal is maximum rent and maximum occupancy, reality dictates that vacancies will be present. In fact, an increase in rent can be expected initially to increase vacancies. With this in mind, the property manager strives for a realistic maximum rent that will minimize the impact on the vacancy rate. Both rents and vacancies must be considered in estimating changes in effective gross income and net operating income that will result from an increase in rents.

Narrative Report. A narrative overview of market trends and observations is generally included in the market analysis. One factor that is usually discussed is the absorption rate in the neighborhood or region. The *absorption rate* of a property type is the amount of space leased compared to the amount of space available for lease over a given period, usually a year. It relates to both construction of new space and demolition or removal from the market of old space. Different property types within the same region have different absorption rates.

If demand exceeds supply, the absorption rate is favorable because vacancy overall decreases. If supply exceeds demand, the absorption rate is unfavorable, and lenders tend to curtail their financing of similar developments, causing an eventual slowdown of growth. A negative absorption rate can also result from other changes in a market. If a major industry is shut down and, as a result, there are not enough jobs, people will move away from the area and the lack of jobs will discourage others from moving in. The amount of residential space available for lease will quickly exceed demand, irrespective of any new construction. The commercial sector may also slow based on this major change. The effect of reduced demand is not always immediately apparent, however. Construction may simply continue because the financing is in place. If financing was obtained when the level of demand was high, market trends may be unfavorable when construction is started and stopping construction may cost more than completing the project. As the new space fills over time, demand will again exceed supply and the absorption rate will again be favorable, encouraging new construction and causing the cycle to be repeated.

Also included in the narrative portion of the market analysis are trends observed in the regional and neighborhood analyses that can affect the subject property. A shift in the demographic profile of the neighborhood would be noted here, along with the manager's conclusions regarding the favorable or unfavorable effects that shift may have on the demand for rental space. If the property manager learned in the regional analysis that a nearby company would be expanding its operations and hiring more people, he or she may reason that demand for rental space will increase. The manager may further reason (from the comparison grid) that the competing buildings in the neighborhood are better suited to profit from the anticipated population growth. These considerations should guide the development of a marketing program for the property that will capitalize on any positive trends that are noted and insulate the property from the impact of negative trends. (Marketing is discussed in chapter 6.)

Many management plans conclude with the market analysis. The research to this point can substantiate a need for a new rental schedule and indicate the increase that can be attained without compromising the competitive strength of the property. In other words, if implementation of a new rental schedule alone will place the property in a condition of highest and best use, that is all that has to be said. However, many properties—particularly commercial properties—demand a more comprehensive examination of their future prospects.

Analysis of Alternatives

Some properties require changes in operations or some form of physical change to justify a rent increase, elevate the occupancy level, and subsequently bring them to their highest and best use. Physical changes can range from rehabilitation or modernization of the current building to outright change in the use of the building or the site. In the effort to improve the performance of a property, the property manager should investigate the range of possible changes and evaluate their anticipated effects—in other words, conduct an *analysis of alternatives*. The intent of the changes proposed in this section of a management plan is to increase net operating income—which is the tangible and measurable benefit of the investment in the property—and thereby increase the property's value. Each proposed change also carries with it a cost, so it is essential for the property manager to conduct an analysis comparing the costs and the benefits of each proposal or combination of proposals made in the analysis of alternatives.

Operational Changes. These are changes that affect procedural methods or efficiency but not the physical makeup of the property. The net effect is to reduce operating expenses and thereby increase net operating income. Operational changes range from adoption of a new rental schedule based on the market analysis to using low-wattage bulbs in common-area lighting. The manager may consider charging back to tenants some common-area expenses such as heating or reducing staff. It may be possible to renegotiate contract terms with certain service providers (e.g., elevator maintenance) or to call for bids on recurring services that are not under contract (landscaping, etc.) as a way to reduce outside service expenses.

Even though the intent of operational changes is to reduce operating expenses, quality should not be compromised. After completing the market analysis, the property manager should be keenly aware of the services the competitors provide. Any recommendation that sacrifices any similar services may be more costly than the savings that are achieved. However, examination of the competition may lead to discovery of new methods that will reduce operating costs yet preserve or enhance service standards.

Structural Changes. The economic life of a property can be lengthened through rehabilitation and modernization. *Rehabilitation* is the process of renewing the equipment and materials in the building. It entails correcting deferred maintenance. *Modernization* is inherent in the rehabilitation process because original equipment will be replaced with similar equipment of more modern design to make the property competitive. New decorations, new carpeting, new appliances, equipment that is more energy-efficient, or any other physical improvement that does not affect the use of the property can be rehabilitative. The list of possibilities in this arena is virtually endless. When physical changes are proposed, the management plan must show how the funds for it will be allocated (an expense budget), and the anticipated impact on net operating income and property value. The owner may also require an analysis of debt service (if the funds are borrowed) and cash flow.

Changes in Use. A recommendation to change the use of a property must be well-founded. Such a procedure is complex and expensive and therefore not very commonly done. However, the rewards of a successful change in use are often substantial. Once a change of use is implemented, it is usually impossible to revert to the original condition. The anticipated improvement in performance expected from a change in use must always be weighed carefully against the risks being taken. The most common changes include adaptive use, condominium conversion, and demolition for new development.

Adaptive use (recycling). Across the United States, old factories, mills, hotels, train stations, post offices, and printing plants have been transformed into offices, shopping centers, apartments, and civic centers. Adaptive use of existing structures is usually more economical than building new. By capitalizing on an existing shell and foundation, the cost of demolition and part of the cost of new materials are eliminated. Adaptive use is usually proposed as a way to reduce development costs, convert obsolete property to meet new market demands, preserve historical architecture, or revive a location that is not achieving its highest and best use. A recycled building may not achieve the same rent per square foot as a new one, but the start-up costs are lower and debt service requirements are usually reduced. Thus cash flow per square foot can be competitive with that of a new building. Old buildings, whole city blocks, and even sections of towns have been preserved and made profitable through adaptive use. As an example, Ghirardelli Square in San Francisco, a charming complex of specialty shops, restaurants, and theaters, was originally a chocolate factory.

Condominium conversion. The primary advantage of condominium conversion is the potential to achieve a high profit in a short period of time. The appeal is even greater when high financing costs reduce cash flow. Converting a rental property to condominium ownership allows the original owner to recapture his or her investment, pay off the mortgage loan, and keep any excess funds as profit. If rent control restricts a landlord's ability to increase rents to market levels, condominium conversion may circumvent the potential loss of income, although current renters may have the right to remain despite the conversion. Review of state and local laws regarding condominium formation and conversion is essential to determine the feasibility of a particular conversion.

Condominium conversion was once limited to apartment buildings. However, the concept has been extended to other property types—even parking lots in congested metropolitan areas are sold by the parking space. Commercial condominium ownership is not very common, but it does exist. However, businesses usually require space for growth, and owning only a portion of a building limits the potential for expansion. Also, the financial obligations that are part of such ownership make subsequent relocation difficult. Consequently, conversion of a commercial property to condominium ownership is less likely to be practical or successful.

The success of a condominium conversion depends on the adaptability of the building to this form of ownership. In most cases, the building and all of its components must be in the best possible condition for the property owner who is doing the conversion to achieve the greatest possible return on his or her investment. Also to be considered is the fact that a condominium is a long-term financial commitment for the buyer—a prospective owner is usually more selective than a prospective renter.

Demolition for new development.   Demolition may seem to be an easy alternative, but it can be a very expensive one. The cost of razing a building combined with the cost of erecting a new one increases the necessity for the new structure to generate a high level of income. A proposal to tear down a building, even if it is in serious disrepair, can lead to a public outcry and tarnish the image of the new structure. If a site is listed in the National Register of Historic Places, demolition of the building is prohibited. The decision to demolish an old building and replace it with something new requires thorough review of more than the financial aspects. The impact on the neighborhood and the possible loss of goodwill are also important considerations.

Mixed-use developments (MXD).   If demolition is concluded to be the most feasible alternative, replacement of the existing structure with a mixed-use development may be a possibility, especially in a city. A mixed-use development commonly has three or more income-generating uses. It represents a more intensive use of urban land than a single-use building on the same site. Examples are Broadway Plaza in Los Angeles, which includes offices, a hotel, retail space, and a large parking garage, and Water Tower Place in Chicago, which has a similar complement of uses plus condominium apartments and several theaters. Because such projects derive income from several uses, they are less likely to falter if income from one of those uses is reduced. However, mixed-use developments require large amounts of land, superb locations, and complicated financing. Because of this, MXDs are *not* commonly recommended in a management plan as replacement for a conventional single-use building.

Cost-Benefit Analysis

Changing a property always involves costs. The amount and extent of the costs depend on the scope of the changes being made. Establishing a new accounting procedure (an operational change) may only require training of staff and replacement of a current form, but these have measurable costs. Rehabilitation or other structural change is costly and can cause interruption of part or all of the rental income while the work is being done. Even a recommendation to maintain status quo has to be justified financially. In order to determine whether a specific recommendation will improve the property's income, the property manager does a *cost-benefit analysis.* Each alternative considered must be evaluated to ascertain that it will indeed yield higher levels of net operating income and cash flow than if the property is left unchanged. There is also the matter of recovering the costs of making the change (plus any financing). Clearly the benefit (increased income—and therefore property value) must outweigh the cost if a recommendation is to be feasible. This means the *payback period*—the amount of time for the change to pay for itself—has to be evaluated as well. As an example, consider a thirty-year-old apartment building with fifty units. The property manager discovers that residents in the neighborhood tend to pay higher rent for apartments with new kitchen appliances. Although the refrigerators and ovens in the subject property are as old as the building, they still operate well. However, new appliances and built-in microwave ovens are standard equipment in comparable buildings nearby.

The property manager calculates that replacing appliances will cost $2,000 per apartment, or $100,000 for the entire building. Its payback period would be calculated as follows: If the property historically has 90 percent occupancy (45 leased units out of 50), then the return on the investment should be based on that number of units. If the improvement is expected to allow an increase in rent of $50 per apartment per month, the improvement would generate $2,250 a month ($50 × 45 units), so the payback period would be approximately 44 months ($100,000 total cost ÷ $2,250 per month). The possibility of a higher occupancy rate because of enhanced desirability of the apartments may reduce the payback period. Operating expenses may also decrease because of reduced repair expenses which may reduce the payback period even more.

Whether a 44-month payback period is reasonable or feasible for such an undertaking depends on the owner and what he or she expects from the property. The cost-benefit analysis should also show the potential increase in property value resulting from the improvement. To determine the effect of the improvement on property value, the increase in NOI ($2,250 × 12 months = $27,000) is divided by the capitalization rate. (Capitalization rate is explained in chapter 4). At a cap rate of 10 percent, the property value should increase by approximately $270,000 ($27,000 ÷ .10) because of the $100,000 improvement, yielding a net gain of $170,000.

Management Plan Conclusion

The length and complexity of the management plan can be made more easily understandable by inclusion of a recapitulation of the major conditions affecting the property and a summary of the primary recommendations that are made in the plan, along with the rationale for specific changes and the expected results. A statement of the anticipated long-term financial performance—the effect on the bottom line—usually helps the owner understand the reasoning behind the management plan. Highlighting this information at the beginning of the document in the form of an "executive summary" may be more valuable in guiding the owner through the text than if it only appears at the end of the report. Recommendations that relate to only one area of the property's operation may not require a very complex management plan. A market analysis may be all that is necessary to assess the condition of a property and recommend maintaining status quo. Any proposed change, including a change in rental rates, requires a cost-benefit analysis as well.

THE MANAGEMENT AGREEMENT

In many ways, the property manager assumes the role of the owner in conducting the day-to-day business of the property. Most tenants regard the manager as "landlord"; often they do not know who actually owns the property. The tenants are correct in thinking of the property manager this way because he or she can have the legal authority to establish leases, set rents, and safeguard the property. The manager operates the property on the owner's behalf and represents the owner to both tenants and others who have business with the property. To formalize this relationship, the owner and manager must agree on a variety of terms and responsibilities.

A *management agreement* is a formal and binding document that establishes the property manager's legal authority over the operation of the property. The manager usually is an agent for the owner, serving as the owner's *fiduciary* or trustee of the owner's funds and assets associated with the property. As a legal contract, the management agreement should be written by or prepared in consultation with a lawyer. The agreement establishes the relationship between the owner and the manager for a fixed period, defines the manager's authority and compensation for services provided, outlines some procedures, specifies limits of the manager's authority and actions, and states financial and other obligations of the property owner. The contents of a management agreement generally include:

> Full names and identification of the property owner and property
>   manager
> Description of the property
> Term of the agreement
> Responsibilities of the manager
>   Financial activities
>   Reports to the owner
>   General property management
> Obligations of the owner
>   Insurance
>   Operating and reserve funds
>   Liability
>   Legal and regulatory compliance
> Compensation for management services

A good management agreement also includes provisions for termination of the arrangement under specific conditions as well as numerous clauses related to general legalities. (The Institute of Real Estate Management offers a Management Agreement Form that includes an explanation of the typical components of an agreement along with possible variations and additions.)

Basic Components of an Agreement

Fundamental to every contract are the names of those entering into it, the purpose of the agreement, and how long it is to be in effect. In a management agreement, these elements are the parties, management of the property, and the term (or duration). In naming the parties to a management agreement (property owner and the management company or an independent property manager), it is important to establish their authority to negotiate and sign such an agreement. In particular, individuals representing a partnership or a corporation must be specifically authorized to sign contracts. The property may be identified uniquely by its street address; however, it may be appropriate to include the legal description of the property according to its title documentation. If the property has a special name, that is usually listed as well. The term of the agreement is the period for which it will be in effect. This is usually stated as a specific number of years and includes beginning and ending dates. Often there is provision for automatic renewal on an annual basis when the initial term expires provided the agreement is not otherwise officially terminated. The duration of the agreement and its renewability are negotiable, as are all its other terms and conditions.

Responsibilities of the Manager

Financial management, reporting, and general property management activities are among the property manager's normal duties. Much of this work is interrelated; reporting and record keeping are natural functions of both financial management and general management. The management agreement formalizes these functions of the manager, often providing specific procedures to follow and sometimes stating intervals of time (monthly, annually) for performing various duties.

Financial Management. Establishment of an operating bank account is an important provision of the management agreement. The property manager usually chooses the financial institution and establishes the account, although the owner may be involved in the decision. The operating account is the one through which receipts and expenditures flow. The management agreement may require that a minimum amount remain in the operating account at all times. It may also call for the owner to advance to the manager an amount equal to the first month's expenses. Apart from the necessity of having adequate funds to pay the operating expenses of the property, a minimum balance may be required by the bank. It is not necessary for the operating account to be anything more than a commercial checking account.

The manager and owner may agree that more than one bank account will be maintained. Security deposits and reserve funds should be kept separate from the operating funds of the property. This measure often makes accounting for security deposits and reserves easier for the manager in addition to protecting these funds. In many states, security deposit funds are required by law to be kept in a separate account. Regardless of the number of accounts necessary to satisfactorily maintain the funds of the property, the management agreement usually mandates that deposits be kept in federally insured accounts. The manager is also obligated to inform the owner if the balance in any account for the property exceeds the federally insured amount.

The management agreement should clearly state that the owner's and manager's funds should not be mixed together (*commingled*). This is a legal requirement and is a matter of both professional ethics and good business practice. All funds directly or indirectly earned by the property belong to the owner. The manager is entitled to compensation from the property's income and, as the owner's agent (or *fiduciary*), is authorized to make those payments to himself or herself. It is important for all financial transactions to be fully disclosed to the owner.

The management agreement authorizes the manager to collect rent and any other income due the property. The manager is also authorized to charge fees for late payments, checks returned for insufficient funds, credit checks, and other administrative work. Fees collected from tenants for these services may be retained by the manager as compensation for these exceptions to regular practices, although that point should be negotiated between the manager and owner.

Payment of expenses is another duty of the manager. These expenses can include debt service in addition to normal operating expenses. The *net proceeds* after all income has been collected and expenses have been paid are sent to the owner on a schedule established in the management agreement. If there is more than one owner, the management agreement should state the proportionate distribution of net proceeds.

The manager usually seeks prohibition from lending funds to the property for any reason. In the event of an operating deficit, the owner is obligated to make up any difference immediately. However, the owner may ask the manager to make up the deficit temporarily with management funds and the manager may elect to do so. To allow for this situation, the management agreement should state that such amounts should be considered as a loan at a specified interest rate. Property owners are usually obligated to maintain a minimum balance in the property's operating account to avert such deficits.

The owner is usually given the right to audit the accounts of the property at any time, although a routine schedule for this procedure may be agreed to and stated in the contract. Audits are performed at the owner's expense unless discrepancies in excess of a predetermined percentage are found; if the manager has erred and a discrepancy greater than the limit has resulted, the manager may be financially responsible for the audit. The management agreement may also state that all ledgers, receipts, and other records pertaining to the property belong to the owner even though they are usually in the manager's possession. When the agreement is terminated, the records are turned over to the owner.

Reports to the Owner. The manager is usually required to report the financial performance of the property to the owner each month. The report itself often consists of several parts, including a summary of operations, a record of income, a record of disbursements, and a narrative report of operations. Budget variances and their causes are important information for both the owner and manager. Although preparation of these reports requires a significant amount of time, the use of computers permits rapid arrangement of data to satisfy both parties and expedites report preparation. The manager is commonly required to prepare an annual budget for operating the property, and the agreement will usually state how and when this is to be done. The number of written reports and their respective formats are negotiable items. Institutional owners often require that manager's reports conform to the institution's forms, a process that can involve a considerable amount of time and expense. Because of this, the reporting requirements should be considered before the management fee is negotiated.

Apart from the financial reports required by the agreement, many situations arise in which a telephone call or personal visit with the owner may be necessary or appropriate. The level and frequency of personal contact depends in part on the owner's personality and requirements. Some owners may request frequent consultation; others prefer to distance themselves from the relationship. The property manager, being contracted as a professional to maintain the property, is generally authorized to handle any crisis. If disaster strikes, however, the owner must be told what has happened. Even so, the manager's priority in any crisis is to gain control of the situation. This means informing the proper authorities, notifying the insurance agent if warranted, and consulting with contractors as appropriate. During a relatively calm moment later, the manager can speak with the owner and describe what is being done to rectify the situation.

General Property Management.   The manager is authorized to advertise space in the property available for lease, such advertising to be at the owner's expense. It is appropriate for the manager and owner to establish objectives for advertising and to state them in the management agreement.

The manager may be authorized to execute leases. This usually includes authorization to select tenants, set rents, and enforce lease terms, in which case, the owner and manager should agree in advance on the lease form, financial requirements for tenancy, and rental rates. For commercial properties, the manager's participation in leasing activities is usually less direct; often there is a separate leasing agent. The complexity of the leases and the rents for commercial space may dictate the manager's specific role.

The manager is usually expected to hire and supervise staff and to administer payroll, but the owner may be the employer of the staff of a property. The staff may include maintenance personnel, site managers, and anyone else who works full- or part-time on the property or in its behalf. The expenses of employment, including salaries, benefits, employment taxes (social security and unemployment), and workers' compensation insurance premiums, are the responsibility of the owner and are paid out of the operating funds of the property. The property manager is not an employee of the owner and the management agreement should clearly state that fact. A property manager provides a service and is either self-employed or an employee of a management company.

The manager is authorized to perform all necessary and ordinary repairs and replacements to preserve the property and to make all alterations that are required to comply with lease agreements, governmental regulations, and insurance requirements. Apart from specific budgeted expenditures, the management agreement usually states a maximum dollar amount the manager can spend for individual items of maintenance without receiving prior approval from the owner—except in the event of an emergency. Because of the agent's authority over the owner's finances, a provision may be included in the management agreement that requires the manager and others who handle the owner's funds under the manager's supervision to be bonded and states the amount of liability involved.

Obligations of the Owner

The owner is responsible for insuring the property, and the agreement should require the manager to be named on all policies as an additional insured party. Premiums and deductibles are expenses of the owner, although the manager may pay them out of the operating funds. The types of insurance required depend on the specific property and local practice. Both owner and manager should consult their insurance agents to determine the most complete coverage for the property.

An important issue to negotiate for the management agreement is establishment of a reserve fund. This is usually a percentage of the property's effective gross income or net operating income to be set aside on a regular basis.

The agreement should state the owner's responsibility for compliance of the property with governmental regulations that apply to it (e.g., environmental laws, building codes) and for any associated insurance requirements. It should also indemnify the agent against liability for noncompliance. If the owner does not cure any discovered noncompliance, the manager—as the owner's agent—could become liable. However, the agreement should require the manager to advise the owner of any noncompliance that is discovered. The owner must then decide (and authorize the manager) to implement changes or corrections.

Compensation for Management Services

The usual compensation for management services is a percentage of the gross receipts (effective gross income) of the managed property. The specific percentage is always negotiated, and it is usually advisable to negotiate a minimum monthly fee to be stated in the agreement to assure the manager of compensation in case there is a shortfall in collections. The manager should take care in setting a fee to be certain of adequate compensation for the full range of services provided. It may be appropriate to negotiate separate fees for leasing a new building, overseeing construction (rehabilitation or remodeling), or other services provided by the manager that are not generally part of the regular management duties.

SUMMARY

The management objectives for a particular property are unique; they are usually spelled out in two documents—a management plan and a management agreement. A property manager must know how to assess the potential of a property and how to explain this assessment through a management plan. Evaluation of data on the region, the neighborhood, and the property itself forms the basis for an analysis of the current market position of the property. Assessment of the structural integrity of the property, its operating history, rent levels, etc., indicates whether and how much change is necessary to bring the property in line with market demand. With every change that is proposed to improve profitability, a cost is involved, and the manager must evaluate the proposed benefit in terms of its cost.

A management agreement is a formal contract between an owner and a manager. It outlines the responsibilities of the manager and the obligations of the owner and authorizes the manager to operate the property on the owner's behalf. Even though the manager is given extensive authority, the owner is ultimately responsible for the property.

Key Terms

Absorption rate	Fiduciary
Agent	Management agreement
Commingle	Management plan
Comparison grid	Market analysis
Cost-benefit analysis	Neighborhood analysis
Curb appeal	Property analysis
Demographic profile	Regional analysis

Key Points

Development of a management plan

Evaluation of a market based on regional, neighborhood, and property analyses

Use of comparison grid analysis to establish a new rental schedule

Achieving highest and best use of a property

Considerations for structural, financial, and operational changes to improve the performance of a property

Major issues negotiated in a management agreement

6

The Cycle of Tenancy

The principles of tenant relations are essentially the same regardless of property type. In fact, there is a cycle of tenancy that is common to all properties. All current tenants were once prospects; they were attracted to the property because of its marketing. They signed a lease and they regularly paid rent to occupy space in the property. When the lease expired, they may or may not have renewed it based on evaluation of the benefit of renewal versus the amount of the rent increase or the expense of relocating. Tenants eventually move out, but satisfied tenants may refer others to the property. In all phases of the cycle of tenancy, the skill and dedication of the property manager are as important to tenants' satisfaction as the location, appearance, and structural integrity of the property.

MARKETING THE PROPERTY

For every product or service there is a market of willing consumers. Identifying prospective customers whose specific needs, wants, and ability to pay will be satisfied by a particular product or service is a function of *marketing*. The objective of marketing rental space is to entice as many potential tenants as possible from the market of renters. This requires thorough knowledge of the property for lease and a clear understanding of the market for that type of space. The features of the property should already be known from the regional, neighborhood, property, and market analyses conducted during development of the management plan (see chapter 5).

**Factors that Determine
Market Size**
* Property type
* Location
* Rental space
* Rental price

Those analyses should have indicated the features and amenities of the property to be highlighted and the type of prospective tenant who will be attracted by them. In the absence of a specific management plan, the same types of analyses should be done before planning a marketing program.

Understanding the Market

Marketing real estate is different from marketing other types of products and services. Real property is immovable and difficult to alter to meet market demands. Specific features of a property may limit the size of its market and the number of potential tenants. Because of this, the property's features and its location must be thoroughly understood before the property manager can identify the market and concentrate promotion in media appropriate to that market. Money spent to reach extraneous markets—those individuals who have no reason to respond to the marketing effort—is money wasted. Careful study of the limitations on the market before the start of a marketing program will reduce the time and expense required to produce results.

The primary factor that limits the potential market is the *property type.* Store space must be marketed to merchants, apartments to people who want a place to live, etc. The second limiting factor is the *size of the rental space.* Supermarkets must have 25,000–45,000 square feet of space, while a gift shop usually requires much less (around 2,000 square feet); the number of people in a household and their income generally define the size and layout of their living quarters. Factors such as these narrow the range of potential tenants for a specific store space or apartment. The third limiting factor is *location*—where the property is situated and how far it is from its market. This, too, is related to the type of property. Shopping centers can seek tenants nationally. Rental housing and office space generally attract prospective tenants from the surrounding neighborhood or region. A time-share condominium in a resort area may attract residents from all parts of the country or the world. Specific features related to location (access to transportation and proximity to local attractions) define the market as well. *Rental price* is the fourth limiting factor. Those in the market must be able to afford the rent and be willing to pay it.

Common Advertising Media
* Classified newspaper ads
* Display advertising
* Signage
* Brochures
* Direct mail
* Broadcast advertising

Once the general characteristics of the tenant profile become evident, the property manager can examine what will attract the greatest number of prospects to visit the site. The effort of the property manager at this point is to make the market for the property aware of its existence, the advantages it offers, and the availability of space in it. This means choosing the medium and the message that will generate the most responses. The greater the number of responses, the larger the number of prospects to choose from, thus ensuring that the property will be leased quickly.

By its nature, a new property attracts attention; its location, size, and state of completion invite curiosity. In this regard, a new development benefits from free publicity it receives simply because it is new. People's natural inquisitiveness can be further encouraged with specific advertising. On the other hand, an older property may not be viewed with much curiosity; however, compared to a new structure, an established property usually has fewer vacancies to fill.

New residential properties usually have impressive model units. A model should reflect the property manager's understanding of the market and the most probable type of resident. Models are intended to help prospects envision the space as their home. While it is important for the furnishings of a model space to suit the market, the furnishings themselves should not be the focus of attention—they should subtly enhance the space, not overshadow it. (Models are rarely used in leasing office or retail space.) The main thrust of any marketing program will be specific advertising.

Developing a Marketing Program

Knowing the marketable features of the property and the profile of the most likely prospects, the property manager can plan a specific promotional message and choose the best medium through which to convey it. Advertising and promotion cost money, so the first step in developing a marketing program is to quantify how much money is available for it. An advertising program generally requires its own budget. Another early step is to determine whether an advertising agency will be used and to what extent. Because of the extra expense involved, advertising agencies are most likely to be used to promote very large developments, especially new ones. If an advertising agency is considered, the property manager and owner must verify the extent of the services to be used, the precise cost of these services, and the length of time the contract will last. Whether an agency is used or not, a comprehensive marketing program includes a variety of media. The advantages and disadvantages of some specific promotional vehicles are discussed in the sections that follow.

Newspaper Advertising.   Newspaper advertising is one of the most cost-effective ways to convey a message to the greatest number of people. One newspaper usually dominates the coverage of a community's business and real estate. That paper should be preferred for marketing space for rent.

Newspapers offer a number of methods for advertising rental space. *Classified advertising* usually appears in a special section of the newspaper and is the most common medium for announcing available rental space. Classified advertisements should be straightforward and identify the space, its location, the rent, and a phone number to call. Purposely omitting any of this information is not necessarily an enticement; it can dissuade prospects. Apartments, condominiums, some office space, and some small retail spaces are successfully advertised in the classified section.

Display advertisements (exhibit 6.1) are larger and more expensive than classified ads. These advertisements must be attractive and well-designed. They are most helpful during initial lease-up of any type of property and are very effective for inviting the public to visit a new or renovated building. When display advertisements are used, their placement on the newspaper page should be as prominent as possible.

Newspapers with large circulations periodically publish special real estate sections that include information on properties, neighborhoods, property owners, real estate brokers, developers, and managers. They are often presented in a magazine or tabloid format and appeal to numerous audiences. The appeal and potential success of advertising in these special sections must be weighed against the extra cost.

Signs.   Every property, whether it has vacancies or not, should display a tasteful sign that identifies the site, shows the name of the managing agent or firm, and tells where or how rental information may be obtained. Those who respond to on-site signage are usually strong prospects; they have seen the property and its surroundings and are already sufficiently impressed to inquire.

Using signs to enhance the prestige of a building is productive. However, signs on the site have an understandably limited effectiveness; only people passing the property will notice the signs, and they may already

E X H I B I T   6.1

Sample Display Advertisement (Residential)

RIVERSIDE TERRACE APARTMENTS

Distinctive Rural Living

1500 North Main Street

- 1, 2, and 3 bedroom apartments from 800 to 2,500 square feet
- Private balconies
- Charming river views from most apartments
- Hardwood floors, woodburning fireplaces
- European-style kitchens
- Private, secured parking
- Choice location near commuter rail station
- Health club, tennis courts, and indoor swimming pool on premises

For Appointment Call 555-5555

EQUAL HOUSING
OPPORTUNITY

know the information that is presented. Billboards announcing the location, type of space, and projected occupancy date can reach a wider audience. Signage is not used alone; it must be accompanied by other forms of advertising.

Brochures. A brochure is usually the most detailed piece of advertising used. A colorful, appealing brochure that fully describes the rental space and includes sample floor plans should be available as a handout to prospects who visit the property. A brochure may also be suitable for mailing to those who inquire by telephone. To minimize the expense of the brochure, the property manager should consider how long it will be in use before the brochure is designed. In particular, a design that allows information on rents to be updated can make a brochure effective for several years. It is important for additions or changes to be printed with the same typeface as the brochure itself. Primary design elements of the brochure (logo, typeface, graphics) are the most likely elements to be adapted for or used in conjunction with outdoor signs and display advertisements in newspapers and trade magazines. Brochures are often a component of direct mail campaigns, and they are most useful in promoting properties that are very large, brand new, or recently renovated.

Signage

The term *signage* means the signs in and on a property. A building's signage conveys an integrated message and impression about the site. Even though signs do not necessarily enhance the appeal of a building by themselves (tenants lease space, not signs), signage that displays a unified theme will not lessen the building's appeal. On the other hand, mismatched signs, handwritten signs, and signs that give commands detract from a building's image. Three types of signs comprise a property's signage: directional signs, identification signs, and informational signs.

* *Directional signs* guide visitors and tenants to where they want to go in the building. The building directory and signs on walls or in hallways leading to various building facilities are directional signs. Buildings with numerous entrances may have signs directing visitors to the main entrance. Off-site directional signs lead prospects to the building and to the on-site office. These types of signs contain few words and may use arrows to indicate direction. Display of the building's logo (if it has one) and use of a single typeface will unify the theme of this type of signage.
* *Identification signs* are often placed on or above doors to indicate entrances, exits, and unit or suite numbers or special rooms (e.g., the office, laundry room). The designs of identification signs usually match those of the directional signs.
* *Informational signs* convey messages, and while they must be used from time to time, they should be kept to an absolute minimum. Many informational signs are negative (Keep off the Grass, Wipe Feet Before Entering). They tend to detract from the building's image, and their effectiveness is open to question. On the other hand, there are legal requirements for posting some types of informational signs. Examples are warning signs concerning safety (e.g., swimming pool rules, emergency procedures, fire exits, etc.). Temporary signs are occasionally needed to warn tenants about a malfunction, a wet floor, or wet paint; however, it is important to remove these signs once the problem is corrected.

Direct Mail.   Every individual is a prospect for housing and most businesses are prospects for office or retail space, but not all of them will be prospects for a particular apartment, office, or store. However, if the legitimate prospects for a particular property can be identified, a direct-mail campaign may be profitable. Identifying prospects with any accuracy is problematic, however. While the production and printing of a direct-mail advertisement is costly, preparing or purchasing the mailing lists is usually even more expensive. Most purchased lists are ineffective for reaching the specialized market of users of office, retail, or even residential rental space. Postage is another concern. Because of the costs involved, direct-mail advertising is *not* a *primary* means of promoting rental real estate.

Press Releases.   The property manager should not hesitate to send a press release about a newsworthy item to the business or real estate editors of local newspapers and broadcast media. Information about a new development can lead to rental inquiries at virtually no cost. To increase the chances of a press release attracting an editor's attention, the following pattern should be employed.

- The name and phone number of a person to contact should be at the top of the page.
- The release should be short—two pages double-spaced at the most; one page is preferable.
- The pertinent information (who, what, when, where, and why) should be contained in the first paragraph.
- The subject should be a legitimate news item, not a veiled advertisement.

Press releases should not be used in place of advertisements; they will not lease space directly. However, they should be planned to maximize their publicity and public relations value.

Broadcast Advertising. Television advertising is occasionally used to lease a new residential development. Television advertising is extremely expensive because both production and air-time costs are high. In certain markets, local advertising is run on cable-access channels. The cost of the air time is usually much lower than network television and the advertisement can be targeted to a specific market based on the programming of the particular channel.

Production and air-time costs for radio advertisements are much lower than they are for television. Radio promotion is used primarily for residential space, although office and retail space may benefit from being advertised on all-news or business stations or programs. Saturday or Sunday afternoon radio commercials may be used to direct drivers to "open house" showings. Weekday "drive time" is also a consideration.

Locator Services and Referrals. Advertising will generally attract the largest proportion of prospective tenants and is therefore the major part of a marketing program. However, two particular methods of *prospecting* for tenants are also valuable. Because both of these services require compensation, use of these services must be budgeted appropriately.

In major cities and many large communities, there are businesses whose sole objective is matching prospective tenants with rental spaces. These *locator services* are more common in the apartment market, and are often called upon to assist people who are relocating into the area. They provide a centralized listing of available rental space, and they usually offer their services directly to the prospect. However, their fee—typically a percentage of the first month's rent—is paid by the owner of the property whose space is rented. In the commercial market, there are leasing agents and real estate brokers who provide a similar service to owners and prospective tenants. These representatives seek out prospects if they work for an owner. If they work for a prospective tenant, they search for office and retail spaces that meet the prospect's criteria. The broker's fee is also related to the negotiated rent and is normally paid by the owner of the leased space.

An excellent source of prospects for any type of property is *referrals.* Satisfied tenants actively discuss their satisfaction with friends and business associates, and this can be encouraged by offering referral incentives. The choice of the incentive to offer and its cost should be evaluated carefully. A rental discount may appear to be the most attractive incentive to offer, but other incentives may be more effective, especially for a residential property. Prospects referred by tenants are usually of the same caliber, and because of this, a referral based on a rental discount may be counterproductive. The most desired referrals are from residents who pay their rent on time and meet the other lease requirements, yet they may hesitate to refer their friends if they feel they are being paid for the referral. On the other hand, residents who have difficulty paying their rent are likely to take advantage of a rental discount offer, and prospects they refer may have similar difficulty paying rent. A good incentive offer is usually indirect (e.g., an improvement to the current resident's apartment, such as a new appliance or fixture, if an acceptable referral becomes a resident). The resident should be required to introduce the referral prospect to the manager in person. This will prevent any questions or conflicts over the referral source or awarding of the incentive. Before instituting any referral incentive program, the manager should investigate any legal limitations on tenant referrals or compensation for them.

Marketing Incentives

The list of incentives and concessions that can be offered to new tenants is endless. Incentives to lease residential space tend to center on courtesies or amenities such as free cable television, a lower security deposit, or interior decorating (paint, wallpaper)—even giving away lottery tickets. Whatever the incentive, it should be in good taste and cast a positive reflection on the property.

Hard times may require strong measures. In areas with high vacancy and a poor economy or a large amount of new competitive space, it is common to offer a period of free rent as a marketing incentive. Such marketing incentives are called *concessions.* Free rent is a costly concession for an owner to make—the reduction in net operating income reduces net proceeds and may reduce the property value. However, if the market is poor and competitors are offering rent-free periods, there may be no choice but to offer such a concession.

Effective Rent

A property manager must understand the concept of effective rent in order to accurately evaluate the ramifications of a rental concession. Effective rent is the cumulative rental amount collected over the term of a lease. If a lease term is twelve months (more common in residential than commercial leasing), the effective rent is the total rent collected during the twelve-month period. When one month's free rent is given as a concession, the effective rent is equal to only eleven months' total rent. Averaged over the entire lease term of twelve months, the rate is less than the quoted rent for the space per month, even though the full quoted amount is collected in those eleven months. However, a period of free rent is preferable to actually reducing the quoted rent because the latter alternative may reduce effective rent for many years, not just one.

Assuming the quoted rent for an apartment is $720 per month and the lease term is twelve months, the total annual rent (effective rent) should be $8,640 ($720 × 12 months). However, a rent concession is necessary to lease the space. If one month is offered rent free, the effective rent will be $7,920 ($720 × 11 months), and the *average* rent collected will be $660 per month ($7,920 ÷ 12 months). On the other hand, if the quoted rent were reduced to $660 per month, the effective rent would also be $7,920 ($660 × 12 months). Because so much income can be lost by lowering quoted rent (in this case over 8%), prudent property management often includes promotion of carefully planned concession packages.

The ramifications of lowering quoted rent are long-term. Suppose greater operating expenses necessitate a rent increase of 5% in the second year. Residents usually anticipate a rent increase when the lease is to be renewed, and 5% probably would be acceptable to most of them. If the rent had been $720 per month, it would now be increased to $756 per month, yielding an effective rent of $9,072 ($756 × 12 months). On the other hand, a $660 monthly rent would yield only $693 per month, an effective rent of $8,316 for the year. Thus reducing the quoted rent in the first year results in even less increased rent in the second year ($756 − $693 = $63, an additional 8% loss of potential income). In order to increase the reduced rent to the level required (from $660 to $756 per month), a 14.5% increase would be necessary. Few residents would be willing to renew their leases under such conditions. That could result in another period of vacancy, and it may be necessary to offer another concession to lease the space again.

The impact of lowering quoted rent is magnified when seen in the context of the whole building or complex. Above all, it reduces NOI and thus the property's value.

Offering an incoming tenant a period of free rent technically reduces the amount of income derived from the rental space. However, the impact of this concession on property value and long-term income is not as great as a straightforward reduction of the rent, provided the rental space is priced competitively. When a financial concession seems necessary, the owner and the property manager must strive to minimize the negative effects of the concession on NOI. At the same time, the owner and the manager must realize that if no concession is offered, the damage to NOI may be more severe.

EXHIBIT 6.2

Weekly Traffic Report (Residential)

Property _____ Week of _____ Prepared by _____

	Mon	Tue	Wed	Thu	Fri	Sat	Sun	Total
Nature of Inquiry								
Telephone call								
Visitor								
Time of inquiry								
Before noon								
Noon to 5 P.M.								
After 5 P.M.								
Referral Source								
Classified ad								
Display ad								
Billboard								
Drive-by								
Telephone directory								
Word of mouth								
Direct mail								
Television								
Radio								
Apartment locator service								
Current resident								
Prior visit								
Apartment Desired								
Studio								
One-bedroom								
Two-bedroom								
Three-bedroom								
Other								

Weather conditions _____

_____

Comments _____

_____

Measuring Marketing Effectiveness

The goal of all marketing programs is to attract as many legitimate rental prospects as possible. The effectiveness of each marketing effort (or advertisement) is measured in terms of the number of prospects who come to the property, the cost to reach them, the number of prospects who become tenants, and the length of time the space remains vacant. The amount of advertising that is necessary depends on the occupancy level. If the property is fully leased and no move-outs are expected, no advertising is necessary. However, most large buildings have continual turnover, and continual advertising is a must.

Location of a property has an effect on the amount of advertising required. The prominence of a property's location may generate enough walk-in traffic to reduce the advertising needed. Less prominent properties may require significantly more promotion to achieve sufficient traffic. No set rule can be used to determine how much advertising is necessary for an individual property, but thinking of advertising as an investment underscores its monetary value. The return on this investment is finding a qualified tenant to fill a vacancy as quickly as possible. With this in mind, advertising expenses should be calculated in terms of the cost per prospect. For example, a property manager spends $100 to advertise in the classified section of the newspaper to fill a vacancy in an apartment building. Because there are very few vacancies in the community, ten prospects respond to this ad, and two of them are intent on signing a lease for this $500-a-month space. The $100 investment certainly would be a value at a cost of $10 per prospect. The number of strongly interested prospects was two out of ten, making the prospect-to-tenant ratio five to one. This ratio is called the *conversion ratio*. The advertising cost, the selected medium, and the length of time before a new tenant is found must be evaluated in relation to the resulting conversion ratio to determine the effectiveness of a particular marketing campaign.

A *traffic report* is commonly used to record what attracted a prospect to visit the subject property. The example shown (exhibit 6.2) is for a residential property, but the same format can be adapted for other property types by modifying the referral sources and the type of space desired. By evaluating traffic reports, the effectiveness of different marketing methods can be determined. The most effective approach is the one that produces the most prospects at the lowest cost per prospect in the least amount of time.

Another management form used to measure marketing effectiveness is a rental inquiry or *prospect card* (exhibit 6.3). The information required in the example can be modified or expanded to meet the needs of any property type. A record of prospects who called or visited a property may be a useful resource if other units become available immediately; it can make additional advertising unnecessary. However, the life of such a prospect list is very short; most potential tenants whose need for space is urgent will usually sign a lease within 30–60 days of beginning their search.

The most that advertising and promotion can do is generate prospects. Prospects become tenants only after visiting the property. The

EXHIBIT 6.3

Prospect Card (Residential)

```
Name of prospect _____
Address _____ Phone _____
Other phone _____
Unit desired _____
Rent desired $_____ Date desired _____
Number of occupants _____
Unit shown _____ Rent quoted $_____
Reason for move _____
Follow-up remarks _____
_____

Date Inquiry Received _____ Inquiry Taken By _____
```

rental space may "sell itself," but regardless of the condition of the available space, there is no guarantee of that happening. The person who shows the rental space to prospects must use sales techniques to try to persuade the prospect that a particular rental space is the best value to accommodate the prospect's particular needs.

There are numerous books about sales techniques, and everyday life offers countless demonstrations of their effectiveness, but three fundamentals must be mastered in regard to leasing.

1. Know the features of the property thoroughly.
2. Discover the needs and wants of each prospect.
3. Demonstrate how the features of the property meet the prospect's needs and wants.

All three are critical; the last is most important of all and must go beyond the obvious. For example, if prospects considering an apartment mention that they have children, simply saying, "There is an elementary school next door," is not sufficient; the prospects most likely noticed the school themselves. Instead, leasing personnel should be able to volunteer detailed information about the school. In fact, they should be thoroughly familiar with the neighborhood (shopping, transportation, etc.) so they can answer specific questions as well as describe the setting in which the property is located. A leasing agent or a property manager leasing office space should be able to inform the prospects about features and businesses in the vicinity that may be of use to prospective office tenants as well as their employees. Examples would be the proximity of business-to-business services such as attorneys and commercial banks as well as information about nearby restaurants, health clubs, public transportation, etc.

Measures of Marketing Effectiveness
* Number of prospects attracted
* The cost to reach each prospect
* Conversion ratio—prospects to signed leases
* Duration of vacancy

Approving a Prospect for Tenancy

In the leasing effort, diligence is necessary to assure that the prospect can and will pay the rent, care for the property, and be a cooperative tenant. Most of this *qualification* process involves financial history, but it should include other pertinent credentials as well. The information to check is usually supplied by the prospect on an application form. Financial records such as existing bank accounts, sources of income, etc., can be verified through a credit bureau. Prospects may be asked to pay a fee for such a credit check, and they customarily leave a refundable deposit with the property manager to reserve the space until such a credit check can be completed. If the prospect is approved, the initial deposit should equal or be applied toward the security deposit rather than the rent, and the remainder of the security deposit should be collected when the lease is signed, if any amount is due. The application form should request the prospect's current and previous addresses so that both landlords can be contacted. The information they can provide about the prospect as their tenant cannot be acquired anywhere else. (Qualification of residential and commercial tenants is discussed in greater detail in chapters 9 and 10, respectively.)

THE LEASE DOCUMENT

The culmination of the marketing activity is a written agreement between the owner and the tenant. By definition, a *lease* is a contract between a landlord (or *lessor*) and a tenant (or *lessee*) for the use or possession of real property for a specified time in exchange for fixed payments (rent). The property manager may sign the lease as the agent of the owner. The contract is legally binding on both parties and should be in writing.

Although any agreement, even an oral one, is legal and enforceable within the bounds of applicable law, provided the intent is clear, good management practice requires a written lease. A written lease offers greater protection to both parties, and it assures the landlord that the space will be occupied for a certain period of time and that a prescribed income can be anticipated for that period. In theory, there should be no financial loss because of a sudden vacancy. The tenant is assured possession of the space for the duration of the lease at a set rental rate. The lease may also outline procedures for rent increases (this is more common in commercial leases).

The lease should reduce or eliminate misunderstandings between the lessor and lessee, so its provisions must be understood by both of them. New tenants should be asked if they have read the lease and understand it. Any provisions that are unclear should be explained at that time.

The property manager should use a lease form that is reasonable, standardized, and suitable for all tenants. As a matter of goodwill, the lease form should not contain clauses to which informed people will object or that uninformed people will ignore. When properly prepared and presented with equal emphasis on the tenant's point of view, the lease has excellent marketing value.

Fundamental Elements of Leases

There are numerous leases suited to different types of rental space, but all leases should describe the *demised premises* (the leased space that is conveyed from the owner to the tenant), the duration of the agreement, and the amount and method of rent payment. The following are the principal contents of a lease.

- *The parties.* The full names of the landlord and tenant, both of whom must sign the lease to validate it.
- *Description of the leased premises.* The apartment number and address of the building for residential units; the amount of space (square feet), location in the building, and street address for offices, stores, etc., often augmented by a legal description and a floor plan.
- *Lease term.* The duration of the lease (including the date it becomes effective and the date on which it ends) and any specific provisions relating to renewal or cancellation. Commercial leases may show separate dates for occupancy and first rent payment when construction is involved.
- *Rent.* The amount of rent to be paid each period and the date it is due. Rent is usually paid monthly and due on the first of the month. The aggregate rent for the entire lease term may be stated (most commonly in commercial leases) to indicate the full financial obligation. Commercial leases often include provisions for rent increases, especially when their duration exceeds one year. (Nonpayment of rent is cause for termination of the lease.)
- *Use of the premises.* Inherent in the lease agreement is a specific use of the space (living quarters, a business office, an apparel store), and any other use may be cause for termination of the lease.
- *Other provisions.* Leases usually include lengthy clauses that detail the rights and obligations of the parties with respect to their relationship to each other (as landlord and tenant) and to the property.

Of particular concern are the responsibilities to pay specific utilities and to maintain the property. The amount and condition for return of any required security deposit is also stated.

Types and Nature of Leases

The type of lease that is used depends on the kind of property. There are three basic types of leases. The first of these is a *gross lease,* under which the tenant pays a fixed rent and the owner pays all of the operating expenses of the property, including property taxes and insurance. The common residential lease is a form of gross lease. Residents are usually responsible for utilities (electricity, cooking gas) *inside* their apartments.

The second type of lease is a *net lease,* under which the tenant not only pays rent but also assumes responsibility for certain expenses connected with the property as a whole. Net leases are used primarily for space in large office buildings, shopping centers, and other commercial property that is rented for longer terms. The itemized pass-through expenses cited in net leases are generally prorated based on the amount of space occupied by the tenant as a percentage of the total leasable space in the building. (Net leases are discussed in chapter 10.)

A third type of lease, the *percentage lease,* is sometimes used for retail properties. Under a percentage lease, the rent is a percentage of the tenant's gross sales made on the premises. The lease usually states a fixed minimum rent, and the tenant pays a percentage of gross sales in excess of that amount, depending on the volume of business.

COLLECTIONS

The crux of effective property management is collecting rent and other amounts due from tenants. As with all other aspects of tenant relations, tact, diplomacy, and goodwill are essential, but the manager must also be firm in requiring rent to be paid on the date it is due. Operating costs, taxes, and other expenses of the property are paid out of the rental income, and they accumulate day to day. Timely collection of rents is imperative for timely payment of the property's bills. In addition, the manager's compensation is usually based on a percentage of the total rent collected, and any decline in that amount reduces the manager's income. These two concerns—operating expenses and personal compensation—are the manager's incentives to collect the full amount of rent on time.

Rental Collection Policy

It is an accepted practice that rent is paid in advance. Monthly rents are usually due on the first day of each month, although some may be paid on the lease date. (If the lease is signed on the 19th of the month, the rent is likewise due on the 19th.) To streamline accounting, rent collections, and payment of the property expenses, all leases should have rent due on the same date. To do this effectively, the first month's rent should be prorated for tenants who do not take possession on the first of a month.

Most tenants pay their rent on the date it is due, but inevitably some will be late. There are two significant reasons for not tolerating any delay in rent payments: (1) Rent is one of the largest expenses of most tenants, and each day's delay increases the chances that the whole amount for that month will not be received. (2) Acceptance of a partial payment increases the tenant's obligation in the following month, and the tenant's financial situation may not be improved.

Some managers and owners state that they expect payment in full by the first of the month, and they impose late fees as a reinforcement of their policy. Late fees may be a residual source of income for management, but the delay in receiving the rent and accounting for the fees tend to cancel any expected benefit. A small late fee actually encourages late payment because such a policy has an inherent grace period associated with it. For example, if an extra charge is imposed for payments received on the sixth of the month or later, there is no compelling reason to pay the rent until the fifth. If late fees are used, they should be large enough to strongly encourage prompt payment. Some municipalities limit the maximum late fee that can be charged on residential rent, and this must be a consideration as well.

Delinquency.   Delinquency, collection, and eviction rights and procedures are *always* controlled by statute. The property manager must be familiar with and understand both the laws and the practices that govern these matters. Local law may be more favorable to tenants than to landlords, and there may even be differences from the laws in nearby municipalities. The property manager's efforts should encourage payment on the first. That policy justifies distributing notices of delinquency very early in the month, followed by a personal contact soon thereafter if payment is not received.

All tenants should have a clear understanding of the rental collection policy before they move in. This includes what action will be taken in case of delinquency. However, the manager must be careful not to compromise any of the owner's legal rights by presenting a policy that is more lenient than the law requires. The policy can be explained in a firm manner that does not jeopardize the extension of goodwill toward the tenant. Some property owners fear that aggressive pursuit of rent will result in vacancies. They hesitate even more when the market is declining and vacancy in general is high. During these periods, managers sometimes tolerate substantial rent delinquencies rather than take action to collect the rent or evict the delinquent tenant. However, a vacant unit is less costly than one that is occupied by a delinquent tenant—when a space is vacant, it is less likely to be damaged and utility costs will be lower. More importantly, the vacancy allows the property manager to find a new tenant who will pay rent.

Even though the great majority of tenants will pay their rent when it is due, the few who do not will be responsible for the majority of the time that must be devoted to collection. The effectiveness of a collection procedure depends on the diligence of the people in control of it. A series of forms is the basis of a good collection system. A notice should be sent to the tenant on the first day the rent is delinquent. This notice should be a strongly worded but friendly reminder. The check may be delayed in the mail, so the reminder notice should simply state that the rent has not been received in the office and ask the tenant to contact the office about the matter. Personal contact by the manager is also appropriate at this point.

Eviction.   If there is no response to the reminder notice and the rent is still delinquent, the next step is to send a further notice (which may be an eviction notice or such other notice as may be required by state or local law to initiate eviction). This notice should be a demand that the tenant pay the rent within a specified period or vacate the premises within that same period. (By law, such a notice may automatically terminate the lease, so the property manager must understand its effect.)

The period of time allowed and the form and content of the notice are prescribed by state and/or local law. If a late fee is permitted, that amount should also be stated. In some states, an owner may accept a partial payment of the amount due without jeopardizing the effectiveness of the notice or the owner's right to bring suit. Because an error can lead to liability of the owner or the property manager to a tenant, an attorney must be consulted to determine the requirements of state and local law.

If a tenant refuses to pay all the delinquent rent specified in the notice or is violating the lease in some other way and has failed to cease or cure the violation within an allotted time period, the manager can begin eviction proceedings. (The property manager should not begin an eviction without the owner's approval. The management agreement should expressly grant the property manager discretion to evict tenants or specify a procedure for obtaining the owner's approval.)

Eviction is ejection of a tenant from the leased premises by the landlord. It is a drastic measure. It can result in the forcible removal of the tenant's possessions from the premises if the tenant refuses to move out. The gravity of eviction and the need for court action virtually mandate action by an attorney. State laws governing eviction vary widely, but most provide for the property owners or their attorneys to serve eviction notices or notices to cure a lease violation within a specified period. Municipalities frequently have laws concerning evictions and tenants' rights as well. The law may preclude the property manager from being involved.

In the case of nonpayment, if the tenant has not responded to the demand for payment within the time allowed, a complaint must be filed with the court, usually by an attorney. The complaint prompts the court to issue a summons to appear in court, and that document is served on the tenant with the complaint. A third party, such as a sheriff or private process server, delivers the summons. If the summons and complaint cannot be delivered personally to an occupant, state or local laws will specify alternate procedures, which *must be followed rigidly*; sometimes a notice may be affixed face-up on the front door of the premises or in a conspicuous place.

The complete form usually includes an affidavit of service (a sworn statement that the notice has been properly served), which is filled out by the person who serves the notice. This affidavit is then presented in court. The form must be filled out and delivered *exactly* as stipulated by the legal procedures specified in it and by state and local law or court rule, or it may be ruled invalid. The internal policy of serving the eviction notice should be reviewed to assure that the notice is being served impartially. Any procedural inconsistency may permit the tenant to avoid the eviction (necessitating a complete restart of the process) or leave the tenant with a claim for a countersuit. The tenant should not be harassed or intimidated—or denied access to or use of the rental unit or specific services; such actions can also be cause for a countersuit.

In court, the tenant may be given an opportunity to pay the rent. At this point, state or local law will determine whether the landlord has a legal obligation to accept the rent. However, if the tenant offers to pay, the judge may direct the lessor to accept payment. If the tenant cannot pay, the judge will usually render a decision or award judgment in favor of the landlord—for possession, for rent due, and (possibly) for court costs. As part of the judgment, the tenant will be given a date by which to vacate the premises. If the tenant does not yield the space by that date, further procedures will be dictated by state and local law—in some jurisdictions, dispossession by the sheriff follows automatically; in others, the owner or the owner's attorney obtains a writ of possession, and if that is ignored, the owner or owner's attorney may have to return to court to obtain a writ of eviction which orders a court officer to physically eject and dispossess the tenant. (State laws vary; some may require only the writ or order of possession to eject a tenant.)

Eviction can involve a considerable sum of money, although it should be possible to negotiate a reasonable fee with an attorney who specializes in evictions. Even in the best circumstances, eviction may require months to complete. Aside from eviction for nonpayment, there are two other types of eviction: Cause (other than nonpayment of rent) and no-cause.

Eviction for cause relates to a breach of the lease (e.g., a resident who keeps a pet when the lease stipulates no pets allowed). No-cause eviction is the landlord calling an end to a lease (used to terminate a month-to-month lease). The primary reason to distinguish the three types of eviction is that they involve three different procedures. It is particularly difficult to win an eviction for cause (other than nonpayment of rent) in court.

The best way to minimize the need for eviction is to be diligent in selecting tenants—perform credit checks and verify credentials for all prospects prior to their signing leases. Although the staff of a property must be diligent and prompt in taking action when rent is late or if any section of the lease is not respected, the most effective means to maintain harmony on the property is to give the tenants the respect they deserve. If tenants are treated properly and professionally, if they are given prompt service, and if their privacy is respected, the great majority of them will faithfully observe the requirements of the lease.

Security Deposits

In addition to rent payments, most residential leases and commercial leases require a *security deposit* to be paid in advance and held as a guarantee to ensure the lessee's performance under the lease. The amount of the security deposit is often equivalent to one month's rent, although it can be any amount. Managers should not permit tenants to apply the security deposit to the last month's rent; if the premises are damaged, the deposit will not cover both repair expenses and the rent. The deposit must be large enough to be an incentive for taking care of the premises, but that does not always necessitate the equivalent of one month's rent. On the other hand, a leased residence that includes furnishings has greater potential for damage, and a larger security deposit is warranted.

If the tenant fulfills all obligations of the lease, the security deposit must be returned in a reasonable amount of time after the tenant moves. This period of time is often dictated by local ordinance. However, the deposit should be held until damage charges can be itemized and deducted. This should be done quickly so the space can be made market-ready right away. If feasible, the property manager should inspect the unit in the tenant's presence on the last day of the lease to explain the need for damage or cleaning charges. (Financial management of security deposits is discussed in chapter 4.)

ACCOMMODATING TENANTS

The most important element in keeping tenants satisfied with their choice of rental space is to make it known that their business is valued. Rent is usually a major expense for tenants, and for that they expect the components of the building to operate properly and efficiently, and they expect the property as a whole to be pleasant, comfortable, and secure.

Between the time that one tenant vacates a unit and another tenant moves in, the property staff should inspect the unit to make sure all components are operating and are properly installed. Thorough inspection and repair at this time will avert dissatisfaction of the incoming tenant. If a repair cannot be completed until after move-in, the new tenant should be told approximately when the task will be finished.

Incoming tenants also should receive a handbook that outlines the rules and regulations of tenancy as well as a list of important names and phone numbers. Emergencies and nonemergencies should also be defined. Management and staff of residential properties in particular may receive calls at any time of day unless guidelines are provided. Although a resident should never be dissuaded from calling about a problem, he or she should be able to distinguish a repair that can wait from one that is a true emergency. A sluggish kitchen drain discovered late at night is annoying but usually can be attended to the next day; a broken water pipe, on the other hand, warrants immediate attention.

In some respects, tenants are more concerned about receiving an honest response than about having a problem corrected immediately. They would much prefer a forthright estimate of when a problem will be corrected over a promised, "We will be right over," when no one will come.

Tenants will at times request improved services or products, and all of these requests must be dealt with respectfully, conscientiously, and promptly; they should not be considered "complaints." Although some tenants may think the motto, "the customer is always right," grants them the privilege to make outrageous requests or demands, most understand the limitations involved in operating a property. All requests should receive a response as quickly as possible. However, requests that are particularly complex may require research, and the tenant should be advised of that fact and told when an answer may be expected. Not all requests can be granted, and it may be tempting to delay a negative response (saying the decision must be made by someone else or that the request is still under consideration). It is never easy to say "no," but delivering bad news as quickly as good news will gain the confidence of most tenants.

Building a business relationship with tenants requires months or even years, especially if the property manager is new to the site and some of the tenants have been there for several years. Any dissatisfaction with the previous property manager or management firm will have to be dispelled. Tenant dissatisfaction can be very damaging in terms of both current occupancy and the property's reputation into the future. Legitimate concerns such as deficiencies in service can be rectified, although it may be almost

---

Reasons to Encourage Renewal
* Eliminate vacancy loss
* Save cost of advertising
* Save cost of new tenant improvements
* Avert dealing with the unknown

---

impossible to regain the respect of the tenants if service was substandard for a long time.

Every communication with tenants is an opportunity to build goodwill. Special events sponsored by the property management (e.g., a picnic or outing for a "tenant appreciation day") can build morale. Newsletters are also used effectively by both residential and commercial developments to update tenants about events on or near the site or to provide other information that pertains to all building occupants.

RENEWAL TECHNIQUES

Lease renewals are very important in the overall economics of property performance. Renewing the lease of an existing tenant is usually more profitable than finding a new tenant for the space for several reasons.

* Renewal eliminates the vacancy loss that occurs when a new tenant does not move in as soon as the current tenant moves out.
* The expense of finding a new tenant (marketing the space) is averted.
* The cost of improvements related to a renewal is usually less than the cost of preparing the space for a new tenant.
* The current tenant is a known quantity (payment history, level of respect for the property and the other tenants), and evaluating prospects entails the investment of both time and money.

Only tenants who are satisfied with the property and the service they receive will renew their leases. In this regard, every contact with the tenant is an indirect renewal contact. There are reasons for not renewing a lease that are beyond a manager's control, but if the tenant is under no pressure to move, renewal of a lease is a reasonable expectation. However, market conditions usually change during the lease term; rents may go up or down, and vacancy may be increasing or decreasing. Lease expiration usually requires negotiating new lease terms. The starting point may be whether the parties are willing to renew the lease, and the conclusion may be whether the proposed terms are acceptable. The principal bargaining points are:

1. The amount of any rental increase.
2. The length of the new lease term.
3. The extent of repairs, service, and rehabilitation to be performed as a condition of renewal.

Both parties usually expect the rent to increase, but the exact amount may be subject to negotiation, depending on market conditions. Renewal terms are more likely to be negotiated for commercial leases, and the negotiations may be as comprehensive as for a new lease.

To facilitate lease renewals, two basic administrative tasks must be performed. First, the manager should make a list of all tenants' lease expiration dates. This should be updated monthly to show renewal progress. Second, a letter should be prepared and mailed to tenants whose leases are about to expire. The timing of renewal negotiation should be adequate for tenants to make their decisions and for the manager to find replacements for those who decide to move. For residential tenants, renewal notices are usually mailed sixty to ninety days in advance of lease expiration; for commercial tenants with long-term leases, renewal negotiations may have to begin a year or more in advance.

SUMMARY

Throughout the cycle of tenancy, a property manager's dedication to goodwill is essential for the property to thrive. The manager must examine the property and its potential tenants to estimate the size and nature of the market and to plan the marketing strategy. By persuasively matching the qualities of the property with the prospect's expressed needs and wants, the property manager attempts to convert the prospect into a tenant. If the prospective tenant's credentials are acceptable, a written lease is executed to protect both parties to the agreement.

One of the most important aspects of tenant relations is collection of deposits and rent. In enforcing the collection policies, the manager must treat all tenants fairly. To meet the expectations of the owner, the manager must firmly uphold the policy on when rent is due. If the tenant is unable or unwilling to pay, or if some other serious infraction of the lease occurs, eviction proceedings must be started.

Tenants frequently ask for repairs and services. These should be handled conscientiously and impartially to provide the tenants with the best service possible. The way the tenant has been treated throughout each phase of the cycle of tenancy will have a strong bearing on lease renewal. The manager should regard lease renewal as both an expression of goodwill toward the tenant and a part of the sound economic operation of the property.

Key Terms

Advertising	Lessee
Concession	Lessor
Conversion ratio	Net lease
Eviction	Percentage lease
Gross lease	Prospect card
Lease	Security deposit
Lease term	Traffic report

Key Points

Marketing plan development and evaluation
Determining the market profile
The range of advertising media
The economics of advertising
Rental collection policy
Eviction notification and procedure
Managing tenant requests for services
Lease renewal as a process

Staffing for Property Management

It is assumed throughout this text that the property manager is employed by a management firm rather than directly by the owner. The responsibilities of a property manager are:

- Assure that all components of the property are safe and operable.
- Maintain the property in good condition.
- Establish rents that are marketable; know the competition.
- Find tenants for properties.
- Collect rent and other fees; properly account for these funds; prepare long- and short-term budgets.
- If authorized, pay any expenses the property incurs.
- Manage employees of the management firm and staff at the site.
- Plan for the property's future.
- Report to the property owner.

Rarely does one property manager perform all of the tasks inherent in these responsibilities. Nevertheless it is the property manager's duty to assure that all of this work is accomplished. There are three ways to do this: (1) hire staff to work on the site, (2) assign employees of the management firm to work at the site, or (3) contract with others to provide the necessary work force. In essence, a property manager may serve as a bridge between the on-site personnel (maintenance, clerical, and site administration) and the property management firm employees (accounting, leasing and marketing, and clerical workers). The property manager may be the supervisor of all of these individuals and may report to a senior or executive property manager in the management firm.

132

In order to hire, develop, and retain a qualified staff, principals of property management firms should consider the reasons a client's property or portfolio is being managed by the firm. The relationship between the property owner's goals and the property manager's goals is the foundation of the relationship between the manager and the staff. The employees must understand the manager's goals and work toward fulfilling them by cooperatively applying their abilities. They must believe that meeting these goals is a worthy endeavor and that they are being treated fairly. In fact, the employees must recognize the relationship between the manager and the owner, understand how the goals of these two entities relate to each other, and appreciate how individual efforts contribute to the success of the enterprise. The owner, the manager, the staff, the tenants, and the property itself should all benefit from the relationship.

REQUIREMENTS FOR SKILLED LABOR

Technically, on-site staff may be employees of the property owner who are supervised by the manager. Employees of the management firm may provide services to more than one property, and their services to a particular property are part of the contractual arrangement with the property owner. Outside contractors are often used for types of work that require skills or equipment that exceed what a single property or even a management firm can utilize on an ongoing basis (e.g., elevator maintenance and repair).

The execution of the tasks necessary to manage the property requires cooperation among on-site staff, management firm employees, and contractors. Each specific task must be assigned to one of these groups. Routine maintenance is most likely done by on-site staff. Lawn care, window washing, and painting may be contracted out. Accounting, marketing administration, and leasing are not necessarily on-site tasks, although visits to the site by marketing and leasing personnel are necessary. Administrative functions may be carried out exclusively by personnel in the property management firm's central office.

On-Site Staff

The on-site staff of a property comprise the human component that makes the property operate efficiently. Such staff members technically may be employees of the property owner rather than the property manager. However, the property manager or other employees of the management firm may actually hire, train, and supervise the on-site staff in addition to processing their payroll, and this sometimes raises a question as to who is the true employer of on-site staff—the owner, the property manager, or the property management firm. Even though a management agreement may stipulate that the owner is the employer of the on-site staff, a court may

E X H I B I T   7.1

Sample Organizational Chart

Staff for a 100-Unit Apartment Building

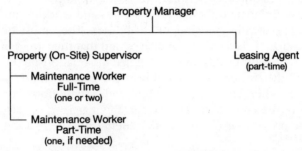

Property Manager

Property (On-Site) Supervisor

Leasing Agent
(part-time)

Maintenance Worker
Full-Time
(one or two)

Maintenance Worker
Part-Time
(one, if needed)

This chart shows the approximate number of staff members and the levels of authority and reporting that may exist for a "typical" 100-unit apartment complex. The age of a building, its layout, and the level of service required all affect the number of personnel needed. An "administrative assistant" may be hired full- or part-time to type correspondence and handle accounting and record-keeping functions. A resident services staff for this size property is unlikely.

rule that they are employees of the manager or management firm because of the circumstances of their employment. Regardless of who employs the on-site staff, their wages are paid out of the operating funds of the property. On-site staff members normally work at only one site. However, if a property owner or management company has several buildings which are near each other, staff members may be assigned to all of the buildings and not just one of them.

The most important factors that determine the size of the property staff are the size and layout of the property and its type. These factors mandate how much work must be done on site. All properties require on-site work, but many are too small to justify a regular part-time or full-time staff member. The cost of hiring a staff member must be weighed against the cost of leaving the work undone or having it done by a contractor. Leaving the work undone is usually the most expensive alternative because the competitive strength and the value of the property will decrease as a result. In actuality, the manager must determine how to have the work completed for the least cost.

If a property requires sufficient maintenance and repair work to occupy one or more people full-time, hiring skilled staff is usually the most economical approach. However, an individual with a single skill (e.g., carpentry, plumbing) would not be hired on a full-time basis. Large properties that include complex operating systems are more likely to employ skilled personnel to routinely maintain these systems. A small property

E X H I B I T   7.2

Sample Organizational Chart

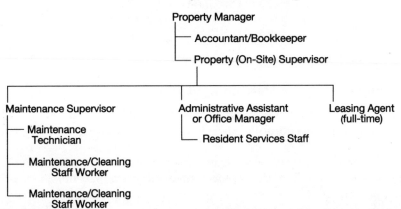

Residential On-Site Staff
for a 300-Unit Apartment Building

Property Manager
— Accountant/Bookkeeper
— Property (On-Site) Supervisor

Maintenance Supervisor
— Maintenance Technician
— Maintenance/Cleaning Staff Worker
— Maintenance/Cleaning Staff Worker

Administrative Assistant or Office Manager
— Resident Services Staff

Leasing Agent (full-time)

This chart shows the approximate number of staff members and the levels of authority and reporting that may exist for a "typical" 300-unit apartment complex. Specific positions will vary with the complexity of the individual property (e.g., resident services staff might include any or all of the following, and perhaps more than one person in each position: lifeguard, concierge, front desk personnel, weight trainer).

that requires only occasional repairs amounting to less than a day's work every week or so will be better served by one or more contracts for skilled labor as needed. A contract laborer usually earns a higher hourly wage than a full-time employee; however, a contract for labor as needed means that money paid is for specific work done and actual hours worked. The need to maintain payroll taxes and forms is also averted.

The most common on-site work is maintenance, but many other duties at a property may require part-time or full-time staff. If the property has its own office, an office manager or full-time clerical worker may be warranted. The presence of recreational amenities such as pools and weight rooms may require part-time employment of lifeguards and trainers in addition to specialized custodial staff. Front desks in large developments must be staffed during times the building is open if not around the clock. Large luxury apartment buildings may have door attendants, concierges, and cleaning personnel. A large staff may also necessitate employing supervisory personnel (maintenance manager, services manager, etc.), all of whom would report to the property supervisor or property manager. For comparison, sample organizational charts for on-site staff to operate representative 100- and 300-unit apartment buildings are shown in exhibits 7.1 and 7.2. (Other on-site duties are discussed in chapters 8, 9, and 10.)

**Factors that Determine
Management Firm Staffing**
* Number of properties managed
* Types of properties managed
* Level of service required
* Size and tenancy of managed properties
* Number of clients (property owners) served
* Location of managed properties
* On-site staff at managed properties

Employees of the Management Firm

The size of a management firm and the range of services it offers depend on the extent of its portfolio. Management firms often begin as two-person enterprises—a property manager starts an independent property management firm with one or a few clients, and most likely hires a second person to do clerical work. This employee may only work part-time; there may not be enough work to warrant full-time employment at first. The clerical employee of a new property management firm may be responsible for several different office activities, such as typing correspondence, answering phones, accounting and record keeping, balancing bank accounts, and making bank deposits. As more contracts are secured, additional employees may be hired—a full-time administrative assistant, and then perhaps a bookkeeper. As the size of the firm's portfolio increases, greater specialization of staff members' roles becomes necessary. Specialization reduces the number of daily interruptions of one specific assignment by an unrelated task that has the same or greater priority. However, it is often necessary to assign numerous unrelated tasks to one individual, especially in small firms with limited economic means.

A property manager in charge of a management firm must continually ask two questions regarding the size of the management firm's staff. (1) Is it large enough to give every client timely and accurate service? (2) Is it adequate to perform its own administrative tasks? When a firm's portfolio is rather small, one or two employees in addition to the property manager may be able to provide tenant services, client services, and routine office administration. However, if the management firm is to expand, or if clients require additional services at some point, the cost of additional staff must be compared with both the service requirements of the firm's clients and the needs of the property management firm itself. The number of staff members and their level of specialization within the management firm depend on six factors:

1. *Number of properties the firm manages.* A fledgling management firm usually has very few accounts, so the expense of a management support staff may be neither justified nor feasible. Most of the

administrative work will be done by the property manager initially. With more accounts, however, it may become necessary to hire additional property managers or property supervisors to handle the day-to-day management of individual properties. Property managers normally oversee several properties; property supervisors usually oversee only a few sites. Managers can be assigned by property type, by owner, by geographic proximity, or by number of units. This level of specialization allows the founding property manager more time to seek new clients. A secretarial staff may be employed in the central office to relieve the property managers of some of their administrative functions.

2. *Types of properties in the portfolio.* Most management firms specialize in office, retail, or residential property, although a number of them manage any type of property with equal ability. A firm with a large number of diverse property types in its portfolio may be organized into divisions according to property type; in which case, each division will most likely have its own leasing and marketing personnel.

3. *Property size and number of tenants per property.* Dealing with tenants in each phase of the cycle of tenancy (chapter 6) requires a significant amount of work, so actual and potential numbers of tenants affect the size of the firm's administrative and support staff. The potential number of tenants is based on the number of existing units in each property that is managed or the capacity for its square footage to be subdivided into leasable spaces. The size of the marketing and leasing staff is influenced by the total number of units or square footage involved and the frequency of turnover; as a general rule, residential properties require more tenant contact than office or retail properties. The number of tenants affects accounting requirements, and that is reflected in the size of the accounting department staff. A property of substantial size may require the assignment of full-time firm employees to that property alone, even though their duties may be performed at the management firm office and not on site.

4. *Number of clients the firm has.* Just as the potential and actual tenant population influences the size of the firm's staff, the number of owners served influences the reporting, accounting, and administrative workload of the management firm. Each client usually requires a separate accounting file subdivided for specific properties. Clients may have unique needs for which time must be allotted. Some property owners—institutional owners in particular—may request or require their reports to conform to their standard formats, and they may request multiple reports to be sent to various investors or partners.

5. *Proximity of the managed properties to each other.* Proximity de-

pends on the type of property being managed. A management firm that specializes in super regional shopping centers is more likely to have a multistate or nationwide clientele than one that manages residential property exclusively. A site manager and some support staff may be required for each property if the properties are located in different counties or states. However, with advances in telecommunications, many functions may be completed efficiently and quickly at the management firm's headquarters. In an urban area where several properties are in very close proximity, a single property supervisor or property manager may be able to manage several properties because travel time is reduced.

6. *Size of on-site staff.* The size of the on-site staff may influence the amount of involvement a property manager has with the property. When there is a large staff working on site, the property manager or property supervisor may have to devote more time to that property alone, thus limiting his or her availability to manage other properties.

The staff requirements of a management firm can grow for many reasons, particularly in areas of responsibility that are not related directly to property management. So much mail may flow through a large firm that a mail room supervisor is necessary. Data entry and retrieval may demand a management information systems (MIS) specialist. While these personnel are not directly involved with property management, their presence means property managers and property supervisors can do their jobs without distraction. The potential for the business of a property management firm to expand is great, and the number of people it employs will grow accordingly. In contrast, the potential for an on-site staff to expand is small—the number of people employed directly at a property rarely increases because changes made to a property are usually not significant enough to alter the size or organization of the staff. (Addition of leasable space would be the exception.) Actually, on-site staff may be reduced as technology lessens the need for specific skills or eliminates jobs altogether—e.g., elevator operators were once essential but are now rare. (Exhibit 7.3 shows a sample organizational chart for a 25-member management firm.)

Contractors

Because hiring employees is expensive, contracting labor for temporary or intermittent tasks can be economical. Contractors can be hired by the property owner or by the management firm, depending on whether the work is limited to one property or is needed by the firm's central office. Contract workers at a site usually perform infrequent maintenance tasks

E X H I B I T   7.3

Sample Organizational Chart
for a Management Firm

Management Firm Owner ————————————— Administrative Assistant
  (Chief Executive Officer)

— Office Manager or Receptionist

— Chief Financial Officer ————————————— Administrative Assistant

  — Accountant

  — Accountant

  — Accountant

— Executive Property Manager ——————————— Administrative Assistant
    (Vice President)

  — Senior Property Manager ——————————— Administrative Assistant

    — Property Manager

    — Property Manager

    — Property Manager

  — Senior Property Manager ——————————— Administrative Assistant

    — Property Manager

    — Property Manager

    — Property Manager

  — Senior Property Manager ——————————— Administrative Assistant

    — Property Manager

    — Property Manager

    — Property Manager

This chart suggests job titles and levels of authority that may be encountered in a
property management firm. Each of the senior property managers may be responsible
for a specific property type (e.g., apartments, office buildings, shopping centers.)

that require special training (elevator maintenance, roof repair, or remodeling). Seasonal services (lawn care, snow removal, decorating, exterior painting, window washing) are often contracted, too. Part-time or
temporary help may be employed in the management office itself, especially for administrative work such as filing or accounting. Temporary employees can be contracted for a day, a week, or longer. Companies that
specialize in providing skilled labor for maintenance, as well as clerical
and administrative duties, are common in large cities.

On site or in a small firm, leasing may be assigned to a staff member in conjunction with other administrative duties. However, very large properties or those with high vacancy rates or frequent turnovers may benefit from having a full-time leasing agent. Initial lease-up of a new or renovated property also demands full-time attention. Leasing is one property management task that is often successfully contracted. A contract with a leasing agent may be particularly economical for a property with few vacancies. Apart from the need for their specialized expertise, a leasing agent or broker on contract is usually paid a commission for each lease successfully negotiated.

Determining Adequate Staff Size

Providing an adequate staff for a property or a management firm—or both—requires careful planning and a close examination of resources. The first step in this process is to list the tasks that must be done and estimate the amount of time required for each task on a weekly or monthly basis. The initial assessment may be very detailed, accounting for everything from the time necessary to pull weeds from flower beds to the time required to collect rent. The final compilation may resemble a budget, except that hours of work per week or per month would be the primary quantitative measures rather than dollars and cents. Analysis of the resulting list should indicate how many workers are necessary for efficient operation and adequate service to the tenants and the property owner.

The size and type of the property as well as particular tenant requirements understandably influence the preparation of this list. Once all functions are noted and the average amount of time for each is calculated, the various duties can be grouped together by category. These groupings may be the basis for job descriptions or for setting up departments (maintenance, administration, etc.). The groupings can also be used to decide how many full-time and part-time workers are needed, as well as which tasks may be completed most economically by using outside contractors. To be accurate, any estimate of the number of workers required must also allow for days off (sick time, vacations). Such time "budgets" may be prepared for each property as well as for the management firm. When there is duplication of duties, further evaluation should be done to decide whether the duplication is necessary or if consolidation is possible.

HIRING QUALIFIED PERSONNEL

One of the largest ongoing investments of property owners and property managers is in the staff they employ. To build a capable and dedicated staff, careful attention must be paid to the recruitment and selection processes. Beyond that, many hours and dollars must be invested in continual

training and development of the staff. There are several ways to find qualified candidates for specific positions, including promotion of current employees, help-wanted advertisements, employment agencies, and personal
referrals.

Promotion is an effective way to retain and increase the value of excellent employees. Some believe that promotion from within doubles the
cost of training because the person who is promoted and the successor to
that person's former position must be trained simultaneously. The initial
training expense may be slightly higher, but promotion can be highly rewarding and is often more efficient. The promoted employee is already
familiar with the company and may even understand the new position
quite well. If time allows, the person who is promoted may be able to train
his or her successor, thus reducing the demands on the trainee's supervisor. Also, the newcomer enters a lower-level position, a situation that
provides room for his or her individual growth within the company rather
than fostering a need to seek opportunities outside of it.

Help-wanted advertisements generate quick responses. Such an advertisement can yield hundreds of candidates, but many of them will be
either overqualified or underqualified for the position. Filtering out the
most qualified candidates is often burdensome. To facilitate the screening
process, the help-wanted advertisement should instruct respondents to
submit a resume, work history, or other pertinent information that
matches them to the position's requirements. Newspapers commonly
offer the opportunity to use a box number rather than the employer's address and phone number. Such box numbers preclude receiving a deluge
of phone calls and letters from hopeful candidates, which require staff time
and other expenses for direct responses and follow-up by the employers.

Employment agencies can also be useful for finding qualified candidates for a position. A detailed job description and a list of minimum job
specifications must be given to the agency so it can screen candidates for
the skills or experience necessary for the available position. The agency
spares the employer the time required for such screening; the employer
interviews only the most qualified candidates. Such time and work savings
can be substantial, especially if the employer's staff does not include a personnel recruiter or if the position to be filled requires specialized skills. A
consideration, however, is the agency's fee, which may be the equivalent
of a month's salary or a percentage of the annual salary for the position
being filled.

Personal referrals from current employees of the company or from
acquaintances of the property manager can be very valuable. Such prospects usually know something about the company already, and they are
most likely capable individuals or they would not have been referred. Another source for referrals is through professional activities. Membership
in professional organizations can provide many contacts that allow prop-

erty managers and other real estate professionals to keep up-to-date with local business activities, including who is working for what companies and how well those people are doing. Established professional relationships can help a property manager locate the right person for a position and check his or her credentials quickly.

In addition to a company's active recruiting, unsolicited resumes and applications may be received at the property or the management firm occasionally. These should be examined when they are received, even if no positions are available. Information sent in this manner is often evidence of an applicant who has sound qualifications and a sincere interest in working for the property or the firm. If such an applicant appears to have the proper credentials, his or her resume or application should be kept on file. All who inquire about possible employment should receive a letter in response, regardless of whether their inquiry will be retained. The reputation of a company is one of its greatest assets, and even a letter of rejection can impress its recipient favorably. Such goodwill is especially important in the property management business. At some point, the rejected candidate may be in a position to affect something the management company wants (e.g., a lease) or the company and the applicant may consider each other for a career opportunity again in the future.

Regardless of how a prospective employee is recruited, all candidates should complete an employment application form. Such a form organizes and standardizes the information needed to make the hiring decision. A personal interview is generally necessary before a final decision on employment is made. In addition to finding out if the candidate is capable, interviews help managers to ascertain if the applicant is compatible with the requirements of the job and willing to work toward the goals of the property owner or the management firm. Those who are not offered the job should receive a rejection letter promptly as a matter of business goodwill, but the letter should not be sent until after the selected candidate has formally accepted the offer of employment.

Although some of the reasons for selecting one candidate over another are subjective, the promise of capability combined with demonstrated reliability are usually the main factors in selecting a new employee. Gender, race, age, religion, sexual orientation, or creed should not enter the decision, nor should such factors ever influence the compensation of a current employee, the compensation offered to an applicant, or any other decision affecting an employee or applicant. Title VII of the *Civil Rights Act,* which is enforced by the United States *Equal Employment Opportunity Commission* prohibits discrimination against employees and applicants for employment.

The importance of nondiscrimination in the workplace goes beyond legal compliance. The population of the United States is extremely varied. People from all races and creeds own and rent property. To provide own-

---

Information for Employees
* Company description and history
* Company policies and procedures
* Employment rules
* Employee benefits
* Department and company organization
* Job description

---

ers and renters with superior service, the staff of the property and the management firm should reflect the diversity of the community. The ability to work with, and for, people whose backgrounds are varied is an asset of incalculable worth.

ORIENTATION OF NEW PERSONNEL

All new employees should undergo training and orientation, regardless of their competence or familiarity with their new duties. Every company has a unique culture and a particular way of doing things. New employees must be properly introduced to the work environment to make them fully productive as quickly as possible. Each employee should have a copy of his or her job description, and all of the employees may benefit from knowing the functions of the various departments. An orientation program can be reinforced with an employee manual that states all of the company policies. An employee manual should include the following:

1. The general rules of employment—hours of work, pay days, holidays, sick leave, vacations, etc.
2. The company's policies affecting internal and external activities— public relations, ethics, employee attitudes, promotion from within, etc.
3. Information about the company—a brief history, a statement of objectives, and an organizational chart.

In addition to the orientation program, regular performance reviews should be scheduled, and they should be conducted when they are promised. These sessions should be structured to help employees increase their value to the firm. Businesses commonly review employees' performance at least once a year. In addition, new employees may be reviewed after the first six months; however, it may be appropriate to review new employees after a shorter period—e.g., three months. This review early in the period of employment can be an opportunity for both employer and employee to reaffirm their employment decisions—or to agree that the decision was not right and go their separate ways. Employees will adapt to their new work surroundings and obligations at their own pace. Depending on the job and the individual, some employees require as much as a year on the job before their productivity reaches the level the employer expects. Conversely, it may be apparent early that an employee is incapable of doing the job he or she is assigned. Comprehensive review of the employee's performance may indicate that his or her talents lie elsewhere. Review of the job description may reveal that the work is too much for one person to do. Additional training or a transfer may be a way to retain an employee who shows promise but is not qualified for the role he or she was hired to perform.

RETAINING VALUABLE EMPLOYEES

Whether the property or the property management company employs one worker or a staff of one hundred, payroll is often the largest business expense. However, a talented and dedicated staff is an employer's most valuable resource. Much effort is invested in developing qualified staff, and it is extremely expensive to continually rebuild a staff because of turnover. Personnel costs can be minimized and the value of individual employees increased if responsible and dedicated people can be retained. Retention of employees is facilitated when compensation is appropriate, communication with employees is open, and individuals are encouraged to grow in their jobs.

Compensation

Pay and benefits are the tangible rewards of dedicated service. By their nature, however, pay and benefits can be stumbling blocks between employer and employee. Compensation must meet market levels to keep employees satisfied. It must also be structured to offer employees security and incentive to strive for greater rewards.

Wages.   The federal Fair Labor Standards Act (FLSA), which is revised from time to time, regulates the minimum wage per hour and the maximum number of hours employees can work per day and per week in positions that are paid an hourly wage. If the maximum number of hours per day or cumulative hours per week exceeds those prescribed, the employer is required to pay overtime—standard wage plus 50 percent. While the minimum wage law must be followed, market demands generally require a higher wage rate to recruit qualified employees. Other incentives such as double-time pay for working on holidays may also be necessary.

To be exempt from the Wage and Hour Regulations of the Fair Labor Standards Act, there are several specific tests that a position must meet. Supervision of others or a position that does not require specific hourly production are among them. Exempt employees are not affected by the hours per day or week maximum. However, the base salary of an exempt worker must be at least equal to what a nonexempt worker would earn by receiving minimum wage and working the maximum number of weekly hours cited for regular-time pay in the FLSA.

Salary adjustments should be scheduled regularly, budgeted routinely, and administered fairly. Reliable and dedicated employees will continue to provide quality service if their good performance is noted and compensated. One incentive to excellent performance—and cost-consciousness—is to link a portion of the employees' compensation directly to the employer's annual profit.

Benefits.   Competition among employers and the selectivity of employment candidates have resulted in extensive benefits packages. Life insurance, employee and dependent health insurance, retirement plans, car allowances or company cars, stock options, savings programs, and paid vacations and holidays are common benefits. Many of these benefits are based on seniority or level of responsibility, and their distribution is often complicated by the effort to avoid or defer tax payments on them. If the employer's goal is to retain employees, these benefit plans must be carefully explained so the employees can comprehend their value.

Other Considerations.   The United States government requires employers to participate in federal programs that provide for workers if they are terminated, retire, or become disabled. The *Federal Unemployment Tax Act (FUTA)* and various state unemployment programs are intended to insure compensation if an employee is laid off or terminated. The contributions are paid solely by the employer, and the amount or rate is based on the number of employees and the number of claims made. There are usually minimum and maximum amounts to be paid—on a per-employee basis and related to the employer's history of layoffs. The federal government collects the FUTA taxes, but unemployment compensation is usually administered by the state. Employers are also required to provide *workers' compensation insurance* to compensate employees in the event of a work-related illness or injury. This insurance is purchased either through the state or from a private insurance company. Privately purchased workers' compensation insurance is commonly associated with a short-term disability plan. In addition to these employer-paid programs, workers collect social security when they retire. Funds for this are collected and administered under the *Federal Insurance Contributions Act (FICA)*, and employer and employee contribute to it equally based on the employee's income. The percentage rate is set by law, and there is a prescribed ceiling on the annual contribution.

Communications

Employees are genuinely interested in the company they work for, and they want to know about the successes, failures, and general activities of the business. Clear communication with employees is a valuable retention tool. Many employees' only source of information about their company is their fellow employees. Their reliance on this news source creates the potential for damaging rumors to spread. To avoid such rumors and their consequences, information that affects the business should be disseminated in a timely manner and explained fully. News of particular significance (i.e., items that may be publicized favorably or unfavorably by the press) should be released to all employees at the same time to avert speculation.

Many companies communicate with employees through a periodic newsletter, and the ease and convenience of desktop publishing can make such a publication visually appealing for little cost. Management most often publishes and controls the newsletter. The writing style should be friendly and personal. Recognition of service anniversaries and promotions and personal news items about their fellow workers are welcomed by employees. A newsletter should be directed to all employees. The quality of the company should be reflected through its copy and design. Employees who work for a company that emphasizes superior quality expect a publication that has an appealing design and is free of typographical and grammatical errors.

Central to the communication program of any company is the policy manual or manuals. This material gives all employees a reference to consult for information on company benefits, work hours, and minimum performance standards for particular procedures. Individual departments may institute policy or procedure manuals for the tasks they perform, but all employees should receive some definitive source of information regarding their relationship with the company as a whole.

Another form of written communication from an employer to an employee is a job description. This document outlines the responsibilities and duties of an individual's job. It may also indicate the direct supervisor and any subordinates.

Grievances are a natural part of life and work. Misunderstandings that arise can result in the loss or dissatisfaction of reliable employees if their concerns are not addressed promptly and sincerely. An "open door" policy for airing work-related problems (and personal problems, if appropriate) that prohibits recriminations against those who use it can preserve a superior working relationship. An open-door policy allows employers to examine their working relationship with their employees. All workers should be expected to use their skills and talents to the maximum in their work. They should be treated with respect regardless of the tasks they perform or whether their position is that of a supervisor or a subordinate.

Promoting Morale

Effective communications are only part of an overall program to maintain employee morale. Recreational activities among co-workers should also be encouraged. Employees who are dedicated to their jobs yet balance their hard work with recreational activities—and can differentiate between the appropriate times for each—usually have a positive attitude about their careers. Company-sponsored baseball teams, golf outings, and bowling leagues are common pastimes among co-workers. The cost of such sponsorship may be very little—a set of matching T-shirts is a nominal investment in employee enthusiasm.

Respect for the individual is also important to good morale. Employers who visit a sick employee or try to cheer one who is depressed are establishing goodwill, which is the foundation of enduring friendships as well as professional loyalty.

Excellent performance should be expected of every employee, and compensation should be given for such performance. However, occasional thanks for a job well done are also important to an employee. Dedicated employees want to know that their work is appreciated and that it contributes to the organization's success. An expression of gratitude, whether it is oral or written, can contribute greatly to good morale in a business.

Continual Training

In the normal pace of business and family life, time is rarely left over for additional training or education. As a result, formal education for many employees ends with high school, trade school, or college. As an incentive to continued learning, many employers institute education reimbursement programs for their employees. The rules and incentives for these programs vary greatly, but the benefits to the employer can be substantial.

In addition to formal coursework, many associations and corporations sponsor seminars and courses in aspects of real estate management as well as other disciplines such as accounting, maintenance, human relations, etc. Seminars teaching management and interpersonal skills foster both personal and professional development. Before sending employees to any workshops or seminars, the cost and quality of such programs should be investigated. If the seminar is to take place in a distant city, a phone call to the sponsor may indicate a closer location or another date that can save considerable expense and time away from work. Sometimes such programs can be brought into the workplace for the benefit of all employees. The size of a company and the resources available to it will determine the extent to which such educational programs can be offered.

Developing Talents

While a job description is a valuable reference for an employer and employee, it can hinder the employee's progress if it is interpreted too narrowly. The job description should define the basic functions of a position but should not set limits on what the person in it can do. Employees commonly desire definite boundaries to their duties, but boundaries can limit more than the number of hours that have to be worked; they also permit employees to concentrate only on the minimum they are expected to do. While boundaries help create a sense of security, they also can be viewed as stifling—people begin to think they are in a "rut" at work. In establishing boundaries, balance is important. If workers resist change too much, their department can stagnate and hinder a thriving business; if they pursue every new opportunity and ignore fundamental procedures, the department or company can founder from the lack of direction.

Most job descriptions gradually change in the course of an evolving business, so workers must increase their knowledge to be able to keep up the pace. Communication and training enable workers to grow with the demands placed on the business; so does encouragement. If employees are encouraged to undertake new tasks and are legitimately capable of mastering the work, they will be productive employees and the employer may not have to hire additional staff in order to expand its operations. The employees also gain if they develop more self-confidence and can base their sense of security on their own growing abilities rather than the minimum their jobs require of them.

EMPLOYEE TERMINATION

The typical American employee no longer makes one place of business his or her lifelong workplace. Seven to ten company changes and four or five different career paths are not uncommon. Turnover is a way of life because of resignations, corporate takeovers, layoffs, and changing client needs. When this occurs, employees should never feel they are just another commodity. Whether an employee retires, resigns, or must be terminated, such a departure is always stressful. Nevertheless, dealing with such matters is a natural part of managerial responsibilities.

Facing a Layoff

When income decreases or expenses increase, or if tenants or clients are lost, a layoff may be the only way to counter the financial shortfall. Whether permanent or temporary, a layoff can be devastating to the employees and their families. The stress on those who remain will increase. They will be concerned about their job security and, because of the staff shortage, they may have to perform additional work without additional pay. The manager in this situation also endures strain. The personal feeling of responsibility and the work that must be done to salvage the business exact a high toll.

The employer who must resort to a layoff has very few options for assisting the terminated employees, especially with finances. However, the manager may have some means for providing assistance if strong training and communications programs are in place. Training in financial management can develop habits of frugality the individual can use on his or her own. Programs that help employees define and expand their job skills can lead to less time without a job in the event of a layoff because the individual has more and better job skills and therefore more to offer potential employers. Business associates of the employer may have positions available, and job-seeker services and resume consultants may be able to help. The most valuable assistance, however, involves being direct with employees about the condition of the business and giving them as much warning as possible about its future.

Providing employees with proper notice of an impending layoff and helping them with the unemployment application forms are a few steps that can be taken if a layoff becomes inevitable. Before notifying any employees, however, the employer must review the personnel list to preclude discrimination against any group as a result of the layoff. In property management, layoffs are usually begun in the departments that are not directly involved in providing service to tenants or property owners, and seniority often determines which employees will remain.

Disciplining Employees

When a firm's policies are disobeyed, the employer is left with two choices—discipline or dismissal. There is a substantial difference between these two alternatives. "Discipline" implies reform; "dismissal" precludes the possibility of reform. Which action to take depends on the infraction involved. The desired result is the same regardless—the employer hopes to remedy or undo any damage from the employee's actions and prevent any recurrence.

Most work rules are absolutes. They should be fairly easy to enforce because of that. Employees are expected not to lie; they should not steal—either time or supplies. They should not be hostile toward others. They should respect the instructions they receive from their supervisors.

Although a thorough and impartial system of discipline should be established, it is impossible to write a comprehensive set of disciplinary measures to cover every possible circumstance. Regardless, all employees must be dealt with individually and fairly, based on the nature of the incident.

Progressive Discipline.   Some of the most vexing disciplinary problems are a result of minor disobedience. The circumstances that require discipline can provoke anger, but employers must restrain their anger. It is important to preserve impartiality and respect for the employee. When a supervisor learns about or witnesses an infraction, he or she should write down what is known about the incident and find out the employee's perspective on the matter. Any required disciplinary action should take place as soon as possible after the offense, and the matter should be discussed in privacy and in confidence. Accusing an employee of wrongdoing in the presence of co-workers neither rectifies the problem nor serves to rehabilitate the offending employee. Moreover, other employees who witness the exchange between supervisor and subordinate may lose their respect for the employer.

A system of progressive discipline can be established to provide ample opportunity for the employee to change or correct his or her behavior. The number of "warnings" or notices given to an employee regarding a particular problem will depend on the type of infraction. One or more conversations calling attention to the company policy and asking for the employee's commitment to eliminating the problem may be all that is needed if an employee is repeatedly late for work or regularly extends his or her lunch period beyond the allowed time. A written memorandum copied to the employee's personnel file would be the next step. However, if the employee's behavior improves within a short period, the employer may decide to keep it off the record.

Some undesirable behavior may require a written notice from the beginning. This is particularly appropriate if an employee is not following company procedure properly, and this results in problems for others on the staff. Sometimes what is needed is a period of *probation* during which the employee is given a fixed amount of time to overcome his or her work-related problem. Probation allows an employer to monitor and report on the employee's improvement. During probation, the employee should be reminded that being on probation may affect his or her next performance review. If the employee corrects the problem before the next performance review, it may be appropriate to cancel the probation officially (in writing). The employee should also be made to understand that if the problem is not corrected, he or she will be terminated. Regardless of how the disciplinary action is set up, pay and benefits should remain intact during a period of probation.

The most extreme action that can be taken against an employee is *termination*. A primary concern for the employer is protection from an unjust termination suit, so termination is usually a last resort. Grounds for immediate dismissal, though widespread, often have legal or social ramifications. Before an employee is terminated, the employer should verify that the event or behavior prompting dismissal is thoroughly documented. (In fact, any disciplinary action against an employee should be recorded.) While terminated employees are usually entitled to collect unemployment compensation, there may be circumstances in which unemployment benefits may be denied. A dismissed employee could sue the employer for denied unemployment compensation or for damages based on discriminatory or other unfair practices by the employer. To avoid such a suit, reasons for dismissal should be recorded carefully and a policy of progressive discipline should be established and applied fairly. Documentation should concentrate on the work performed (or not performed), not on assumptions regarding its cause (e.g., substance abuse).

SUMMARY

In property management, relations with employees are central to maintaining good relations with tenants and with the property owner. All staff members, whether supervisors or subordinates, are colleagues and should work toward fulfilling the owner's goal for the property. The size of a property management firm's staff depends on specific attributes of the properties being managed as well as the attributes of other properties in the firm's portfolio. People working at a property may be employed by the property owner or the management firm. Contractors may be hired for specialized work. All these workers must perform their duties harmoniously and cooperatively.

Wise selection of staff members is as crucial to successful property management as it is to any other business. The key to hiring superior employees is searching for qualified candidates who possess the appropriate skills and are willing to share the same goals as the property manager. Continual training and encouragement to pursue additional education fosters individual productivity. Such programs are good investments when companies can afford to implement them.

Employees can be retained by treating them fairly, respecting them, and regarding them as colleagues. This includes providing fair compensation and benefits. Honest communication and genuine concern should be at the forefront of employer-employee relationships. The rules in these relationships differ very little from any other human relationship involving mutual respect.

The true skills of an employer will shine through in difficult times. Employees may be lost through their own volition or through a layoff. Discipline is also problematic, primarily because the employer wants to assure that disciplinary actions are fair. If it is necessary to discipline or terminate an employee, all infractions of the rules and regulations as well as job performance (or nonperformance) must be properly recorded.

Key Terms
Contractor
Job description
Layoff
Probation
Performance review
Social security
Workers' compensation insurance

Key Points
Determining adequate staff size
Recruiting and selecting qualified personnel
Wages and employee benefits
Differences between exempt and nonexempt employees and
    requirements for overtime compensation
Orientation and training
Disciplinary action, probation, and termination

8

Maintenance and Structural Preservation

The reasons for maintenance are obvious. Maintenance is the key to superior presentation and optimal function; it preserves—and sometimes improves—the condition and, therefore, the value of the property. Regular cleaning and repairs are also necessary to keep tenants comfortable. The objective of maintenance, like every other aspect of property management, is to meet the goals of the owner.

A comprehensive maintenance program can provide the following benefits for the owner.

1. *Tenant retention.* If the property is immaculate and the building components are in good working condition, tenants will be comfortable in their surroundings. The subsequent tenant satisfaction will result in a lower vacancy rate. The owner will have less expense for turnover of rental space because tenants will be inclined to renew their leases.

2. *Reduced operating costs.* Maintenance and repair costs may be a large part of a property's operating expenses, but other operating costs—utilities, rubbish removal, insurance premiums, etc.—may be reduced as a result of the investment in maintenance and repair. Rental income may increase because of increased tenancy in a well-maintained property. If the property manager investigates reducing maintenance expenses, he or she should also consider the indirect savings and improved income that good maintenance programs can produce.

153

Objectives of Maintenance
* Tenant satisfaction
* Optimal function of the property
* Lower operating costs
* Higher tenant retention
* Maximized property value

---

3. *Preservation and enhancement of property value.* If the property manager establishes a comprehensive maintenance program, the property's value will be preserved and enhanced during the course of regular operations. Neglected maintenance may cause the greatest loss an owner can suffer on a real estate investment. Even if the property is consumed by fire or determined to be a complete loss because of a natural disaster, the financial investment usually can be regained if the property is properly insured. However, there is no insurance against neglected maintenance; cleaning and repair must be a daily concern of the property manager.

All maintenance procedures can be categorized in one of four ways: as custodial, corrective, preventive, or deferred maintenance. *Custodial maintenance* is the day-to-day cleaning and upkeep that should be part of every property's ongoing program to retain value—and tenants. *Corrective maintenance* is the ordinary repairs that must be made to a building and its equipment on a day-to-day basis. *Preventive maintenance* is a program of regular inspection and care to avert problems or at least detect and solve them before major repairs are needed. *Deferred maintenance* is ordinary maintenance of a building that is *not* performed at the time a problem is detected. If left unchecked, deferred maintenance will eventually diminish the use, occupancy, and value of the property.

SCHEDULES, INSPECTIONS, AND MAINTENANCE WORK

In the effort to minimize monthly operating expenses, some property managers unwisely have cleaning and maintenance work done only when they are absolutely necessary or in an emergency. On any property, some deferred maintenance is inevitable, but too much of it will eventually result in excessively costly repairs. As an example, not heeding the manufacturer's recommendations for maintaining a motor may temporarily delay the expense of a service call or replacement parts, but temporary loss of service from the motor as well as excessive wear on it will eventually cost much more, including premature replacement.

Because of budget constraints, the property manager may find it necessary to tolerate some deferred maintenance. When this occurs, the maintenance to be deferred should be listed in order of priority and incorporated into the list of routine maintenance procedures. In this way, the property manager and staff can gradually reduce the list of deferred projects while they keep pace with ongoing maintenance.

Schedules and Inspections

Planning is the first step in any maintenance operation. A list should be made of every component that requires maintenance, the type of maintenance each requires, how often each procedure is to be done, and how much time a procedure requires. To develop this list, the property manager should survey the condition of all functional components of the property. From the list, the manager can develop schedules for inspections and routine service.

Scheduling of inspections and cleaning is crucial. Some building components (corridors) require day-to-day cleaning or maintenance, while other components (fan motors) need only periodic maintenance to function optimally; the roof may only require annual inspection. These considerations, assembled in a master maintenance chart, can be used to establish a regular and efficient pattern of inspection, cleaning, and repair. An *inspection report* (exhibit 8.1) usually lists all of the major components of a property (grounds, foundations, exterior walls, electrical network, etc.), with numerous subentries under each major component. For example, transformers, circuit breakers, fuse boxes, wiring, wall plugs, light switches, light bulbs, etc., may be subentries under *electrical system.* Space is also provided to record the condition of the component, specific work to be done to it, an estimate of the cost of the work, and when it should be inspected again. Inspection reports are coordinated with a maintenance schedule to assure timely follow-up. The *maintenance schedule* (exhibit 8.2) usually lists specific tasks and their frequencies. Spaces may also be provided for assignment of specific personnel and a specific time of the week, month, or year for the task to be completed.

The organization of inspection reports and maintenance schedules depends on the design of the structure and its surroundings, the individual components that require service, and the availability of personnel qualified to do the work. All of these factors must be synthesized to develop a logical and efficient program for maintaining the property. It may take time and experimentation to perfect effective schedules, especially for an older property whose service records are incomplete. A new property should have available a complete set of owner's manuals and manufacturer's recommendations for its equipment; these documents make it easier to develop a maintenance schedule.

E X H I B I T   8.1

Sample Property Inspection Report

Property _____

Initial Inspection By _____ Date _____

Item	Condition	Repairs Needed	Estimated Cost	Next Scheduled Inspection
Grounds				
Foundations				
Exterior walls				
Roof				
Gutters and downspouts				
Windows and casings				
Lobby				
Common areas				
Elevators				
Stairways				
Boiler or furnace room				
Air-conditioning plant				
Electrical system				
Plumbing				
Gas lines				
Fire safety equipment				
Garbage disposal area				

Custodial Maintenance—Housekeeping

Custodial maintenance or housekeeping is the process of keeping the building clean for tenants, prospective tenants, and visitors. This element of maintenance is most noticeable because it relates to people's sensory perceptions, particularly sight and smell. Custodial maintenance is the simplest form of corrective maintenance. It is also the first level of defense in averting deferred maintenance by discovering a need for more extensive corrective maintenance. A schedule of what must be cleaned on a daily or weekly basis establishes a pattern for inspecting every part of the building. This can also ensure early discovery of damage or wear.

Quantifying the level of traffic passing through each section of the building will help the manager schedule housekeeping. Some areas of the building may require hourly attention; others may require only an occa-

E X H I B I T   8.2

Sample Maintenance Schedule

Date _____

Property _____

Project	Frequency	Month of Year
Patch parking lot and other concrete	Once per year	
Clean upper story windows	Twice per year	
Inspect and oil exhaust fans	Once per quarter	
Clean gutters and downspouts	Once per year or after heavy rains	
Inspect and test fire safety equipment	As needed, at least monthly	
Recharge fire extinguishers	Once per year	
Inspect common area lighting	Once per week	
Clean or replace HVAC filters	Once per month	
Polish chrome and brass in lobby	As needed	
Wax lobby floors	Three times per year	
Prune hedges	Twice per year	
Touch-up exterior paint	Twice per year	
Touch-up interior paint	As needed	
Vacuum swimming pool	Twice per week	

sional spot inspection. Nevertheless, all rooms and sections of the common areas in the building should be listed in the housekeeping schedule so that they will be inspected regularly and kept clean. This should include the supply room. Maintenance personnel may question the purpose of cleaning a supply closet that is not seen by the public, but an orderly supply room saves staff time in finding supplies and helps to protect materials stored in it. It also reminds the staff of the importance of cleanliness throughout the building. The following sections describe some of the areas of a property that require frequent custodial (and corrective) maintenance.

Walks, Driveways, Parking Areas, and Grounds. The schedule of housekeeping duties for the property grounds will depend partly on the time of year. In winter, it is important for all driveways, parking areas, and sidewalks to be free of ice and snow. Doormats must be regularly inspected and cleaned. In spring or during periods of thaw, the grounds should be cleared of litter that accumulated beneath the snow. Most of the custodial maintenance of the grounds is done in the summer, however. Keeping the lawn mowed and weeded and regularly weeding any flower beds will add greatly to the curb appeal of the property. The staff should look for cracks in the concrete or asphalt pavement and patch them if necessary. Weeds growing in these cracks should be pulled. Litter should be picked up as it is noticed. Bushes, shrubs, and trees should be watered and pruned regularly and replaced if they are dead or dying.

Exterior Walls and Components.   The level of traffic around the outside of a property and the exterior finish of the building will determine the frequency of custodial maintenance. In addition to cleaning dirt from outside walls of the building, signs and lights also should be cleaned regularly. Touch-up painting may be necessary as a part of the regular maintenance of some parts of the property exterior.

Windows and Casings.   Cleaning all of the windows and window casings of a building may not be done routinely, but those on the lobby level require frequent attention. Because these windows are in high traffic areas, they are the first ones seen and they are the ones that become dirty most rapidly. They should be washed daily, if necessary. The interior and exterior of other windows may require cleaning semiannually or annually. Trained window washers are usually contracted to clean window exteriors on multistory buildings.

Interior Walls.   To avoid frequent painting or cleaning of interior walls, they should be finished with washable paint or wall coverings and cleaned regularly.

Elevators, Lobbies, and Other Common Areas.   Elevators and lobbies require daily attention. Buildings that have information desks in their lobbies have the advantage of personnel in attendance to keep these areas free of litter or report their condition to the appropriate personnel. In addition to daily cleaning of lobbies and elevators, brass or other metallic surfaces must be polished regularly, and tile floors should be stripped and waxed periodically. Corridors will require the same level of attention, especially in high-traffic areas.

Amenities.   The amenities of a building usually have unique requirements. People are attracted to amenities such as swimming pools and fitness centers. At the minimum, these areas require daily attention because of health and sanitation considerations. Swimming pool maintenance is often contracted. Swimming pools must be vacuumed frequently and the chlorination level must be monitored. Periodic testing of water samples may be required by law. If the facility supplies towels, they must be collected, laundered, and sanitized. Locker rooms and showers must be cleaned and disinfected frequently.

Preventive Maintenance

Preventive maintenance is the effort to assure reliable functional performance of the building and its components. Exterior maintenance requirements vary with the climate. For comfort, safety, and efficiency, all parts of the building must be regularly inspected and maintained. The number of maintenance personnel and their levels of skill and training will indicate how much of this work should be done by outside contractors. For reasons of safety, equipment availability, licensing requirements, and special skills involved, some preventive maintenance should be done by contractors regardless. The following sections discuss components of a property that require regular preventive maintenance.

Walks, Driveways, Parking Areas, and Grounds. Most sidewalks, driveways, and parking lots are finished with asphalt, brick, or concrete. The effects of traffic, vibration, water freezing in winter, and extreme heat in summer cause these materials to crack and crumble. Occasional patching or resurfacing will extend the life of these surfaces, but they will eventually have to be replaced entirely. Parking lots have to be restriped periodically to mark parking stalls and fire lanes. Landscaping that has been neglected may have to be redesigned to be more aesthetically pleasing. Lawns may require reseeding or sod replacement in the spring to restore areas where grass has died.

Foundations. Building foundations should be inspected periodically for evidence of water penetration, settlement, cracks, and other signs of deterioration. To prevent further deterioration, problems should be corrected when they are discovered. Professional engineers should be consulted when problems are severe.

Exterior Walls. Preventive maintenance of exterior walls depends on the construction or finishing material. Because of repeated freezing and thawing, cracks develop in the mortar of brick walls. The periodic replacement of mortar is called *tuck-pointing*. Painted walls should be examined for cracked or peeling paint; occasional touch-ups will protect a painted surface, but complete repainting will have to be done eventually. Wood surfaces should be inspected for splintering, decay, and termite damage. It is often possible to replace portions of a wooden surface without completely refacing the building. To prevent reinfestation, termites must be exterminated before repair work begins. Concrete walls must be checked for cracks or chipping.

Roof. A roof endures extremes of heat, cold, and moisture. Over the years, a building may be reroofed many times. Severe weather may weaken areas of the roof, necessitating occasional patching. A property manager should routinely inspect the surface of the roof for wear (at least once a year and usually accompanied by a qualified roofing contractor).

Gutters and Downspouts. Many buildings have exposed gutters and downspouts. These prevent accumulation of water on the roof and protect the exterior walls from excessive water flow. Gutters usually have to be replaced as often as the roof. They should be inspected frequently, especially after heavy rains, and kept clear of leaves and other accumulating debris.

Windows and Casings. In addition to cleaning, windows require maintenance of their moving parts and frames. Older buildings may have rope and counterweight systems; frayed or broken ropes should be repaired or replaced. Separate storm windows may have to be installed in the autumn and removed in the spring. When windows must be replaced, the manager should investigate double-paned windows which serve as their own storm windows. They are energy-efficient in all seasons and require less maintenance.

Elevators. Elevator maintenance should be contracted. The elevator timing should be recorded and the property manager should work with the contractor to develop a system that is most efficient for handling the volume of traffic in the building. To discourage use of passenger elevators for freight, and vice versa, the freight elevator should be separate from those for passengers. In buildings lacking a freight elevator, there is a risk of damage to passenger elevators if they are used for freight. However, it may be possible to reserve one of the passenger elevators for that purpose and make it accessible only to appropriate personnel who must have a key. Another possibility is to provide pads for the elevator walls and designate particular times of the day when the elevators may be used for moving freight. This will avert disruption during periods of peak traffic.

Stairways. No matter how they are constructed, stairways require close attention because they are frequently the site of accidents involving injuries. Step surfaces show wear over time, and this alone can be a potential hazard because the surface (tread) is no longer smooth or level. Stairs should be checked for any loose or deteriorating steps. All staircases should have an easily grasped banister, and all banisters should be securely fastened to the wall or staircase. The most common challenge is keeping stairways free of debris. Stair edges should be clearly marked if it is difficult to distinguish the surfaces of successive steps, and all stairwells should be adequately lighted.

Heating, Ventilating, and Air-Conditioning (HVAC) Equipment.
Controlling the climate in buildings is an ongoing challenge. In addition to temperature, HVAC equipment regulates humidity, supplies fresh air to the building, and removes stale air. Regulating all of these conditions requires a system of controls and precise monitoring of each room or floor in the building. A malfunction or error in programming this equipment can cause tenants extreme discomfort. Maintenance staff may be trained to clean and replace filters, lubricate portions of the mechanical equipment, or monitor thermostat settings. However, maintenance and repair of HVAC equipment is usually contracted unless the size of a property justifies the skilled labor needed for this work. Local ordinances may require licensing of boiler operators. Heating and air-conditioning systems usually require special maintenance for start-up and shutdown when the seasons change.

Electrical Network and Plumbing. As demand for electrical service grows, the property manager must monitor whether the capacity in the building can meet that demand. In particular, prospective commercial tenants should be asked about their electrical requirements to determine whether they can be accommodated. Any changes in wiring should be done by licensed personnel and appropriately documented. In addition to periodic inspection of the electrical wiring, all electrical pumps and motors should be inspected regularly. All property staff should know the location of transformers on or near the property and where to find the transformer identification number and the telephone number of the electrical utility company. The main shutoff switch should be identified; employees should know where it is located and the circumstances that warrant disconnecting the property from its power supply.

Plumbing should be inspected regularly and work to clear drains, repair leaks, and otherwise maintain the integrity of the system should be done immediately. Residential properties usually have the most plumbing fixtures of any property type. Consequently, they have the most plumbing problems. To minimize service calls and reduce the amount of toxic drain cleaner released into the environment, residents should be taught responsible and proper use of plumbing fixtures. The main water shutoff valve should be identified, and employees should know what circumstances warrant its use.

Gas Lines. Maintenance of gas lines should be done only by trained personnel from the gas company. Maintenance staff should be reminded to check for gas leaks and to report them to the proper authorities—initiating appropriate emergency procedures in the meanwhile. If the property is equipped with a primary shutoff valve and the gas company provides instructions on how to use it, that information should be conveyed to employees.

Fire Safety—Additional Considerations

Thousands of buildings catch fire every year and thousands of people lose their lives in these fires. Property managers must know how to minimize the risk of fire and, in the event of a fire, how to properly react to minimize injuries and property damage. A fire prevention and safety program may start with a call to the local fire department—many fire departments will conduct inspections of properties. An inspection of the site by the fire department will identify potential fire hazards and equipment that must be installed or upgraded to comply with safety standards or codes.

Lights in exit signs should be inspected regularly to assure they are functioning. It may be advisable to consider installing emergency lighting in corridors that automatically turns on in a power failure, and these lights must be inspected regularly as well.

Fire extinguishers and smoke alarms can be installed in common areas. Sometimes local law will require smoke alarms to be placed in each unit. However, if local law does not require the installation of fire extinguishers or smoke alarms in discrete leased space, the property manager may want to encourage tenants to purchase these items themselves. Because the cost of alarms and extinguishers is nominal compared to the cost of lives and property, the manager may even want to encourage the owner to install this equipment in every unit.

The local fire department may also help a property manager prepare a fire safety training program for site staff and tenants. Such a program includes prevention advice (e.g., proper storage and use of combustibles) as well as procedures to follow to escape from a fire. The core of any safety program is to establish an evacuation plan and to begin evacuation as soon as a fire is discovered. Management staff and tenants should know how to call the fire department and how to activate the building alarm system if they discover a fire. Advice from the fire department and occasional fire drills help to ensure the appropriateness of an evacuation plan. Many safety tips about exiting a burning building may seem to be common knowledge (e.g., knowing where the nearest exits are located, touching a door with the back of a hand before opening it, staying near the floor for fresh air, closing doors when possible to contain the fire, etc.), but they should be reiterated frequently. If the fire department does not offer safety training, it may have brochures available that list safety procedures, or it may direct a property manager to the nearest resource for this information.

Cogeneration Equipment. On properties that produce electricity using a cogeneration plant, the maintenance staff may be responsible for certain routine tasks. However, most preventive and corrective maintenance must be done by authorized contractors.

Fire Prevention and Safety Equipment. To minimize the threat to life and property from fire, the property manager should inform everyone in the building about fire safety procedures, make sure that the associated equipment is functioning properly, and verify that all equipment meets local fire codes. All fire exits and fire doors should be marked clearly and kept free of obstructions. Proper operation of fire doors, alarm systems, fire escapes, and interior sprinkler systems should be verified at least once a year. Certificates of inspection may be required, and maintenance may have to be contracted. Most jurisdictions require installation of smoke alarms; batteries will have to be checked and replaced in smoke detectors that are not connected to a central system. Fire extinguishers should be recharged and tagged as prescribed by the manufacturer; this is done by an outside service. Fire extinguishers in the United States are classified by the extinguishing material they contain. The extinguishers should be placed in the building by class according to the combustibles nearby—a water-based extinguisher should not be used on an electrical fire. All property personnel and tenants should be routinely drilled on how to summon the fire department and evacuate the building.

Pest Control.   An ongoing concern among property managers is control of insect pests and other vermin. Most properties contract for regular extermination service, and many states require pest control operators to be licensed. The frequency of the exterminator's visits depends on the severity of infestation, the season, and the locale. Cockroaches are ubiquitous and particularly difficult to exterminate. Other troublesome insects are termites, carpenter ants, and fire ants. Because these insects burrow into foundations and wooden beams, they may be spotted only after extensive damage has been done.

To eliminate an infestation, fumigation may be necessary. However, if only one unit is fumigated or sprayed after a tenant has vacated, the pests may not be killed; they may merely relocate to adjoining units. To ensure complete extermination, the entire building or a large section of it should be sprayed at one time. Properties whose tenants include restaurants or food stores are especially prone to vermin infestations. However, most food stores and restaurants are required by local health departments to spray periodically for pests.

The most effective way to control pests is to remove their food sources. Mice, rats, and cockroaches thrive in unsanitary conditions. The property manager should stress to tenants the proper frequency and method for disposing of garbage on the premises. If there is no place outside of the building to maintain dumpsters, garbage must be stored inside the building. The garbage storage room or area should be inspected regularly—cracks in the walls and other types of damage provide conduits for pests to spread throughout the building. To control odors and inhibit bacterial and fungal growth, routine cleaning and disinfection of the "garbage room" are mandatory. The garbage room should be insulated from heat, especially if the room is near the furnace or boiler. Good illumination and walls painted in a light color imply to tenants the desire to keep the room clean; it is also easier to spot insects on the walls. Regardless of where garbage is stored, a program to sort trash for recycling may also help control pests by concentrating the organic garbage in fewer containers.

By establishing and enforcing strict standards for custodial and preventive maintenance, corrective and deferred maintenance can be reduced significantly.

OTHER ASPECTS OF MAINTENANCE

Regulations enforced by local, state, and federal governments establish minimum standards for the safety of employees and building occupants and affect many maintenance procedures. Laws governing minimum standards change frequently, so the property manager must stay abreast of new laws and court interpretations of them. In addition, properties must be in compliance with current environmental regulations, and such compliance relates to the safety, health, and well-being of tenants through maintenance practices. Energy is conserved as a result of both operating economies and maintenance procedures. Maintenance is also the key to building security and crime prevention.

Safety

The Occupational Safety and Health Administration (OSHA) of the U.S. Department of Labor establishes job safety standards and is authorized to conduct inspections and to cite businesses for violations. The property manager should know the OSHA standards that apply to activities on the property and should explain them to the employees who work there. Unsafe work practices should be corrected. The manager should provide employees with proper equipment for their duties and be sure they know how to use it correctly. Appropriate and approved protective devices for equipment and personnel (shields on power saws, safety glasses, rubber gloves, etc.) should also be readily available.

Protecting the Environment

Understanding proper ways to handle wastes and to dispose of them assures safety, compliance with regulations, and preservation of the environment, yet waste disposal is only one aspect of environmental protection. Many materials once considered safe for use in buildings have been found to be harmful to humans. The U.S. Environmental Protection Agency (EPA) and state and local governments have enacted regulations to protect both people and the environment. The property manager must know whether harmful materials are present on the property and whether they are po-

---

Hazardous Materials in Buildings
* Asbestos-containing material
* Radon gas
* Polychlorinated biphenyls (PCBs)
* Formaldehyde gas
* Lead-containing paint
* Chlorofluorcarbons (CFCs)
* Leaking underground storage tanks

---

tentially hazardous in their current state. The presence of hazardous materials can lower the value of a property, even if the materials do not pose a threat. Liability for leaving such materials in place or removing them has received considerable attention. Of primary concern to the property manager are asbestos, radon, and polychlorinated biphenyls (PCBs). Formaldehyde gas is another concern. Chlorofluorocarbons (CFCs) used in chiller components of many air-conditioning and refrigeration systems are also of concern, as is lead-containing paint in older buildings, which is especially hazardous to children who live there.

* *Asbestos* is a fibrous mineral that was used in buildings for flooring, insulation, and fireproofing. Assessing the condition of asbestos-containing material (ACM) in a property and removing it (*abatement*) or leaving it in place (*containment*) can only be done by contractors licensed to do so.
* *Radon* is a colorless, odorless, tasteless gas that occurs naturally in the radioactive decay of radium and uranium. It became a problem with the advent of energy-efficient buildings that allow only minimal transfer of air between the building's interior and the outside. If high levels of radon are discovered, a qualified contractor can identify the sources and recommend ways to seal them or ventilate the building.
* *Polychlorinated biphenyls (PCBs)* in electrical transformers are relatively harmless if left undisturbed. However, if a PCB-containing transformer leaks or burns, lethal dioxin gas may be released. Transformers that contain PCBs must be disposed in a licensed location and by an authorized waste hauler. The property owner is liable for any PCB contamination caused by the transformer even after it has been removed from the property.
* *Formaldehyde gas* is a foaming agent once used in foam insulation and still present in adhesives used in making pressed-wood products. It is another material whose presence can be harmful. Manufactured homes are most susceptible to high levels of formaldehyde gas because of the amount of pressed wood and the type of insula-

tion used in them. Although formaldehyde gas will eventually dissipate, it may be necessary to remove some of the formaldehyde-containing materials or to increase interior ventilation to hasten the dissipation and eliminate harmful effects.

Many older buildings maintained their own fuel supply for their boilers, usually in storage tanks on the premises. The threat of contamination of groundwater by leaking underground storage tanks (LUSTs) has led to regulations requiring inspection and replacement of tanks that are still in use. Those no longer in use may have to be removed. The presence of "extra" pipes may indicate a forgotten underground tank. If an abandoned tank is found on the premises, the alternatives for making it completely safe are to remove it or fill it with cement. Local authorities should always be contacted regarding the legally correct procedure to use when dealing with environmental issues.

Controlling Energy Consumption

Managing energy usage is an ongoing aspect of maintenance, and any amount of energy savings that can be achieved reduces operating costs and increases potential profit for the property. Energy conservation is a way to ensure comfort and reduce fuel consumption.

Some energy programs cost very little to implement. A reminder to tenants to report leaky faucets can reduce wasted water and fuel. A maintenance program that emphasizes energy management can begin generating savings with the following month's fuel bills. Although new energy-saving equipment can be expensive, some devices have the potential to reduce energy consumption by more than half. As a simple example, low-wattage fluorescent light "bulbs" can be used to replace conventional incandescent bulbs. The cost of one of these fluorescent bulbs is higher than the cost of an incandescent bulb, but its life expectancy is also many times greater. The savings results from much lower energy consumption—the fluorescent bulb produces the same intensity and quality of light as a conventional incandescent bulb but uses about one-fourth the wattage.

The goal of energy management is to strike a balance between the initial cost of an energy-saving device or program and the amount of time before it pays for itself. There are numerous controls that can be installed on existing equipment; replacement with completely new equipment is another possibility. A *retrofit* is the replacement of an old building component with a new energy-efficient one—installation of a new boiler, for example. Retrofitting can be very expensive, but the installation will eventually pay off, especially if the component was due for replacement anyway. Although the payback may take years, such a retrofitting can become a strong competitive advantage if energy costs soar.

A manager should learn about the energy consumption of a property, the billing procedures used by utility companies, and the energy control devices available on the market. Alternatives can be compared and appropriately implemented. To optimize energy conservation, a property manager must think creatively about energy costs and usage. Low-flow shower heads greatly reduce consumption of water and fuel. Motion or infrared sensors on parking lot lights may reduce consumption without compromising security. A combination timer-thermostat on a boiler can match high water temperature with peak demand. Routine cleaning and oiling of machinery results in better performance, longer life, and lower energy consumption. Frequent inspections of the property and routine maintenance are essential to prevent energy waste.

Maintaining Property Security

Successful maintenance programs contribute to a building's security. Although it is very difficult to prevent crime in buildings, many crimes do not result from forcible entry. Complacency about security measures provides greater opportunities for crime. Regular inspections and thorough preventive measures are the best defenses against crime at a property.

Some property managers and owners may consider a security staff or surveillance equipment crucial. Before making such an investment, however, the issue of liability should be considered. The presence of a security force or monitoring equipment—or the promotion of these services when marketing the property—may be construed as a "security guarantee." If that "guarantee" fails, the owner and the manager may be liable. Despite this risk, security personnel are crucial for some types of property, especially office buildings and shopping centers. In residential properties, it may be most appropriate to provide residents with security devices they can use themselves (e.g., deadbolt locks).

Whatever security program is in place, it should be continually monitored to make sure it works exactly as planned. The property manager should advise tenants and staff to consider the ramifications of their actions. Doors that lock automatically should not be propped open; burned-out bulbs should be replaced as soon as they are discovered; and immediate priority should be given to repair of any component that may provide access to a property.

MANAGING MAINTENANCE WORK

The property manager and the owner must choose the most effective method of maintaining the property. Personnel to do the work may be provided in three ways (see also chapter 7).

1. *On-site staff.* This is a customary practice and is an effective way to quickly address custodial and preventive maintenance. The size of the building usually determines the number of people and the range of specialized skills required.

2. *Management firm employees.* The property manager or management company may manage enough properties to sustain a full-time maintenance staff of their own. When nonroutine maintenance is provided to a managed property, labor and parts are billed to the property owner. This is in addition to the regular management fee. The difficulty with such an arrangement is that disputes may arise between the owner and the manager over the amount of extra charges, so it may be more appropriate to negotiate a totally separate fee or billing arrangement if the management company provides maintenance services.

3. *Contractors.* For maintenance that requires specialized skills or licensing of those who do the work (e.g., elevator maintenance), contractors may be used in addition to or in place of on-site staff. Regular janitorial services may also be contracted. Security guards on site are usually contracted through an independent security agency. All contractors should be bonded, and if their particular duties require licensing, the manager should verify that their licenses are current. Contractors should also be required to show proof that they have adequate and appropriate insurance.

Before choosing a contractor to perform a certain job, the property manager should draft precise *specifications* for the work. The specifications should describe the work to be done, the materials to be used, any special equipment or tools required, and any time constraints that may apply. The manager should then invite contractors to *bid* on the job. They will submit *quotations* that state their analysis of the job, the amount of time it will take, and what the cost will be. After receiving the quotations, the property manager can select the contractor who will provide the necessary level of quality for the fairest price. In some instances, a firm price cannot be stated, especially if a job—elevator repair, for instance, could take on a different character after work is begun. The contractor may submit an *estimate* showing known costs (as for parts) and specific rates to be charged for variable components of the job (an hourly rate for labor; mileage charges for travel, etc.).

Whether the maintenance work is done by on-site staff, employees of the management firm, contractors, or a combination of the three, the record-keeping requirements are essentially the same. Each specific maintenance or repair activity assigned should have an individual *work order* (exhibit 8.3) that indicates what is to be done, when to do it, and who will do the work. The work order form usually consists of an original and two

EXHIBIT   8.3

Work Order

Work Order Number _____ Assigned To _____

Property _____ _____ Date _____

Maintenance required _____

_____

_____

Location on property _____

Maintenance performed _____

_____

_____

Materials used _____

_____

_____

Time required _____   Cost of labor $_____
                                        Cost of materials $_____
                                                   Total $_____

Maintenace performed by _____
Unable to complete because _____

_____

_____

---

copies. The original may remain with the property manager, the maintenance supervisor, or the person who files the orders. The second and
third copies are for the maintenance worker. After the job is done, the
worker should complete the work order and return it to the property
manager or the maintenance office.

A *work log* (exhibit 8.4) is commonly used to record maintenance jobs
on a cumulative basis. Two sets of work logs may be used. The property
manager may keep a master work log for all property staff and contractors
listing what has been scheduled for each of them. Staff members receive
individual logs and check off the tasks as they complete them. They should
also report any variance between actual and allotted time as well as the
reasons for the variance.

Although a staff member who is not directly involved with maintenance may complete a *purchase order* for supplies or equipment, this
record has a direct effect on the maintenance staff and maintenance efficiency. A purchase order should show the name of the vendor; the date of
the order; the kind, quantity, and price of each item ordered; the delivery
date and terms of acceptance, and whether any substitutions are allowed.
Purchase orders are especially useful to monitor inventory levels and assure an adequate supply of replacement parts. Tracking inventory through

E X H I B I T   8.4

Work Log

Worker's Name _____ Clock or Contractor Number _____
Property _____ Date _____

Assignment	Location	Allotted Time	Completed (Yes/No)	Actual Time

purchase orders can prevent purchasing too many or too few supplies and spare parts. Both situations are costly. Overstock represents cash that is not available for other uses, and having too many parts on hand can lead to pilferage by employees or tenants. Inadequate inventory is also expensive, especially in terms of the staff time involved in making a special trip to purchase a part. To verify inventory levels and to track the frequency with which items are restocked, the property manager may develop an inventory control system, such as a checkout list in the supply storeroom. Each item is recorded as it is removed from inventory, and the remaining inventory count (item total) is reduced. Regular review of the list will indicate what needs to be restocked and when.

SUMMARY

Maintenance involves more than cleaning and repairs. A good maintenance program also anticipates malfunctions and schedules regular examination and care of building components. Appearance is the best marketing tool for any property, so the site must be immaculate at all times. Housekeeping can be scheduled optimally by monitoring traffic flow through various parts of the building and by making sure the maintenance staff know how often inspections are required under differing conditions. Preventive maintenance lowers repair costs overall. It can help deter crime by assuring that security devices (door locks, alarms) and strategic lighting (in parking lots, stairwells, etc.) are operational.

Maintenance and repair of equipment poses risks and hazards to staff; to minimize these and provide a safe working environment, one must comply with OSHA regulations. The variety of chemicals used in cleaning and maintenance must be disposed of safely, so it is essential to know the proper procedures. If hazardous materials such as asbestos are found on the premises, the property manager must know what to do about them in order to comply with federal, state, and local environmental regulations.

Keeping accurate records is an integral part of maintenance and management. Use of purchase orders and inventory controls can save the owner the costs of excessive or inadequate inventory. Records are also necessary to track specific maintenance work and when or whether it has been completed.

Key Terms

Asbestos	Polychlorinated biphenyls (PCBs)
Corrective maintenance	Preventive maintenance
Custodial maintenance	Purchase order
Deferred maintenance	Radon
Formaldehyde	Work log
HVAC	Work order

Key Points

The effect of maintenance on value preservation and enhancement
Differences between routine (custodial, corrective) and preventive maintenance
Reasons for a maintenance routine and schedule
Relationship between maintenance and security
Importance of inventory control

Managing Residential Property

Residential property offers some of the greatest opportunities for property management because of the diversity and number of properties involved. In the public's perception, rental apartments are most commonly associated with professional management, and apartments come in a wide variety of sizes and configurations. One primary difference that managers face in managing rental housing is whether it is a conventional site (a market-based operation) or government-assisted (residents or owners may receive some sort of assistance which affects policies or procedures). Management of all types of rental housing requires that the manager select qualified residents and enforce lease terms. Condominium and cooperative housing also require management and can place their own special demands on managers. Mobile home parks, where residents commonly own the mobile homes they live in but lease the land on which they are set, offer a different type of management opportunity. The same is true of specialized housing for the elderly. This diversity creates numerous challenges and opportunities for property managers who specialize in residential management.

RENTAL HOUSING

Rental housing possibilities range from apartments of various sizes in high-rise buildings to single-family houses. Unlike commercial property, rental housing is in use twenty-four hours a day and must meet all of the

---

**Types of Residential Housing
that are Managed Professionally**
* Apartment buildings
* Government-assisted housing
* Single-family houses
* Condominiums
* Cooperatives
* Mobile home parks
* Housing for the elderly
* Planned unit developments (PUDs)

---

needs of residents' daily lives. This continuous occupancy of residential property tends to increase the demand for maintenance and repair. When housing is rented, there is an expectation that management will provide specific services such as yard work, window cleaning, snow removal, etc. If service lapses for any reason, the property manager may become the personification of the problem in the resident's mind. This is unavoidable at times and is not necessarily a reflection of the ability of the property manager or the quality of service. Because the resident considers the place he or she lives as "home," there is an investment of emotion as well as money. As a consequence, managers of residential property must have superior "people skills" in addition to proficiency in the administrative functions of the profession. Because the manager's compensation is usually based on the rental income of the property, the manager's efforts will be focused on maintaining the highest levels of occupancy. Satisfied residents are likely to want to renew their leases.

Management of residential property requires specific applications of the principles of real estate management already outlined in this book. The personal nature of the use of the leased space places special demands on the staff who work at the property. The following sections discuss characteristics of rental housing that make managing it unique.

Multiple-Unit Rental Housing

Technological advances have changed the concept, design, size, and features of apartment buildings. At one time, a prospective resident could tour numerous apartments of about the same size and never see the same floor plan twice. Newer apartments usually have more standardized floor plans; variety appears in the types of amenities that are built into the individual units and the building or complex. Although new complexes are generally more popular with renters, a fairly large portion of the rental population seeks "vintage" property, especially in urban areas. Location, size, age, and amenities make every apartment building unique. The challenge of property management is to recognize and accentuate the positive characteristics of the individual property. This creates a more pleasant residence and helps to enhance the property value.

High-rise apartment buildings are popular in major cities where land is at a premium and intensive use of the land is a necessity. The minimum number of stories that constitute a high-rise apartment building varies by region, but most buildings that are between ten and fifteen stories tall would be classified as such. The largest high-rise apartment buildings can contain hundreds of apartments and house thousands of residents. These buildings may have a variety of recreational amenities such as fitness centers, tennis courts, swimming pools, saunas, hot tubs, etc. Parking on decks or in underground garages connected to the building may be another amenity, although the number of parking spaces allotted per resident or apartment may be limited. A high-rise apartment building may warrant a continuously staffed "front desk" or have all-night attendants on duty when the on-site office is closed. Large high-rise apartments may also include retail space for convenience stores or newsstands on the ground floors.

One type of multiple-unit development that is found in both cities and suburbs is the *mid-rise apartment building*. These are between four and nine stories tall and may include recreational facilities. A central lobby and mail room are fairly standard. Mid-rise apartment buildings in urban areas are not likely to provide parking, but their counterparts in small cities and suburban areas usually have parking available. Most buildings that are four or more stories tall have elevators, although older four-story apartment buildings may have stairs only. Such a building may be referred to as a *walk-up*.

Garden apartments are often located in suburban areas where land is comparatively less expensive. Garden apartment complexes may occupy several acres and consist of numerous *low-rise buildings* one to three stories tall, with each building having as few as four apartments. A separate building may house laundry facilities, the management office, or recreational amenities. Such amenities are often comparable to those in high-rise apartment buildings. Part of the attraction of the suburban garden apartment complex comes from its appealing landscape.

Traditional smaller properties with two to twelve units have profited from a resurgence in popularity. Most of these buildings do not have elevator service and consequently are rarely more than three stories tall. Many of them have been rehabilitated, especially in urban areas. Even though these small properties do not provide the recreational amenities found in other types of apartment buildings, they generally offer greater privacy along with the conveniences most apartment dwellers expect in return for rent.

The architectural design of multiple-unit apartment developments and their size directly affect the complexity of managing them. For instance, high-rise apartment buildings include sophisticated elevators, centralized HVAC equipment, and other systems that require specialized maintenance. Large garden complexes offer a different set of management challenges because they have more spacious lawns and separate equipment in each of several buildings. Small apartment buildings usually provide few extra services and facilities and consequently are less "management-intensive." However, these structures are usually older, and their general maintenance may be time-consuming. Older structures usually require a greater amount of work per apartment as well. In addition to the physical upkeep that apartment buildings require, administrative time is influenced by the number of properties in a manager's portfolio. The preparation of an operations report on 300 apartments may be a relatively light exercise if all the units are in one building owned by a sole proprietor. On the other hand, 300 apartments in thirty individually owned 10-unit buildings will require more involved reporting.

Government-Assisted Housing

Government-assisted housing is defined as any residential rental property in which the lessor receives part of the rent payment from a governmental body. As a general rule, governmental housing subsidies are either resident based or property based. In the former arrangement, the government pays a portion of the resident's rent to the owner; in the latter, the government buys down a portion of the owner's mortgage and thereby reduces the interest rate on the loan. In this circumstance, the owner must agree to reduce rents to comply with the program. In another type of program, the local housing authority may lease a portion of a rental complex from the owner or use a voucher program to pay a certain percentage of some residents' rent. In this manner, the government achieves the goal of *mixed-income housing* by providing more housing choices to citizens who have very low to moderate incomes. *Public housing,* on the other hand, is generally owned and managed through a local or state governmental agency. Regardless of the level of government involved, government-assisted housing challenges the creativity of the real estate manager.

Rental property in which a subsidy is provided usually is owned by private investors. The common forms of real estate ownership (partnerships, corporations, REITs, etc.) also apply to subsidized housing, and the owners' desire for a fair return on their investment is the same as in conventional housing. However, a portion of the return on investment in subsidized housing may result from additional tax advantages that were granted for development, for leasing part of the property to residents eligible for housing subsidies, or for leasing to the local housing authority. Lower debt service payments due to special loan arrangements can also increase the return so that the investment is competitive with conventional housing. Another common arrangement is for the developers and investors to build the complex and sell it to the housing authority or to a religious or charitable (nonprofit) organization that specializes in subsidized housing.

The need for effective management of subsidized and public housing creates a strong demand for property managers who are skilled in balancing the interests of all the parties involved—owners, governmental agencies, residents who receive subsidies, residents who do not, citizens' action groups, and resident (tenant) associations. In addition to understanding the principles of real estate management, managers of subsidized housing must thoroughly understand all applicable regulations. They must also understand the role and structure of the governmental agencies involved and work within budgets that are limited because of lower rental income. Under most federal, state, and local housing programs, an extensive series of forms and reports must be submitted. These reports are often time-consuming to complete, and if they are filled out improperly, they may have to be redone before compensation will be sent.

Property managers who work with public or government-assisted housing often think of themselves as a special breed. Their specialization extends beyond the ability to work with governmental agencies. Interactions with residents are often more demanding than in other professionally managed housing because the objective of assuring resident comfort has additional social, political, and fiscal dimensions. In subsidized housing, the manager must establish lines of communication to overcome a multitude of barriers—ethnic, economic, social, and linguistic. In addition to maintaining peaceful coexistence at the property, the improved relations that result help the community and society at large.

Federal Housing Programs. Government-assisted housing evolved from the post-Depression New Deal plan to rebuild the United States' economic strength. The initial programs were designed primarily to stimulate construction, but subsequent housing programs have shifted the government's emphasis toward programs that benefit residents more directly. The Housing Act of 1937 was passed to meet the needs of people with lower incomes, and most federal government-assisted housing legislation enacted since then has perpetuated that goal. However, the Housing and Community Development Act of 1974 changed the federal government's role in housing and urban development. Since the passage of that Act, *Section 8* has become a major program for federal government housing assistance. There are four major Section 8 programs.

1. The *existing housing program* gives its recipients greater choice in the housing market. An eligible individual or family finds an existing apartment in the private market, and the apartment is inspected

to verify that it is of standard quality. The amount of the rent subsidy and the amount the resident pays depend on the resident's income level—residents pay a percentage of their income for rent and the remainder is paid by the government. They are usually responsible for utilities the same way conventional renters in the building are. Although the program has worked rather effectively and can be administered through nearly any local agency with minimal difficulty, there are drawbacks. The federal government can change the program at any time for any reason, and such changes have wide-ranging impact. Another drawback is that the rent rate is set by the government at a "fair market value" for the space, a rate which may in some cases be low.

2. The *new construction program* guarantees to private developers, before construction of new housing projects, that eligible prospects who apply directly to the owner will be subsidized.

3. The *substantial rehabilitation program* operates in the same manner but is a form of assistance in the renovation of existing structures.

4. The *moderate rehabilitation program* has the same net effect but does not require as great an amount to be spent on the rehabilitation.

In addition to these Section 8 programs, there are many other federal housing programs. In most cases, they are available to a particular segment of the population (for example, the Section 202 program covers housing for the elderly and disabled).

Selecting Qualified Residents

One of a residential manager's most important responsibilities is qualifying prospects for residency. Before agreeing to establish a lease, it is essential for the property manager to obtain certain information about a prospect.

- Does the prospect have sufficient resources to pay the rent and his or her existing obligations?
- Will the prospect pay the rent on time?
- Will the prospect respect the privacy and property of others?
- Will the prospect maintain the rental space?

The answers to these questions are usually provided by the prospective resident on a *rental application* form (information guidelines are outlined in exhibit 9.1). With the exception of the financial data, some of this information may be difficult to verify. The amount of information that is

---

EXHIBIT   9.1

Information Commonly Requested on an Apartment Rental Application Form

Property/Lease Information
- The space to be rented (street address and apartment number)
- Rental rate (dollars per month)
- Duration of the lease term (if applicant approved)
- Amount of security deposit

Applicant Information—Personal
- Name and social security number of principal applicant (and all adults who will sign the lease)
- Name(s) of all other occupants, including minor children
- Description(s) of any pets (if allowed)

Applicant Residency Information
- *Current* address and phone number
- Name and phone number of current landlord; address (if different from applicant's)
- Duration of current tenancy
- Reason for leaving
- The same information for *prior* residence

Applicant Employment Information
- *Current* place of employment (company name, address, and phone number), job title, years with the company, immediate supervisor(s), and salary
- Same information for *prior* employer

Applicant Financial Status
- Institution names and account numbers for bank savings and checking accounts, credit cards or charge accounts, automobile and other outstanding loans

Other Information
- Identification of any requisite deposits or fees to be paid at the time the application is completed (e.g., for processing the credit check) and their refundability
- A statement of authenticity of information provided and grant of permission to verify it
- Applicant signature
- Spaces for initials of staff who process the application and the date

---

actually validated may be left to the discretion of the property manager. In particular, inquiries pertaining to prospective residents' behavior must be made cautiously and without any bias; a decision that can be perceived as discriminatory can lead to liability. Of utmost importance in the selection of residents is understanding of local, state, and federal fair housing laws.

Fair Housing Ground Rules.   The federal Fair Housing Act of 1968 (Title VIII, Civil Rights Act of 1968) prohibits housing discrimination on the basis of race, color, religion, national origin, or sex. The Fair Housing

Amendments Act of 1988 further prohibits discrimination on the basis of familial status (children) or mental or physical disability. Interpretation of these laws has been very strict, partly because very few people overtly say to a prospective renter, "I will not rent this apartment to you because. . . ." Even an unwitting breach of the law can result in a discrimination lawsuit, an event that can end a career and result in a substantial monetary fine. One of the most common discriminatory practices involves a prospect who inquires about available property and is dissuaded from living at a particular site or is encouraged to look elsewhere. This is called *steering* An applicant from whom some vacancies are hidden is also a victim of steering.

The intent of the fair housing laws is to give every resident an *equal opportunity* to live where he or she desires. To uphold the spirit of this law, it is important to maintain consistency in all phases of the relationship with prospects and residents. To maintain such consistency, all employees who interview prospects at the property or at the management firm should receive thorough training in this matter, and all policies should be clearly stated in writing. For example, if it is decided that income level compared to rent is an important selection criterion, the formula to calculate the ratio should be standardized, documented, and applied to all applicants consistently. Fair housing laws are subject to change, particularly as states and local jurisdictions enact their own rules. The latter are often more stringent, and the most stringent law in place locally is the one that applies, so state, county, and municipal codes can supersede federal acts. Consultation with an attorney and reading on the subject of fair housing are two ways to remain informed on these important laws.

Rent-Paying Ability.   A prospect's past payment record, sources and amount of income, and level of indebtedness are the main considerations in determining rent-paying ability. The amount of rent as a percentage of the individual's income is not by itself a definitive indicator of someone's ability to pay rent. The size of a household and the number of its members who are employed affect the amount of money available for rent.

Most occupants of rental housing in the United States pay their rent from current income. Reserves or proceeds from financial investments are not commonly used. The resident who loses a job may soon be unable to pay the rent because he or she does not have enough cash in reserve to meet living costs for an extended period. Housing may be considered essential, but in times of financial difficulty, other essentials such as food, clothing, and transportation may take precedence over rent payment.

It is fair and necessary to examine prospective residents' sources of income to verify their ability to pay rent. Factors to consider are the length of time that a worker has been in a position with a company, the amount of income and frequency with which it is paid, and the nature of the employer's business. Individually, these factors may not qualify or disqualify a prospect, but taken together they can be a good indicator of personal financial strength.

- *Length of service.* The longer someone has been in a position, the more likely it is that employer and employee are mutually satisfied with each other's performance, increasing the probability of the prospect's job security.
- *Amount of income.* Although the amount of rent as a percentage of income can be used to estimate the prospect's ability to pay the rent, it is not the only deciding factor. In addition to wages or salary, the prospect should be asked about other financial resources.
- *Frequency of payment.* Because rent usually is paid from current income, knowing how often the prospect is paid can be helpful in predicting the timeliness of rent payments.
- *Nature of the business.* It was thought at one time that some jobs were more secure than others, that workers paid by the hour were at greater risk of being laid off than salaried workers. The changing economic climate from decade to decade indicates there are no guarantees. Anyone can be laid off at any time. Because the prospect probably works in or near the community, the property manager can easily learn about the company, its outlook, and its reputation as an employer.

Review of these factors may cast a favorable light on a prospect, but none of them indicates whether he or she manages money wisely. A large family with limited means may be very frugal while someone with a large income and a secure position may not. Just as it is important to verify sufficient income, it is also important to check the applicant's payment record for loans and revolving credit programs. Regular and timely payments signify responsibility and ability to manage money.

Property managers generally hire credit bureaus to conduct the financial investigation of an applicant. Businesses are willing to provide a reputable credit bureau with accurate information because they may rely on the credit bureau for information themselves or foresee a use for the service. A credit bureau's reputation for maintaining confidentiality is also well known in most circumstances, and reputable organizations know precisely what to ask without inadvertently requesting information that cannot be given out. However the information is to be acquired, the Fair Credit Reporting Act requires that the prospect must be advised that his or her credit is being checked. A standard rental application form usually includes a statement that the prospect permits verification of the information provided.

Respect for Property and Neighbors.   While financial investigation of all applicants is important, it is equally important to verify that applicants will be good neighbors and treat the property with care. However, this information is more difficult to verify. It is usually beyond the scope of a credit bureau's investigation, although other local firms may perform such background checks. Such firms may also scan public records for evidence of evictions and checks returned because of nonsufficient funds.

The definitive sources for verification of an applicant's respect for property and neighbors are his or her previous landlords. A phone call or visit to the prospect's present landlord is often the best way to learn about the prospect's rental payment record, respect for neighbors, and treatment of the premises. However, the manager should interpret a current landlord's comments carefully. The present landlord may commend the prospect even if he or she has not been an ideal resident; knowing there is a place for a problem resident to move is one way to assure the problem will soon be gone. (Within a small network of property managers and landlords, such a tactic would result in few referrals and hinder professional cooperation.) If a landlord's responses seem dubious, checking with an earlier landlord may remove any doubts. A former landlord may be more candid because the prospect is no longer a resident.

Length of residency is additional evidence of reliability. A succession of moves may imply instability, while long-term occupancy tends to indicate that the prospect is dependable.

Permanence Potential.   Although it is difficult to predict how long a prospect may be a resident, those whose records indicate prior long-term occupancies will probably reside in a new rental space for a long period as well. Most stable households dislike moving, yet turnover in residential properties is common. Frequent turnover reduces income and increases costs for repair, cleaning, and leasing. That is why long-term residents are greatly desired.

The Residential Lease

A lease is a contractual agreement between a landlord and a residential tenant to provide the resident with a private dwelling and the landlord with regular payment in the form of rent. A lease is important because it protects the resident's interests as much as it protects the landlord's. In an attempt to dispel negative connotations of the word "lease," a residential lease is sometimes called an *occupancy agreement.* However, an occupancy agreement is just as binding legally; in fact, it is a lease.

The lease for any rental property is based on intended use of the space and any special provisions for that usage. Residential leases by na-

---

Principal Clauses of a Residential Lease
• Names of parties (landlord and residential tenant)
• Description of leased premises
• Amount of security deposit
• Amount of rent and due date
• Late fees and other charges
• Term of lease
• Subleasing
• Rules and regulations clause

---

ture are not complicated, but there are some provisions and clauses that must be included. These are discussed in the following sections.

Lease Clauses and Provisions.   Printed lease forms include specific clauses that define the leased space, govern the payment of rent and handling of security deposits, and state the responsibilities of and the relationship between the landlord and the resident. These forms usually include various protections for both parties. The items discussed here are especially important.

Lease Term.   While there is no standard *lease term* for residential property, one year is the usual period that is cited; six-month and month-to-month terms are also seen. The length of the term is often based on what is popular in a given market. In most markets, residential units that command high rents are covered by a written lease lasting at least one year.

Establishing the term of the lease has both advantages and disadvantages. When a lease is signed, the rent is probably the highest the market will bear at the time for the amount of space leased. If market demand rises during the lease term, the owner has essentially undersold the space; if the market declines, the resident has agreed to a rent that may exceed the rate for comparable space.

Although a residential lease term of more than one year is uncommon, the property manager should always remember that the length of the lease term can be used to advantage. The incentive of a free period of rent and adjustment of the lease term to compensate for that period have already been discussed. Other circumstances may also justify a modified lease term. For example, a prospect who needs to find a place to live during the winter and an owner who wishes to fill a vacancy during this period are both limited in their options because winter is a period in which there is little turnover, especially in northern regions. If a qualified prospect is found, a sixteen- or seventeen-month lease may benefit both owner and resident even though the time period is unusual. The longer lease term would preclude the unit becoming vacant the following winter and protect the resident from having to move again in the cold.

When nonrelated adults occupy a unit, each resident should sign a lease. While individual leases for several adults sharing one rental unit may seem extraordinarily troublesome, the action prevents friends of the residents from becoming long-term guests. If one resident is irresponsible or behind in paying rent, his or her eviction is more easily managed if a lease is issued for each roommate.

Condition of Premises.   A *statement of condition* is usually a reflection of what has been noted during an inspection of an apartment just prior to a resident's moving into it. Incidental damage may be noted so a new resident will not be charged for it on move-out. This statement may also include information about what charges for damage will be assessed at move-out and what will be considered normal wear and tear. This is a delicate subject because of varied interpretations of the word "damage" by the manager and the resident. Finally, a statement of condition may establish the overall state to which the apartment is expected to be restored at the time of move-out. Information regarding condition may be included in the lease or in a policies (house rules) handbook given to residents.

Pets.   Animals can be a nuisance and can damage property. That is why property managers and owners often prohibit pets on the property. However, such a policy can also limit the potential market for an apartment. A *pet clause* is necessary regardless of whether pets are allowed. Instead of outright prohibition, thorough guidelines can be established that specify what is allowed and what is not. Alternatively, these may be stated in a separate *pet agreement* that the pet-owning resident signs, or they may be listed in the residents' handbook. The provisions in a pet agreement may only reiterate local ordinances, but if they are a stipulation of the lease or of house rules, they are easier to enforce. Guidelines often set limitations on the type, size, and number of pets allowed; list requirements for damage deposits, use of leashes, and cleanup of animal wastes; and reiterate legalities related to licensing and vaccinations.

1. *Type of animal.* There are arguments for allowing some types of animals and excluding others. Barking dogs may be considered a nuisance by other residents. Cats have a tendency to roam when let out and to scratch woodwork indoors. Exotic pets, if not illegal, may be too large for the premises. Pets also produce odors that linger. These are elements to consider in deciding which animals to permit.
2. *Size of pet.* Specific weight and height requirements should be

stated so that extremely large dogs or exotic animals can be excluded.

3. *Number of pets.* A maximum number of pets may be instituted to preclude residents from having too many animals.

4. *Pet deposit and registration.* It is appropriate to require an extra deposit for each pet. This deposit should be sufficient to cover any damage to the leased space or the property as a whole and to deter the resident from allowing the pet to cause damage. The pet should be registered with the property manager. This links a specific pet to the deposit and verifies the number of pets on the premises. An instant photo of the pet for resident files is an added measure of verification.

5. *Leash requirement.* It is wise to state that all pets taken outside must be kept on a leash. Pets may break loose from their leashes occasionally; such a statement is not intended to penalize a resident for this rare occurrence but to encourage residents to take extra care with their animals and not allow them to roam.

6. *Cleanup.* Animal wastes are a danger to health and sanitation, and many communities have passed ordinances requiring pet owners to clean up after their animals. This should be a policy of managed residential property as well.

7. *Vaccinations and licenses.* It should be a requirement of the property that all animals receive appropriate vaccinations and are licensed as required by law. Neutering or spaying may also be required.

Although such a pet policy may appear rather harsh when itemized and listed in an agreement, the property manager can remind the resident that these measures are similar to advice given by pet associations and humane societies. In addition to protecting the owner's property, these policies safeguard the pet and all residents of the property from the nuisance and danger that animals can sometimes pose.

Subleasing. A prospect may request inclusion of a *transfer clause* that allows the lease to be broken without penalty in case of a job transfer. If that is the case, the property manager should request documentation from the resident's employer to that effect. Instead of a transfer clause, a *sublet clause* should be written into the lease, stating that in order for the resident to vacate the premises before the end of the term, whether because of a transfer or other extenuating circumstances, he or she must find a suitable resident to sublet the space for the remainder of the lease obligation. This person will have to be approved by the property manager, and either the resident or the subtenant will have to pay for the credit check. In the event of a job transfer, the employer may use its resources to help find a subtenant or, on the employee's behalf, pay a negotiated penalty for breaking the lease without finding a subtenant.

Utilities. Occupants of rental apartments are usually responsible for payment of utilities such as cooking gas and electricity, for which they are billed directly by the utility provider. The lease should state specifically what utilities are the resident's responsibility. This is especially important when residents pay for their own heat. If some utilities are charged to the property, a system for prorating such expenses (based on apartment square footage) and billing each resident may be implemented. Because of the time involved in prorating utilities, it is usually easier and more economical to include them in the rent. This is a common practice in older buildings in which the apartments are not individually metered.

Rules and Regulations. To assure residents' safety, protect their rights, and protect the physical integrity of the property, a set of rules and regulations may be distributed to new residents. These rules may be part of a *residents' handbook.* In addition to recapitulating information in the lease (such as when rent is due), it is also an appropriate format in which to state policies regarding trash disposal, laundry room use, permissible or prohibited furnishings (e.g., water beds), etc. To encourage all residents to abide by these rules, the handbook may come with a form for the residents to sign that states they have read and understand the rules. In addition, a clause in the lease stating that the resident understands and will abide by the house rules is often appropriate. To make the house rules more palatable, they may be called "policies" rather than rules and regulations. Positive statements are more readily accepted than a list of what is not allowed. Following are some items that may be listed in a residents' handbook.

- When rent is due and how delinquencies are treated (what constitutes late payment, fees that will be assessed for late payments, etc.)
- The purpose of the security deposit and conditions for its return
- Limitations on occupancy by visitors and persons other than those named in the lease
- Limitations on parking by residents and visitors
- Pet agreement conditions
- Limitations on particular furnishings, wall hangings, etc.
- Use of laundry room, pool, and any other amenities of the property
- Fundamental maintenance and upkeep the resident is expected to perform (i.e., resident provides and replaces own light bulbs within residence; resident is expected to replace the battery in the smoke detector when necessary)
- Whom to call for emergency repairs and other services

- Which utilities are the resident's responsibility
- Insurance the resident is expected to carry
- Evacuation procedures and exit routes from the specific apartment
- Requirements for notice of renewal, nonrenewal, or termination of the lease
- Procedures for management inspections of the premises before move-in and after move-out, the effect of the latter on security deposit refunds (amounts charged for cleanup and repairs to restore the apartment to move-in condition), and requirements to restore the property to the original rental condition
- Need for and right of the landlord to enter the premises and conditions that would require the landlord to enter the premises without notifying the resident first
- Rules governing subletting
- What constitutes grounds for eviction
- Other limitations or proscriptions on the residents' actions

The residents' handbook may also include information regarding proper care of built-in appliances such as ovens, refrigerators, air conditioners and furnaces, or thermostats. Such instructions (e.g., do not use a sharp object to defrost the freezer compartment of the refrigerator; always run cold water when using the garbage disposal, etc.) can avert damage or minimize wear on the appliances. Other suggestions, particularly those pertaining to energy conservation (e.g., replace air-conditioner filters regularly; keep windows and doors closed in the winter or when operating the air conditioner in the summer, etc.), will reduce the residents' utility bills or the owners' expenses for master-metered fuel.

Compliance with Landlord-Tenant Laws.   Most if not all local jurisdictions have laws that affect the rights of residents; these are known collectively as "landlord-tenant laws." They state the rights and obligations of both landlords and residents and what either party can do if the other does not comply with the lease or the law. Landlord-tenant laws usually govern issues that are addressed in the lease, its clauses, or the policies (or rules) for the property. In particular, they regulate the handling of security deposits. They may also set the maximum late fee that can be charged, state provisions and requirements for subleasing, and specify procedures for eviction.

Certain locales have *rent control laws* that set a ceiling on the amount of rent that can be charged. Rent control is a concept that is seen in some metropolitan areas—as a way to maintain "affordable" housing—but it benefits neither owners nor residents over the long term. If rent is held below what the market will bear, the income of the property may not be adequate to maintain it properly. The result will be a greater concentration of undesirable residential space. Properties that are not maintained lose value. Depressed property values also reduce municipal income because of the lower property taxes they yield. Because it reduces or precludes the potential for financial success, rent control also discourages new construction.

Encouraging Renewals.   Reputable residents are the most valuable assets of any income-producing residential property. A resident whose lease is nearing expiration should be contacted two to three months before the expiration date. Some managers send out a new lease. Others send only a renewal notice stating the rent and noting any specific changes in terms and conditions of the prior lease. Personal contact regarding renewal is a good management tactic. Hand delivery of a renewal lease or a follow-up visit is a way of showing residents that their tenancy is valued.

Even though residents generally anticipate a rent increase, they may protest it. Because of the potential for reaction, managers often focus on lease renewal as the time to improve the unit. Upgrading is a sound business practice and can be an incentive for the resident to renew. The upgrade may be a new appliance, painting one or more rooms, or some other work. (Some improvements may be necessary in the unit regardless of the resident's decision.) At least three benefits can be gained from improving a unit as part of a lease renewal.

1. *Good resident relations.* Even if the improvement is not necessary for the resident to commit to a new lease, the extension of goodwill strengthens the relationship with a good resident. If the improvement alone wins the renewal, it is most likely a cost-effective means of keeping the unit leased. The cost is usually equivalent to or less than one month's rent. If the improvement averts a rent loss because of temporary vacancy, it also averts the expense of advertising and marketing. The improvement may be necessary anyway to keep the unit competitive in the market if the lease cannot be renewed.

2. *Increased property value.* A comprehensive program of individual unit improvements will increase the value of the property as a whole, which may lead to higher income both short- and long-term. The investment may increase the resale value of the property by much more than the actual cost of the improvements.

3. *Tax benefits.* Apartment upgrades can be tax deductible in either of two ways. An improvement that will increase the value of the property and will endure for more than one year may be depreciable over several years. On the other hand, the cost of repairs done to preserve the integrity of the property may be deductible as an operating expense for the year in which it is paid.

CONDOMINIUMS AND COOPERATIVES

Managing condominiums and cooperatives is quite different from managing residential rental property. A *condominium* is a multiple-unit residence in which the units are individually owned. In a *cooperative,* ownership of shares in the cooperative corporation entitles an individual to inhabit a unit. Condominium and cooperative ownership does not preclude the necessity of professional management; in fact, it usually increases the need for it, especially in large complexes. Technically there is no difference in construction among the various types of residential property—cooperative, condominium, and rental apartment buildings can have identical floor plans. Unit ownership is what makes the management of condominium and cooperative properties unique.

Condominium Fundamentals

The word "condominium" literally means "joint dominion"—the domains (homes) are arranged together in a single property. One who owns a unit in a condominium development actually owns the space bounded by the floor, walls, and ceiling of a particular unit. The rest of the property (hallways, lobby, grounds, and any other part of the property that is not individually owned) is called the *common area.* The individual owners technically own a percentage of the common area, and this percentage is usually based on the square footage of their living areas compared to all of the living area in the building. It may also be based on the desirability of the individual unit—irrespective of square footage, some units will have higher values because of various amenities and therefore represent a greater percentage of the entire property value. However, common area ownership is *undivided,* so no owner can claim a particular section of common area as his or her own.

State law requires that condominium unit owners form a *condominium association,* a not-for-profit corporation comprised of all of the individual owners; it is a body that discusses and acts on common concerns of the property owners. All owners are association members. The association elects a board of directors from among the membership. From the board of directors, individuals are elected to serve as president, vice president, secretary, and treasurer. The remaining board members who are not officers are at-large members. The board is responsible for the management of the property and it normally hires the property manager. In addition to hiring and communicating with the property manager, the condominium association upholds and fulfills the tenets of the *governing documents,* which usually include the following:

- *Declaration.* The declaration commits the land to condominium use, provides for the association's creation, defines the method to determine each owner's share of expenses, and outlines the relationship between the individual owners and the association. The declaration is effectively the constitution of the association.
- *Bylaws.* While the declaration establishes the broad administrative framework for the association, the bylaws provide specific procedures for handling routine matters such as accounting, maintenance of common areas and individual units (the unit owner being responsible for repair and maintenance within his or her unit), election of officers (and their duties), votes by the association members, collection of assessments, and other administrative business.
- *Unit deed.* The individual unit deed is the document that legally transfers to the purchaser the title of a condominium unit and its undivided portion of the common areas.

Other documents relate to the establishment and operation of a condominium. The *articles of incorporation* state that the condominium association is a corporation under the laws of the state. House *rules and regulations* are the guidelines for day-to-day behavior on the premises and for settling disputes that may arise. Although there are many rules that are common among condominium properties, each association is likely to establish some rules that are unique. The rules may cover anything from pets to noise to parking.

The bylaws or a separate document usually specify the percentage of the property owned by each unit owner by taking into account the amount of living area—and possibly the desirability—of each unit. These percentages are the multipliers used to calculate the monthly *assessment* paid by each owner. The monthly assessment is used to pay the operating expenses for the whole property—common-area services, maintenance, reserves, and management. If the board determines that operating expenses for the whole property are $4,000 a month and the bylaws state that the owner of unit 6B owns five percent of the property, then the owner of 6B will pay the association at least $200 every month.

Reserves also must be factored into the regular assessment collections. Reserve funds may be used to pay for anticipated and unanticipated capital expenses. If a capital expense is required and there are not sufficient reserve funds to pay it, or if the association chooses not to deplete reserves to pay the expense, a special assessment will be necessary to defray the cost. For example, if the property needs a new roof and $30,000 of that cost will not be paid from the reserves, the owner of unit 6B (who owns five percent of the property) will be required to pay a special assessment of $1,500.

The *timeshare condominium* is a specialized form of condominium found mostly in resort areas. As the name implies, the owner has the right to occupy the unit for a specific period. There are several ways to set up a timeshare condominium. In order to provide the owner with an actual share of property and its accompanying tax advantages, he or she may co-operatively own a percentage of a condominium unit. In other words, a person who owns one month's possession of one unit every year may own $^{30}/_{365}$ of a unit. On that basis, a 100-unit building could have 1,200 or more owners.

Cooperative Fundamentals

Cooperative ownership differs from condominium ownership in that the cooperative incorporates itself to purchase or build a multiple-unit dwelling and issues shares in the corporation to represent the proportion of ownership of the entire property. Shareholders receive a *proprietary lease* that entitles them to occupy one unit. A single mortgage covers the entire cooperative property. Managing a cooperative differs from managing a condominium in several ways. Residents tend to be long-term—the resident profile is highly stable and homogeneous. Decisions for the cooperative are made by a board, which is comprised of shareholders in the corporation.

Cooperative boards can be more active than condominium boards, and sometimes they enforce greater restrictions on the property—new residents must be interviewed and approved by the board; the board may have the right to approve or deny improvements to units; the board may stipulate that all sales of shares must be on an all-cash basis, and the board may state that only shareholders may reside in units (i.e., they cannot be bought as investments and leased to others).

The Role of Management

Perhaps the most important attraction to owning and occupying a portion of a multiple-unit building is that advantages of apartment living are combined with advantages of homeownership. The owner of a condominium unit reaps all of the tax advantages of homeownership and his or her equity in the property grows as the mortgage on the unit is paid down. As with maintenance of a single-family house, the owner can make repairs and improvements to his or her individual unit.

The condominium or cooperative association may manage the property on its own, but larger complexes require full-time supervision, which is usually why a property manager is hired (or retained as a consultant). Unlike rental property, condominiums and cooperatives have no effective

gross income; their monthly assessment collections are based on anticipated expenses—including management fees and funds for reserves. Because of this, compensation for management is usually a fixed monthly
amount, which is prorated into the owners' monthly assessments. However, the manager may negotiate separate fees for specific additional services or for attending after-hours' board meetings.

Owner Relations. Because each encounter between a staff member
and a resident is an encounter with one of the property owners, all employees must understand their relationship to the owners. Their efforts to
extend goodwill should not compromise the agreement between management and the board of directors. Because the residents actually own the
property, they may think the staff is at their service for any maintenance or
repairs in their individual units. However, condominium and cooperative
residents usually have to pay for these services separately. (Depending on
the management agreement, the residents may have to call an independent service of their choosing or pay the association to have the work
done by staff.) To be fair to the other unit owners, the association must be
reimbursed for an employee's work on an individual unit. As a convenience, some properties may provide service in individual units at no
charge to residents. However, the association members must agree that
such a benefit is worth higher assessments for everyone.

Working with a Board of Directors. The association most likely elects
a board and new officers each year, or there may be an annual election
with staggered multiple-year terms to ensure consistency of board decisions. The meetings are usually held after-hours in one of the resident's
units or in an office or common room available on the premises. Because
the board meeting is also a gathering of neighbors, the agenda may yield
to tangential discussions. The proximity of the board members, by virtue
of living in the same building or complex, may also encourage frequent
meetings. The property manager is usually required to attend *some* meetings. However, the amount of time the manager must spend at these meetings can often be minimized if the management agreement includes an
hourly fee for attending meetings.

The board makes management decisions, but the manager may be the
one who carries out those decisions. This may require the manager to me-
diate differences of opinion among the board members. With regard to
issues of property management, the property manager is probably better
qualified to decide which course of action to take. However, property
management decisions may provoke dissent because some board members may consider the manager's viewpoint biased. These differences of
opinion can be extremely frustrating for a manager and can impede suc-

cessful management. To prevent conflicting demands on the manager, the board should be asked to name one individual—usually the president—to be responsible for communication with the manager.

Maintenance. As owners of the property, the residents will be especially attentive to maintenance of the building and grounds. While a rental property must be sold as a whole, the units in a condominium or the shares of a cooperative may be bought and sold independently. Rental property can tolerate some deferred maintenance for a limited time without losing value. However, once the owner decides to sell a rental property, its deferred maintenance must be corrected to assure the highest sale price possible. In contrast, any deferred maintenance of a condominium or cooperative, whether in a particular unit or in a common area, will lower the individual unit or share value. The board or the president may have to be reminded of that fact occasionally, especially when a repair is extremely costly. Because resident-owned properties are investments and resale potential is paramount to the resident-owners, management must be aware of a heightened demand for housekeeping in condominiums and cooperatives. The property manager should work diligently with the association to assure that funds for maintenance of the property are budgeted adequately and that there are sufficient funds in reserve.

Fiscal Affairs. The assessments paid by condominium and cooperative owners are intended primarily to cover the operating costs of the property that is owned in common (e.g., insurance, utility costs, etc.). These costs must be kept under control to minimize the residents' individual assessments. However, assessments should not be so low that there is no provision for reserves. Low monthly assessments usually result in requirements for special assessments every time there is a major repair. If only one or even a few residents do not have the money available to pay a special assessment when it is levied, the necessary work may be jeopardized. For this reason alone, it is important to accrue an adequate reserve fund through the regular assessment. The board should be encouraged to develop ample reserves because it is in the owners' best interests to preserve the value of the property as a whole, and, if possible, enhance it. Prospective buyers recognize the value of a large reserve and will be more inclined to pay a higher price for a condominium unit or shares of a cooperative because of it.

As a general rule, a condominium or other homeowners' association can apply for tax-exempt status under the Internal Revenue Code if (1) a prescribed percentage of its gross income comes from unit owner assessments; (2) a prescribed percentage of its expenses are for managing, maintaining, and caring for common areas; (3) substantially all of the units are used as residences; and (4) no part of the net income benefits any individual member of the association. Some sources of income—interest earned by reserve funds, fees received for special use of amenities, and the like— are not exempt under any circumstances. Tax exemption protects the principal of the reserve fund. Without exempt status, reserves collected as part of the assessment could be construed as the association's profit and taxed accordingly. A tax specialist should be consulted periodically for updates on rules governing tax exemption of a homeowners' association.

OTHER RESIDENTIAL PROPERTY

Variations on traditional rental and ownership arrangements abound. These include single-family houses, mobile home parks, specialized housing for the elderly, and planned unit developments. Few property managers are involved in working exclusively with these variations, but they represent a large part of the housing market; in some localities, one of them may be the dominant type of available housing.

Single-Family Houses

References to "the American dream" frequently conjure notions of owning a house surrounded by a yard. However, many houses are not owned by their inhabitants but are in fact leased. A *single-family house* is defined as having its own entry. Therefore townhouses, which by definition share a common wall but have private entrances, are also classified as single-family houses.

An extension of the American dream is the investment in a second or third house to rent to others. A house requires a smaller financial commitment than a multiple-unit dwelling; the percentage required as a down payment is often lower; and a house usually can be resold more quickly and easily than a larger property. Some first-time real estate investors start in this manner. Another group of investors are those who buy a house to live in when they retire and retain their original house as a source of rental income. Because these investors may live far away from their rental properties, they often seek professional property management.

Houses as rental units are generally more time-consuming to manage, primarily because they are rarely next door to each other. If an owner demands a level of maintenance that exceeds what can be required of the resident, the general upkeep of the premises can be as time consuming as for a larger property. Marketing and leasing take more time because the manager has to travel to the individual units. In all likelihood, each rental house in a property management company's portfolio will be individually owned, and the manager will have to report to numerous owners, many of whom do not live nearby. Despite these seeming disadvantages, some managers have marketed their skills exclusively to the single-family house rental market with great success. Managing rental houses can be very rewarding financially—because of the value placed on greater privacy, more-accessible parking, and a private yard, a house usually commands more rent than an equivalent-sized apartment.

Mobile Home Parks

A mobile home (also called "manufactured housing") is usually built at a factory and, depending on its width, is transported to the installation site in halves or as a whole. At the site, final assembly and connection of the mobile home to gas, electrical, water, and sewer facilities takes place.

Zoning laws commonly prohibit manufactured housing in neighborhoods where there are conventionally built houses. Manufactured housing is found in areas zoned for *mobile home parks*. Residents of these parks generally own their homes, but they rarely own the land beneath them. They lease the land and may have to pay an access charge for the utility connections. The ground rent usually provides for maintenance of park roads and amenities; residents are responsible for maintaining their homes and private yards. Utilities may be billed directly to residents by the utility company, but it is also common for the park to serve as a distributor and bill residents for utilities used. Mobile home park "condominiums"—an arrangement in which the owner purchases the lot in addition to the manufactured housing unit and pays an assessment for community services and amenities—are becoming popular, especially in resort areas.

The form of management for manufactured housing depends on what precisely is being managed. Property managers may be contracted by park owners to lease lots, collect rents, manage park staff, and supervise the placement of homes on sites in the park. Depending on the type of residents—families, retirement community, etc.—the manager may be responsible for maintaining a clubhouse or other recreational facilities, supervising an activities director, and overseeing any other special services that are offered by the park.

Housing for the Elderly

As people reach and surpass retirement age, their lifestyles change dramatically, often changing the type of housing they seek. Some retirees have more time for recreational activities and may be more affluent than other age groups. As they age, people require more medical care and have a higher mortality rate. All of these considerations influence the type of housing the elderly seek. Housing options range from "aging in place" to full-scale assisted living. Of course, there are many alternate housing choices in between these two extremes. When residents age in conventional rental housing, managers can be confronted with a changing tenant profile—they may have to spend more time with residents, alter building services or building components, and be more aware of the public services available to their residents. Property managers also become involved with developments specifically built for senior citizens. These developments often provide arrangements for independent or assisted living. When the level of service increases in these sites, managers find that they must broaden their skills to include knowledge of recreational amenities, food service, transportation options, and social, psychological, and medical services. In general, management of this type of housing is characterized by a greater diversity of services and greater interaction with residents and their off-site families—all the while providing basic property management for the site.

Planned Unit Developments (PUDs)

The residential *planned unit development (PUD)* combines the concept of the conventional neighborhood subdivision with characteristics that are similar to condominium ownership. Most residents purchase their dwelling, the property it is on, and an undivided share of the common area within the PUD (roads, parks, recreational amenities). A monthly assessment is paid by the residents to maintain the common areas. The assessment may also pay for lawn care, snow removal, etc., for individual units.

A developer normally designs a PUD as a single entity before ground is broken, much as the plans of a building would be completely drawn prior to construction. Unlike a single building, however, the PUD may be constructed in stages over several years. A characteristic of planned unit developments is that as much attention is paid to the location of open space as to the placement of the buildings in the development. Although open spaces are emphasized in PUDs, land is used more intensively than in conventional subdivisions because townhouses and multiple-unit dwellings are more common than single-family houses. This concentration of land use benefits three groups in particular:

1. *The developers.* The profit margin on land resale is higher, both because there are more living units per acre and because careful planning of the development as a whole makes it aesthetically attractive.
2. *The community.* More property taxes can be collected per acre.
3. *The residents.* Assessments for common area services are minimized because of the large number of residents per acre and because the intensive use of the land reduces the amount of common area to maintain.

A PUD is a departure from conventional residential zoning; therefore, the term "planned unit development" also refers to a special zoning apparatus that permits the undertaking. Because it is a unique zoning form, public officials can be heavily involved in the site plan review and may play a key role in determining the nature and shape of the PUD.

In addition to dwelling types that may range from detached houses to rental apartments, a very large PUD may include retail and service facilities if these are not immediately accessible from its location. In most cases, the PUD is governed by a homeowners' association. This organization is comparable to a condominium association, except that the developer may be more prominent in the homeowners' association of a PUD, especially if there are rental units in the property. Because only property owners can be association members in PUDs with both privately owned residences and rental residences, renters would not have a voice in the association.

Collection of assessments for common area maintenance is a major responsibility of the property manager of a PUD. The association may rely on the property manager to create the assessment structure, which may provide for a variety of separate collections, including standard assessments, special assessments, rental security deposits, and rents. Maintenance services provided may encompass landscaping as well as general upkeep and repair of apartments, building exteriors, roads, and amenities.

MAINTENANCE ISSUES

Maintenance of residential properties is usually more intensive than that for other types of property because of the amount of wear and tear on them. When maintenance is required within a unit, it is imperative that the staff inform the resident prior to entering the premises. If not, a court of law may interpret the entry as trespassing. Some local or state ordinances require that written notice be given a certain number of hours in advance of entering a unit. However, if property or safety is threatened by a malfunction in a leased unit, entry is permissible without advance notice to the resident.

After one resident moves out and before another one moves in, there is an opportunity to do extensive maintenance and repairs in a vacant apartment. This work may be done principally for marketing purposes. To minimize vacancy periods and maximize rental income, all units must be attractive and all components in them operational. Even though a vacancy period that lasts a month or more reduces income, it affords a significant amount of time to paint and repair the unit. In other circumstances, the period between one resident's vacating an apartment and another's taking possession of it may be less than a day. However, such a limited amount of time should not reduce the thoroughness with which maintenance is done.

Curb Appeal of Residential Property

Curb appeal greatly affects the value of every property, but it is particularly important to residential sites. "Curb appeal" is defined as the overall condition of a property as viewed from the outside—from the street or curb. Favorable curb appeal depends on many factors that make the property as a whole inviting to residents and visitors. The effort to make a property appealing on the inside must be complemented by an effort to make the property appealing on the outside.

To maintain or improve the curb appeal of a property, the manager should examine the building exterior and grounds through the eyes of a prospective resident. A prospect who visits the site most likely has not seen it before and will naturally form an impression about the building or complex and its grounds. Most residents take pride in their dwellings—where one lives makes a statement to society about a person and his or her character. Therefore, a prospect's initial impression of a site will weigh heavily in the decision whether to rent an apartment in the building.

After a prospect who is impressed by the curb appeal of a property leaves the site, he or she may find it difficult to remember precisely what features created the favorable impression. Curb appeal is an overall impression of the state of all exterior property components. People will not necessarily notice subtleties such as sidewalks without cracks, clean glass and light fixtures, chip-free paint in entrance areas, coordinated signage, or tidy garbage dumpsters. However, they will notice—and remember—any individual component that leaves the slightest negative impression (overloaded garbage dumpsters, for example). Besides high standards for maintenance, obvious enhancements of curb appeal such as flower beds, understated seasonal decorations, or a fountain in the courtyard will also be remembered. The property manager must be careful to avoid excessive additions, but a few well-placed enhancements of this nature can be very appealing. Once such an enhancement is placed on the grounds, it is vital to maintain it. A watered, pruned, and weed-free flower bed can improve curb appeal considerably, but an uncared-for or dying flower bed will detract from it. In fact, an untended flower bed may lessen curb appeal more than if no flower bed had been planted in the first place.

To avert service calls and assure the resident's comfort, the unit should be presented to an incoming resident in superior condition. A vacant apartment should be inspected every day, not only as a check on its condition for marketing and showing to prospects, but to assure that an uninhabited unit remains free of damage. A *unit make-ready report* (exhibit 9.2) can be a useful guide for the staff as they inspect and repair a vacant apartment. After repairs are completed, a final inspection using the completed make-ready report for reference verifies that the unit is ready either to be shown or inhabited by a new resident. Printed unit make-ready reports may be available for purchase, but the unique features of a property may require development of a special make-ready report form.

Some facilities are unique to residential property and require special care and monitoring. The laundry room is a particular source of concern. Because an on-site laundry room is an amenity, it should be as clean and inviting as the rest of the property. If it is tastefully appointed, it will also

EXHIBIT   9.2

Residential Unit Make-Ready Report

Property _____ Date _____

Unit _____

Date vacated _____ Date to be occupied (if known) _____

Initial inspection by _____ Date _____

Checklist Before Move-In

☐ Check that all plumbing in unit (toilets, faucets, etc.) works properly. Make sure there are no leaks or drainage problems.

☐ Check all appliances (run dishwasher once on each cycle; check for proper operation of refrigerator, disposal, range). Make sure that all appliances and kitchen cabinets are clean.

☐ Inspect all windows and screens (no breaks in either). Verify that all sliding components work correctly and easily. Clean out tracks of all windows and sliding glass doors. Clean inside of all window panes.

☐ Check paint surfaces for chipping, peeling, discoloration, and stains. Determine whether repainting is necessary.

☐ Check all walls for holes, seams, cuts, cracks, and nail pops.

☐ Check venetian blinds for proper operation and clean.

☐ Check flooring (all floors cleaned and waxed, parquet block floors or wood strip and asphalt tile included; vacuum carpet).

☐ Clean bathroom(s) (tub, toilet, basins, vanities, mirrors, medicine cabinets, wall and floor tile).

Special Instructions

_____
_____
_____
_____
_____
_____
_____
_____
_____
_____
_____
_____
_____
_____
_____
_____
_____
_____
_____
_____
_____
_____
_____
_____
_____
_____
_____
_____
_____
_____
_____

be easier to keep clean. Maintenance of the washers and dryers is often contracted to a company that specializes in this service, and the cost is paid out of the revenues from the coin-operated machines. Maintenance of the room itself is a management responsibility. The laundry room should be inspected regularly. Air ducts and drains may become clogged with lint; trash may accumulate in the area, and wet or soapy floors can cause a fall.

E X H I B I T   9.2   (continued)

Checklist Before Move-In	**Special Instructions**

☐ Verify that all towel bars, toilet paper holders, and soap dishes are secure and clean.

☐ Check tile in bathroom(s) for cracks or flaws.

☐ Make sure that all baseboards, cabinets, shelves, electrical outlet plates, and smoke detectors are properly installed and secure.

☐ Verify that thresholds and metal strips are installed properly where needed.

☐ Check that all doors close properly and that there is no rubbing or warping.

☐ Check that all vents and registers are properly installed.

☐ Check heating and air-conditioning units to verify that they are working properly. Clean or replace air-conditioning filter.

☐ Make sure that all lighting fixtures work properly and have new bulbs.

Other _____

_____

Other _____

_____

Other _____

_____

Final inspection by _____ Date _____
Approved by _____ Date _____

A storage area may be provided for residents' use. Storage spaces that are not attached to the units are usually located in a common area, often in the basement. Typical storage spaces are enclosed by wooden or wire floor-to-ceiling partitions that the resident can secure with a padlock. Storage spaces should be protected from seepage and flooding, mildew, and vermin.

Many large complexes offer indoor or outdoor swimming pools for residents and visitors. Although these can be a great attraction, pools also pose a serious danger. To minimize the risk, rules for pool use (including hours of access) should be posted and enforced. The chlorination level must be monitored and regular vacuuming of the pool is necessary. For reasons of safety and security, fixtures such as fences, gates, and ladders must be checked periodically.

While the foregoing maintenance considerations are specific to rental properties, condominiums or cooperatives—especially older properties converted from rental use—may have similar facilities and similar requirements for maintenance. Mobile home parks and PUDs will have road repairs in addition to maintenance of amenities, and all properties that provide parking must maintain the parking lots or garages.

INSURANCE ISSUES

The wisest choice a property owner and manager can make to avert a financial loss from damage to the property is to consult a capable and knowledgeable insurance expert. Unique aspects of a property will require inclusion of certain provisions in its insurance coverage. For example, a residential property in an area that is not prone to earthquakes most likely will not require earthquake insurance; however, insurance for property along the southern California coast must include this type of coverage. Likewise, a condominium association would not require insurance to protect against the loss of rent in the event of damage to its building, but rent loss coverage should be included in the insurance of a rental property. In fact, the mortgage holder may require such protection. If the building sustains a physical loss, insurance covering the building will pay to restore the premises. During restoration, however, the property may be partially or completely uninhabitable, resulting in little or no income. Rent loss coverage provides some income to the owner during restoration and thereby reduces the prospect of foreclosure.

There are two principal types of insurance. *Actual cash value (ACV)* insurance is the least expensive and leaves the owner the most vulnerable. It pays a claim based on a depreciation of the original value of the item, and the amount may be substantially below the cost of replacement. The alternative, *replacement cost coverage,* pays the cost of the new or equivalent replacement item. Thus, a claim for a desk that cost $1,000 when it was purchased three years ago and is priced at $1,700 today would be reimbursed at the current cost. Naturally, the premiums for this type of coverage are higher.

An option for lowering the premium cost is to carry a *deductible,* which is a certain amount the owner agrees to pay before insurance pays for any of the claim. This practice benefits both the insurance company and the property owner. The owner pays a lower premium, and the insurer does not have to investigate or pay small claims. A deductible may be for $50, $500, or $5 million, depending on the circumstances, the policy, and what was negotiated, and it may be per occurrence, per building, or per year.

Most insurance policies for damage to a property have *fire insurance* as their basis. Fire insurance is especially important for residential property because of the numerous opportunities for fire to start in a private residence. Smoking, stoves, outdoor grills, and carelessness on the part of children are just some of the causes. Fire protection itself is not enough, nor will fire insurance necessarily pay for fire damage under every circumstance. For example, it may pay for direct loss from a fire but not for related smoke and water damage.

Greater protection is provided by adding *extended coverage* insurance, which usually encompasses damage from windstorms, hail, explosions, riots and civil commotion, aircraft, vehicles, and some types of smoke. Coverage is still limited, however, and broader coverage may be desirable.

All-risk insurance would seem to be the most comprehensive coverage available because of its name; however, "all-risk" is a misnomer. In fact, all-risk insurance pays for anything that is *not* named as an exception, and anything can be excluded. Common exceptions include earthquakes, floods, sewer backup, water seepage, boiler explosions, war, and nuclear contamination.

To maximize coverage, each residential property usually requires a unique insurance plan. Level of coverage and type of policy vary with the insurance carrier. Insurance for one property may come from several different insurance companies, and there may be numerous *endorsements* or *riders* to assure protection against particular circumstances that the basic policy does not cover. Possibilities for endorsements are unlimited. If the property has a rare sculpture on its grounds, an endorsement may be added to the basic policy to insure against theft or damage of that particular piece of art. To obtain the best possible coverage for the lowest premium, the costs and benefits of each type of additional coverage (endorsement) should be carefully calculated.

Administration of such complex insurance coverage is likewise complicated. The responsibility to hold the policies, file claims, and assure that premiums have been paid is usually given to the property manager by the owner although some owners elect to do this work themselves. The property owner is named as the primary insured party in all such policies. However, as the owner's agent, the manager acts in the owner's stead with regard to the property. For this reason, the owner should agree to name the manager as an additional insured or named insured party on all policies related to the property. This will protect the manager in his or her operation of the property and expedite the handling of claims for which the manager must contact the insurance company directly.

Physical damage to the structure is only one type of risk that must be guarded against by owners and managers of real property. *Liability* is another. In particular, if an individual is injured or dies on the premises, the manager or owner may be deemed liable. Liability is determined in a court of law, usually in response to a lawsuit. The expense of court time and the prospect of a judge or jury awarding damages to a plaintiff make liability insurance essential. Liability insurance protects the owner from financial ruin; its pays the expense of defense against the claim and, if the owner is ruled liable, it pays the settlement. The premium for liability coverage is usually quoted as a flat rate per $100,000 of coverage. Additional coverage may be obtained by carrying *umbrella liability insurance,* which is a separate policy that will pay claims that exceed the basic liability coverage. Because the owner is not the only possible defendant in a liability suit, the property manager should always insist that he or she be named as an additional insured party in the owner's liability insurance. This will protect the manager in case of a lawsuit involving the management of the property.

Regardless of the amount of insurance or the types of coverage a property owner carries, the owner's insurance only protects the property, the owner, and the manager. Personal possessions of the residents are not covered. For this reason, all residents should be encouraged to carry renters' or homeowners' insurance, depending on the nature of their residency.

SUMMARY

Managing residential property is particularly challenging and rewarding. Rental properties are the ones most commonly thought of as professionally managed. Apartment buildings range in size from a handful of units to high-rise buildings with thousands of units. Although the principles of management are the same regardless of property size, each property has the potential to create unique situations that require specialized management skills. Government-assisted properties require additional administrative paperwork and compliance with legalities.

In rental properties, someone other than the resident is the owner. When the residents are the owners, as in condominiums and cooperatives, the manager is employed by the condominium or homeowners' association. The cost of operating the property is paid from assessments on the owners, and the manager is compensated by a flat fee rather than a percentage of rental income.

Single-family houses usually require resident participation in their maintenance, and management of units that are not adjacent to each other is more time-consuming. In mobile home parks, the land is usually leased to residents who own their homes, and residents may pay the park for their utility services. Housing for elderly people is specially designed to accommodate their diminishing independence; rental arrangements may include meals, and varying levels of health care may be available. Planned unit developments (PUDs) include both rental and resident-owned housing. Maintenance of residential properties is highly demanding because of the round-the-clock nature of occupancy. The range and complexity of facilities provided along with the living space will also influence maintenance requirements.

Insurance of residential property is complex and often necessitates creation of unique insurance packages. Liability and loss of rents coverage should be carried in addition to property damage protection, and the manager should be listed as an insured party on all policies for the property.

Key Terms

Actual cash value insurance

All-risk insurance

Assessment

Condominium ownership

Cooperative ownership

Deductible

Endorsement

Fair housing laws

Garden apartment complex

High-rise apartment building

Liability insurance

Mid-rise apartment building

Pet agreement

Planned unit development (PUD)

Replacement cost coverage

Steering

Sublet clause

Umbrella liability insurance

Key Points

Differences among types of rental housing

Government assistance programs

Elements to consider when screening prospects

Residential lease clauses

Management differences between resident-owned property and rental property

Advantages and disadvantages of actual cash value versus replacement cost coverage insurance

Managing Commercial Property

The term "commercial property," in its broadest definition, encompasses all real estate development that is not exclusively residential. Office buildings and shopping centers (retail space) are the types of commercial property most often managed by professional property managers. Other types of commercial property that commonly require professional management include industrial and research parks, warehouses, and buildings designed for medical and other professional services. While management of commercial property is similar in many ways to that of residential property, there are also a number of important differences.

Two of the most striking differences between residential and commercial property management are length of the lease term and complexity of rent payments. As a consequence, the involvement of a manager with prospective commercial tenants is much greater than that with prospective residential tenants. A prospective resident applies for occupancy, and from the information he or she supplies on an application, financial and other data are checked. If these meet approval, the prospect is usually offered a standard lease (with a term of one year or less) for a particular residential unit. In leasing commercial property, prospects are sought out more aggressively. While prospective residents are usually found by advertising in the newspaper, the manager of commercial property narrows the promotional focus to attract specific types of tenants. Often prospects are sought through "cold calling," which is the process of gathering information about prospects and then actively recruiting them. In a further effort to entice prospects, the property manager may demonstrate how a particular space can be reconfigured to suit a specific prospect's requirements. Leases for residential property are rarely negotiated, but negotiations with commercial prospects are commonplace, and many clauses in the lease may be negotiated specifically. Negotiation of leases for commercial space is complex because the financial risks are greater for both the tenant and the property owner.

OFFICE BUILDINGS

The office building as it is known today started with the advent of the "skyscraper" in the late nineteenth century. The first skyscrapers were only ten to twenty stories tall, but this innovation in construction made it possible to concentrate many office workers in a central location. Skyscrapers built near a city's courthouse attracted legal professionals. Brokers settled in buildings near the stock exchange and ultimately produced the financial districts of major cities. The concentration of skyscrapers within a community eventually became known as the *central business district (CBD)*. Within the last half of the twentieth century, people in the largest cities have witnessed the development of multiple business districts within the cities and outside of them, in the suburbs. The high price of land and increasing congestion of the CBD have fueled this development.

Property Analysis by Class of Structure

The first skyscrapers of a century ago are dwarfed by new buildings in most modern city skylines. Insignificant as ten- or even twenty-story buildings may seem in a city's skyline, each one most likely requires full-time management, and each of these structures may be the site at which the property owner, manager, tenants, and their employees earn their incomes. The so-called "trophy" properties—e.g., the World Trade Center, the Chrysler Building—represent only a fraction of the office buildings requiring professional management.

When a management agreement is signed between a building owner and a property manager or management firm, the property must be examined objectively to discern its marketable qualities. The property manager must learn how the tenants, prospects, and others in the market perceive it in terms of desirability. The property manager must not delude himself or herself into believing a property has a greater or lesser strength in the market than it actually has. For this reason, the integrity of the property must be studied, and the first procedure in this assessment is to examine the building for the purpose of classifying it. While there is no definitive standard for what constitutes a specific class of office building, the people and publications in the real estate profession commonly refer to office buildings in the following way:

- *Class A.* These buildings usually command the highest rents because they are the most prestigious in their tenancy, location, and overall desirability. They are usually new structures with the latest amenities. Class A buildings generally have a complete service staff, including full-time maintenance and security personnel.
- *Class B.* The rents in these buildings are usually less than in Class A buildings, but the buildings themselves may not differ greatly from Class A buildings in structure. The rents are lower for any of several reasons (e.g., the building is in a less-desirable location, fewer amenities are available, etc.).
- *Class C.* These buildings (once Class A or B) are older and reasonably well maintained but they are below current standards. They are priced to match the rent-paying ability of a lower-income tenancy, and may be located on the CBD perimeter.

Age and obsolescence are the two prevailing issues in building classification. An older building has the potential to be notable and appealing, but only if it can accommodate current business needs. If a building cannot be retrofitted for advanced office systems or if the space cannot be configured for efficient use by current standards, the class of the building is likely to decline.

The classification of a building is an estimate at best. It is easy to visualize the differences between Class A and Class C buildings, but the distinctions between Class A and Class B buildings can be very subtle. Regardless, the building classification can be useful to convey in general terms the desirability of the building. Not surprisingly, the criteria that influence building classification are those evaluated by prospective tenants as they select office space to lease; current tenants also review these criteria when they consider renewal. There are twelve fundamental criteria for classifying office buildings—location, ease of access, prestige, appearance, lobby, elevators, corridors, office interiors, tenant services, mechanical systems, management, and tenant mix. Most of these factors are interdependent, but examining them separately illustrates their relationship and importance.

Location.   The desirability of an office building is largely measured by its proximity to other business facilities; this desirability can change over time as one section of a city becomes more popular than others. Evidence of this is recorded in the history of most large cities. As the central business district is developed, most of the buildings on the two main streets are Class A. With each block that is farther away from the main intersection, the property values and prestige diminish, although the buildings may still be Class B. As the area of the CBD is expanded, some locations on the perimeter may become less desirable because the expansion of the CBD is in the opposite direction. What was once a Class B building may now be Class C because of location alone. The effects can be reversed as well. As growth of the CBD continues, areas adjacent to the CBD may become popular again because they offer relatively inexpensive land and opportunity for expansion. If so, occupancy rates will increase once the buildings in the area have been rehabilitated or the land redeveloped. This will lead to an increase in income and a better property classification.

Buildings developed outside the central business district of a metropolis may also be Class A. Companies that left the city because land prices and rents were lower in the suburbs have generated a new demand for offices in the outlying regions, resulting in development of discrete business centers (office parks) near airports, major highways, and other suburban attractions. Population growth in outlying suburbs has also provided a large pool of workers from the local area.

Desirability on the basis of location is influenced by the attractiveness and cleanliness of neighboring sites. An office building that is well-constructed and maintained may rate a Class A designation only if its surroundings are attractive and clean.

Besides the attraction of the central business district or a similar suburban location, the presence of a major corporation can influence suppliers and other associated businesses to settle nearby or in the same building. A major bank may attract investment counselors, brokers, and accounting firms to the site. Likewise, a bank that works closely with large businesses may consider proximity to its major customers when choosing a site.

The desirability of a location because of prestige or convenient access can overshadow most other factors. A strategic location near transportation, within walking distance of major business and financial centers, or adjacent to government services can make a 100-year-old building in sound condition as desirable to the prospective office tenant as the newest construction.

Accessibility. Multistory buildings may contain thousands of workers. Because they must have an efficient and rapid way to arrive at and leave the office, access to transportation affects building classification. Office buildings that are served by several transportation alternatives (buses, commuter trains, elevated and subway rapid transit lines, highways, etc.) generally have greater value because employers benefit from the availability of a large labor pool. The availability of parking is also a consideration of accessibility. In general, buildings in CBDs cannot offer as much parking as those in outlying regions; however, buildings centrally located in large cities usually do not require as much parking as those in suburban locations because of the availability of public transportation.

Prestige.   Image and reputation are important factors in business, and location can enhance prestige. A young, ambitious lawyer may want an office in the same building as the city's leading law firms or at least in the same area. The directors of a financial institution will want it to be located in the most desirable building in the financial district or as close as possible to such a center. Because of this, the building with a prestigious address and reputation ranks high on the scale of desirability. Although much of the prestige may stem from location alone, the ownership, reputation, management standards, and services offered to tenants of the building can enhance its status. Building size also contributes significantly to prestige. A building that is prominent in the city's skyline may command higher rent, and a large building can include more extensive amenities, which will further enhance the prestige of the site.

Appearance.   The architectural design of a building and the way it is maintained are two physical attributes that affect its desirability. In the 1960s and 1970s, advances in technology and economical construction techniques resulted in buildings with few distinctive features; multistoried office buildings of this era were characteristically cubical or rectangular structures of glass, steel, and stone. Their use of space is highly efficient, but their uniformity of appearance makes it difficult to distinguish them from each other. As a result of a resurgence in architectural creativity, however, office buildings from the 1980s and 1990s have distinctive visual appeal.

Lobby.   The appearance, floor plan, and lighting of a building's lobby establish its character. The entrance to any building is part of the setting in which each tenant's business is conducted. A lobby that appears outdated, worn, or uncared-for will detract from an otherwise attractive building. Attention should be paid to the primary services that tenants, employees, and visitors expect from a lobby; an updated, well-maintained building directory and unobstructed access to elevators or stairs are essential.

Elevators.   Vertical transportation is vital to multistory office buildings, and each additional story increases the demand for efficient and rapid service. Several factors influence the perception of elevator quality; location is one of the most important. The desirability of space in the building will be lessened if tenants, employees, and visitors must walk a long distance from the main entrance to the elevators and then walk an equally long distance to their destinations after they arrive on the appropriate floor. Such inconvenience and apparently inefficient use of space create negative impressions about the building.

The appearance of elevator entrances and cab interiors also can affect the perception of the office building as a whole. Adequate lighting, proper ventilation, understandable controls, and well-maintained floor coverings are expected in an elevator. To create the illusion of a larger space, a mirror or other reflective surface on the back wall of the cab is sometimes helpful. Any lessening of aesthetic and maintenance standards in the elevator can raise doubts about the quality of the building's tenancy and may even provoke questions about safety in the minds of the elevator passengers.

The most important standards of elevator service are safety and speed, but for passengers, speed includes more than travel time in feet per minute. They judge the amount of time their elevator trip takes from the moment they press the call button to the moment they arrive at their destination. The time spent waiting for the elevator to arrive and the number of stops it makes en route usually influence the perception of quality more than actual rate of movement does.

It may be possible to control the timing of elevator movement to increase efficiency. If the building is exceptionally tall, the number of elevators serving a particular floor can be limited. In a forty-story building, for example, one bank of elevators may serve only the second through twentieth floors, while the other bank serves the twentieth through fortieth floors. If one or a few floors in the midsection of the building are served by all the elevators, passengers will not have to descend to the lobby to go from one half of the building to the other.

Corridors. All hallways in a building should be subtle in their decoration and appointments. As much as possible, the corridors should appear to be an extension of the tenants' offices. They should be well-lighted and decorated in neutral colors. If artwork or wallcoverings are hung in the halls, they should reflect the visual appeal of the rest of the building. Corridors must be diligently maintained in immaculate condition. Signage should be clear, discrete, up-to-date, and uniform throughout the building.

Office Interiors. Office suites are usually reconfigured to accommodate new tenants' needs and aesthetic choices. Desirability depends less on existing interior design than on alternative floor plans. Numerous factors can limit possibilities for changes: the size and number of windows in a given space and their relative locations, existing lighting, the depth of the space from the corridor to the outside wall, the width of the space between supporting columns, and even the view. Most buildings constructed prior to 1945 have more load-bearing columns, and this limits efficiency of use and flexibility of the space. Newer office buildings usually have wider column spacing, permitting numerous alternative configurations and more efficient use of space.

In addition to layout, the perception of interior quality depends on decoration, wall finish, light fixtures, illumination, and ceiling height. All of these will be judged on their conformity or lack of conformity to the "ideal" office interior, which is generally represented by what is available in the most prestigious building in the market. As with any other property, rental value of office space is ultimately based on what else is available in the market.

Tenant Services.   Prospective tenants judge an office building by the quality and variety of the services that are either included in the rent or can be obtained. Most important among these are custodial or housekeeping services, security, prompt response to service requests by on-site maintenance personnel, after-hours access to the building, and HVAC maintenance.

Some office buildings provide special amenities for tenant use (for example, auditoriums and conference rooms with extensive audiovisual equipment, exercise facilities, etc.). The presence of retailers (drugstore, newsstand) that serve needs of workers in the building may also be an asset. In some parts of the United States, new office buildings may include concierges and even day-care services, although the latter may be a building tenant. These amenities, and their direct or indirect costs, are noted by the selective tenant who is shopping for new office space or simply considering a move. The availability of amenities will often influence the prospect's decision.

Mechanical Systems.   Advances in office technology place increasingly greater demand on the electrical wiring and HVAC systems in an office building. Often the mechanical systems of a building are a crucial consideration in a prospective tenant's search for space to lease. New buildings are usually constructed with up-to-date systems that can keep pace with user demands. They may incorporate computer controls into the electrical and HVAC networks to monitor and regulate energy usage, and many include telecommunications systems. Buildings that do not meet the infrastructure demands of new technology may be considered for retrofitting. However, many buildings—even relatively new ones—cannot be easily retrofitted to accommodate technological advances. In some cases, the costs of retrofitting may be prohibitive; in others, the design of the building may preclude efficient or cost-effective operation of the retrofit. Some buildings cannot be retrofitted at all. This obsolescence is one reason Class A buildings can become Class B or Class C despite good locations and high management standards.

Management.   The quality of a building's management adds to the value of its space. Business people are very aware of the influence management has on the appeal of a property and the efficiency of its services. Of special importance is the level of maintenance. This is often provided as a building service and is a direct indicator of management's professional dedication. A well-maintained building with bright wood, polished tile, clean washrooms, dust-free cornices, and general tidiness is more attractive to current and prospective tenants. A prospect who discovers anything less will select a property that is better maintained. Upkeep of mechanical systems and the extent of building security are also indicators of management quality. The effectiveness of management influences demand for space in the building and contributes to the reputations of the firms whose offices are in it.

Tenant Mix.   Image and reputation are crucial elements in business, and fellow tenants in an office building can enhance (or detract from) these qualities in each other. For this reason, both prospective tenant and property manager closely examine the *tenant mix* in an office building. A prospect guards against locating in a building whose other tenants will not contribute to its reputation.

The tenant mix of a building is usually governed by its principal lessee. For example, if the major tenant in a building is a bank, other financial enterprises (investment and mortgage bankers, brokerage firms, accounting services) may seek space in the building because of that tenant's reputation in its industry and in the community. Sometimes the name of a major tenant may be applied to the building, and that may further encourage a particular type of tenant to lease space there.

Tenant mix is more vital to retail properties (discussed later in this chapter), but property managers of office buildings must be wary of prospects whose businesses may detract from the image and reputation of the property. Such a tenant may have a negative effect on the businesses of other tenants, resulting in a decline in the property's reputation and its income.

Tenant Selection

Just as an office tenant anticipates being in a building for several years, the property manager and the owner seek tenants who can and will commit to a long-term relationship. The major criteria to consider are the prospect's type of business and reputation, its financial stability and long-term profitability, its space requirements, and its need for specific services. Because these types of information are published or readily available, it is often less difficult to check the credit of commercial prospects than residential prospects. However, the information is more complex and the consequences of inadequate research can be more damaging.

Business Reputation and Financial Status.   The value of an office building is founded partly on the business reputations of its tenants. The manager must recognize the impact of each tenant's reputation on the building. The prospect's business should be compatible with the mix of tenants already in the building, and its reputation should enhance or at least reinforce the reputation of the building as a whole.

The financial stability of the business should be investigated. The manager must ensure that the tenant can perform under the terms of the lease and that rent will be paid on time. A prospective tenant should fill out an application that lists, among other things, the type of business, the length of time the tenant has been at its current address, its preceding address, the principals of the business, where the business is incorporated (if a corporation), where the home office is located (if it is a branch office), the type of space the business is seeking, who its bankers are, and credit references (which are usually vendors). Financial statements, a Dun & Bradstreet rating, the local chamber of commerce or business organization, and the prospect's bankers and suppliers are sources of credit and financial information. Every potential tenant, no matter its size or renown, should be scrutinized; large multinational firms are as subject to takeover and bankruptcy as are small ones.

Space Requirements.   One of the most complex issues of tenant selection is determining whether the building has adequate space for a specific prospect. Efficient use of space is crucial, and some prospects may not qualify as tenants simply because the available space cannot be designed to comply with their requirements. Three factors must be considered in determining whether the available space is suited to a prospective tenant.

1. *Configuration of the available space.* There is no guarantee that a prospect currently occupying 10,000 square feet of space can operate efficiently in the same amount of space in a different building. Exterior walls, pillars, elevator shafts, and stairwells cannot be moved or altered to suit the requirements of individual tenants, so these structural elements usually determine whether a specific space can be configured to meet a prospective tenant's needs.
2. *The nature of the prospect's business.* Some organizations require many executive offices, and usually these are placed along exterior walls of the building because the lighting and view are a sign of personal prestige. An organization with a particularly large clerical staff can be expected to have a lesser demand for exterior walls.

3. *A prospect's plans for future expansion.* If a company expects to grow significantly in the future, consideration must be given to whether and how the building can accommodate that growth, especially if the prospect will need contiguous space.

In general, an allowance of 150 to 200 square feet of floor space per worker will provide a large enough area to accommodate clerical staff in particular, along with necessary space for cabinets, required equipment that is not part of the employee's work area, and aisles between desks. (Individual work stations with movable partitions may enclose only 50 to 60 square feet of floor area.) However, if a large number of private offices is to be included in the design, the square footage of individual offices should be taken into consideration along with separate allowances for conference rooms.

Service Requirements.   The special services that are necessary for a prospective tenant to be able to conduct its business should be thoroughly known and considered in the qualification process. In most cases, the requirements of a prospect that prompt the property manager to conduct extra research are: (1) a higher level of security than is currently provided; (2) an extraordinary need for electrical power or HVAC; (3) business hours that differ radically from those currently established for the building; or (4) any other service that differs significantly from standard operations. If such factors are not given proper consideration, the building may operate at a loss as a result of a particular prospect's tenancy. However, before rejecting a prospect outright, the property manager and the owner should consider accommodating the prospect and analyze the actual costs and the cost-benefit ratio over the long term. Who will pay for the proposed accommodation is one of the lease terms to be negotiated. For example, a prospect who has a large mainframe computer may warrant such specialized consideration. Mainframe computers consume large amounts of electricity and can strain the capacity of a building's wiring. Some require separate, additional cooling systems, and additional structural support may be needed to bear the weight of the equipment. Meeting these requirements may necessitate a large investment, and retrofitting of mechanical systems cannot always be done successfully. However, evaluation of accommodation is warranted for the following reasons: (1) The first installation of this kind will make a future installation less difficult; it can also make it easier to secure tenants with similar computers. (2) The prospect most likely understands the amount of work and the expense involved in installing the equipment and is therefore more likely to seek a long-term lease in order to avoid repetition of this investment.

Office Rent

Office space is commonly leased as *shell space*—enclosed by outside walls and a roof, with a concrete slab floor and utilities brought in. The plumbing and electrical installations are unfinished, and there are no partitioning walls, ceiling tiles, wallcoverings, or flooring. Commercial clients generally have unique requirements for space they lease, and it is easier to design and *build out* an unfinished space. (Construction of *tenant improvements* can be done according to the incoming tenant's specifications.) Even a previously rented space may be gutted and rebuilt for succeeding tenants. Rent is usually charged on a square-foot basis and may include repayment of monies advanced to finance tenant improvements to the leased space. Some operating expenses of the property (e.g., property taxes, insurance, common area utilities and maintenance) may be included in the rent or charged separately on a pro rata basis; tenants' electricity may be metered individually and billed directly by the utility company.

Measuring Rentable and Usable Space.   Accurate measurement of the space is crucial to assure that rental income and market value of the property are maximized. Three concepts are central to the measurement of office space. The *gross area* of a building is its entire interior floor area. The *rentable area* of a building is its entire interior floor area *less* vertical penetrations through the floor (air shafts, elevators, stairways). The *usable area* is the rentable area *less* certain common areas that are shared by all tenants (corridors, storage facilities, washrooms, etc.). Usable area is the actual space occupied by tenants.

In order to establish profitable rental rates, the manager must know how much space in the building generates revenue (rentable area) and how much of that can actually be occupied (usable area). Accurate measurement of the rentable area is extremely important. In a building that has 100,000 square feet of rentable area, a one-percent error would amount to 1,000 square feet. If the average rent is $10.00 per square foot per year, that one-percent error would result in a loss of $10,000 in rental income each year. The resale value of the property would likewise be reduced—at a capitalization rate of 10 percent, the $10,000 shortfall would lower the property value by $100,000.

The *usable area of a tenant's leased office space* is the area bounded by its *demising walls* (the partitions that separate one tenant's space from another) and is available for the tenant's use exclusively. This area may occupy a portion of a floor, an entire floor of a building, or a series of floors. Although the usable area is the amount of space that is in the tenant's sole possession, rent is usually quoted on the rentable area. The *rentable area of a tenant's leased office space* usually includes certain common areas in addition to its usable area. In a multistory office building, the tenants on each floor would pay rent for the common areas on their respective floors. Each tenant's *pro rata* share of the common area is the percentage represented by the ratio of the tenant's usable area to the usable area of the entire floor (the sum of all defined usable areas on that floor). In addition, all tenants in an office building pay for the upkeep of the ground-floor lobby and any other areas that benefit all tenants mutually. If a separate assessment is made for these additional common areas, the amount is prorated based on the tenant's percentage of the usable area of the entire building.

To avert discrepancies, a standardized method of measurement is employed. The one most commonly used is the one adopted by the Building Owners and Managers Association International (BOMA), a trade association that serves the mid- and high-rise office building industry (exhibits 10.1 and 10.2).

The BOMA system of measurement computes rentable area by multiplying a tenant's usable area by an *R/U ratio,* which is the rentable area of a floor divided by the usable area of that same floor. The larger the R/U ratio, the greater the rent paid for the common areas. Prospects are usually more inclined to choose rental space that has an R/U ratio close to one. High R/U ratios are usually found in older buildings. This is another characteristic that is used to classify buildings (Class A, Class B, and Class C are described earlier in this chapter).

In some markets, an *add-on factor* (or load factor) may be used to account for the proration of the common areas among individual tenants. This may or may not be equal to the ratio between the rentable and usable areas. Some markets may establish a standard or accepted add-on factor. In other words, the R/U ratios of buildings in the CBD may range from 10 to 13 percent, but a standard add-on of 11 or 12 percent may be applied to all usable area rents in the market. This can effectively eliminate one point of negotiation on a market-wide basis. (Exhibit 10.3 on page 218 is an example of an add-on factor based on the R/U ratio.)

Establishing Rates. The rental rate for a building depends on local practice and market conditions. Rent for office space is commonly quoted per square foot, either per month or per year. To determine the rent, it is first necessary to establish a base rate. (An economic analysis will indicate the lowest acceptable rate per square foot that will offset debt service, operating expenses, and vacancy loss—and yield the owner's desired return on the investment.) If the base rate is greater than what the market will bear, the manager will have to examine alternatives for reducing expenses so the base rate can be lowered. In ideal circumstances, market conditions will allow for rents to be higher than the base rate. The marketplace will also dictate whether and which operating expenses are included in the rent or charged directly to tenants on a pro rata basis.

E X H I B I T   10.1

Usable Area (BOMA Method of Measurement)

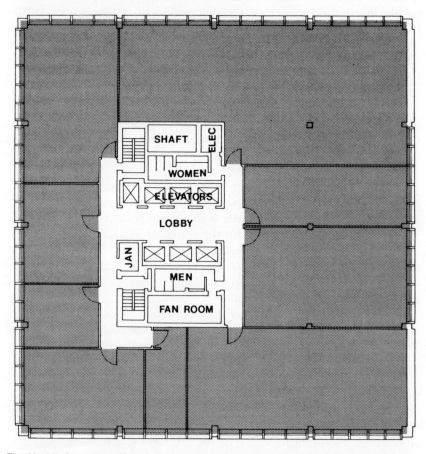

The *Usable Area* of an office shall be computed by measuring to the finished surface of the office side of corridor and other permanent walls, to the center of partitions that separate the office from adjoining Usable Areas and to the inside finished surface of the dominant portion (glass line) of the permanent outer building walls. No deductions shall be made for columns and projections necessary to the building. The Usable Area of a floor shall be equal to the sum of all Usable Areas on that floor.

Reproduced with permission from *Standard Method for Measuring Floor Area in Office Buildings* (ANSI Z65.1–1980)—Secretariat—Building Owners and Managers Association, 1201 New York Avenue, NW, Washington, DC 20005, 202-408-BOMA.

EXHIBIT   10.2

Rentable Area (BOMA Method of Measurement)

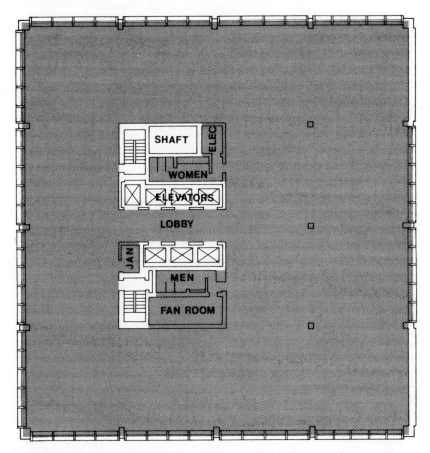

The *Rentable Area* of a floor shall be computed by measuring to the inside finished surface of the dominant portion (glass line) of the permanent outer building walls, excluding any major vertical penetrations of the floor (elevators, stairwells, air shafts, etc.). No deductions shall be made for columns and projections necessary to the building. The Rentable Area of an office on the floor shall be computed by multiplying the Usable Area of that office by the quotient of the division of the Rentable Area of the floor by the Usable Area of the floor resulting in the "R/U Ratio."

Reproduced with permission from *Standard Method for Measuring Floor Area in Office Buildings* (ANSI Z65.1–1980)—Secretariat—Building Owners and Managers Association, 1201 New York Avenue, NW, Washington, DC 20005, 202-408-BOMA.

E X H I B I T   10.3

Use of an Add-On Factor

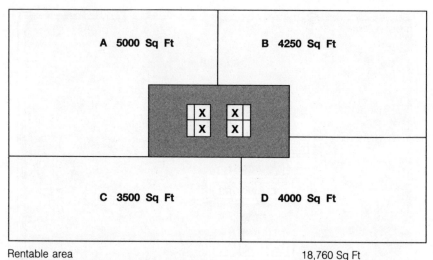

Rentable area	18,760 Sq Ft
Common Area	2,010 Sq Ft
Usable Area (Total)	16,750 Sq Ft

$$\frac{\text{Rentable Area (18,760 Sq Ft)}}{\text{Usable Area (16,750 Sq Ft)}} = \text{R/U Ratio} = 1.12$$

Usable Area × 1.12 = Rentable Area
Tenant A: 5,000 × 1.12 = 5,600 Sq Ft
Tenant B: 4,250 × 1.12 = 4,760 Sq Ft
Tenant C: 3,500 × 1.12 = 3,920 Sq Ft
Tenant D: 4,000 × 1.12 = 4,480 Sq Ft

Total: 16,750 × 1.12 = 18,760 Sq Ft

Use of *rentable area* as the basis for calculating rent recovers operating costs for the common areas of a building. In some markets, an add-on factor that is not equivalent to the R/U ratio may be used.

As with any other property, the rent that can be earned by an office building depends on its condition and its location. Also to be considered is the location of a particular office within the building itself, especially in a high-rise building. In most markets, higher floors and better views command higher rental rates. In terms of height, both extremes of the building must be examined. The anticipation of high income from upper floors often has to be tempered with lower expectations for office space closer to the ground. Although a fifty-story office building will most likely generate a considerable amount of income from its upper floors, that amount may not be sufficient to yield a high income for the building overall. For instance, a property manager may calculate a base rate of $18.00 per square foot per year for a fifty-story, Class A office building. A spectacular view in this structure creates high demand for space on the upper floors, most of which can easily be leased at rates between $20.00 and $24.00 per square foot per year. The lower floors cannot be expected to command such a high rent, however, and space on these floors may have to be leased for rates that are at or below the base rate of $18.00 per square foot per year. Ideally, the lower rates should be offset by the income produced by the upper floors; if the *average* income per square foot is equivalent to or slightly above the base rate, income production overall will be sufficient.

Space Planning and Tenant Improvements. Businesses seeking office space are concerned about the comfort of their employees and efficient use of the space they lease. The tenant who pays for unused space is essentially wasting money, but crowding too many employees into an office may waste the same amount of money through inefficiency. A property manager often can help a tenant determine an optimum square footage through a process called space planning.

Space planning is the translation of the prospect's square footage requirements, organizational structure, aesthetic preferences, equipment needs, and financial limitations into the design of a specific floor plan that indicates how office equipment, rooms, and hallways will be placed in the rental space. Usually a space planner, designer, or architect is contracted to prepare preliminary drawings. Computer-aided design (CAD) equipment makes it possible to explore different space arrangements quickly and economically. Once lease negotiations are completed, detailed plans will be prepared.

Payment of the cost of constructing (building out) the tenant's space is often a significant point of negotiation between the leasing agent (or the property manager) and the prospective tenant. Usually there is a *tenant improvement allowance* to cover standard items that will be installed at no cost to the tenant (e.g., one telephone jack for every 125 square feet leased, one door for every 300 square feet, etc.). If such a quantitative approach is *not* used, the allowance may be stated as a certain amount of money to be provided by the owner per square foot of leased space.

Which party (either the owner or the tenant) pays for construction costs that exceed the standard tenant improvement allowance depends on market conditions and the occupancy level in the building. One of four alternatives is possible: (1) the owner pays; (2) the tenant pays; (3) both owner and tenant pay a portion; or (4) the owner lends the incoming tenant the funds for the construction, and the loan is amortized over the life of the lease (paid back as part of the rent). While a loan paid back via rent is fairly common, the tenant may also seek financing from other sources or pay for the construction outright. Tenant improvements will be used as an incentive more frequently in a renter's market than in an owner's market. Because a commercial lease is usually a long-term contract, sacrifices early in the term may have lasting rewards for both tenant and owner. However, incentives that are too liberal may attract prospective tenants who are less than ideal candidates for the space, and this can burden the property with excessive expense for many years.

No matter how payment is arranged, the owner and the property manager retain final authority on all construction in the building, and the owner (or the property manager on the owner's behalf) usually contracts the construction firm to complete the build out. This is actually to the tenant's benefit; owner supervision of construction assures that the integrity of the property's image will be maintained. It tends to ensure high-quality workmanship at lowest cost. It also can aid realistic scheduling so that move-in is on schedule.

Leases and Lease Negotiation

The rights and obligations of the office tenant and the building owner are defined in a written lease, which is a legal contract between the two parties. Because of the complexity of the arrangement and a length of term that normally lasts more than one year, there are usually lengthy negotiations before a lease is signed. The property manager often participates in the negotiations. Even though the manager represents the owner, he or she may be instrumental in clarifying the tenant's perspective or suggesting possible compromises.

The starting point of negotiations is usually a proposal, followed by the presentation of a standard lease form, which the building owner has developed and which contains clauses that apply to all of the leasable space in a property. However, the negotiation of each individual lease will generate a unique document that reflects the relationship between the owner and a particular tenant. Many clauses require only minimal discussion. The concerns of both prospective tenant and property owner usually center on a few specific points. Tenant improvements and any allowances for them are almost always negotiated at length. Other clauses that usually prompt negotiation relate to rent increases (escalations), pass-through charges, services, and tenant options.

Standard Clauses.   In developing a standard lease form, one of the owner's objectives is to minimize expenses associated with the rent received. The incoming tenant, on the other hand, wants to maximize the rights and services it receives for that rent. To accommodate these differing desires, a number of specific clauses are common to leases for office space.

Because a commercial lease is often in effect for several years, an *escalation clause* to provide for a regular increase in rent is commonly included. Such a clause may refer to a standard index such as the *Consumer Price Index (CPI)* to determine the amount of the increase. (The CPI is also discussed in chapter 2.) The CPI is computed for major metropolitan areas and for the nation as a whole. The metropolitan indices provide an accurate record of the effect of inflation on the cost of living locally. However, fluctuations in the CPI can make it difficult for tenants to accept it as a basis for rent increases, and the tenant and the property manager may prefer to agree on a fixed annual increase for the duration of the lease or on specific rates for set intervals. Annual escalations might be stated specifically ($10 per square foot in year one increasing to $11 in year two and $12 in year three) or as a percentage (8 percent per year); a very long lease might be negotiated to state specific increases only every three or five years.

In a commercial lease, not all operating expenses of the property are necessarily collected in the rent; under a *gross lease,* the owner pays all expenses of the property and must recover these costs through the rent, but this arrangement is uncommon in large office buildings. Usually some expenses are billed to the tenant on a prorated basis in the form of a *pass-through* charge. When any operating expenses are passed through to a tenant, the lease is called a *net lease.* The pass-through charges are in addition to the base rent charged for the leased space.

Three types of net leases are common; they are called net (or single-net), net-net (or double-net), and net-net-net (or triple-net). In any locality, a single-net lease for office space constitutes the smallest number and a triple-net lease the largest number of pass-through expenses; the specific expenses covered under each type of net lease may vary from region to region. In general, the higher the level of net lease in a region, the lower the base rent. In other words, a gross lease for office space will state a comparatively high rent because the owner will pay all operating expenses from that rent; the "all-inclusive" rent for that space is its "base" rent. A single-net lease on that same space will state a lower "base" rent because the tenant will pay part of a certain operating expense or expenses. If a double-net lease is employed, the base rent for the space will be even lower because more operating expenses will be passed through to the tenant. Under a triple-net lease, the base rent on the space will be lowest of all because of the large number of pass-through expenses. (The three types of net leases are also used for industrial and retail space, and there are fairly standard definitions for those uses, as described later in this chapter.)

The specific pass-through expenses and the method of computing the tenant's pro rata share are stated in the lease. The most common pass-through expenses are utilities and common area maintenance in addition to real estate taxes and insurance. Capital improvements in the common areas may be passed through as well. The lease may include an *expense stop* which makes the property owner responsible for a certain dollar amount of operating expenses. The expense stop may be calculated per square foot per rental period (e.g., $4.00 per square foot per year) or stated as a grand total (e.g., $150,000 per year), and any amount exceeding the expense stop is prorated and charged to the tenants.

Concessions and Tenant Options. A *concession* is an economic incentive given by the owner to the prospective tenant. It usually provides a monetary incentive but should not reduce the quoted rent. Concessions may be in the form of free rent for a specified time period, financial assistance with moving from the former location, payment of penalties for breaking a former lease, or payment for above-standard tenant improvements. A concession may be an advance of funds that allows the tenant to invest in certain improvements or incur other costs initially and pay the money back to the owner over the term of the lease. This permits the quoted dollar rent per square foot to stay as high as the market will bear.

Other concessions may be sought by prospective tenants or by current tenants negotiating a lease renewal. A tenant anticipating growth may bargain for an *option to expand* that requires the owner to offer specific additional space at a stated time in the future, often at the end of the lease term. Except in very perilous market conditions, such an option is rarely granted because it can mean the expansion space will be vacant for some time before the option is exercised. As an alternative, the owner may offer a *right of first refusal,* which gives the tenant first choice to lease contiguous space or other space in the building if it becomes available (the area is specified in the lease clause). Sometimes a tenant may seek an *option to renew* on the same terms and conditions as the original lease. However, owners are disinclined to grant renewal options for several reasons. In the first place, a multiple-year lease usually does not account for all possible market changes during its term—even with escalations still in effect, the actual rent may remain below the market rate. Also, a renewal option does not guarantee that the tenant will remain. Under some circumstances, an *option to cancel* may be sought. This grants the tenant the right to cancel the lease before expiration and, if granted, usually requires a financial penalty. Because these options favor the tenant, ownership is understandably reluctant to grant them. However, it may be necessary to grant options so a property can be competitive and reflect market conditions.

RETAIL PROPERTY

Leased retail space ranges from storefront sites in older office or apartment buildings to modern shopping malls that enclose a million or more square feet of space and are promoted widely enough to attract shoppers from several states. Numerous historical factors have created the diversity of retail space in existence today. Major retail districts were originally established in downtown areas—the central business district. As automobiles became more affordable and roads were built to the outlying areas, suburban populations grew. Population growth on the fringes of the cities set the scene for the emergence of chain stores as major retailers from the CBD established branch stores to serve their suburban customers. At the same time, widespread use of consumer credit encouraged the purchase of goods, and better manufacturing techniques increased mass production and distribution so that standard brands of items could be purchased anywhere for about the same price. As competition intensified, self-service stores came into being as a way to reduce labor costs and thus lower retail prices. This allowed larger stores to be developed. The principle of self-service, combined with the tendency of retailers to cluster their establishments close to each other, led to the development of the modern shopping center.

Property Analysis

A shopping center differs from a retail district in that it is usually a single project in a suburban area with on-site parking. Usually a shopping center has a unified image, and the property is planned, developed, owned, and managed on the basis of its location, size, and type of shops as they relate to the trade area the center serves. So-called shopping centers are no longer located exclusively in suburbs, however; major cities are fostering their development downtown, both as new buildings and as adaptive use of old ones.

The definitive measure of retail space is its square footage, expressed as *gross leasable area (GLA)* in reference to both the center as a whole and the individual store interiors. (In an enclosed mall, the *gross floor area* includes the *common areas*—courtyards, escalators, sidewalks, parking areas, etc., which are not used exclusively by individual tenants—in addition to the mall's GLA.)

Most shopping centers have at least one *anchor tenant*. Retailers such as department stores or supermarkets whose space requirements are very large are common anchor tenants. *Ancillary tenants* occupy the smaller store spaces in a shopping center and may, because of their specialization (jewelry or stationery, for example), attract additional customers to the center. For the property manager responsible for a shopping center, the classification of the property, the size and strength of its trade area, its location, and its accessibility by automobile and public transportation are all important considerations.

Shopping Center Classification. Shopping centers are categorized according to the nature and variety of merchandise they offer and the size of their trade areas. There are five primary categories of shopping centers.

1. *Regional shopping center.* These large centers contain 400,000 to 1,000,000 square feet of GLA and have one or more full-line department stores as anchor tenants. The presence of a department store tends to attract such ancillary tenants as men's and women's apparel stores, optical shops, electronic equipment stores, and jewelers. Often there are several stores of one type (for instance, three to five shoe stores). Many regional centers include small fast food outlets arranged in a *food court.* Some also have cinemas. Regional centers usually serve a population of 150,000 to 300,000.

   The same pattern also exists on a larger scale. *Super regional centers* have 1,000,000 or more square feet of GLA and include three or more full-line department stores. Ancillary tenants are usually the same types as in regional centers, only there are more of them. Super regional centers, as well as some regional centers, may include separate buildings on sites called *outlots* or *pads.* Banks, restaurants, automotive service centers, and movie theaters are common tenants for these spaces. A super regional center serves a population of 300,000 or more.

2. *Community shopping center.* Centers of this type range in size from 150,000 to 400,000 square feet of GLA and are usually anchored by junior or discount department stores. Alternatively, the anchor may be a supermarket or a large hardware store. Men's and women's apparel stores, book stores, card shops, family shoe stores, and fast food operations frequently comprise the ancillary tenancy. These types of shopping centers usually require a population of 100,000 to 150,000 to sustain them.

3. *Neighborhood shopping center.* The most common anchor tenant in a neighborhood center is a supermarket or a discount drug store or a combination of the two. Ancillary tenants include dry cleaners, bank branches, video rental stores, and card and gift shops. The GLA of a typical neighborhood center is between 50,000 and 150,000 square feet. The growth in the size of the supermarket from 25,000 square feet of GLA in the 1950s to more than 50,000 square feet of GLA in the 1990s has increased the size of centers anchored by them. A neighborhood center usually thrives in an area with a population of 5,000 to 40,000.

4. *Specialty shopping center.* These types of centers are characterized by a dominant theme or image. Those in downtown areas are often the result of adaptive use of a historic building. They do not always have an anchor tenant, and many rely on tourists for most of their sales. Some of these centers can be as large as 375,000 square feet of GLA, and most require an area population in excess of 150,000 in order to survive. Two variations of specialty shopping centers focus on lower-priced merchandise. An *outlet center* is comprised of at least 50 percent factory outlet stores that offer name-brand goods

at lower prices by eliminating the intermediary wholesale distributor. At an *off-price center,* retailers offer name-brand merchandise at well below normal retail prices. Such large discounts can be given because the merchandise consists of factory overruns, seconds and dated items, overstocks from other stores, and consignment purchases from manufacturers.

5. *Convenience center.* This type of center usually has no more than 50,000 square feet of GLA and more typically contains 20,000 or less. The principal (anchor) tenant is a convenience food store, although a combination gas station and food store is also common, and most stores of this nature are open all day and all night. When additional store spaces are available, other tenants may be coin-operated laundries, barber shops, dry cleaners, or liquor stores. Convenience centers are often designed in a line, so they are sometimes called "strip centers." That term can be used to refer to other types of centers as well. A convenience center can succeed in an area with a population of 1,000 to 2,500 if it is well-located.

New forms of shopping centers are also being developed. *Megamalls* are three to four times larger than a regional center, and some contain five million or more square feet of GLA. Megamalls are often connected to or contain hotels, amusement parks, or nightclubs in addition to numerous anchor tenants and hundreds of ancillary tenants. *Hypermarkets* appeal to shoppers looking for discounts by combining the elements of a supermarket with those of a discount warehouse store that offers low prices on household items. These stores often encompass 150,000 or more square feet of GLA. Another shopping center innovation is the *power center.* These have GLAs ranging from 250,000 to 700,000 square feet. Compared to conventional centers, power centers have a much higher ratio of anchor space to ancillary space—there may be three to five anchors and only a few ancillary tenants. Discount food stores, super drug stores, sporting goods stores, home and garden centers, large toy stores, and electronics stores are common anchor tenants in these centers. The name "power center" comes from its power to attract customers from a much wider radius than similar-sized community shopping centers.

Trade Area Analysis. The *trade area* of a shopping center is the geographic area from which it draws most of its customers. Trade area analysis includes a *demographic profile* showing the number of people who are likely customers, their shopping habits, and purchasing power. This indicates the potential for a shopping center to succeed in a particular location. A new center does not create new buying power; it must attract customers away from other shopping centers, so evaluation of the competition in the trade area is important.

Most trade areas are subdivided into three zones—primary, secondary, and tertiary. The *primary trade area* is the immediate area around the site and accounts for 60–75 percent of the center's sales. The *secondary trade area* usually extends 3–7 miles from the site (for a regional center) and accounts for 10–20 percent of sales. The *tertiary trade area* may extend 15–50 miles from a major center and account for 5–15 percent of sales. Every shopping center, no matter its size, has a trade area and trade zones, the sizes of which vary with the type of center and its location. People will usually travel only one to two miles for food, but they will travel three to five miles for apparel and household items and eight to ten miles to comparison shop for major purchases.

Aesthetic Appeal, Location, and Parking.   The property analysis so far has centered on the size of the site and the proximity of potential customers. The aesthetic appeal of the center also plays a strong role in attracting customers, particularly for regional and super regional centers. People who shop at convenience and neighborhood centers live nearby, and proximity is their primary reason for shopping there. Small centers are not dependent on attracting people from a considerable distance, so aesthetic factors are not as critical. Larger centers must blend function and design to create an attractive place for people to spend a long period of time. Important decorative features are lighting, seating, colors, landscaping, and flooring.

Within the trade area, the value of one location over another may depend on the customers' means of transportation. Because most people who shop at large centers travel by car, the center must be easily accessible and provide parking for large numbers of automobiles. Simply being adjacent to a major thoroughfare is not a guarantee of accessibility, especially if a left turn must be made at an uncontrolled intersection, or if no turn or exit is possible. Also contributing to accessibility are distinctive and appropriate signage to identify the center, clearly marked entrances and exits, and internal traffic controls (i.e. stop signs).

Parking must be convenient; therefore, the plans for a parking lot or garage must be given a great deal of forethought. The amount of land that is necessary for parking can be gauged in two ways. The *parking area ratio* is the relationship between the size of the parking area and the size of the retail building. In the past, the ratio was required to be 3:1—a 500,000-square-foot regional mall would have to have 1.5 million square feet of parking area. That is approximately equal to thirty-four acres of land. Since the 1960s, however, parking has been related to the gross leasable area (GLA) of a shopping center using a *parking index*. The Urban Land Institute (ULI) recommends four parking spaces for each 1,000 square feet of GLA for centers having 25,000 to 400,000 square feet of GLA. A center that has 400,000 to 600,000 square feet of GLA should have between four and five spaces per 1,000 square feet of GLA. One that has more than 600,000 feet of GLA should provide five spaces for every 1,000 square feet.

Parking ratios and indices are merely guidelines; many other factors must be considered in developing a viable parking plan. Local zoning ordinances generally establish the parking ratio for a shopping center, and almost all centers are designed to provide the minimum amount of parking allowed. Different parking angles and varied widths of driving lanes between parking bays affect the numbers of stalls that can be included in an area. The needs of specific retailers must also be considered. For example, supermarkets may require a drive-up lane for loading. Video stores and fast food restaurants require more parking spaces because of the frequent turnover of their customers. Shopping centers that include offices must provide long-term parking for employees of both the offices and the stores in addition to parking for customers. Certain retailers within the mall may have more extensive parking requirements than others, or they may have a higher demand for parking at particular times during the day or week. Cinemas in shopping centers pose a different problem. Parking for nighttime showings will not conflict with regular daytime customer parking, but matinees would require additional parking—at the expense of parking for shoppers. Also, shopping centers are required to provide parking for handicapped shoppers, so wider stalls and access ramps near entrances are necessary. Parking for downtown centers is usually provided in multistory garages incorporated in or adjacent to the retail building, and shoppers may be given a discount on parking if they make a purchase.

Tenant Selection

In choosing tenants for retail space, the manager will weigh many factors. Apart from consumers' natural curiosity, the manager must anticipate what will actively attract customers to the center. The ideal tenant will offer appealing merchandise whose price and quality are a good match with the goods and services of the other tenants. In addition, the ideal tenant's merchandise should fill a need in the market that is not met by competing shopping centers. All of these factors are in keeping with the demographic profile of the trade area. The retailer's reputation and financial status must be scrutinized to address issues of quality and responsibility as well as ability to pay the rent. Requirements for store space and support services, as well as products or services that the retailer offers, must also be considered—particularly as they affect where the retailer can or will be located in the center.

Reputation. One of the most important factors to consider when choosing a retail tenant is reputation. Because reputation results from public perception, it is important to learn how a retailer treats customers. This is fairly easy to ascertain for a store that is part of a franchise or chain or one that is planning to move from one site to another. Assuming the role of a customer and making a purchase, then asking to return or exchange the item, will reveal the quality of a retailer's *customer service*. Observation of the treatment of other customers in the store and asking them about their perceptions of the store can also help one learn how the prospective tenant conducts business.

A consideration in addition to customer service is *merchandise presentation*. A slim inventory of dusty items suggests a poor sales record while fresh merchandise presented carefully implies the opposite. Salespeople who know their stock and present themselves well in both dress and attitude are an asset to the retailer and will be the same for the center. How much the retailer advertises indicates what is being done to establish and maintain reputation.

The inclusion of a unique business in a center whose other tenants are well-known can give the center a competitive edge. While the risks involved with a new business are greater, the rewards may surpass the risks. An innovative enterprise may quickly gain a healthy customer base because of its difference from established retailers and chains. A new or developing enterprise may not have an identifiable reputation, but it is not impossible to find out how it will operate. An individual or company that presents a clear plan of action for developing a new business, including investment in inventory and a pricing structure that is in line with the demographic profile of customers in the trade area, will probably be a better prospect than one whose plans are vague. Knowledge of its probable clientele and understanding of its competition are also important. Prior retailing experience is almost essential.

Financial Integrity.   There was a time when the decision to accept a prospective tenant could be based primarily on reputation—the name "Bloomingdale's" was once sufficient to solidify a deal. In an age of buyouts and takeovers, however, property managers should carefully investigate the financial health of all prospects. While an established store in a chain may be doing exceedingly well, that one store may not be an accurate reflection of the success of its parent company or the parent company's parent company or the other interests of the owner. If the related enterprises are foundering, the individual store may be sold to raise cash. While such an occurrence may not affect a prospective tenant's business, any change in ownership of a complex retailing operation increases the risks to the individual store and may create a vacancy in the center.

The greatest cause of business failures is undercapitalization, which is one reason for investigating new or proposed retail businesses very carefully. The costs of operating a retail business include not only rent, utilities, and maintenance of the store area, but also inventory, payroll, store design, fixtures, and advertising. For an established business, moving costs and the loss of business resulting from the move must be considered as well. Prospects should have sufficient reserve funds to be able to weather an initial lean period after they relocate.

Tenant Mix and Placement.   The combination of retailers and service vendors leasing space in a shopping center constitutes its *tenant mix.* A center anchored by an upscale department store will attract shoppers that seek—and can afford—its lines of merchandise. A center anchored by a discount department store will attract people seeking bargains. The best tenant mix for each center will follow the anchor's lead. In other words, the merchandise of the ancillary tenants must not clash with that offered by the anchor tenants. For example, a furrier probably will not succeed in a shopping center anchored by a supermarket or a hardware store. On the other hand, a dry cleaner may flourish in such a center because it, too, serves immediate needs.

Another consideration relating tenant mix to merchandise is destination versus impulse shopping. People usually have a specific purpose in mind when they are visiting an optical shop or a jewelry store in a shopping center; their search for a particular item or service has led them there. If they buy an ice cream cone in the process of going to or coming from their destination store, that is an impulse purchase. A good tenant mix serves both destination and impulse shoppers and increases sales of the center as a whole.

Shopping centers with more than one anchor tenant must ensure that the merchandise offered by each of them is a good match and complementary to the offerings of the ancillary tenants. An effective way to create a workable tenant mix is to view the specialty shops and department stores in the shopping center as parts of one big store.

Where the tenants are located in relation to each other in the center is also vital. Shoe stores are a natural complement to retailers selling men's or women's clothing. An ice cream parlor often does well next door to a sandwich shop. When new centers are built, careful attention is given to positioning of tenants in order to maximize their potential to attract customers to and through the center as a whole.

Tenant Requirements.   The retail tenant's primary concerns will be the availability of adequate space for its business, visibility of its location, and the volume of customer traffic a center generates. In addition, some tenants will have special requirements. Food service operations have unique garbage disposal and pest control problems that have to be addressed. Furniture and appliance stores require specialized loading docks. Supermarkets need large areas for short-term parking. A bank may want to provide drive-up services for its depositors. Whether and how these unique tenant requirements can be met are the subject of lease negotiations. However, the manager must know in advance what types of accommodations are possible so that unrealistic promises are not made during prospecting.

Special services arranged for one tenant that are beyond those normally provided can lead to a concern on the part of other tenants, even if the tenant requiring the special service is paying for it. The best way to counter these concerns is by explaining positive outcomes. For example, if a movie theater in a shopping center has a last showing that begins at what is closing time for the stores in the center, the common areas leading to the theater must be left open so its patrons can exit after the show. Even if the entrances to the stores are closed with heavy chain-link gates and locked, tenants whose stores are adjacent to the theater may be fearful that late hour theater patrons may try to damage their stores. The manager should understand this concern and act on it. One way is to make it a condition of the theater's late showing that a guard (paid by the theater) will be present until all its patrons leave. Limiting access to the center—by a single entrance only—is also helpful. The manager should also point out to other tenants that the theater's last showing may be responsible for a swell in business before the stores close because theatergoers may arrive early to do some incidental shopping.

Retail Rent

Rents for retail space are based on the gross leasable area (GLA) of the individual spaces. Like offices, stores are usually rented as open shell space to be set up as the tenant requires. Shopping center leases state rent for the space as *base rent.* In addition, retailers usually pay pass-through expenses that cover the cost of operating the center (including taxes and insurance) plus *common area maintenance (CAM)* charges. They may also pay a portion of their sales revenue as *percentage rent.* Some retailers may be able to negotiate to pay percentage rent only, but this exception is made rarely and then only for large establishments with very high levels of sales.

Base Rent.   Base rent, also known as *minimum rent,* is usually calculated on a per-square-foot-per-year basis and is commonly stated in the lease as equal monthly incremental amounts. Base rent assures the property owner a minimum income regardless of the merchant's sales success.

Percentage Rent.   When percentage rent is charged, the property owner shares in the success of the retailers that lease space in the property. Percentage rent is generally based on gross annual sales, but payments may be made monthly or quarterly. Because this type of rent is based on the retailer's sales volume, the amount can fluctuate significantly from month to month, so percentage rent is usually in addition to base rent.

There is no universally applied percentage rent rate—it depends on the type of business and the locale—but there are accepted ranges of percentage rent. For example, supermarkets have a very large sales volume and very low profit margins, yet one percent of their gross sales will yield a large amount of percentage rent. Conversely, gift shops have comparatively small sales volumes but high profit margins, and ten percent of their gross sales may be appropriate. The actual percentage is always negotiated, and it is usually collected on sales in excess of the amount of base rent and referred to as *overage*. In other words, the base rent for a store may be $120,000 a year, payable in equal monthly amounts of $10,000; if five percent of gross sales is charged as percentage rent, the tenant's gross sales must exceed $200,000 a month before percentage rent applies ($10,000 ÷ .05 = $200,000).

In the preceding example, the $200,000 a month in sales is the *natural breakpoint*. If the store produces $250,000 in gross sales in a month, its rent will be the $10,000 base rent plus five percent of sales above the natural breakpoint—in this case, 5 percent of $50,000, or $2,500, meaning the total rent for that month will be $12,500. However, the prospective tenant or the property owner may negotiate an *artificial breakpoint* to use as the threshold for paying percentage rent. The artificial breakpoint may be higher or lower than the natural breakpoint—a downward adjustment of the breakpoint would increase the owner's income. An artificial breakpoint may be used to accelerate payback to the owner of funds advanced for tenant improvements.

Pass-Through Expenses and Net Leases.   As in office leasing, under a gross lease for retail space, all operating expenses are the responsibility of the property owner who must recover them fully in the rent. However, most retail tenants have net leases, meaning that *some expenses of operating the property are passed through to the tenant*. The type of net lease offered by the owner determines what the tenant pays, and pass-through expenses are prorated based on the GLA of the individual store as a percentage of the GLA of the center as a whole. The various types of net leases are differentiated as follows:

- *Net lease.* The tenant pays a prorated share of property taxes only.
- *Net-net lease.* The tenant pays a prorated share of property taxes and insurance costs.
- *Net-net-net lease.* All operating expenses including taxes, insurance, utilities, maintenance, and common area fees are prorated and passed through to the tenant. Under a *modified triple-net lease,* which may be used in shopping centers, the owner is responsible for structural repairs to the building and for payment of management fees.

There are numerous other—mostly regional or local—definitions of the expenses that are passed through to the tenant under a particular type of net lease, so it is most important to delineate the pass-through expenses when describing a type of net lease. Major retail tenants may also negotiate with landlords to set a "cap" (an expense stop) on certain expenses, most often on common area expenses. This ceiling assures that the retailer will pay only a certain dollar amount per year for the particular pass-through expense or expenses to which the cap applies. Unlike an expense stop in an office lease, which sets a ceiling on how much the property owner pays, a cap in a retail lease defines a limit on how much the tenant pays.

Escalations. Because retail leases have long terms (a twenty- or thirty-year lease for an anchor tenant is fairly common; ancillary tenants' leases usually have three- to ten-year terms), escalations have to be written into the lease in order for them to take effect automatically. As in leases for office space, provisions for rent increases may be based on an index such as the Consumer Price Index (CPI) or negotiated as a periodic percentage increase. An escalation provision applies only to the base rent. The lease for an anchor tenant whose sales generally surpass the agreed-upon breakpoint may mandate an escalation in base rent only once every five years; ancillary tenants' leases usually call for annual increases.

The Retail Lease

The standard form lease for a shopping center includes a number of clauses that are specific to this type of property and address concerns and contingencies that can arise over the number of years covered by the lease. (The lease for a freestanding store or for space in a small shopping strip may not have such specific provisions.) In addition to the specific clauses and considerations described in this section, the lease will specify rental rates and other charges and state when and how payments are to be made.

Use. A shopping center is carefully designed and leased to appeal to a specific market in a specific location. Should any tenant change its merchandise or its image (e.g., specialty lines to general merchandise, upscale to discount), the tenant mix of the center may be altered. A use clause prevents a tenant from using the premises in a different way than originally intended.

Exclusive Use. A clause covering exclusive use may be sought by a prospective tenant to prohibit another tenant in the shopping center from selling a similar product—in other words, to minimize competition. However, some competition within the center is generally beneficial, and an exclusive use clause can be counterproductive. It may also violate anti-trust laws enforced by the Federal Trade Commission, which make restraint of trade illegal. However, temporary limits on certain product lines or on competing store sizes may help a retailer meet its obligations for rent, etc., or give a new business a head start. Because it is desirable to have several types of tenants in each retail category in a regional center, and because the merchandise carried by each retailer in a category tends to complement the others' merchandise rather than compete with it, exclusive use is rarely granted.

Radius. This clause prohibits a tenant from operating a similar store or from developing a similar chain of stores within a certain distance from the shopping center—typically three to five miles. Its intent is to prevent the tenant from directing customers to a nearby store in order to reduce percentage rent. A compromise may be negotiated whereby the tenant agrees to include in the percentage rent calculation part or all of its gross receipts from a permitted nearby store.

Store Hours. Among tenants of the same shopping center, variation in store hours should be minimal. This clause authorizes the management of the property to set store hours for the center as a whole. Some anchor tenants such as supermarkets or large drug stores may remain open twenty-four hours a day. These stores usually are located in open centers where the ancillary tenants maintain their own hours. A store hours clause may also include provisions for seasonal adjustments and special hours for Christmas shopping.

Common Area Maintenance. This clause specifies exactly what constitutes the common area of the shopping center and what expenses the tenant will pay. It also gives the property owner the right to expand, reduce, or otherwise alter the common area. The common area in an enclosed mall includes the mall "corridors," parking lots, escalators, landscaped areas, and other parts of the property that are used in common. (In a neighborhood center, the "common area" may be limited to the parking lot.) As noted earlier, common area maintenance (CAM) fees are normally prorated based on the percentage of gross leasable area of the center that is occupied by the individual store. On that basis, a store with 3,000 square feet of GLA in a 300,000-square-foot (GLA) shopping center would pay one percent of the center's CAM costs.

Advertising, Signs, and Graphics. The property owner retains the right to restrict the size, location, lettering, and language of all signs in the center. Large malls establish uniform graphic images and seek to maintain consistency in the caliber of signage. This is especially important for signs that are permanently mounted on the exterior of the building or placed in the center's interior. Tenants may be required to spend a certain percentage of their gross income on advertising to promote their stores—and the center.

Concessions.   As in office leases, concessions may be offered to a prospect to secure a new lease or retain an established tenancy. Because concessions are a special part of the lease negotiation process, they are usually stipulated in the applicable clauses rather than included as a single specific clause or, if there is no applicable clause to amend, they may be listed in separate documents incorporated in the lease by reference (addenda). Ideally, any concession granted will not lower the quoted rent. It is important to remember that any reduction in rent also reduces the value of the property. One type of concession, a *tenant improvement allowance,* is money the owner provides for modification of the leased space before the tenant moves in. Other concessions include payment of a new tenant's moving expenses or a period of free rent.

Other Clauses.   Requirements for *continuous occupancy* (staying in business for the full term of the lease) and *continuous operation* (keeping the business operating smoothly and consistently) are common clauses in retail leases. Provisions regarding *alterations* to the store space and *insurance* coverage for the retailer's business are also common. *Parking* is a concern for some businesses, and a separate clause may address the tenant's specific rights and limitations. Most shopping centers have promotional campaigns for the center as a whole and, to support these campaigns, may require tenants to participate in a *merchants' association* or *marketing fund,* usually through a specific lease clause. Options similar to those described for office leases—to renew, to expand, to cancel—may also be a part of retail lease negotiations.

Management of the Shopping Center

Management of a shopping center requires intensive work and a tireless staff. In addition to keeping the center up-to-date, clean, and safe, and generally maintaining the common areas, the manager must deal with the tenants and their concerns. The tenants' economic survival depends on customers coming to the center and patronizing their stores. Competition among tenants is sometimes intense and can result in strained relations unless the property manager serves all of them in a fair and consistent manner.

   In addition to the physical and financial management of the property, managers of shopping centers become intensively involved with the marketing of the site and, by that means, with the marketing of each store. In general, managers of shopping centers are more involved with the ongoing activities of their tenants than are managers of office buildings or residential properties. Management of shopping centers can be as dynamic as retailing itself. So, to be successful, managers of shopping centers must have a knowledge of retailing and merchandising comparable to their knowledge of real estate management.

It is not unusual for a shopping center to be visited by thousands of shoppers every day. Their continued patronage will be assured by careful attention to their comfort while they shop in the hope that they will leave with a favorable impression. However, such large numbers of people can lead to concerns about crime, and shopping centers are vulnerable to many forms of criminal activity. Some anchor tenants may employ their own security forces, but most malls of significant size contract with a security agency to guard the premises. While the importance of such personnel cannot be understated, the efforts of the property manager should be directed toward educating tenants and their employees about ways to prevent crime and reduce opportunities for criminal activity.

MARKETING COMMERCIAL SPACE

The methods to attract prospective tenants, as outlined in chapter 6, are true for commercial properties: The principal effort is to create enough interest in the subject property so that the space in it can be leased. However, the effort expended in attracting prospects for commercial space is generally more intensive than that for residential rental space, primarily because of the difference in the types of tenants and the duration of commercial leases. Businesses are not inclined to move very often; when one does, it usually intends to remain at its new location for a long time. Because of the infrequency of moves, and because a multiple-year lease translates into many thousands or millions of dollars in rent over its term, it is common for commercial tenants to be recruited directly, although conventional advertising and promotion cannot be overlooked. To assure optimum occupancy, it is necessary for a property representative to make direct calls on potential tenants. This is particularly important for proposed developments; lending institutions usually require a certain percentage of a planned property to be *preleased* (in other words, leased before construction of the building begins or while the construction is taking place) before construction loans will be approved.

A property or a management firm may employ (either temporarily or permanently) a leasing agent whose sole purpose is to seek out potential tenants for the subject property. The leasing agent accomplishes this through a process known as *cold calling* or *prospecting*—he or she calls

---

Other Commercial Properties

Other commercial space that is professionally managed includes medical buildings, industrial sites, and warehouses. Each poses distinct challenges to the property manager because of the unique requirements of its tenants.

Buildings whose space is leased primarily to medical and dental professionals must be modified to meet these tenants' needs for additional—sometimes specialized—plumbing and electrical wiring. The nature of their clients (patients who may be ill) and the services they provide mandate special care in housekeeping and waste disposal. Entrances and other common areas—including parking—must accommodate handicapped and ailing individuals. Doctors and dentists are not the only possible tenants in a medical building. Pharmacies, biomedical laboratories, physical therapists, optical services, and health maintenance organizations are just some of the others.

Research facilities and factories often use hazardous materials that require special storage facilities and special waste disposal equipment and procedures. Tenants in an industrial park may establish a tenants' or owners' association to oversee road maintenance and grounds keeping, budgeting and collection of fees for "common area" operations and maintenance, and any other routine management activities.

Warehouses lease storage space for inventory, records, excess raw materials, etc. Warehouse management services may include shipping and receiving, with charges based on gross weight of materials handled or the number of packages shipped and received. The storage environment (control of temperature, humidity, etc.) is critical for many materials, and federal and other laws mandate labeling to identify specific hazards of materials transported in interstate commerce. These requirements may affect management procedures.

Individuals and businesses may choose to store and secure their goods themselves in self-service storage facilities that resemble rows of attached garages. Many of these facilities include living quarters for an on-site manager. The storage areas are rarely insulated and therefore storage is at the lessee's risk.

---

on the principals of businesses (individuals or corporations) to discuss the possibility of moving their operations to the subject property. In order to achieve success with such a program, the leasing agent must conduct research on different businesses in order to direct his or her efforts toward the most likely prospects. This is especially important for retail properties; specific types of tenants are sought to fill a particular product or service niche in the tenant mix of a large shopping center.

Information regarding businesses that may be considering a move can come from many sources, including the chamber of commerce, company annual reports, and referrals from business acquaintances. The most likely prospects are businesses that anticipate expansion and those whose leases are nearing expiration.

Unlike residential property, which is usually marketed on the basis of personal appeal, the marketing emphasis for office and retail space is usually on the dollar value the prospect will receive for the rent paid. In this case, value directly affects the prospect's profit margin. There are four principal ways to market space based on value:

1. *Price advantage.* Well-managed businesses are always striving to improve net profits. If a leasing agent can demonstrate a price advantage in a location that fully meets the prospect's expectations or prerequisites, the likelihood of at least stimulating preliminary interest is great.

2. *Improved efficiency.* More convenient access for employees or customers, lower utility costs, and better tenant services are some measures that may turn a prospect into a tenant. Better operating efficiency is also a form of price advantage. The expectation of more efficient operations usually must be illustrated with office space plans and layouts or other visual aids. A demonstration of space adaptability is a tangible and especially strong incentive. Such a demonstration, coupled with data on the probable reduction of expenses, may justify the prospect's move. Also, with the growing dependency of business offices on technology, many businesses move to buildings with superior mechanical systems so they can upgrade their operations and equipment.

3. *Increased prestige.* In terms of business value, prestige is a marketable commodity. The rent for prestigious space will certainly be higher, but greater visibility may increase the prospect's business so that the amount of rent as a percentage of gross income is actually lower. Prestigious locations can also help to attract employees.

4. *Economy.* When price advantages are mentioned, a lower cost on a comparable item is implied. In office space, however, economy refers to space that is lower in price and not necessarily equivalent to the space currently occupied. Sometimes a business located in a Class A building could just as well have part or all of its operations in less expensive space without compromising its strength or reputation. During periods of inflation or slow business activity, a prospect may consider less luxurious space or outlying locations to control costs.

INSURING COMMERCIAL PROPERTIES

When someone makes a "small investment" in commercial property, the purchase price of the store or office building may be several million dollars. "Large investments" do not necessarily have an upper limit, but property valued between $100 million and $1 billion can be found in most major U.S. cities. Whether the investment is small or large by industry standards, the expectation is for the property, over its lifetime, to generate income well in excess of its purchase price. In fact, the ability of the purchaser to retain ownership usually depends on the periodic income the property generates.

If the lifespan of the property were abruptly ended because of damage, even a so-called small investment could bankrupt the investor. Protection from financial ruin due to the loss of use of the property is provided through comprehensive insurance coverage. However, no single policy can completely protect the investor; even if such a policy were available, the premium cost would be prohibitive.

While almost anything can be insured, the owner must balance the cost of the premium against the risk of leaving all or part of the item's value uninsured. To illustrate, windows are easily broken and expensive to replace, so most basic insurance policies exclude plate glass windows from coverage or limit the amount paid in any year for window breakage. If this coverage were included in every policy and no upper limit were placed on the amount that could be claimed, owners of skyscrapers that may replace numerous windows in a year because of breakage would benefit at the expense of owners of buildings with few windows that have to be replaced only rarely. (The insurer would have to charge very high premiums in order to pay the claims, and the cost to insure a small building would be prohibitive.) To avoid such an inequity, plate-glass coverage is excluded altogether. However, a separate plate-glass policy can be purchased, or an *endorsement* can be added to the primary policy to pay for plate-glass damage. An owner of a building with thousands of windows probably would investigate the value of paying for the coverage; for a smaller building, the windows may be left uninsured, and payment for the occasional replacement can be made as an operating expense.

As with income-producing residential property (chapter 9), the owner of commercial property insures it against loss of income, structural damage, and liability. The owner is listed as the insured party and the property manager is named as an additional insured. A major difference for commercial property, however, is that insurance premiums are an operating expense that may be prorated and passed through to the tenants.

Because insurance for the property as a whole does not cover the contents of tenants' individually leased spaces, most commercial leases require tenants to carry enough insurance themselves to cover their inventory and whatever furnishings and equipment they have in their leased space. The commercial tenant's insurance coverage should be sufficient to both preserve the business and meet the obligations of the lease in case of disaster. They may need other types of insurance as well. Commercial tenants are usually required to carry their own liability insurance, and the lease may obligate them to name the owner of the property as an additional insured party. Retail leases may specifically require tenants to be insured against plate-glass damage and business interruptions. Federal law requires that employers carry workers' compensation insurance to cover on-the-job illness and injuries of employees.

The relationship of an insurance company with its customers technically gives it the right to sue an entity in the name of the insured party in order to recover a settlement it has paid if there is evidence that the other entity is liable. This right is called *subrogation*. Suppose, for example, that an electrical fire damages a building, and the property owner's insurance pays the claim. If later evidence proves that an employee of a tenant left a space heater on overnight and it ignited the carpeting, a suit may be filed against the tenant or its insurance company to recover the amount of the claim. The existence of this right can make it very difficult for both the tenant and the owner to obtain insurance, so both parties are usually obligated to sign a *waiver of subrogation* to prohibit exercise of this right.

SUMMARY

Commercial space is defined as rentable space that is not intended for residential use exclusively. Long lease terms, complex rents, and tenants' desires to maximize the ability of their businesses to prosper in the spaces they rent make lease negotiations crucial to successful management of commercial property.

Office space is primarily concentrated in the central business district of a city, but it is commonly found in suburban areas as well. Whether a building is 100 years old and small in size or the newest 100-story skyscraper, the value of its rental space to tenants depends on its location, structural components, proximity to transportation, prestige, tenant services, management standards, and tenant mix. Office rents are based on the square footage of the leased space and may cover a proportionate part of the operating expenses for the common area (a gross lease). However, many operating expenses of the property are passed through to the tenants on a prorated basis and paid in addition to rent (a net lease).

Shopping centers are the most common form of retail property that is professionally managed. They are usually located in suburban areas, although urban shopping centers are becoming more common. Each shopping center is planned as a single project; on-site parking is provided, and there is a unified image. Shopping centers are classified by size and by types of tenants. The most common forms are regional and super regional centers, community centers, neighborhood centers, specialty centers, and convenience centers. As in office buildings, rent is based on the square footage of the leased space, and some operating expenses of the center are passed through to the tenants as a separate charge in addition to base rent. Retailers may also be required to pay a percentage of their gross sales as additional rent.

Marketing is more aggressive for a commercial property than it is for a residential property. The property manager or leasing agent targets specific businesses as prospective tenants and calls on them directly to sell the benefits of relocation to the property he or she represents.

All property owners, property managers, and commercial tenants must be insured, both to protect their own interests and to protect the interests of all others involved with the property. As with residential space, the diversity of commercial property types does not permit development of a definitive insurance policy to cover all of the damage that may occur at an individual property. As a unique combination of policies and endorsements is planned, the premiums must be balanced against the cost of self-insuring (replacing an item outright) so that an insurance program can be designed that is both economical and effective.

Key Terms

Anchor tenant

Ancillary tenants

Artificial breakpoint

Base rent

Central business district (CBD)

Concessions

Consumer Price Index (CPI)

Demographic profile

Escalation clause

Gross leasable area

Gross lease

Marketing fund

Merchants' association

Natural breakpoint

Net leases

Options

Parking area ratio

Parking index

Pass-through expenses

Percentage rent

Pro rata

Radius clause

Rentable area

Subrogation

Tenant improvements

Tenant mix

Trade area

Usable area

Key Points

Management differences between commercial and residential property

Determining the value of office space

Usable area and rentable area and how they are measured

Space planning for commercial property

Differences between gross and net leases for both office and retail space

Difference between an expense stop (office lease) and an expense cap
   (retail lease)

Property analysis and definitions of retail space

Points to negotiate with retail tenants

Different types of rent charged to retail tenants

Types of insurance and considerations of cost versus benefit

11

The Business of Real Estate Management

In most cases, those who choose property management as a profession begin their careers with an established property management firm. To develop a complete perspective on all of the career opportunities and functions of real estate management, an overview of the typical management firm is necessary. The property manager must understand how a property management office is organized, how its business is acquired, how management fees are determined, and the types of collateral services that a management company may offer its clients. The property manager is a representative not only of his or her employer (the management firm) but also of the property owners who are the management firm's clients.

THE ORGANIZATION OF A PROPERTY MANAGEMENT FIRM

Many of the same criteria that make real property desirable (e.g., location, design, amenities) also affect the value of a property management business. The company office should be convenient and comfortable for the firm's clients, the tenants of the properties it manages, and its employees. The people in charge must be conscious of the clients' perceptions in particular, because clients entrust their investments to the firm. An office with dirty ashtrays, stacks of paper, mismatched furniture, tattered carpeting, and dingy walls will not inspire a prospective client to sign a management agreement. On the other hand, the most prestigious office in town may raise other concerns. Because management fees pay for the company's office space, clients may think the firm's fees are too high if the offices are luxurious—even if the fees are competitive with those of other firms. Successful management companies understand what their clients expect and reflect that in their own offices.

Location

Two elements of location are most important for property management firms to recognize: where the on-site office is located in a building, and where the management firm's central office is located with respect to the buildings it manages. Not all management firms have multiple offices; some may have all operations in one on-site office or they may have an on-site office in each property that is managed. On the other hand, a management firm could have a central office in addition to on-site offices or, if the firm has only small properties in its portfolio, it may have only a central office and no on-site locations.

In a residential property, vacant apartment space may be utilized for an on-site management office, but most new apartment complexes have space planned and designated as an on-site office. If a vacant apartment serves as the office, however, this should not be the most luxurious unit available for two reasons: (1) potential rental income will be reduced, and (2) the more luxurious apartments are usually in low-traffic areas and therefore less convenient for residents and prospects who must visit the office.

An on-site office in commercial property must be easily accessible by visitors and tenants, but such locations are usually in the section of the building that commands the highest rent. Ground-floor locations and other high-traffic areas are desirable as both retail and office space, and their potential for rental income must be evaluated before a location for the office is chosen. Management offices in retail developments are often adjacent to but not in the midst of primary traffic areas. In all types of properties, directional signage is necessary to guide people to the management office.

In ideal circumstances, the central office or headquarters of a large management firm is located close to many of the properties it manages. However, that may not always be possible. A firm that manages residential property exclusively may have to have its main office in another part of town because of zoning restrictions where the apartment buildings are located. Some management companies have offices in buildings they own, and these are not necessarily near their client's buildings. Working for clients whose properties are in other cities may necessitate opening branch offices or assigning regional property managers who are based at the main office but visit the out-of-town properties periodically.

Layout and Design

The management office should reflect the efficiency of the firm and the quality of management that clients receive. Above all, the office should be comfortable. It must have sufficient space for the various business functions—in this case, accounting, record keeping, and dealing with suppliers, architects, tradespeople, and others in addition to present and prospective tenants and clients. Prospective commercial tenants may pay close attention to the space planning in a management firm's office because the property manager is often involved in the planning of tenants' offices.

Office procedures, equipment, and operations should be scrutinized. The areas occupied by bookkeeping and accounting personnel should be set apart where they will be quiet—to prevent distraction and allow concentration. Individual work spaces and offices as well as the office common areas should have adequate room for personal comfort and efficiency. Files and storage cabinets should be located conveniently. Overall size of the area can be visually enhanced by using light colors for walls and furnishings; neutral colors are usually best. Lighting should be adequate and appropriately placed so it is neither too bright (causing glare) nor too dark (causing eye strain). Furniture should be selected with comfort and the job function in mind. Properly designed chairs suited to employees' work activities will maximize comfort and efficiency. Attention should also be paid to desk size and height. An appropriate amount of work area should be provided for the task being performed. Employees who use computers at their desks should have furniture designed to accommodate this equipment.

If rent payments are collected at an on-site office—more common in residential than in commercial properties—a high counter may be appropriate. A counter provides a barrier that limits tenants and other visitors to a specific portion of the office and a work area for the tenants who would normally stand as they make their payments.

Private offices and conference rooms should be included in the basic plan. Private offices are generally located farthest away from the main entrance, while conference rooms are usually close to the main entrance in a central portion of the office. In addition to being used for employee meetings, a conference room may be a more comfortable environment in which to meet with a client or tenant. Clients may think the property manager has a "home-field advantage" when they sit on the visitors' side of the manager's desk, and a private office may be too imposing for tenants, especially residential tenants. A conference room places everyone on equal footing and affords the necessary privacy.

Office Equipment and Procedures

As a result of technological advances, numerous time- and labor-saving devices are available for use in the management office. Word processors have replaced electric typewriters. Hand-held calculators have largely replaced adding machines. Some telephones serve as their own answering machines, and they record more than incoming calls (e.g., the day and time of the call). Some answering machines can be activated by a touch-tone code to replay messages. This feature permits one to retrieve messages while away from the office. Copy machines have virtually eliminated other types of duplicating equipment, and there are machines that address mail, weigh it, and apply proper postage. A vast array of equipment is available to perform an equally vast array of office functions. However, efficiency and economy should be major criteria for selecting office equipment, and it is important to remember that the most sophisticated models are not always the most appropriate ones.

Computers.   Perhaps the greatest innovation in office equipment has been the evolution of the personal computer, or PC. Unlike a mainframe computer that may be linked to numerous terminals in different locations, the data processing and storage capabilities of a PC—its memory—are generally contained in a small piece of equipment called a central processing unit (CPU) that can be placed on a desk or near the terminal. A PC can be linked to other computers via cables or telephone lines (modems), and diskettes can be used to transfer data and programs between computers. These capabilities are particularly important to management firms that use computers to link on-site offices to the central management office, and to transmit data directly to their clients in addition to or instead of sending hard-copy reports.

In comparison to a mainframe computer, data storage in a PC is definitely limited, and storage of multiple programs reduces the capacity to store data. As new generations of PCs are developed, they will invariably have more built-in memory and greater capability to expand that memory and to add peripheral equipment. The cost of a fairly sophisticated personal computer and printer is within the financial reach of most management firms, even those that are newly founded. A single personal computer may serve as typewriter, adding machine, and bookkeeping ledger while the number of clients is small. As the number of clients grows, the firm will have to grow, and additional computers will be required. Eventually, some PCs may be programmed for dedicated functions (e.g., word processing, financial report processing) or a more sophisticated system—possibly a mainframe computer—may be necessary.

For optimum performance of a computer, three elements must be considered: the hardware, the software, and their compatibility. In contrast to the computer *hardware,* which is the machinery (CPU, keyboard, printer, etc.), the *software* consists of the programs that permit the generation, storage, and manipulation of data. In order to assure maximum efficiency, reliability, and capability of the hardware and software to perform the office procedures for which they are purchased, the manager should compare product specifications and consult with people who use computers before making a purchase. There are numerous software programs that perform real estate-related functions, particularly for property management. Care must be taken to choose the best software for a particular management operation. Software is costly and not something that is replaced on a whim.

Accounting Systems and Equipment.   Much of the activity in a property management office is related to management of the funds collected for the properties. Each property may have one bank account for security deposits and one for general operating funds. Such separation of funds may be mandatory, especially if security deposits are required by law to be held in escrow. The size of the property, the owner's requirements, and applicable laws will mandate how many bank accounts are required for a specific property. Limitations on federal deposit insurance coverage of accounts may also be a consideration. In some situations, separation of clients' funds may be accomplished solely through accounting and bookkeeping procedures. If separate accounting is used instead of separate bank accounts, care should be taken to avoid using one owner's funds for another owner's property. In addition, owners' funds should not be commingled with the management firm's funds. Commingling owner and agency funds is unethical and illegal.

The equipment necessary to operate an accounting department efficiently depends on the number of accounts to be maintained. This, in turn, depends on both the number of properties being managed and the number of accounts maintained for each property. While separate bank accounts may distinguish security deposits from operating funds, the latter will be accounted for variously. As income is deposited and expenses are paid out each month, the specific amounts will be recorded as a type of income or expense identified in the *chart of accounts* (see chapter 4). Small firms whose accounting needs are simple may be satisfied with manual (hand-posting) systems for recording accounts, although computerization has made most manual accounting procedures obsolete. A new firm with limited means can rely on hand-posting and be just as effective as one that uses computers; as the firm grows, accounting and record keeping will inevitably require computer assistance. A *spreadsheet* program that performs computations in a format of columns and rows (just as they are done manually in a typical ledger) usually will allow text or word entries in addition to numbers for calculation. The ability to sort data by one factor (tenant's last name, date of payment, amount paid) can facilitate comparisons of similar data. Sort functions may also assist in maintaining accuracy. Discrepancies that occur in totals when data are sorted in a different manner usually signal an incorrect entry, and additional use of the sort command may help isolate the error.

Accuracy is of utmost importance in accounting. No matter what type of system is used or how well-qualified the staff, mistakes can occur. The management firm can protect itself against financial liability from an administrative oversight by carrying professional liability insurance (also called *errors and omissions insurance*). This type of insurance is very expensive because of the size of the financial awards that may result from adjudication of specific claims. In order to exclude small claims, errors and omissions coverage usually has a large deductible, and the policy carefully delineates what constitutes an error or omission.

Communication Equipment. Other technologically advanced devices can make office operations more efficient. Communication between the central office and on-site personnel is of particular importance. A property management firm with numerous remote offices may be able to improve efficiency by placing a facsimile machine in each office or installing an electronic mail system in all its computers to avert lengthy (or missed) telephone calls.

Management offices sometimes use portable pagers to communicate with on-site maintenance personnel. Such a system can ensure prompt service, but it has the potential to cause delays if the person being paged is working on another call. Conventional two-way radios may be more convenient; they allow immediate communication between the maintenance worker and the dispatcher without taking the worker away from the task at hand. Cellular telephones, which have revolutionized interpersonal communications, can be very useful. They can also be very expensive; all calls are charged by the minute—local and long-distance, incoming and outgoing.

Office Procedures. Office machines can save both time and money, but overuse of them can reduce efficiency. The definition of "overuse" will be different for every company—a procedure that is efficient in one company may be inefficient in another firm. The key to efficient use is to combine the equipment with effective office procedures. Costs can be controlled by establishing specific procedures for routine business activities and setting limits on the use of more expensive systems and services. For example, a facsimile machine may save time, but if a lengthy document must be sent from one part of the country to the other quickly, an overnight courier service may be more economical.

HOW MANAGEMENT BUSINESS IS ACQUIRED

Recruitment of prospective clients is similar to seeking prospective tenants, a topic that has been discussed at length elsewhere in this book. Management firms usually specialize their services based on the type of client, the type of property, or both. Such specialization tends to minimize the increase in administrative duties as the firm's portfolio grows. The difference between managing one office building or two, for example, is not necessarily a doubling of the workload overall. Site management responsibilities may be doubled, but similarity of administrative tasks reduces the cost of establishing procedures and reports for each property.

Identifying Prospective Clients

Any individual or organization that owns income-producing real estate is a prospective client of a management firm. However, not all of them are legitimate prospects. The property manager should study the types of owners who are most likely to seek professional management as well as the situations that may cause an owner to become a client. This identification process will enable the firm to concentrate on a particular type of client and may aid in specializing the business by property type.

Quite often, new management business arises from problem properties. If a property is not profitable, it becomes a liability to the owner instead of an asset, and the owner will investigate alternatives to strengthen the return on the investment. One of these alternatives may be new management. The owners of properties undergoing a downturn are therefore a potential market for professional management. Telltale signs of financial hardship are the loss of a major tenant, a vacancy rate higher than that in comparable properties, bankruptcy, or foreclosure. Evidence of deferred maintenance may also indicate an opportunity. Even though such property may provide an opportunity to acquire a new client, the manager and firm must proceed with caution. Thorough analysis is necessary before any promises or proposals are made. If space in a property is not leasable, any investment in such a property by a management firm can divert attention from other clients and properties that will benefit from dedicated management.

New buildings present a different type of management opportunity. Often a management firm is contracted by a developer before ground is broken, and the manager is involved in the planning process early. Research of zoning changes, demolition permits, and sales of vacant land, coupled with insights from the media, colleagues, and acquaintances can identify such opportunities so the management firm can promote itself for consideration to manage a new property.

Some types of owners naturally seek professional management, primarily to free themselves from the responsibility of caring for the property. In most cases, management firm clients can be categorized either as owners by choice or owners by circumstance.

Owners by Choice.   Individuals, partnerships, corporations, foreign investors, and others who intentionally invest in real property are owners by choice. Their goals for an investment may differ, but all such owners offer distinctive and profitable opportunities for the property manager.

Individuals who actively engage in their own professions may have neither the time nor the inclination to collect rents, handle leasing activities, perform maintenance, or do any of the other tasks that are essential to effective property management. Sole proprietors who do not reside or work in the immediate area of their investment property almost always require the services of local managers.

Partnerships are groups of investors who seek profit from a real estate investment but require professional guidance and attentive property administration to achieve their goal. A management firm may create a partnership (a syndicate in such a case) to purchase a property in order to manage it. Other forms of multiple ownership (REITs, joint ventures, and other investment-based ownership arrangements) almost invariably seek professional management of their properties.

Some corporations own and are responsible for operating income-producing property but they are not large enough to create an organization for that purpose. Sometimes corporations erect buildings to house their own operations and build much larger structures than they need. They may do this to gain rental income or provide space for future expansion, or merely for prestige. To operate such a building, the corporation may hire a property manager as a staff member, but many engage a management firm.

The owners' association of a condominium or cooperative is usually a corporation, but the individual owners rarely have the ability to supervise the property in which they live, let alone an interest in doing so. Nonprofit corporations such as colleges and universities often hire managers to operate and maintain their academic and residential buildings. They may also own income-producing property acquired through bequests, and these properties require management as well.

Foreign investors commonly rely on professionals to manage their real property holdings in the United States. This dependence stems from more than geographic distance; foreign investors rely on the native property manager to advise them on legal and cultural implications of actions involving their property. Naturally, this requires the property manager to understand the laws and culture of the foreign investor's homeland.

Owners by Circumstance.   Sometimes individuals and institutions become owners of real property that they did not purchase. These owners by circumstance may be geographically removed from their property or unwilling or unable to manage it themselves. They present a unique opportunity for professional management. An individual who inherits an apartment building in another state is an example.

Estates themselves are another source of management opportunity. Whether a property is put in trust after its owner's death or is held by the estate for some other reason, professional management may be necessary to maintain the value of the property, assure a regular income, or both. Some lawyers representing owners or estates that have properties requiring administration will occasionally assume the management of these properties, but most will engage a professional manager.

Financial institutions (banks, savings and loans, trust companies, mortgage banks, investment houses) often own real property as a result of mortgage foreclosures. Often they try to sell the property as quickly as possible to terminate the unpaid mortgage. However, properties they cannot sell must be managed to retain value and, if possible, generate income in order to meet specific financial obligations (i.e., taxes). Because they do not seek to hold the property for a long period, financial institutions rarely seek to improve the property (or increase its market value) unless improvements must be made so the property can be sold and the loan repaid.

Federal, state, and local governments are important factors in the local real estate economy and therefore prospective clients for property managers. A housing authority may acquire property or, as a principal lender, become the owner of foreclosed property. Other agencies or departments become "owners" of real property through seizure. Property may be seized to cover unpaid taxes, or because the money used to purchase the property was obtained illegally—or the financial institution holding the property may have been declared insolvent and its assets seized to liquidate the institution. The U.S. government became a major property owner through the Resolution Trust Corporation (RTC) as part of the savings and loan bailout. Regardless of how they become owners of income property, most governmental agencies will engage private professional property managers rather than set up their own management departments.

Litigation in the courts involves naming receivers, trustees, etc., and the professional property manager is qualified for all of these roles. The manager who is acquainted with the local heads of agencies that own real property and with the courts that have jurisdiction over properties in receivership is a likely candidate to manage them.

Promotion of the Management Firm

Identifying potential clients is just the beginning. The challenge is to convert these prospects into clients of the management firm. There are several methods for achieving this conversion. However, most prospects become clients as a result of direct solicitation, established reputation, personal referral, institutional advertising, and good public relations.

Direct Solicitation.   The best way to acquire business is to ask for it. However, before asking for management business, the manager should be familiar with a specific property or an owner's portfolio as well as that owner's investment goals and prepare a brief proposal stating the general advantages of professional management as well as specific advantages of management for the particular property or portfolio. This means that before a prospect is called on, the manager will have carefully examined the building and evaluated its operations—the proposed service must be understandably justified. The manager should also know as much about the owner as possible. When the prospect is finally contacted, he or she should be given an appealing and clearly understood sales kit that outlines the qualifications of the management organization and the kinds of services it offers.

Direct solicitation requires much persuasion and perseverance. A prospect's property is a major investment, and it is unlikely that he or she will award a management contract to a new manager after only one call; usually many calls are required. Managers who solicit business directly must understand that rejection is more common than acceptance. However, the reasons for rejection can become obsolete over time, and repeated follow-up can lead to success because an owner may eventually be willing to reconsider a manager who presented a proposal previously.

Reputation.   One of the most important ways to achieve success in property management is to establish a favorable reputation. Professional reputation is the overall opinion of the business community regarding the character and capability of the manager or the management firm. This opinion is based on successful results and on personal and business characteristics such as ethical practices. While a good reputation in the community is important to a management firm, it is also important for the individual manager. Personal reputation is the cornerstone on which an individual manager can build his or her own property management company. Neither management firms nor individuals can rest on their laurels for very long. An accomplished manager should work as hard to preserve a good reputation as a newcomer must work to create one.

When an owner turns a property over to a management firm, it is because he or she trusts the integrity and capability of that firm. Establishing worthiness of that trust should be the highest priority in the property manager's efforts to obtain business—and retain it. This is done in part by developing as many solid credentials and good references as possible. The CERTIFIED PROPERTY MANAGER® (CPM®) and ACCREDITED MANAGEMENT ORGANIZATION® (AMO®) designations from the Institute of Real Estate Management are two such credentials.

Referral.   The adage that "nothing succeeds like success" certainly applies to expanding the business of a property management firm. A proven record of managerial success and a reputation for diligence can lead satisfied clients and other business acquaintances to recommend the manager and the firm to owners who could benefit from management services. They may also identify prospects directly to the management company or the individual manager. Licensed real estate agents who sell various types of income property naturally encounter new owners and established investors, and they are an important source of referrals. (It is fairly customary for real estate agents to receive a referral fee if a management agreement is signed as a result of their referral.)

Institutional Advertising.   Advertising can be used effectively to promote management services. However, such advertising is usually designed to increase name recognition and build reputation rather than to promote a specific service. Three types of institutional advertising have proved effective.

Display advertising in community newspapers reaches a wide circulation and, if handled effectively, enhances institutional prestige. However, advertising in a newspaper reaches its entire readership, most of whom are not in the market for property management. Because those who own property or who have control of property in some manner are the potential prospects, it may be more cost-effective to advertise in the real estate, business, or financial section of a newspaper. Display advertising in real estate and other investment-related periodicals is another way to direct the message to the appropriate audience.

Direct-mail advertising may be used to promote the firm exclusively to those who are likely prospects for management. The promotional material should be of superior quality and personalized as much as possible. The quality of the presentation and the care with which the mailing list is created and maintained determine the success of direct-mail advertising.

Signs on buildings the firm manages are a significant source of new business. Prospective clients are influenced by the judgment of other building owners, and the buildings it manages are direct evidence of the quality of service the firm offers. In this regard, building signs should be carefully designed, and the signs as well as the buildings must be meticulously maintained.

Public Relations.   In addition to purchased advertising, a thoughtfully conceived public relations program is a valuable promotional adjunct. *Public relations* relates to public knowledge, approval, confidence, and preference. An effective public relations program acquaints as many people as possible with the existence of the management company—what it does and what it stands for—and encourages general acceptance of the company. Because a property management firm provides a service, a sound public relations program is very important. People usually give more credibility to what they read or hear if the source of the information is not an advertisement, so a property management firm should take every opportunity to garner favorable publicity. Familiarity and cooperation with members of the press can help in this regard, especially when the firm issues a press release about a new contract, a new major tenant, changes in management personnel or practices, or any other newsworthy item. The management firm's "public" includes its clients, and copies of press releases or a periodic newsletter mailed to them can be used as a means to promote new or expanded services to established clients and to prospective clients as well.

Good public relations also requires introspection with respect to personnel, office environment, and clients' properties. The firm should review its operations regularly and make appropriate changes as necessary. Personnel represent the company, so they should reflect credit on it. Their duties and responsibilities should be reviewed in terms of their public relations impact. The office should be attractive and efficient. To maintain this impression it should be redecorated from time to time and remodeled when necessary. The buildings it manages are also a reflection on the firm, so the company's management portfolio will require periodic review. As part of prospecting for clients, buildings selected for management should be a credit to the firm.

All promotional efforts of the property management firm should be continually monitored to measure their success. Cataloging the source of each business contact is the primary method of identifying those public relations activities that are most effective. Site managers and leasing agents should ask prospective tenants what inspired them to consider renting in the property. Those who come to the office should be asked what prompted them to visit. Based on these responses, the firm can assess its public relations efforts and determine which programs should be enhanced, which should remain as they are, and which should be reduced or discontinued.

**Common Client Expectations of
Property Management Firms**
* Detailed reporting
* Thorough long-range planning
* Sophisticated financial accounting
* Thorough analysis of property's performance
* Frequent communication
* Rapid response time
* High net operating income

Ultimately, responsibility for establishing public acceptance rests with the personnel of the organization. They should be able to communicate effectively to bring credit to themselves and their company. Individuals within the firm should be encouraged to participate in professional activities and to establish themselves as respected authorities in particular fields. They should also be encouraged to participate in civic affairs, and, when they do, to perform the duties they are assigned.

HOW MANAGEMENT FEES ARE DETERMINED

Before an individual or a firm considers acquiring the management of a particular property, the amount of income that can be collected from the property must be estimated. The specific fee is negotiated with the property owner, and the amount depends on the type and extent of services provided. In most circumstances, a property is managed for a percentage of its gross receipts (the total amount collected during a reporting period—the effective gross income), sometimes with a minimum monthly amount being stated in the management agreement to ensure compensation for services regardless of the property's income. A management fee of two percent of gross receipts with a minimum monthly fee of $2,000 would require gross receipts to be less than $100,000 a month for the minimum fee to apply. Individual property managers may be employees of an institutional owner or of a management firm and compensated with a regular salary, although an independent property manager (one who is not employed by a management firm) can contract to manage properties himself or herself on a percentage-fee basis. Percentage fees usually apply only when rents are the principal source of income. Compensation for management of condominium or other association-operated properties is commonly a flat fee. These properties do not have rental income as such; residents are assessed a prorated amount to maintain the property.

In addition to a management fee, separate compensation may be sought for other specific services such as lease-up of a new building or rehabilitation of an old one. However, normal leasing activity in an existing building is usually included in the regular management fee. The services that are compensated by the management fee should be itemized in the agreement so the owner understands that a request for other types of services will result in additional charges. Some firms establish a schedule of fees for services not included in the management contract. For example, standard procedure may be to provide one copy of a financial status report to the owner each month, in which case, a charge for additional copies or more frequent reporting would be appropriate. Such a schedule of fees may be incorporated in the management agreement by reference and attaching a copy to it.

ADDITIONAL CLIENT SERVICES

The property management firm that offers a wide variety of services is attractive to many property owners. Typical services offered include property appraisal, real estate brokerage, management and investment consultation, corporate fiscal service, tax preparation, and insurance. All of these services can command separate, additional fees and are therefore good sources of income for a property management firm. Because so many of these services are necessary when properties are purchased, offering them is a good way to build management business. There is an increasing demand for *asset management,* and many collateral offerings of a property management firm may lead to providing this service. While the objective of asset management is similar to that of conventional property management, asset managers may oversee the financial operation of an investor's entire real estate portfolio—a duty that may involve the investigation and recommendation of financing alternatives and the participation in real property acquisition, development, and divestiture. The asset manager may also assist a client in defining his or her short- and long-term goals for real property investment. An asset manager's investment responsibilities exceed the normal property management involvement with maximizing net operating income and property value, but these property management objectives are also basic to asset management. Even though asset managers may be more attuned to the financial investment an owner has in a property than to its day-to-day management, those asset managers who possess strong site management skills in addition to investment ability are more likely to maximize the value of an investor's portfolio.

Appraisal

Real estate management and real estate appraisal can be closely linked activities. Property managers are expected to exercise business and economic judgment in the interest of their clients. Property owners ask about the future of their properties and wonder what they should do with their real estate investments. These questions are best answered by an *appraisal*. This involves gathering information to determine the highest and best use of the property and its greatest potential value. The testing procedures used by appraisers are similar to those the property manager uses to justify recommendations made in the management plan. An appraisal is an estimate of the property's value. To arrive at this estimate, data on competitors, economic conditions and trends, population movement, neighborhood trends, and market conditions must be reviewed in addition to conducting an in-depth analysis of the property itself. The accuracy of the appraisal depends on the qualifications of the individual who performs it.

Real estate professionals recognize three methods of establishing value—cost approach, market approach, and income approach. The *cost approach* estimates property value based on the value of the land plus the cost of reproducing the improvements on it. In this approach, the cost of construction is adjusted to reflect observed or measured depreciation of the existing improvements as well as the owner's intent, which may be to *replace* the building with a similar facility (using modern materials) or to *reproduce* it (build an identical facility using precisely the same materials). The value of the land is estimated based on sales of nearby vacant property or comparable properties. In the *market approach,* value is established by comparison of the subject property with similar properties that have been sold recently. Similarities in terms of location, lot size, construction materials, zoning, physical condition, etc., are important to the comparison because substantial adjustments of the value must be made for differences in these elements. The appraiser must obtain as much information as possible about the comparable sales to accurately perform a market approach appraisal. The *income approach* bases value on the flow of income from the property. For an appraisal of income-producing property, this is a major consideration. The income approach may be used to calculate estimated current value and to project estimated future value. *Highest and best use* of the property will be indicated by the projection showing the largest amount of income that can be expected from the property. These projections are central to any recommendations to alter, rehabilitate, modernize, or otherwise change a building or its operation. Such recommendations are also influenced by the length of time the owner expects to own the property and the payback period that a change would require.

Usually no single one of these approaches is sufficient to accurately estimate the value of an income-producing property, nor is averaging the results of these different methods. However, the results of the income approach are given more emphasis. Because the *techniques* used by the property manager and the appraiser are similar, a management business and an appraisal business may operate from the same office. The two activities can be interrelated because tax work, estate tax appraisal, condemnation appraisal, and other special-purpose appraisals are necessary for professionally managed real estate. Management of property provides numerous opportunities to solicit appraisal jobs, assuming the manager or management firm is qualified to conduct appraisals.

Management Consultation

Some property owners do not require ongoing management service, but they may seek professional advice on specific problems. Property managers can accommodate these owners by offering consulting services.

Based on experience in the real estate industry, a property manager can advise owners on ways to manage their properties to achieve maximum profits. Most consulting work relates to converting property to other uses or enhancing the investment through rehabilitation or modernization. At other times, owners who wish to buy, sell, or refinance property may request management plans, proposals, or budgets. Developers sometimes call on property managers to assist in determining the feasibility of a proposed project. A developer may also hire a property manager to recommend rental schedules, marketing programs, and leasing policies for proposed projects. Cooperative and condominium associations that do not require a full-time property manager may occasionally consult a professional manager to ensure sound operation of their properties.

The changing national economy and the increasing complexity of real estate transactions have created an environment in which demand for such consultation will continue to grow. Potential clients for management consulting services include buyers and sellers, investors, developers, homeowners' associations, corporate owners of real estate, financial institutions, and other lenders.

Real Estate Investment Counseling

Successful property managers usually have an intimate knowledge of the real estate market in the region. They often know which investors want to buy property and which ones are likely to sell. They know what property is available in the market, the level of demand for it, and the probable value of the property in the future. Understanding the market and knowing the investment profiles of their management clientele, property managers are in a position to counsel clients on potential real estate transactions and sometimes to participate in them.

Investment Partnerships.   A partnership can be formed to acquire, develop, manage, operate, or market real estate, or to undertake any combination of these activities. In a *limited partnership,* the general partner or partners manage the real estate operation and are liable for all of its debts.

The liability of the limited partners for the debts of the partnership is confined to the capital they have invested in the business. Limited partners do not have a voice in the management of the partnership; they merely invest money and receive their share of the profits, usually based on the percentage of their investment.

Property managers may form and promote such limited partnerships in order to participate in the business venture. In this case, the property manager assumes the role of the general partner. The manager who forms a limited partnership must be familiar with the laws (both federal and state) that govern real estate investment and operation. Conditions are not always favorable for forming limited partnerships, and the Tax Reform Act of 1986 removed much of the potential tax shelter of such investment entities.

The risks inherent in participation in a limited partnership can be substantial, especially if current clients have been recruited to participate in the venture with the management firm and the investment property operates at a loss. The other participants' confidence in the management firm may weaken; they may hire new management for their other properties and leave the firm with responsibility for the faltering property owned by the partnership. To minimize the risks, the subject property should be carefully appraised (by a professional appraiser), and a detailed management plan should be prepared before the opportunity is presented to any investors.

Joint Ventures. Another means by which the property manager can participate in the ownership of a property being managed is a *joint venture* (an association of two or more persons or legal entities conducting a single business enterprise for profit). Real estate enterprises that require large amounts of investment capital frequently are operated as joint ventures. Such an arrangement creates a pool of equipment, skill, knowledge, and talent as well as financial resources. A property manager may participate in a joint venture by offering professional management skills in exchange for the opportunity to share in the property's success.

Acquisitions for Clients. Property owners may seek additional property for their investment portfolios, and they may hire a property manager or a management firm to find suitable investments. Compensation for this type of service is usually the brokerage fee; a separate fee may be charged for preparing a management plan, proposal, or budget. If the property is located within the community, it is also likely that the management firm will manage the property.

In order to acquire property for clients, it is necessary to know what the client is seeking from the investment. A property suffering from obsolescence or deferred maintenance may be a suitable short-term holding if repair, rehabilitation, or modernization will lead to a rapid appreciation in value. Investors who prefer long-term ownership may desire a property that is in good physical condition and has a proven record of market strength. Type of property may be another consideration. Some investors may want to diversify the types of properties they own, and others may choose to divest themselves of one type and reinvest in an entirely different type of property. Acquisition as a management activity is a function of asset management.

Corporate Fiscal Service

The real estate manager employed by a corporation often must be prepared to administer not only the property it owns but other corporate affairs as well. The latter involves responsibilities beyond those inherent in the management of real property. The management firm that provides complete fiscal service may be required to plan meetings of the corporate board of directors. It may also be required to send a representative to the meetings to furnish information and advice on a property's operations. Stockholders in real estate-owning corporations often have questions about the properties, and their inquiries may be handled by the management firm that is providing fiscal service.

The management firm also may have complete charge of the books and records of the corporation. This accounting activity transcends maintenance of operating records on the buildings owned by the corporation and may involve supervision of the filing of capital stock tax returns, preparation of income tax returns, and preparation and filing of other taxes and government forms.

Tax Service

Investors are increasingly likely to turn their real estate investments over to a property management firm for complete administration, including collateral services such as payment of taxes associated with real property, because the scope of property management has expanded as real estate transactions have become more complex. Appropriate records must be kept so that tax reports can be filed for clients, and tax calendars and reserves should be prepared to ensure availability of funds and prompt payment of the taxes involved. The scope of tax service will vary with the size of the management firm. Small firms are mainly concerned with basic routines and will consult tax specialists when necessary. Large firms may have tax experts on staff.

Real Estate Tax.   Real estate tax is an *ad valorem tax,* meaning it is based on the value of the real property. The local assessor periodically reassesses the property to adjust the tax according to the property value.

Because of this, it is important to analyze the real estate tax bill, especially if it has changed from the previous year. The manager must verify the measurements, the age of the property, the amount of depreciation allowed, the classification of the property, and the unit replacement cost. The next step is to validate the computations of the total tax by applying the tax rate to the assessed valuation. If this analysis indicates excessive assessment, there may be reason to protest. The property manager should prepare and submit such a protest to the assessor, or, with the owner, contract a professional agency to file the protest. If the protest is disallowed, an appeal to the next higher authority may be justified.

A primary duty of a property manager who handles the taxes of the property is to make sure that adequate funds are available to pay real estate taxes by the due date. Whenever possible, a reserve fund should be established for this purpose, or real estate taxes should be budgeted specifically by setting aside a prorated amount each month.

Personal Property Tax.   Where personal property taxes are imposed locally, it may be necessary for the manager to file with the assessor a schedule of personal property that is subject to tax. The real estate manager must understand both local laws and accepted practices. Here again, the manager becomes responsible for timely payment of this tax.

Federal Income Tax.   Most individual property owners handle their own income taxes and include the earnings or losses from real property on their personal returns. Corporations, however, may rely on the accounting department of the property management firm to prepare and file federal income tax schedules on their real estate holdings.

Besides preparing the schedules, all property managers should be familiar with state and federal income tax laws. In a large management firm, at least one individual should be fully informed about income tax laws and their impact on real estate investment. However, property management professionals should stay within the bounds of management responsibilities. Accounting or legal issues should be referred to qualified accountants or lawyers.

Payroll Taxes.   The property management firm may file tax payments as well as the appropriate forms for some of the property owner's employees in addition to those for its own employees. To file these forms and make these tax deposits, the property manager must have power of attorney for the owner.

Excise Tax.   Managers of office buildings and other large properties may have to collect federal excise taxes which are levied on the production, sale, or consumption of certain commodities. These are indirect taxes on the ultimate consumer. When the management of a building includes the operation of separate merchandise or service departments (restaurants, bars, drugstores, or telephone switchboards, etc.), management should investigate its responsibility concerning excise taxes.

Sales Tax. When taxable sales are transacted in states and cities where sales taxes are imposed, a return must be prepared and the tax paid. These taxes may apply to electricity resale; hotel, food, and beverage operations; gasoline and oil sales; and other types of sales (i.e., on all taxable goods sold in subsidiary operations under the manager's direct administration). Sales tax regulations should be checked when assuming management of property in which goods are sold.

Insurance Service

A difficulty associated with real estate ownership is underwriting the risks as much as possible. The risks vary in different localities and under different operating conditions, so it is customary to expect the real estate management firm to determine the extent of the risks involved and to know with what agency or corporation these risks may be safely and adequately insured. The level of involvement has prompted some real estate managers to write insurance as a service to clients.

Although the real estate manager may be an insurance broker, he or she always represents the insurance buyer. In this capacity, the manager determines the risk from the buyer's point of view, investigates the insurance market for the best and most economical protection, and then recommends the proper insurance for the client to purchase.

While added services may increase the income of the manager, they also increase his or her responsibility. The duties of representing a client in insurance matters are extremely important and must be carried out with utmost care. The real estate manager must have sufficient knowledge of all aspects of insurance underwriting to provide the client with the fairest and most economical insurance coverage possible. The manager is also responsible for keeping records of the policies so that renewals can be handled in ample time. Knowing the expiration dates far enough in advance permits the property manager as insurance broker to continually research other agencies and companies for more economical coverage.

Regardless of whether the property manager is also an insurance broker, the manager must have enough familiarity with the policies and their limitations to assure the client constant and adequate coverage. To accomplish this effectively, schedules must be established to inspect clients' properties to determine whether there have been any changes that may increase the risk that is underwritten. This is especially true in the case of commercial and industrial properties, where changes in types of merchandise carried or kinds of goods manufactured may alter the coverage cost or jeopardize the effectiveness of the coverage. The same considerations apply if the manager is writing insurance for the occupants (tenants) rather than the owners of the property.

SUMMARY

Most property managers begin their careers with property management firms. Understanding the operation of a management firm is important to gaining a complete perspective on the property management profession and the numerous career opportunities available. Many of the criteria used to evaluate property can be applied to the management firm itself in an effort to maximize its efficiency and make it attractive to prospective clients. In this respect, the offices of the firm must be conveniently located, carefully designed, well-maintained, and somewhat understated in decor.

As a result of technological advances, many innovations have been introduced into the modern office. Equipment such as copy machines, personal computers, facsimile machines, and cellular phones can improve the efficiency and reduce the cost of administrative functions, but only if they are combined with carefully planned and executed procedures.

Management firms must promote themselves both to invite new business and to retain established clients. Promotion encompasses much more than advertising; direct solicitation and a good reputation are often the definitive factors in successfully promoting a management firm. Other means of obtaining clients are personal referrals and public relations.

When prospects become clients, a management fee must be negotiated. Owners of rental property usually pay a percentage of gross receipts for management services, and a minimum fee may be stated in the management agreement as well. Other management arrangements are compensated by a flat fee.

The complexity of property management often creates opportunities for a firm to diversify its business and offer collateral services to clients. Appraisal, management consultation, investment counseling, corporate fiscal service, tax service, and insurance brokerage are possible related services. The availability of these services is not restricted to management clients; such services as consultation may be sought by owners who do not require ongoing management but do need occasional advice.

Key Terms

Ad valorem tax	Errors and omissions insurance
Appraisal	Institutional advertising
Asset management	Management fee
Computer hardware	Public relations
Computer software	Referral
Direct solicitation	Spreadsheet program

Key Points
Important elements in organizing a management firm and office
Procedures and equipment for efficient administration
Acquisition of property management business
Ownership by choice versus ownership by circumstance
Compensation for management services
Different approaches to property valuation
Real estate investment counseling

Glossary

Absorption rate The amount of space of a particular property type that is leased compared to the amount of that same type of space available for lease within a certain geographic area over a given period.

ACCREDITED MANAGEMENT ORGANIZATION® (AMO®) A designation conferred by the Institute of Real Estate Management on real estate management firms that are under the direction of a CERTIFIED PROPERTY MANAGER® and comply with stipulated requirements as to accounting procedures, performance, and protection of funds entrusted to them.

ACCREDITED RESIDENTIAL MANAGER (ARM®) A professional service award conferred by the Institute of Real Estate Management on individuals who meet specific standards of experience, ethics, and education.

Accrual-basis accounting The method of accounting that involves entering amounts of income when they are earned and amounts of expense when they are incurred (even though the cash may not be received or paid). (Compare *cash-basis accounting*.)

Actual cash value (ACV) Insurance that pays a claim based on the purchase price of the item, usually allowing for depreciation because of age and use. (Compare *replacement cost coverage*.)

Adjustable-rate mortgage A type of variable-rate mortgage for which the interest rate can be adjusted (raised or lowered) only at specific intervals (e.g., semiannually or annually). The adjustment is based on a predetermined index (such as the prime rate plus 2 percent). (See also *variable-rate mortgage*.)

Ad valorem tax   A tax levied on the basis of the value of the object taxed. Most often refers to taxes levied by municipalities and counties against real property and personal property.

Agent   A person who enters a legal, fiduciary, and confidential arrangement with a second party and is authorized to act on behalf of that party.

All-risk insurance   Insurance that pays for any losses unless they are specifically excluded in the policy.

Amortization   Gradual reduction of a debt, usually through installment payments.

Anchor tenant   A major shopping center tenant that will draw the majority of customers.

Ancillary tenant   A shopping center tenant that occupies a smaller space and a location that is secondary in relation to the anchor tenant.

Appraisal   An opinion or estimate of the value of a property. An estimate of value that is calculated by a certified or accredited appraiser. Three methods of appraisal are common: The *cost approach*, based on the estimated value of the land plus the estimated cost of replacing the improvements on it less depreciation; the *income approach*, based on the net operating income of the property; and the *market approach*, based on a comparison to similar properties in the market that have been sold recently.

Assessment   An amount charged against each owner or tenant of a property to fund its operation.

Asset management   A specialized field of property management that involves the supervision of an owner's real estate assets at the investment level. In addition to normal property management responsibilities that include maximizing net operating income and property value, an asset manager may recommend or be responsible for or participate in property acquisition, development, and divestiture. An asset manager may have only superficial involvement with normal daily operations of the site (e.g., supervision of personnel, maintenance, tenant relations, etc.).

Balloon mortgage   A loan with a constant monthly rate of repayment and a much larger (balloon) payment at the end of the term to fully amortize the loan.

Bankruptcy   A state of financial insolvency (liabilities exceed assets) of an individual or organization; the inability to pay debts.

Base rent   The minimum rent as set forth in a (usually commercial) lease.

Base-unit-rate approach   A method of establishing rental rates in which the typical unit within a specific submarket (either an actual unit or a perceived ideal) is used as a standard against which all similar units are measured.

Board of directors   The governing body of any corporation, including condominium and other homeowners' associations. (See also *corporation*.)

Breakpoint   In retail leases, the point at which the tenant's percentage rent is equal to the base rent and beyond which the tenant will begin to pay overages; also called *natural breakpoint*. Sometimes a tenant and owner will negotiate an *artificial breakpoint* which requires the tenant to begin paying percentage rent either before or after the natural breakpoint is reached.

Budget   An estimation of income and expenses over a specific time period for a particular property, project, or institution. (See also *capital budget* and *operating budget*.)

Bylaws   Regulations that provide specific procedures for handling routine matters in an organization such as a condominium association.

Capital budget   An estimate of costs of major improvements or replacements; generally a long-range plan for improvements to a property.

Capital improvement   A structural addition or betterment to real property; the use of capital for a betterment that did not exist before.

Capitalization   The process employed to estimate the value of a property by the use of a proper investment rate of return and the annual net operating income produced by the property, the formula being expressed:

$$\frac{\text{Net Operating Income}}{\text{Rate}} = \text{Value}$$

Capitalization rate   A rate of return used to estimate a property's value based on that property's net operating income. This rate is based on the rates of return prevalent in the marketplace.

Cash-basis accounting   The method of accounting that recognizes income and expenses when money is actually received or paid. (Compare *accrual-basis accounting*.)

Cash flow   The amount of cash available after all payments have been made for operating expenses and debt service (mortgage principal and interest).

CERTIFIED PROPERTY MANAGER® (CPM®)   The professional designation conferred by the Institute of Real Estate Management on individuals who distinguish themselves in the areas of education, experience, and ethics in property management.

Chart of accounts   A classification or arrangement of account items.

Collateral   Property pledged as security for a loan or debt.

Commingle   To mix or combine; to combine the money of more than one person or entity into a common fund. A prohibited practice in real estate.

Common area   Areas of a property that are used by all tenants or owners; in a condominium, the areas of the property in which the unit owners have a shared interest (lobbies, laundry rooms, etc.).

Comparison grid A form for price analysis in which the features of a subject property are compared to similar features in comparable properties in the same market. The price (or rent) for each comparable property helps to determine an appropriate market price (or rent) for the subject.

Concession An economic incentive granted by an owner to encourage the leasing of space or the renewal of a lease.

Condominium A multiple-unit structure in which the units and pro rata shares of the common areas are owned individually; a unit in a condominium property.

Condominium association A not-for-profit corporation comprised of the unit owners of a condominium that governs its operation.

Consumer Price Index (CPI) A way of measuring consumer purchasing power by comparing the current costs of goods and services to those of a selected base year. Used as a reference point for rent escalations in some commercial leases.

Conversion ratio The average number of prospects who visit a rental property compared to the number who sign a lease.

Cooperative Ownership of a share or shares of stock in a corporation that holds the title to a multiple-unit residential structure. Shareholders do not own their units outright but have the right to occupy them as co-owners of the cooperative association and through proprietary leases.

Corporation A legal entity that is chartered by a state and is treated by courts as an individual entity separate and distinct from the persons who own it.

Corrective maintenance Ordinary repairs that must be made to a building and its equipment on a day-to-day basis. (See also *deferred maintenance* and *preventive maintenance*.)

Cost-benefit analysis A method of measuring the benefits expected from a decision (e.g., a change in operating procedures) by calculating the cost of the change and determining whether the benefits outweigh the costs.

Curb appeal General cleanliness, neatness, and attractiveness of a building as exemplified by the appearance of the exterior and grounds and the general level of housekeeping.

Debt service Regular payments of the principal and interest on a loan.

Declaration A legal document that creates a condominium. The document describes the condominium, defines the method of determining each unit owner's share of the common elements, and outlines the responsibilities of the owners and the association.

Deductible In insurance, a specified amount the insured party must pay before the insurer pays on a claim.

Default Failure to fulfill an obligation; the nonperformance of a duty.

Deferred maintenance   Ordinary maintenance of a building that, because it has not been performed, negatively affects the use, occupancy, and value of the property. (See also *corrective maintenance* and *preventive maintenance.*)

Deflation   An economic condition occurring when the money supply declines in relation to goods, resulting in lower prices. (Compare *inflation.*)

Demised premises   That portion of a property covered by a lease agreement, usually defined by the walls and other structures that separate one tenant's space from that of another.

Demographic profile   A compilation of social and economic statistics (including population density, age, education, occupation, and income) for a specific population, usually within a geographic area (as a neighborhood or region).

Department of Housing and Urban Development (HUD)   A department of the federal government that supervises the Federal Housing Administration (FHA) and a number of other agencies that administer various housing programs.

Depreciation   Loss of value due to all causes, including physical deterioration (ordinary wear and tear), structural defects, and changing economic and market conditions (see also *obsolescence*). The tax deduction that allows for exhaustion of property.

Effective gross income   The total amount of income actually collected during a reporting period; the gross receipts of a property.

Eminent domain   The right of a governmental body to acquire private property for public use through a court action called condemnation. The court also determines the compensation to be paid to the owner.

Endorsement   An attachment to an insurance policy that provides or excludes a specific coverage for a specific portion or element of a property; also called a rider.

Environmental Protection Agency (EPA)   The agency of the United States government established to enforce laws that preserve and protect the environment.

Equal Employment Opportunity Commission (EEOC)   A U.S. governmental body that enforces Title VII of the Civil Rights Act, which prohibits discrimination in the workplace.

Equity   The interest or value that an owner has in real estate over and above the mortgage against it.

Errors and omissions insurance   See *professional liability insurance.*

Escalation clause   In a lease, a provision for increases in rent, often based on a standard index such as the Consumer Price Index.

Eviction   A legal process to reclaim real estate, usually from a tenant who has not performed under the agreed-upon terms of the lease.

Eviction notice   A written notice to a tenant to cure a breach of the lease immediately or vacate the premises within a specified period.

Expense stop   In an office lease, a clause obligating the property owner to pay operating costs up to a certain amount per square foot per year; tenants pay their pro rata share of any costs in excess of that amount. In a retail lease, a clause obligating the tenants to pay a pro rata share of operating expenses up to a certain amount (expense cap) per year; the owner pays any costs in excess of that amount.

Extended coverage (EC)   An endorsement to a standard fire insurance policy which adds coverage against financial loss from certain other specified hazards.

Fair Credit Reporting Act   A federal law that gives people the right to see and correct their credit records at credit reporting bureaus. It also requires property managers to inform applicants if a credit bureau is contracted to investigate their credit.

Fair housing laws   Any law that prohibits discrimination against people seeking housing. There are federal, state, and local fair housing laws. Specifically, Title VIII of the Civil Rights Act of 1968 prohibits discrimination in the sale or rental of housing based on race, color, religion, national origin, or sex; the Fair Housing Amendments Act of 1988 further prohibits discrimination on the basis of family status (children) or mental or physical disability.

Fair Labor Standards Act   The federal law that establishes minimum wages per hour and maximum hours of work. It also provides that certain employees who work in excess of forty hours per week are to be paid one and one-half times their regular hourly wage. This act is frequently referred to as the Wage and Hour Law.

Fair market value   The price paid, or one that might be anticipated as necessarily payable, by a willing and informed buyer to a willing and informed seller (neither of whom is under any compulsion to act), if the object sold has been reasonably exposed to the market.

Federal Housing Administration (FHA)   An agency, part of the U.S. Department of Housing and Urban Development (HUD), that administers a variety of housing loan programs.

Fidelity bond   Insurance guaranteeing one individual against financial loss that might result from dishonest acts of another specific individual.

Fiduciary   One charged with a relationship of trust and confidence, as between a principal and agent, trustee and beneficiary, or attorney and client, when one party is legally empowered to act on behalf of another.

Financing   The availability, amount, and terms under which money may be borrowed to assist in the purchase of real property, using the property itself as the security (collateral) for such borrowing.

Fire insurance   Insurance on property against all direct loss or damage by fire.

Fixed-rate mortgage   A loan for real property in which the interest rate is constant over the term of the loan.

Floor area   See *gross leasable area*.

Foreclosure A court action initiated by the mortgagee, or a lienor, for the purpose of having the court order the debtor's real estate sold to pay the mortgage or lien.

Garden apartment building A low-rise building designed for multifamily living, usually located in a suburban area.

General partnership The business activity of two or more persons who agree to pool capital, talents, and other assets according to some agreed-to formula, and similarly to divide profits and losses, and to commit the partnership to certain obligations. General partners assume unlimited liability. (Compare *limited partnership*.)

Gross leasable area (GLA) The total square feet of floor space in all store areas of a shopping center, excluding common area space; also called floor area. The size of a retail tenant's area of exclusive use in a shopping center, usually expressed in square feet.

Gross lease A lease under the terms of which the landlord pays all operating expenses of the property and the tenant pays a fixed rent. (Compare *net lease*.)

Gross possible rental income The sum of the rental rates of all spaces available to be rented in a property, regardless of occupancy; the maximum amount of rent a property can produce.

Heating, ventilating, and air conditioning (HVAC) system The unit regulating the even distribution of heat, refrigeration, and fresh air throughout a building.

Highest and best use That use of real property which will produce the highest property value and develop a site to its fullest economic potential.

High-rise apartment building A multiple-unit dwelling which is ten or more stories in height.

Household All persons, related or not, who occupy a housing unit.

Housekeeping The regular duties involved in keeping a property clean and in good order, sometimes called custodial maintenance.

Inflation An economic condition occurring when the money supply increases in relation to goods, resulting in substantial and continuing increases in prices. (Compare *deflation*.)

Institute of Real Estate Management (IREM) A professional association of men and women who meet established standards of experience, education, and ethics with the objective of continually improving their respective managerial skills by mutual education and exchange of ideas and experience. The Institute is an affiliate of the NATIONAL ASSOCIATION OF REALTORS®. (See also *CERTIFIED PROPERTY MANAGER®*.)

Insurance   An agreement by one party (the insurer, carrier, insurance company, etc.) to assume part or all of a financial loss in the event of a specified contingency or peril (e.g., liability, property damage) in consideration of a premium payment by a second party (the insured).

Joint venture   An association of two or more persons or businesses to carry out a single business enterprise for profit.

Landlord   One who owns real property that is leased to a tenant. (See also *lessor*.)

Landlord-tenant law   Laws enacted by various jurisdictions that regulate the relationship between landlord and tenant.

Lease   A contract, written or oral, for the possession of part or all of a landlord's property for a stipulated period of time in consideration of the payment of rent or other compensation by the tenant. Leases for more than one year generally must be in writing to be enforceable. A residential lease is sometimes called an occupancy agreement.

Leasing agent   A person who is directly responsible for renting space in assigned properties.

Lessee   The tenant in a lease.

Lessor   The landlord in a lease.

Liability insurance   Insurance protection against claims arising out of injury or death of people or physical or financial damage to property.

Lien   The legal right of a creditor to have his or her debt paid out of the property of the debtor.

Limited partnership   A partnership arrangement in which the liability of certain partners is limited to the amount of their investment. Limited partnerships are managed and operated by one or more general partners whose liability is not limited; limited partners have no voice in management. (Compare *general partnership*.)

Low-rise apartment building   Multiple-unit residential dwelling of three or fewer stories. (See also *garden apartment*.)

Management agreement   A contract or agreement between the owner(s) of a property and the designated managing agent, describing the duties and establishing the authority of the agent and detailing the responsibilities, rights, and obligations of both agent and owner(s).

Management fee   The monetary consideration paid monthly or otherwise for the performance of management duties.

Management plan   An outline of a property's physical and fiscal management that is directed toward achieving the owner's goals.

Market analysis The process of identifying the specific group of prospective tenants for a particular property and then evaluating the property by that market's standards for rental space.

Marketing All business activity a producer uses to expose potential consumers to available goods and services, including selling, advertising, packaging, etc. For rental property, methods used to attempt to lease space.

Marketing fund In a shopping center, an account controlled by the landlord that is specifically for funding shopping center promotions and advertising. Merchants in the center contribute to this fund based on a predetermined amount stated in their leases. (Compare *merchants' association*.)

Merchants' association An organization formed in shopping centers and controlled by the tenants to plan promotions and advertisements for the good of the center as a whole. Usually all tenants are required to participate and both tenants and landlord pay dues. (Compare *marketing fund*.)

Mid-rise apartment building A multiple-unit dwelling ranging from six to nine stories tall.

Miscellaneous income See *unscheduled income*.

Mixed-use development (MXD) A single property, often found in central business districts, that has more than one use, including retail, office, and hotel space, among other possibilities.

Mobile (manufactured) home A dwelling that is built in a factory, transported to and anchored on a site, and used as a year-round residential unit. All manufactured homes must be in compliance with the federal Manufactured Home Construction and Safety Standards Act of 1974 (the HUD code) which became effective in 1976. (Usage note: The term "mobile home" is commonly used to identify all manufactured homes even though the legal nomenclature is "manufactured homes" for units built after the enactment of the HUD code.)

Modernization The process of replacing original or outdated equipment with similar features that are of up-to-date design.

Money supply The total volume of currency in circulation plus the total amount of demand deposits (checking and savings accounts) in all of the nation's banks, sometimes differentiated as M1 and M2.

Mortgage A conditional transfer or pledge of real property as security for the payment of a debt. The document used to create a mortgage loan. (See also *collateral*.)

Negotiation The process of bargaining that precedes an agreement; in commercial leasing, the bargaining to reach a mutual agreement on rental rates, term of the lease, and other points.

Neighborhood analysis A study of a neighborhood and comparison with the broader economic and geographic area of which it is a part to determine why individuals and businesses are attracted to the area.

Net lease   A lease that requires the tenant to pay a share of specific property operating expenses in addition to base rent. The terms net-net and net-net-net (or triple net) are also used, depending on the extent of the costs that are passed through to the tenant. Used most often for commercial tenants, the definitions of the terms vary with location and types of property (e.g., office, retail). (Compare *gross lease*.)

Net operating income (NOI)   Total collections less operating expenses.

Obsolescence   Lessening of value due to being out-of-date (obsolete) as a result of changes in design and use; an element of depreciation. *Physical obsolescence* is a condition of deferred maintenance; *functional obsolescence* is a condition of obsolete design or use of a property; and *economic obsolescence* is the state of a property that cannot generate enough income to offset operating expenses.

Occupancy agreement   See *lease*.

Occupational Safety and Health Act of 1970 (OSHA)   A law requiring employers to comply with job safety and health standards issued by the U.S. Department of Labor.

Operating budget   A listing of all anticipated income from and expenses of operating a property, usually projected on an annual basis.

Operating expenses   All expenditures made in connection with operating a property with the exception of debt service and income taxes.

Overage   See *breakpoint* and *percentage rent*.

Parking area ratio   The relationship between the size of the parking area and the size of the building it is intended to serve.

Parking index   For a retail property, the number of spaces per 1,000 square feet of GLA.

Partnership   See *general partnership* and *limited partnership*.

Passive activity income   See *Tax Reform Act of 1986*.

Passive loss rules   See *Tax Reform Act of 1986*.

Pass-through charges   In commercial leasing, operating expenses of a property that are paid by the tenants, usually on a pro rata basis and in addition to base rent.

Percentage rent   In retail leasing, rent that is based on a percentage of a tenant's gross sales or net income, often set against a guaranteed minimum or base rent and therefore considered *overage*. (See also *breakpoint*.)

Planned unit development (PUD)   A zoning classification that allows flexibility in the design of a subdivision, usually setting an overall density limit which allows clustering of units to provide for common open space.

Preventive maintenance A program of regular inspection and care that allows potential problems to be prevented or at least detected and solved before major repairs are needed. (See also *corrective maintenance* and *deferred maintenance*.)

Principal In real estate, one who owns property; in property management, the property owner who contracts for the services of an agent; in finance, the amount of money that is borrowed in a loan as distinct from the interest on such loan.

Professional liability insurance In property management, insurance to protect against liabilities resulting from honest mistakes and oversights (no protection is provided in cases of gross negligence); also called errors and omissions insurance.

Property analysis A study of a property referring to such items as deferred maintenance, functional and economic obsolescence, land location and zoning, exterior construction and condition, plant and equipment, unit mix, facilities, and expected income and expenses.

Property management A profession in which someone other than the owner (a property manager) supervises the operation of a property according to the owner's objectives or consults with the owner on the definition of those objectives and the property's profitability.

Pro rata Proportionately; in real estate ownership and leasing, based on the size of individually owned or leased spaces in relation to the whole. Condominium owners and commercial tenants commonly pay proportionate shares of operating expenses and other costs.

Prospect A potential tenant or management client.

Public housing Housing owned by and/or managed for a local or state governmental agency; the principal form of low-income housing available in the United States. (Compare *subsidized housing*.)

Qualification The process of judging a prospective tenant's financial or credit information. The process of determining whether a prospect can afford the unit applied for and has a good history of bill payments.

Radius clause An article in a retail lease that prevents a retailer from opening and operating a similar—and therefore competitive—business within a certain radius from the shopping center.

Real estate Land and all improvements in or on it.

Real estate investment trust (REIT) An entity that sells shares to investors and uses the funds to invest in real estate.

Receivership Court-ordered turnover of a property to an impartial third party (receiver) so that it may be preserved for the benefit of the affected parties.

Regional analysis   A detailed study of a region, usually surrounding and including one or more neighboring cities, to determine the force of various factors affecting the economic welfare of a section of the region, such as population growth and movement, employment, industrial and business activity, transportation facilities, tax structures, topography, improvements, and trends.

Rent   In real estate, payment made for the use of space; periodic payments made under a lease.

Rentable area   The area in an office building on which rent is based and which generally includes the space available for tenants' exclusive use plus identified common areas less any major vertical penetrations (air shafts, stairways, elevators) in the building. The term is applied to the building as a whole, individual floors, and portions of floors. (See also *usable area*.)

Rental agreement   See *lease*.

Rent control   Laws that regulate rental rates, usually to limit the amount of rent increases and their frequency.

Rent ledger   A record of rent received, date of receipt, period covered, and other related information for each individual tenant.

Rent roll   A listing of all rental units, showing for rented units the rental rate, tenant's name, and lease expiration date but usually not including the status of rent payment; also called rent schedule. (Compare *rent ledger*.)

Replacement cost coverage   Insurance to replace or restore a building or its contents to its pre-existing condition and appearance. (Compare *actual cash value*.)

Reserve fund   Money set aside to provide funds for anticipated future expenditures.

Resident   One who lives (or resides) in a place. Referring to residential tenants as "residents" is preferred by many real estate professionals. (Compare *tenant*.)

Resident manager   See *site manager*.

Residential manager   One who manages a residential property or properties.

Retrofit   The replacement of fixtures or facilities in a building with new equipment that is more efficient, usually in terms of energy consumption, fire protection codes, or accommodations for new technology.

Rider   See *endorsement*.

Section 8 housing   Privately owned residential rental units that participate in the low-income rental assistance program created by the 1974 amendments to Section 8 of the 1937 Housing Act. Under this program, the U.S. Department of Housing and Urban Development pays a rent subsidy to the landlord on behalf of qualified low-income residents so they pay a limited portion of their incomes for rent.

Security deposit An amount of money advanced by the tenant and held by an owner or manager to ensure the faithful performance of the lease terms by the tenant. Part or all of the deposit may be retained to pay for rent owed, miscellaneous charges owed, unpaid utility bills, and damage to the leased space that exceeds normal wear and tear. Limitations on withholding may be imposed by local and state ordinances.

Shopping center A generic term applied to a collection of retail stores enclosed in one building or adjacent to each other in separate buildings. Shopping centers are categorized as either convenience, community, neighborhood, regional, super regional, or specialty centers based on their gross leasable area, type of tenancy, and the extent of their geographic trade area (customer base). Variations such as megamalls, power centers, and hypermarkets are also called shopping centers.

Site manager An employee who oversees and administers the day-to-day affairs of a property in accordance with directions from the property manager or the owner and may live in the building being managed (resident manager) or off site.

Sole proprietorship A business enterprise carried on by one person.

Space planning The process of combining functional efficiency and effectiveness with a pleasing appearance in creating office interiors.

Steering An illegal discriminatory practice that encourages a prospective tenant to look at another site for housing or conceals vacancies from a prospect.

Sublet The leasing of part or all of the premises by a tenant to a third party for part or all of the tenant's remaining term.

Subrogation The substitution of one creditor for another such that the substituted person succeeds to the legal rights and claims of the original claimant; in insurance, the right of an insurer to attempt to recover amounts from an at-fault third party for claims paid to the insured party.

Subsidized housing Residential rental property in which the lessor receives part of the rent payment from a governmental body—either directly from the government or from the residents. (Compare *public housing*.)

Syndicate A group of individuals or companies who together undertake a project that they are unable or unwilling to pursue alone. Syndication enables very large projects to be undertaken and spreads the risk among many investors. One who organizes a syndicate and oversees its operation is called a syndicator.

Tax An amount assessed by government for public purposes, usually based on the relative value of property or income.

Tax Reform Act of 1986 A resolution that restructured federal income tax and its associated deductions. Of primary importance in real estate are its definitions of passive activity income (and loss), which include real property income, and its restrictions against using passive losses to offset active income (i.e., salary). The Technical and Miscellaneous Revenue Act of 1988 delineated technical corrections to the Tax Reform Act of 1986.

Tenant   One who pays rent to occupy real estate. Property managers often limit the use of the term "tenant" to commercial tenants and refer to residential tenants as "residents." (See also *resident*.)

Tenant improvement allowance   In commercial leasing, an amount a landlord agrees to spend to improve the leased shell space for a tenant before move-in. A *standard tenant improvement allowance* is a fixed dollar amount allowed by the owner for items that may be installed in the leased premises at no charge to the tenant. Payment for tenant improvements is part of the lease negotiations.

Tenant mix   The combination or types of businesses and services that lease space in a shopping center or office building.

Term   The duration of a tenant's lease; the duration of a mortgage (e.g., a thirty-year term).

Trade area   The geographic area from which a shopping center obtains most of its customers, its size depending on the type of center, location of competition, and other factors. Trade area is generally divided into primary, secondary, and tertiary zones based on distance from the center, travel time, etc.

Traffic report   A record of the number of prospects who visit or make inquiries at a property and the factors that attracted them to it.

Umbrella liability insurance   Extra liability coverage that exceeds the limits of one's basic liability policy.

Unit deed   A document that legally transfers title to a condominium unit and a share of the common areas from one owner to another.

Unscheduled income   Income a property produces from sources other than rent, such as coin-operated laundry equipment, vending machines, late fees, etc.; also called miscellaneous income.

Usable area   The area in an office building that is available for the exclusive use of a tenant. (Compare *rentable area*.)

Valuation   An estimation or calculation of the worth of an object.

Variable-rate mortgage   A mortgage in which the lending institution can raise or lower the interest rate of an existing loan depending on prevailing loan rates or a prescribed index. (Compare *adjustable-rate mortgage*.)

Wage and Hour Law   See *Fair Labor Standards Act*.

Workers' compensation insurance   Coverage obtained by an employer to pay compensation and benefits awarded to an employee in the event of employment-related sickness or injury.

Zoning   Regulation of the character and use of property by areas or "zones," usually by local (municipal) government.

Index